"What is you want *this* time?" Grigori snarled. Even after so many years of torment, he was defiant. *How many centuries?*

The gargoyle preened, his long, stony talons caressing the edge of his wings. For while most of the golem's form was gray stone, the upper edges of his wings were composed of bone-white stone. "You've moved again. I thought you *liked* London?"

He had *loved* London. He had been forced to flee. The list of places he had been forced to leave stretched long, to the limits of his memory.

"I wanted to see Chicago. I've heard it's a beautiful city."

"Perhaps a century ago," replied the gargoyle. "When it was freshly burned. I think they should do it again . . . "

◆══ ══◆

Also by Richard A. Knaak

THE DRAGONREALM SERIES

Firedrake
Ice Dragon
Wolfhelm
The Shrouded Realm
Shadow Steed
Children of the Drake
Dragon Tome
The Crystal Dragon
The Dragon Crown

King of the Grey

Published by
WARNER BOOKS

RICHARD A· KNAAK

FROST WING

ASPECT

WARNER BOOKS

A Time Warner Company

WARNER BOOKS EDITION

Aspect is a trademark of Warner Books, Inc.

Cover design by Don Puckey
Cover illustration by Den Beauvais
Hand lettering by Dave Gatti

Warner Books, Inc.
1271 Avenue of the Americas
New York, NY 10020

 A Time Warner Company

Printed in the United States of America

First Printing: January, 1995

10 9 8 7 6 5 4 3 2 1

I

THE GARGOYLE CAME TO HIM IN HIS DREAMS DURING HIS third night in Chicago.

Grigori Nicolau knew that he was dreaming despite the fact that his eyes were open and he was standing in the middle of his hotel room. He knew that he was dreaming despite having been wide awake only moments before. Yet he also knew that this was not a normal dream—although similar experiences had plagued him so many times in the past, perhaps that meant they *should* be considered normal. He recalled his eyes suddenly growing heavy. There had been a second of dizziness. Nothing more. That was enough, though, that and the gargoyle himself.

"Aaah, Grigori, Grigori . . . I have missed you of late," rumbled the stony figure perched incongruously atop one of the elegant reading chairs of his room. The fact that the gargoyle was huge, taller than most men, did not make it impossible for Nicolau's Morphean visitor to remain where he was. After all, this *was* a dream.

Unfortunately for Grigori, Frostwing was all too real.

When the human failed to respond in what the gargoyle evidently thought a suitable time, the macabre creature shook his horned head and grinned. Frostwing always grinned; his mouth being carved in that manner, he had no choice. "Surely you have not forgotten me, Grigori! It has been only a little more than two weeks . . ."

"If I've forgotten, it's because you made me forget."

Frostwing chuckled and seemed to wink. It was hard to say whether he truly did wink or not. Unlike the still, stone forms perched atop Notre Dame Cathedral in Paris, the face of Grigori's tormentor was an incomplete study in sculpting. Whatever mad fool had freed the gargoyle from the rock from which he had been spawned had failed to finish the creature's visage. Frostwing's eyes were little more than two heavy brow ridges overlooking shadowy craters. Of his nose there was even less to observe—a slight protuberance under which a pair of downward slashes ran. In comparison, the footlong pair of horns atop his head and the winged ears on each side were almost extravagant.

The rest of the horrific creature was as incomplete as his face. Frostwing had arms and legs, with claws worthy of the best of his kind, but they lacked detail. Even his massive wings hung like curved slabs of unhewn rock, though they somehow bent with grace whenever the gargoyle spread them, as he did now.

With speed and litheness that belied his formidable size, the gargoyle fluttered across the room to another of the chairs. His jagged claws toyed with the fine fabric, but did not so much as snag it. Frostwing could be delicate when he so desired . . . which was not often.

A full-length mirror decorated with wooden scrollwork hung behind his loathsome companion's new vantage. Grigori stared back at Grigori. Dark eyes narrowed under heavy black brows. A shock of almost pitch-black hair topped his head.

His features were eastern European, although Nicolau would have been hard-pressed to say exactly where his ancestry lay. He wore no mustache or beard, and while he did not consider himself more than ordinary in appearance, Grigori was aware that many women found him handsome, especially when he was dressed for the evening, as he was now. His Italian suit went well with his steel-blue eyes, or so the attractive young woman behind the hotel's front desk had brazenly informed him.

He cursed silently as he tore his gaze from the mirror and returned it to the leering gargoyle. Frostwing had chosen his new perch because he had known that the mirror would draw his victim's attention. It was not out of vanity that the man stared, however, and both of them knew it.

"What is it you want of me this time?" snarled Grigori. Even after so many years of torment, he was able to dredge up defiance. Futile defiance, true, but the fact that he was able to muster any resistance to Frostwing allowed him to go on . . . that and the fact that he really had no choice *but* to go on.

How many centuries? He could not recall. His dread companion had stolen that knowledge along with so much else.

The gargoyle preened before answering, his long, stony talons caressing the edges of his wings. As they spread, the wings revealed perhaps the most arresting of Frostwing's features. Where most of the golem's form was of a gray, unremarkable stone, the upper edges of his wings, most notably around the shoulders, were composed of a peculiar, bone-white stone. Veins of the same white stone spread from his shoulders, streaking the top quarter of each wing. It had, at some point far in Grigori's forgotten past, made him think of ice upon a statue, and so he had come to call his adversary Frostwing. Whether the gargoyle had another title, Grigori did not know. Possibly he had forgotten it.

He had forgotten so much else . . . and all thanks to the monster before him. Now Frostwing said, "You have moved again. I thought that you *liked* London."

He had *loved* London, *loved* Great Britain. He had been forced to flee them, though, like every other place he had come to love. There were always questions, damnable questions, and, worse, a terrible compulsion which did not allow him to remain anywhere for very long. The list of places he had been forced to leave behind stretched long, the count ending only at the limits of his poor memory.

Grigori purposely walked away from the gargoyle and over to the mini-bar of his room. He removed a small bottle of whiskey from its place, then seized a glass and poured himself a drink. He swallowed the contents in one gulp, entirely unaffected by the strength of the liquor. Drinking was a pastime wasted on him, for no matter how much he downed, no matter how strong the drinks, they might as well be water. He could not become drunk if his life depended upon it.

It was also impossible for him to grow insane, a thing Grigori had always regretted. No matter what horrors he faced, he never sank into the protection of madness. Frostwing had once informed him that he would not allow Grigori to escape that way.

"I left London because I've always wanted to see Chicago," he finally remarked, his back still to his tormentor. "I'd heard that it's a beautiful city."

"Perhaps a century or so ago," returned the gargoyle. "When it was just freshly burned. I think that they should do it again. Fire is so cleansing."

Ignoring the comment, Nicolau poured himself another drink. He could just barely taste the alcohol. "You have your answer. There's really no need for you to remain."

Throughout their conversation, both had spoken accentless English. In the past, they had conversed in perfect Italian,

Greek, French, Chinese, Indian, and at least a dozen more tongues. Whatever land he visited, Grigori Nicolau knew the language, but at the cost of forgetting the others. His own name was Rumanian, yet had he chosen to visit one of the northwestern Chicago neighborhoods populated by immigrants from that country, he would have been as lost in a conversation as any newborn child. Grigori knew Rumania only as a country still struggling to free itself from the vestiges of the old Communist system . . . and as the supposed home of Transylvania and Dracula. Neither bit of knowledge aided him in any manner.

It was even possible that Grigori Nicolau was not his true name. Frostwing *liked* to play games with his memory. His name might be just one more of the devilish gargoyle's jests.

He heard the slow tearing of cloth, a sound that nearly made him drop his glass. Grigori glanced at his hands and found them shaking. The sound of cloth being methodically ripped held many different memories, many forgotten, but too many more still recalled. There were some things he wished his tormentor *would* take from his mind, but then that was why they remained in his head. The gargoyle generally took only what was treasured by his victim, not what tortured him.

Slowly, Grigori turned back to the monster. Frostwing removed his talon from the chair, revealing four slashes across the headrest. The gargoyle flashed a toothy grin.

''Poor little Grigori! You know that I *always* come for my due . . .''

Nicolau dropped the glass and raised his left hand, the open palm toward the demonic creature.

One by one, every electrical device in the room burst into blazing light as they short-circuited. A green aura surrounded the perched gargoyle.

Frostwing chuckled. He raised a taloned hand.

The aura faded, to be replaced by a sickly red light of no

discernible source. Grigori tried to run, but discovered that he could not move.

"Still hopeful as ever! It is good that you can still entertain me after so long, my dear Grigori!"

Rising from his perch, the huge stone figure darted across the room to where his hapless prisoner stood frozen. To Grigori's silent terror, Frostwing fluttered to a point just behind him and then seized hold with his arms and legs, wrapping himself around the man like some horrific child demanding a ride from his parent. The strain of so much weight upon him was almost more than Grigori could bear, but his legs refused to buckle—thanks mostly to the spell Frostwing had cast upon him.

"Naughty, naughty Grigori!" mocked the gargoyle, the side of his head pressed against the man's own. "After all we have been through together! After all I have done for you! How many centuries now? Five? Six? Seven? If you had been forced, like most men, to remember your past, the weight of all those memories would crush you! Think how good it is of me to take from you that which would *only* fill you with pain!"

I would gladly have it all, Nicolau desired to say. *I would gladly take upon myself the centuries of memory if it meant I would know what you've hidden from me about myself.*

Frostwing, of course, would have never granted such a request. It was not in the gargoyle's nature to be so benevolent.

"What shall I take from you this time, my old and untrusted friend? Will it be what remains of Trier in 1904? What of the last bits of Cairo in 1883? Paris in 1790?" One claw toyed with the hair hanging down over Grigori's forehead. "Do you still remember Muscovy? Wallachia, even?"

He recalled little of any of the places or times, but that was how Frostwing desired it. The last two names meant nothing to Grigori. He repeated them over and over in his mind. Perhaps, if luck was with him, he would recall them later, when he might have time to fit them into the puzzle that was his past.

"King Gustav, then," whispered the monster in his ear. "Do you recall his shining glory? Do you recall the day the *Vasa* sailed . . . and sank?"

The talon touched his forehead and brought back to him memories of the day that Grigori Nicolau . . . had that been his name then, too? . . . watched a ship he himself had helped build begin its maiden voyage from the harbor in Stockholm. There had been a broadside, a salute to both the king, who awaited his new royal warship in another city, and to the great navy of Sweden.

But the ship is top-heavy! Grigori wanted to cry again. *Too little room for ballast! Too many great guns above!*

The memory grew clear, and with its clarity came a bitter feeling of helplessness.

A breeze had blown up. Not a wind, but only a breeze.

The Vasa, *new pride of the mighty Swedes, had listed.*

Many of the crew had been below deck, and the gunports had still been open.

The sea had seized the opportunity with lusty abandon and had filled the Vasa's *bowels. The cold, inky waters of the harbor had greedily received the magnificent folly of King Gustav, making no distinction between the ship and the poor unfortunates aboard.*

Grigori had known more than a few of the thirty or so seamen who had joined the flooded ship in her chill, deep grave. Although frozen where he was, Grigori could still cry. Fresh tears for men dead more than three hundred years trailed down his face.

"Yesss, I think that I shall remove those awful memories from your mind! I am nothing, you know, if not sympathetic."

The theft was as simple as it was cruel. Merely once more

the touch of the gargoyle's talon on his forehead. The spell prevented him from protesting the loss of . . . of . . .

Of what?

Grigori noted the moisture on his face and concluded that once more he had lost some tragic piece of his past. It was futile to wonder what it was; he had tried too many times not to realize that once the memories were gone, they were gone.

The gargoyle placed his head on the other side of Nicolau's own. "A deliciously terrible thing that one was. So . . . *moving*. Not filling enough, though." Frostwing hissed in delight. "I think I will take from you another."

Another? His heart pounded even harder. Something was terribly wrong. Frostwing had never taken two memories during the same dream.

"Shall I tell you something?" asked the gray demon. "Shall I tell you that I am the reason you felt compelled to come to this city at this time? Shall I tell you that I am waiting for you here? That I have *always* waited for you somewhere? Shall I tell you *why*?"

Grigori had no time to ponder the revelations the gargoyle had offered so casually, for the moment he stopped speaking, Frostwing fluttered from the man's back and came around so that they faced one another. The monstrous golem towered over Grigori. He reached out with one clawed hand and drew the frozen figure to him, not stopping until Nicolau's face was only inches from his own. Frostwing's other hand came up and began stroking the side of Grigori's head, threatening to remove the dark man's ear and flay several inches of flesh from his face.

"Poor Grigori . . . you look *so* tired. In honor of our long friendship, I shall go easy on you this time." The shadowy pits that were Frostwing's eyes stared into Grigori's own. "I shall take from you only the memory of *this* encounter. Yesss,

I think it would only be a service to allow you to forget that I am waiting somewhere in the city for you."

Waiting for him somewhere in the city . . . Grigori Nicolau tried desperately to secure that knowledge deep within his own mind, to leave himself a warning that might afford him a feeble hope. He did not understand exactly what the gargoyle meant, for Frostwing had always come to him in his dreams and dreams had no physical boundaries. Yet, the creature was not jesting, not now. Somehow, Grigori knew that Frostwing had spoken true this time.

But what did he mean?

The hand that had been stroking his face moved to his forehead. The gargoyle chuckled. "Promise me that you will not forget me, dear Grigori?"

Grigori gasped—

—And woke to find himself sitting on one of the chairs in his hotel room. He opened his eyes wide. The lights around him all burned brightly, and for some reason this bothered Grigori. He was sweating and his mouth was dry. Grigori could recall neither sitting down nor falling asleep; his last memory had been of dressing for a rare evening out. Grigori had planned to see the Chicago Symphony. They were playing Bruckner tonight. It was one of the few vices he allowed himself, the occasional concert or play. Most of the time it was safer and less painful to remain secluded.

He no longer had any desire to see the symphony. After so long, Grigori had come to recognize his reactions. He had been asleep. He had been dreaming.

Frostwing has been here . . . to steal from me again! What bit of my life has he stolen this time? It was hard to know how deep the gargoyle might have gone for a memory. In truth, the content of the memory was not so important as the simple fact that one more piece of Grigori's past had been stolen from him.

It was odd that he could not recall the dream itself. That would mean that his nemesis had stolen the recollection of his visitation, something he had never done before. At least not that Grigori could remember.

Perhaps he had been mistaken and Frostwing had not been here. Perhaps his recent crossing from London to Chicago had taken more out of him than he had realized. Grigori leaned back to think and noticed something peculiar about the chair's backrest. It felt ragged and uncomfortable. He twisted around to see what was wrong.

"God in Heaven," he snarled. The slashes across the top of the chair were new. The gargoyle had been here.

Rising, he stepped away from the chair. It was then that he noticed the small glass lying on the carpet. An open bottle of whiskey sat on a counter nearby. Dreams the gargoyle's visits might be, but Frostwing always left physical signs of his visitation. Somehow he could reach through from the lands of Morpheus and actually touch the world . . . and Grigori.

Why, though, has he left me so many signs of his passing? Why take the memory but leave the evidence? Nothing that he had ever attempted had allowed Nicolau to record Frostwing, but then, how did one record a dream . . . especially without its consent? This era was a marvel when it came to devices, but he could hardly have asked his Fury to ignore an array of wires and machines.

Something was different. Something in the centuries-old game had changed. Grigori knew that he would have to discover just what that change meant . . . which was likely just what the gargoyle desired.

"And so it begins again," he whispered. Removing his suit coat, Grigori stalked over to a desk against the far wall. Seating himself, he opened the top drawer and, moving aside a small paperback book, pulled out what at first glance might have seemed a hand-held electronic game. Grigori had no interest in such, however, the game of life taking too much of his time.

So much progress and still nothing to help me free myself of this curse . . . The device was an electronic notebook, a marvel to him, yet still a toy in comparison to so much else that this era had wrought. Grigori picked up the small pen that went with the device and started to write. His brow furrowed as he tried to summon up what meager information he could recall about this latest encounter with the monster who had controlled his life for the past six hundred years or more.

His hands shook. After several seconds of staring futilely at the machine, Grigori put it down, rose, and walked over to the television. It also played any radio station in the area. Grigori flicked it on.

An entire symphony orchestra joined him in the room. He paused for a time to listen. Mahler. Almost as good as listening to Bruckner, he decided. Grigori had been fortunate to find a station that played what was rightly termed classical music. Searching for such a station was one of the first tasks he set for himself whenever arriving in a new place.

Nicolau retained a single memory of the time he had heard the premiere of Bruckner's Fourth in Vienna, during the winter of 1881. It had not been the original version, but a revised one. Anton Bruckner had never been satisfied with his work. Only a few years later he would revise parts of it again, but as far as Grigori was concerned, the version he had heard had been the definitive one.

Music and reading. They were his two most consistent pastimes. They were, it could have also been said, his life lines. Bereft of both, Grigori Nicolau would have been lost.

With strains of Mahler flowing through the hotel room, Grigori at last began to calm. He returned to the desk and sat down again. After a moment or two more of staring at the notebook, he attempted to write.

This time, he had more success. Scribbled words became perfectly typed as he wrote on the glass panel. The machine had not taken long to become attuned to his rather archaic style of handwriting.

Frostwing came to me in my dreams again this night . . .

II

WHEN HE WOKE THE NEXT MORNING AFTER A SLEEP FILLED with troublesome but normal nightmares, Grigori found the electronic notebook atop the desk. He had not left it there the night before. It should have been in the drawer, surrounded by wardings.

The notebook was on, but the panel was blank. Not only had his entire entry disappeared, but the entire program, as well. Grigori pressed several buttons, but the screen remained empty. Everything had been erased.

Nicolau ran a hand through his sleep-rumpled hair. The destruction of the notebook and his entry in particular was disappointing, but not unexpected. Frostwing tended to be very thorough.

There was no need to wonder how it had happened. Likely it had been Grigori's own hand that had cleared the notebook. It would not be the first time. For years, Grigori had burned his paper writings, not realizing it until the next day when he would wake to find a pile of ash smoldering on the floor and gray soot smudging his fingertips. Through the years, he had tried a thousand tricks to keep his journals intact, but each ploy had failed because he was combating not only Frostwing, but *himself*. He was the instrument of the demon's compulsion, the tool by which the gargoyle prevented Grigori from leaving himself a written history of his life. Somehow his words were always destroyed. Any safeguard he put up was easily defeated because he had already identified its weaknesses. He had even tried outside safeguards, but those had proven just as ineffective.

"Can't you leave me anything?" he whispered not for the first time to the absent gargoyle. "What did I ever do to you to deserve this fate?"

He had posed that same question to his tormentor. Frostwing, of course, had not deigned to reply.

And so I go on . . . Grigori threw the electronic notebook in the wastebasket. The device was useless. It could have been repaired, Grigori supposed, but he had no real desire to have the work done. He had owned the machine for several weeks, had even jotted down a few notes about possible enterprises, and the fact that Frostwing had taken no action had given him slight hope that he had finally discovered a technology the gargoyle could not foil so easily.

He should have known better.

When had it all begun? *Why* had it begun? He still asked himself those questions, even after centuries. Grigori Nicolau could not recall the first time he had been visited by the gargoyle; that memory had probably been the second Frostwing had devoured. The gargoyle seemed to have no purpose for the trials he inflicted upon his victim. After several centuries there should have been some possible conclusion, some culmination. Yet, he was forced to go on and on and on . . .

Fragmented though his memory was, he could still recall portions of his journey through history. Much of it had been in the cities of Europe, but he had visited other lands as well,

including parts of Asia and Africa. Occasionally he found
work that he could perform. Other times he subsisted on the
poor powers he had been granted, using his rare abilities to
manipulate games of chance and business transactions.

Ever Frostwing had found him. Grigori often wondered
whether he chose where he went or actually followed the
secret commands of the hideous golem.

*I have seen more than anyone could ever dream, watched
the rise of men from the darker ages, and yet I myself have
nothing to show for that time! Six hundred years, perhaps
more, and no purpose but to be the plaything of a creature
from Hell!*

Why?

Suddenly, Grigori felt an overpowering need to leave
his hotel room. It was a waste of his abilities to clean and
clothe himself, but this morning he chose to do so. A part
of him regretted that decision even as he worked the spell.
Showering generally gave him a sense of renewal, a fresh
start to his life. That was an illusion, of course, but Nicolau
took what solace he could from day-to-day living. In fact,
not only did he shower in the morning, but he also often
bathed at night, the better to wash away the day's oppres-
sive weight.

Gone was his robe, to be replaced abruptly by a dark
business suit and deep-blue tie. The day was supposed to be
a chill one, and so he conjured a long trenchcoat to cover
the suit. Grigori's hair, now neatly combed, was half-hidden
by a brimmed hat. Hats were not so popular these days, but
Grigori preferred them.

Smetana was playing in the background. "Hakon Jarl,"
the symphonic poem. For some reason known only to
Frostwing, Grigori's musical knowledge remained nearly
intact. Grigori did not question why; it was enough that he
had his music.

Nicolau had left the radio on all night to aid his troubled

slumber. He contemplated turning it off before he left, but decided better of it. At the moment, the thought of standing even for a few brief seconds in the room with no music to comfort him was too much.

Two minutes later found him departing the hotel lobby. A bellman opened the door for him and tipped his hat. Grigori nodded toward the man, then forgot him. He was anxious to lose himself in the morning crowd and pretend that he was just one of them too.

They led such brief, hurried lives. Hands in his coat pockets, Grigori observed those around him as he walked. Ever rushing through life and often not accomplishing anything worth their trouble, they were still enviable. Most of them had some control over how they spent their limited time. True, their decisions might be poor ones, but the point was that they had, however small, the *opportunity* to choose.

Nicolau had no choice. He could not die. Injure himself badly, yes, but he always mended.

Once, more than three hundred years ago, he had attempted suicide. He remembered that, although the reasons for the desperate act—other than the obvious—had been stolen from him. Grigori had failed, of course, and the agony he had suffered until he had mended had convinced him never to try it again.

What had been almost as terrible as the pain had been the gargoyle's mocking presence throughout the entire recovery. The winged golem had haunted his every moment during that period. It was in part because of his dread companion that Grigori had struggled harder to heal. He did not feel any gratitude toward the gargoyle for that, however. If Frostwing had desired him to mend it was only so that the curse could continue.

Grigori's anxiety lessened as he walked. It would never completely leave him, but he knew from those times that he could recall that he might lessen his stress to a more tolerable level. The centuries had taught Grigori one thing: it was useless to lose his wits after one of the gargoyle's visitations. It had never done him any good in the past; it would do him no good now.

He had passed shop after shop without paying heed to what they offered within, but now Grigori paused before a bookstore that was just opening, something in the window catching his eye. A closer look revealed it as a regional atlas. The cover promised the most up-to-date information on the Windy City, as Chicago was known. Much of the basic information he already knew. Chicago was a huge metropolis, smaller in size only to New York and Los Angeles, but first in many other ways. The tallest building in the world, the Sears Tower, reigned from here. Some of the finest cuisine could be found in the city. The information and business aspects of the midwestern goliath were respected worldwide. There were countless reasons why Nicolau had chosen this city of roughly three million.

Grigori stepped closer to the display window and studied the book. An idea formed in his head, a notion concerning something that he had not considered since departing Great Britain. This was the fabled New World, where modernism and technology prevailed. Yet, this was also a land of immigrants from many places around the globe. Anyone who wanted to begin anew came to America. *Anyone*.

Nicolau abandoned his walk and stepped inside the bookstore.

In a small cafe near the bookstore, Grigori chose a secluded booth and sat down. From a bag marked *Kroch's & Brentano's* he removed not only the atlas but a pair of maps and a guide book. There were other books in the bag, all mysteries. That had become his passion of late, but they were of personal interest only and would be of no assistance in what Grigori planned now.

It would be better to perform this spell back in his hotel room rather than in a public place, but Grigori could not bring himself to return there so soon. It was foolish, of course, to stay away. Since no one else noticed Frostwing, the gargoyle could appear anywhere, at any time based solely on his own whim. It was even possible that he might materialize before Nicolau while this spell was underway.

Grigori swallowed. *But he never returns quickly after a visitation. I should have a week, maybe more.*

Of course, it was dangerous to think he could predict what Frostwing would do. The fact that the stone golem had stolen the memory of their most recent confrontation was proof enough that Frostwing changed his patterns from time to time.

Yet, still he hoped.

He was contemplating how to begin when an attractive young waitress came over to take his order. She wore no identifying tag and did not offer a name, but did, at least, smile at him.

"I almost didn't see you there! Do you want some coffee?"

Grigori realized that he had not eaten yet. For what he planned, it was wise not to be too full. Still, raw energy would benefit him. "No coffee. Give me something with sugar."

"A coke?" From her tone, the young, brunette woman did not sound certain. Grigori could almost read her thoughts simply by studying her expression and tone of voice. *Most people*, she was likely thinking, *drank coffee or juice in the morning, but some people did drink soda*. From the way she had reacted, he knew that she was not one of the latter.

"Yes, please." He considered. "Also a sweet pastry. Give me something coated."

"Something—you want a cinnamon roll with frosting?"

"That would be perfect."

She bit the pen she had been writing with. "You sure you don't want something more? I know I shouldn't say this, but it's not good for your health to eat like that."

Grigori gave her a smile that only he knew was bittersweet. "I think that I'll survive this once."

The waitress disappeared to place his order. Grigori resumed arranging his purchases. The maps he unfolded and spread across the table. One depicted the metropolitan area, the other the surrounding suburbs. From the maps' perspective, Chicago appeared akin to a mighty kingdom surrounded by countless smaller principalities.

He briefly inspected the guide book, then put it aside. Its role would come later. He was just opening the atlas when the waitress came back with his order.

"Do you need to find someplace special?" she asked, gazing at the maps. "I know the area pretty good."

Grigori made some room on the corner for his drink and his food. "No, thank you. I am just familiarizing myself with your city."

"With Chicago? Good luck! If you've got any questions, feel free to ask, okay?"

"Thank you. May I pay you now?"

"If that's what you want." She reached into an apron pocket for his bill. Grigori took it from her, inspected it briefly, then paid her, including the woman's tip with the rest of the money.

She looked at the extra money. "This is almost as much as your bill."

"It's yours. I won't need anything else."

"Well, if you do, just wave for me, okay?" With a parting smile, the waitress left him alone.

Grigori watched her move on to another customer, briefly admiring her youth and beauty. Now and then he allowed himself brief liaisons, but this was certainly not the time. He was also not one to use his power in that manner.

At least, as far as he could recall. The uncertainty made him pause before he reminded himself that it was futile to worry about actions he could no longer recall.

Thumbing through the atlas, Grigori found the section detailing the area where he and his hotel room were situated. He adjusted the atlas so that it would stay open, then put it on top of the uppermost map.

His next step was to devour the roll and drink the entire glass of soda. This Grigori did in little more than a minute. The meal left him with a faint, sickly sweet taste in his mouth, causing him to briefly contemplate ordering a glass of water. That could wait until afterward, however. For now, it was important that he had taken in the extra sugar. What to most people were simply health debilitating pleasures for the tongue were to him the necessary fuel he needed in order not to deplete his strength.

From his pocket, Nicolau removed a small pendant. It was not remarkable in any way save by its age. He had carried it with him for . . . for . . . at least two hundred years. The pendant consisted of a silvery metal chain and a small, green gemstone. It had not been fashioned to please the eye, but rather to perform a function. With it, Grigori Nicolau planned to see whether or not he was alone.

To the best of his knowledge, his command of the power had never been more than fair. He had mastered numerous minor abilities, such as raising and manipulating small objects in midair or altering his clothes. Grigori could also influence the minds of the unsuspecting, something he hated doing but found forced into at times to protect his anonymity. He could, with effort, transport himself some short distance. Most folk would have been awed by his "magical" skills, but to Grigori those abilities were laughingly limited. They caused him as much ill as they did good.

Why he bore such power, Grigori did not know. Among the explanations he had pondered during the centuries, the only one that made sense to him was that some people were more closely tied to the natural forces of the world. These few, either trained, naturally adept, or simply lucky, learned to manipulate those forces to some degree.

There were others who wielded powers like his, some with much greater ability. Very few of them were to be trusted. Grigori avoided them as readily as he wished he could avoid the gargoyle.

There was another group that drew his interest just now. Those people Grigori *wanted* to find, but he doubted that they would be as easy to discover as the first group. He did not know if any of them were in the region at all.

He took the pendant in both hands and let the gemstone slip down so that it swung back and forth over the open page of the atlas. Grigori took one last look around to see if anyone was watching, then, satisfied that his appearance seemed innocent enough, he lowered his head as if reading and began to concentrate.

The gemstone stopped swinging, but it did not hang straight down. Instead, it froze at a slight angle, one that pointed the stone's tip directly at the center of the area outlined on the map.

Show me! Grigori demanded. *Am I alone?*

Slowly, a small pinprick of light, very faint at first, appeared in the upper left corner of the map. It remained weak but steady. Far across from it and very near the North Shore area of Lake Michigan, another light, this one more intense, flickered into being.

Two. Any more?

Near the bottom of the map, yet another pinprick of light sprouted. Grigori leaned forward to see where this one was located.

The pendant abruptly swung downward, as if gravity had finally demanded its due. The three gleams vanished. For a moment, a haze hung over the map.

Then . . . nothing. The haze vanished, and the map was as it had been before the spell.

That was not right. Not at all. He glanced around, fearing that Frostwing had returned, but he could neither sense nor see the cursed monster. There was no trace of any other power, either—at least that he could detect. Grigori was well aware of the limitations of his abilities, but he felt safe none the less.

What had happened?

Pushing aside the atlas, he studied the fold-out map of the city. The main map revealed not only Chicago, but the first villages and towns just beyond its official borders. Grigori positioned himself before it, then brought the pendant forward again.

All went well at first. The pendant swung forward, the tip of the gemstone focusing on the very center of the city.

Then, as quickly as it had risen, the gemstone swung back to its original hanging position. Once more, Grigori sensed a haze covering the map.

More curious now, he roughly pushed aside the first map and began the rite on the remaining one.

The results were the same.

An uneasy feeling crept over him. He had never confronted anything so confounding. The territory around and including the city was blanketed by something. A part of him wanted to leave Chicago there and then, perhaps even leave the United States if need be, but Grigori was also curious. It was a trait that had made his harried existence both tolerable and impossible. It had placed him in danger, yet had led him to dozens of fascinating discoveries over the centuries.

But the cliché is that curiosity killed the cat. Death did not frighten Grigori, but there were worse fates than death. Experience with those others who wielded power had taught him that long ago.

Grigori Nicolau leaned back for a minute. The work with

the pendant took much out of him, but the soda and the roll had given him the excess energy that he had required. Despite the seeming simplicity of the spell, utilizing the gemstone in a search was one of the most difficult acts he was capable of performing.

Returning the pendant to its resting place, Nicolau began folding the maps. They were still of use to him, if only to guide him around Chicago. He put the maps and the atlas back into the bag, then contemplated his next move.

The truth of the matter was that his situation would likely be unchanged no matter where he went. There was always the threat of others and *always* the gargoyle's visits in his dreams. No matter where he journeyed, those two things would remain true. Chicago, then, was as good a place to be as anywhere else. Grigori had, after all, wanted to come here. He had read much about the city and admired it. It was an excellent region for both business and life, not to mention being a good central location for journeying to other parts of the continent. In a city of over two million, it would also be easier to go unnoticed by others . . . at least, Grigori hoped so.

He had just finished replacing the articles in the bag when his waitress returned.

"Are you through, already? Did you find what you wanted or can I be of some help after all?"

Grigori considered simply thanking her for her concern and departing, but a new notion entered his mind. "Perhaps, yes. Is there some place nearby where I might purchase a newspaper?"

"I've got a *Tribune* back there I'm done with," she offered, indicating the counter far behind them. "I was just going to recycle it, but if you need it, I'll get it for you."

"You don't have to do that."

She smiled again. Her features had just a little too much

character for the present fashion look, the nose especially being a bit too flat, but Grigori's tastes were more basic.

"I don't mind," the woman continued. "Sure you don't want anything else?"

The brief but intense work had left him thirsty. The combined sweetness of the Coke and the roll also still assailed his tongue. "A glass of water, perhaps, but that's really all."

"All right."

She returned but a moment later, both drink and paper in hand. Nicolau thanked her for both and, despite her protests, paid her for the newspaper.

Most of the sections he ignored as having no consequence to his new goal. In fact, only one section interested him at all, and that he finally found at the bottom of the stack.

In the *Tribune*, the Classified section was a separate little paper. Grigori pushed aside the other parts of the newspaper and read the index. The first listing was for those seeking employment. Nicolau did not need that; his financial state was excellent at the moment. Between his writing and some slightly manipulated gambling, he would be comfortable for at least the next half year. He had silent investments in various other ventures, a few of which he planned to liquidate in the near future.

He had never really suffered financial straits. That had always been one of the odd things about his already much too odd existence. It would have made perfect sense to Grigori for Frostwing to leave him a pauper, a man with no home, no money or chance of relief, yet, evidently such was not part of the demon's plan.

Once more he reminded himself that there was no predicting the ways of the marble golem. Frostwing was quite mad, and madness had a logic all of its own.

The time would come when he would have to choose an occupation, if only to keep from sitting around all day thinking of the beast's next visitation. Gambling could easily have filled his needs, but Grigori preferred work. It gave him at least some satisfaction.

Grigori finally found what he was searching for immediately after the employment advertisements.

Almost every major newspaper across the world contains a section where people can leave short messages for anyone to read. Many writers thank God or some saint for miracles. Others plead for information concerning some event or some person. There are messages from one lover to another. Anything anyone desires to say, provided the wording doesn't offend the editors, might be found in this section.

To one who knew where to look, there were messages for those like Grigori. Those with power.

Some communication was necessary. In the modern world, the methods were boundless, but one of the most dependable was the newspaper. A newspaper could be found almost anywhere, at almost any time. Such messages were not, of course, the most confidential. There were other ways in which more important missives traveled. Yet, the information one might find in the newspaper could prove very important.

However, his search through the paper proved just as fruitless as his work with the maps. There was nothing, no hidden message or even an identifying mark. Although his work with the pendant indicated there were at least a few others of power in and around the city, no one was using the newspaper to relay information. That did not necessarily mean anything; perhaps none of the others had had anything to say. Unless circumstances demanded it, Grigori would not contact them. If unbothered, they were more likely to leave him be. Most power wielders respected one another's privacy unless provoked.

The uneasiness remained. Nonetheless, Grigori knew that it was time to proceed with his own plans. He had learned to live with fears and anxieties. For the time being, the region would provide him with a new home, a place from which he could plot.

The centuries had not broken him. Grigori still hoped to free himself of his nemesis. Perhaps in Chicago, he would find a way.

He smiled grimly. Sometimes it amazed him, the way hope never completely faded away.

Returning to the paper, Grigori sought out the Housing section. He could not stay at the hotel forever. In a city this size, there would be a great number of apartments or even homes to rent. Price did not matter; one way or another he would find what he needed.

Grigori located the beginning of the Apartments column and guided his finger along the entries. The speed at which he scanned the list would have been impossible for anyone else. But by the time he was finished, Grigori would know everything he needed to know in order to locate a place sufficient for his needs.

Midway through the listings his finger froze.

It was not a message, not, that is, of any sort that he could comprehend. Grigori's index finger seemed transfixed on the small advertisement. It was not even for a single location, but rather for an agency.

The home you have always been seeking! Apartments, condos, and houses throughout Chicagoland! Rent or buy today! We're waiting for you today at Sentinel Real Estate, Chicago's fastest-growing realtor and leasing company!

There was more text after the blazing announcement, but Grigori Nicolau noted only the address and telephone number. They became etched into his mind, but, just in case, he ran his index finger around the advertisement. As if cut with a pair of scissors, the advertisement lifted loose of the page.

Grigori had no explanation for the strange feeling. It was

not a compulsion, not exactly, but he felt a great urge to visit the agency. There was some connection between the realtor and himself. It was not the first time he had felt such a link, but this was somehow different.

A trap? He doubted it. Even if it were, Grigori intended to find the realtor.

"Sentinel Real Estate . . ."

When the waitress glanced up a moment later to see if the slight, dark man might want something more, the booth was empty. She stood at the counter and stared for a time, trying to recall just exactly when he had gotten up and somehow walked past her without her seeing him leave.

III

THERE WERE THREE MEN IN THE DIMLY LIT ROOM, ONE OF whom was bound to a chair of silver and iron. A single light overhead illuminated only the immediate region around the chair and the pair of standing figures. The bound man was tall and angular, almost cadaverous, with graying black hair and a swarthy look. He was dressed very elegantly in a suit that matched his steel-blue eyes. The others were clad less aesthetically, their rumpled brown suits and scuffed shoes an indication that they spent much time on the move. Both men had nondescript faces, the kind that went unnoticed at the proper times, and were clearly of the type for whom strength attempted to make up for a lack of original thought.

It was clear, too, that the bound man, despite his seeming helplessness, inspired great fear in them both.

"Another buyer slipped through your grasp." The bound man's voice was calm, almost soft, yet each word struck the listener like a harsh slap. His words echoed through the dark room, repeating over and over his quiet condemnation of his subordinates.

The two men shifted uneasily.

"The house grows stronger with each failure, gentlemen." Each word was spoken with precision, yet now and then, a hint of accent could be heard. Oddly, it was not always the same accent.

Neither figure attempted an excuse. They knew that excuses would only make their recent failure more egregious in the eyes of the man strapped securely to the high-backed, ancient chair. And even in his present position, the bound man held their lives in his hands.

"Something new has entered the playing field."

The news both worried and cheered them. This development meant that they had one more opportunity. Yet if the bound man considered this a new situation, all they had been taught might now be useless.

"Go out and take your positions. This time, however, there will be other eyes to aid your own. They will watch with you. They will also watch *you*."

From the darkness came the sound of many tiny feet skittering back and forth. A squeaking noise made the bulkier of the two men start.

Neither amused nor unamused, the bound man continued. "My life is already staked on the outcome of this, gentlemen. Rest assured that yours are, too."

Although the figure in the chair gave no command, the two underlings knew that they had just been dismissed. Bowing, they backed into the darkness. Steel-blue eyes watched the men depart long after the blackness had swallowed them up. After several seconds, the bound man finally turned his head and spoke to the shadows.

"Follow them closely."

There were answering squeaks, then the sound of hundreds of tiny feet padding across the concrete floor.

The bound man closed his eyes and sighed.

Sentinel Real Estate was located just at the edge of one of the city's residential areas, but close enough to the commercial sections to make it accessible. The realtor took the bottom floor of a small office center. A neon sign in the window continually repeated the company's claim of being the fastest growing realtor in the Windy City. Samples of its current offerings dotted the rest of the pane.

From across the street and just to the right of the realtor's window, Grigori Nicolau studied the office. The cab that he had taken had let him out around the corner, as per his instructions. Nicolau was not so foolish as to go rushing into the office without first learning what he could from a safe vantage.

Unfortunately, he was learning almost nothing. The office looked innocuous. Grigori could detect no underlying force, no source of the compulsion he had felt from the advertisement in the newspaper.

Even so, he felt a renewed urge to enter. It seemed not so tied to the building as to something or someone inside.

Grigori braced himself and walked across the street to the doorway. From here he could see that the office was almost empty. One or two indistinct figures sat in the back, but that was all. Better in some ways, but suspicious in others. Of course, six or seven hundred years of looking over one's shoulder could make anyone paranoid. It was possible that there was nothing to fear.

Possible.

He opened the door and stepped inside. A bell jingled as

the door swung open, alerting one of the figures seated in the back.

"Hello! Welcome to Sentinel! How can we be of service to you?"

The young man started toward him. He could not have been in the real estate business long. The man was shorter than Nicolau, wearing an inexpensive brown suit, and much too eager for his own good. He did not even look as if he had been an adult for very long, but then, to Grigori most people seemed a bit on the young side.

The man was also not the person or thing that he had been seeking. Grigori dismissed him without saying a word, his gaze shifting to take in the rest of the office. Nothing he saw called to him. Everything was what it appeared. The door to another office stood behind the desks, but what little he could see of the back room revealed nothing significant to him. The other figure in the front office, an older man engaged in paperwork, was also not the source of the call.

"Is there someone in particular you're looking for?" asked the young man, trying to make eye contact with Grigori.

Nothing. Yet, the feeling was still there. It was almost as if what he sought was—

When she stepped out of the back room, all else seemed to fade away for Grigori. It was not that she was the most striking woman he had ever met, although she was certainly attractive. Rather, he felt immediately certain that *she* was the source. She was the one who had called him here.

It was also quite apparent that the summons had not been sent with any specific intention; when she looked his way, she smiled with politeness and faint yet innocent interest. Grigori smiled back, but the smile withered a little as he noticed the color of her eyes.

Steel blue. The same as his own. The same as those of a few others he had encountered in the past, souls who had called to him somewhat the same way she had, yet without nearly the intensity. Never had Nicolau felt such magnitude. Small wonder he had not recognized the call for what it was.

Over the centuries Grigori Nicolau had met them. There had been one in Budapest, another in Moscow. Grigori could recall perhaps six, but did not doubt that there had been others Frostwing had caused him to forget. He had never, to his spotty recollection, discovered the reason for the link. He knew only that it felt as if he had found a piece of himself, a piece he had not even known was missing.

"Sir?"

Grigori realized how he must look, staring so wide-eyed at the woman. Swiftly he gathered his thoughts. "Her. I spoke to—" he glanced at the nameplate on the desk the blonde woman was walking toward. The plate read *Teresa Dvorak* "—Miss Dvorak. Forgive me, I couldn't recall her name at first."

As he finished speaking, Grigori attempted to exert his will ever so slightly on the young man. He did not enjoy using his power this way. Often it did not work. But all Grigori desired now was for the man to take his word.

The suggestion seemed to take hold . . . or perhaps the young man had simply believed him. Nodding, the novice real estate agent turned toward the slim figure of Teresa Dvorak. "Terry! This gentleman says that he talked to you. Are you free?"

She looked up at Grigori Nicolau, who could feel her slight confusion. "I'm free."

"Come this way, Mr.—"

"Nicolau."

"Mr. Nicolau. Terry was top agent last month. She'll certainly be able to find something to suit you."

"Thank you." Grigori followed him to Teresa Dvorak's desk. Teresa rose as he neared, indicating that Grigori should take one of the seats in front of the desk. He removed his hat as he started for a seat.

His young guide quickly moved around so as to help him with the chair. "Can I take your hat and coat?"

"Thank you, but no." Nicolau sat down and cradled the hat in his hands. The young man nodded and returned to his own desk.

"It was Mr. Nicolau?" asked the woman. Grigori nodded, taking the opportunity to study her more closely. Her shoulder-length blonde hair curved around a strong, almost sculpted face with cheekbones that would have been the envy of many women. Her lips were slightly fuller than average, but somehow that seemed right for her. She reminded him a bit of a Valkyrie out of Wagner's *Ring*, save that while she was obviously on the athletic side, Teresa Dvorak was still most definitely feminine. The elegant suit dress she wore revealed just enough to tell him that.

Dangerous thoughts blossomed in his mind, thoughts he ever fought to keep in check. He dared not make his interest too evident; the link that had drawn him here from the restaurant worked only on him. Never had any of the others noticed the supernatural bond between himself and them. Grigori had discovered that the hard way, after frightening away the first few.

The others . . . the others had all eventually disappeared. Where, he did not know . . . or at least recall.

She glanced over her desk, as if looking for something. "I don't recall the conversation, Mr. Nicolau. Was it today?"

"No, it was a few days ago. Please, call me Grigori."

Her eyes returned to his. He felt a charge go through him that he had not felt in more than a century. Again, it was as if he had found a part of him that had been missing. But the sensation was more powerful than any previous encounter.

Nicolau stared into Teresa Dvorak's eyes and saw that she

was nobody's fool. It was obvious that she was fairly certain that the two of them had not talked before. "Perhaps if you remind me of what it was we discussed, Mr.——Grigori." She paused. "An interesting name. Is that Russian?"

"It is a name of many lands, Miss Dvorak."

"Call me Teresa," she said with a professional smile. "You speak perfect English. You have no accent whatsoever."

"Thank you." He added nothing. She was suspicious of him, suspicious almost to the point of unreason.

"So, what was it you wanted? A house, an apartment?"

In truth, the longer he sat before her, the more lost Grigori Nicolau became. He had journeyed to the office because of the call. Now that he had discovered the source of that call, he had absolutely no idea as to what to do. Grigori desperately wanted to maintain contact with her; although they had only just met, that which bound him to her made the thought of leaving and possibly never seeing her again almost too much to imagine.

There was also the matter of Teresa Dvorak's reaction to him. His rather peculiar entrance notwithstanding, her wariness went deeper than it should have.

He *did* need a more permanent place to stay. That was why Grigori had looked at the Housing section in the first place. Fate smiled upon him for once. "An apartment was what I was looking for, Teresa."

The reaction his response produced was startling. The blonde woman sat straight. Her eyes widened, and she almost blurted something out. Clearly, the young woman had expected him to choose something other than an apartment. She had mentioned houses; was there some hidden significance in that?

Teresa was quick to recover. He admired her for that. At the same time he wondered how well she would have reacted if he had told her that he was interested in purchasing a house.

The temptation to change his response was great, but not enough to risk alienating her further.

"An apartment? We do handle a number of openings throughout the city and surrounding areas." Teresa's attitude toward him changed. She grew more open, more real. "Part of our leasing program. The owners pay us a fee for every resident that is approved. Did you have any particular region in mind? Lincoln Park, maybe?"

"I have not decided on any particular area, Teresa." How much brighter the office was now that she had opened up to him. He felt his spirits lighten. "Perhaps if you can give me an idea of what is available."

She gave him an amused smile. "In Chicago? If you're willing to pay the price, Grigori, you can find just about anything! What do you want from your apartment? Tell me that, and I can tell you what sort of price range that you're going to be looking at."

For the first time since meeting her, Nicolau looked away. His gaze drifted to the wall beyond the attractive agent, but in his mind he saw the sky. "Something high. As high as possible."

Grigori did not know if there was a Heaven, much less a place for him there. Yet, childish as it seemed, he wanted to be as close as was physically possible.

"Something high up." Teresa smiled again. "I've always liked apartments like that. I've got a wonderful view from my place."

"Is there anything available there?"

She grew just a little distant. "Nothing that I know of."

He had pushed too hard. She was suspicious of him again. "I'm sorry if you took that the wrong way, Miss Dvorak. I only thought that anywhere someone like you, in your profession I mean, decided to live had to be exceptional. I didn't mean any harm."

The tension dissipated. "Forgive me, Grigori. Things have

been a little . . . hectic . . . of late. I shouldn't have reacted like that . . . and *please*, call me Teresa.''

"Thank you, Teresa.''

The realtor reached for a thick folder on the left side of her desk, then opened it. The contents proved to be a series of magazines and pamphlets. There was also a stack of computer pages almost an inch thick. Teresa swiftly thumbed through the magazines, discarding some, putting others in a pile to the right of the open file. When she was finished with the magazines and pamphlets, she looked up at her client. "You still haven't mentioned a price range, or how long of a lease you want. In terms of leases, I have everything from a week to a year, with a few going beyond that.''

"A year would be fine. As for price, I am not a millionaire, but if the apartment suits my needs, I am willing to pay.''

"What sort of business are you in . . . if you don't mind my asking?''

Grigori was tempted to give her a list of the occupations he could still recall from his several centuries of working, but thought better of it. "I am an entrepreneur with varied interests. I have made investments here and there.'' A rare smile escaped him as he added, "I prefer long-term investments.''

She returned his smile, unaware of the bit of personal humor. "You must do well for yourself. Maybe you could give me some stock tips.'' Teresa picked up one of the pamphlets. "Would you prefer a view of the lake?''

The question produced a shudder of fear throughout Nicolau's body. The titanic lake conjured up images of ships sinking and men drowning, but Grigori could not recall any such event in his lengthy lifetime. Either his imagination had gotten the best of him or . . . or he had forgotten something.

What have you stolen from my memory, Frostwing, that I should suddenly fear the water so? Responding at last to

Teresa's question, he shook his head and said, "No view of the lake. I would much prefer something further inland, please."

Teresa removed several pamphlets and one magazine from her stack. She then gathered up the computer printout and folded over the first several sheets.

Steel-blue eyes met steel-blue eyes. Teresa reached for the topmost apartment guide from her much-dwindled pile. "Looks like we can get started."

Sifting through the information took more than an hour. Even then, they had eliminated only the least likely choices. Grigori hardly noticed the time go by. His attention was focused more on his companion than the apartment listings she reviewed with him. He was careful not to let his interest become too evident, although at times it was difficult, especially since Teresa Dvorak was not very forthcoming about herself. The questions he peppered into the conversations concerning the apartments met with little response. Teresa proved adept at turning away anything that concerned her background, which only intrigued Grigori more. Somehow, he needed to find out what she was trying to hide.

The young woman organized her papers, then looked at a slim, gold watch on her right wrist. She exhaled in mild surprise, then turned her attention back to her client. "We can do this one of a number of ways, Grigori. You've given me some idea as to what you're looking for. Let me review the places left on the list, make some inquiries, then give you a call at wherever you're staying. That will save you a lot of useless running around." She handed him a small card and a pen. "Could you fill this out? Just your name and the place you're staying. If it's a hotel, note the room number. Oh, and the hotel's phone number, if you know it offhand."

He was being dismissed. Grigori fought back his distress as he wrote down the information Teresa had requested. As he returned the completed card to her, he asked, "Can we do no more today?"

Teresa was apologetic. "I would, but I have to show some places this afternoon. If you're in a hurry, we could schedule something tomorrow. I should be able to make at least some of the phone calls by then."

"Yes . . . yes, that would be fine." It was foolish to press any further. Nicolau cursed himself for acting like a lovesick idiot, but that was close to the truth. What he had come to learn of Teresa Dvorak in the short time they had spent together only strengthened the link's intensity. She was clever, humorous, and kind. She was also a bit reserved, perhaps shy, beneath all of that. It was a wonderful combination. Some of his past encounters had been with souls not so admirable.

Grigori was certain that, even under ordinary circumstances he would have found her enchanting.

But if you had been a normal man, you would have died centuries ago, he bitterly reminded himself.

Teresa paged through her calendar. "Tomorrow morning is busy, but I have time about three in the afternoon."

"Three would be fine."

"Good. I'm sorry that we can't keep going; I hate leaving things half-done. It's just that, ever since we started this rental and leasing program, we've received twice the business we were accustomed to." She indicated the other two agents. "This isn't even half of our staff. We're here to guard the fort until some of the others come back. In an area like Chicago, a service like ours is in high demand. Still, I can promise you that we'll do our best to get you the place you want, at a reasonable rent."

"And I appreciate that." Grigori did not rise until she did, wanting to make the moment last as long as possible. On the one hand he felt like a child because of his irrational behavior.

On the other . . . Nicolau simply did not care. During his brief time with Teresa, he had felt more alive than he had in years.

He was afraid to consider how long that sensation might last. Frostwing did not approve of happiness.

Teresa handed Grigori a few pamphlets. "Why don't you look these over? They're some of the places closest to your preferences, probably the ones we'll be discussing in more detail tomorrow."

"Thank you." As he took the papers, Grigori allowed his hand to gently touch hers. She took no notice of the action, for which he was grateful.

"Let me see you out."

As they walked toward the door, Grigori contemplated asking Teresa to join him for dinner. He dismissed the notion quickly. Doing so would push her too far too soon. Patience was what was needed now.

Something else nagged at him, then. Nicolau tried to force the feeling down, but it resisted. It was a question, a question that had been lurking at the back of his mind since early in his encounter with Teresa. He did not want to ask it, for fear that she would withdraw again, but he had to give it voice for his own peace of mind.

He paused before the door, trying his best to maintain a casual tone. "Teresa, I hope you do not mind an awkward question, but I was wondering why you seemed so surprised when I said that I was looking for an apartment."

Her face darkened and her manner grew frosty. For a moment, she looked ready to throw Grigori out, but then her expression softened. "I didn't know that it'd showed. I'm sorry about that, Grigori. I've had some trouble with one of our sale properties, and my mind was on it when you came in. I shouldn't have taken it out on you. Will you accept my apologies?"

"No apology is needed. I shouldn't have asked." There was some truth to what she had said, but there was more to it. He knew that even without the benefits of his abilities, Grigori did not pry further.

She smiled and offered her hand. "Thank you for coming, Grigori. I'll see you tomorrow at three?"

He returned her smile with the best of his own that he could offer. "I look forward to it."

To his barely concealed pleasure, she reddened slightly.

He walked across the street and around the corner, not stopping until he was certain that no one in the realty office could see him. Grigori paused, turning to stare back in the direction of Teresa Dvorak's office.

Away from the full influence of her presence, he was able to think with a little more rationality. The course that Grigori had chosen was a futile one. He knew that. There could be no happiness for him as long as Frostwing haunted him through his dreams. Yet, Grigori still had every intention of returning on the morrow and, if things worked well then, arranging for further meetings. It would take him a very long time to find a suitable dwelling place; of that he was certain.

His reverie was broken by a sudden sensation in his mind. It was minute and fleeting, gone almost before it could be noticed. Grigori gasped and immediately harnessed his power in a search for the source of the intrusion. Although he was quick to scan his surroundings, he could find no sign of any other person of power. He could sense the presence of Teresa, but she was not the source.

A trick of his own besotted mind . . . or perhaps the gargoyle toying with him already. Nicolau shivered and started to walk. It could not be the stonework demon. Not so *soon*. No matter how often he repeated this, though, he could not convince himself.

Did Frostwing know of Teresa Dvorak, then? Grigori almost turned around and started back to the office, but decided better of it. It was Grigori Nicolau who Frostwing wanted, Grigori Nicolau who was the nightmarish golem's plaything.

A green taxi came into sight down the street. Grigori raised a hand to hail it, at the same time exerting just enough influence to make the driver notice him. He watched with no sense of triumph as the vehicle stopped before him.

As he entered, he preempted any talk from the driver by immediately giving him the name and street of his hotel. Then Grigori simply settled in on the fading vinyl seat in the back and tried to calm himself again by focusing inward. A Brahms concerto began to play in his head.

He neither saw nor sensed the tiny, furred form that scampered back into the sewer vent below curbside as the cab pulled away, a tiny form that had been regarding him. Had Grigori noticed the creature, he might also have noticed its most distinctive feature.

Its eyes, too, were steel blue.

IV

GRIGORI ATE DINNER AT THE HOTEL RESTAURANT, FEASTING with his eyes well as his mouth. He always chose a table that would allow him the best view of his surroundings. The panorama before him included everything from the activities of the servers to the idiosyncrasies of the various guests. There were tourists, business people, children, elderly folk and more. Limited as he was by Frostwing's unpredictable companionship, Grigori Nicolau dared not grow close to people. However, much like his morning walks, this allowed him to pretend to be one of them.

At last even that pleasure proved lacking, for Grigori's thoughts continually turned to the young blonde woman with eyes much like his own. Teresa Dvorak haunted his thoughts, a thing much preferable to the gargoyle haunting his dreams. As for the brief sense of intrusion that had followed his encounter with her, Grigori had finally attributed that to his own nerves. If it had been Frostwing, Nicolau certainly would have known it; the winged horror was not so timid in his assaults.

It was time to face his room. Grigori had not returned to it since morning. Now, however, dinner was over and night was falling. Changing rooms would be a waste of time; he had given up such futile gestures centuries ago. Frostwing would find him no matter where he hid.

Grigori Nicolau paid his bill in cash, credit cards requiring too much intrusion into his background. He also found the concept rather unsettling. One spent only what one could afford to spend. It was a state of mind that reminded him that he was of another time, another place.

At his door, Grigori brought out one of the magnetic cards that the hotel used as keys. He could still recall when he had first come across them. To Grigori, a key should be a solid piece of metal that opened an iron lock. The modern system seemed so flimsy. How could it prevent anyone from walking into his room? Fortunately, he did not have to rely on such technology. Wards protected his room.

The darkened room was silent, the maid evidently having dealt with the music. Nicolau quickly turned on the light, glanced around out of reflex, then stepped inside. Closing the door behind him, he started toward the radio.

The wall to his left suddenly bulged outward. The bulge swiftly took on the form of a man, as if the wall had *swallowed* someone whole, someone who now sought escape. Yet it was clearly not escape the bulge wanted, but rather Grigori.

He backed away, at the same time attempting to counter the attack of the wall with his power.

Apelike arms decorated in the pattern of the wallpaper wrapped around his chest from behind him. It was almost impossible to breathe. Grigori struggled, but the arms held him tight. It was all he could do to remain conscious.

The bulge separated from the rest of the wall. As it did, the thing of wallpaper and woodwork became a hulking, brutish figure in a rumpled suit and coat. Grigori, still gasping for air, glanced down at the arms pinning him and saw that they, too, now appeared human.

" 'Bout time you got here," grunted the man before him. The man was a mongrel. Several different physical types had combined to create his features. None of them had meshed well. Even without being able to see the countenance of the second villain, Grigori was certain that he would have a similar look. "Yell all you like. No one's going to hear. We've made certain of that."

"There—there's no need to hurt me," Grigori gasped, stalling for time. "I'll tell you where all my valuables are."

"Valuables. Right. Maybe later."

There was something about the way the man's lips moved that was not right. His words were out of sync with the movements of his mouth. That was disturbing, but not nearly as disturbing as the fact that, even now, Grigori could not sense either man in the room. He might have been the prisoner of ghosts. Grigori could sense neither their minds nor their lifeforces. His power should have enabled him to note their existence on either of those two levels. They were too solid to be illusions, which meant that they were shielded by either their own power or some device given to them by another.

The mongrel looked to his companion. "Chair."

Grigori was thrown bodily into the nearest chair and secured with an expertise that impressed him. These men were professionals of a sort. Yet neither of them could be the true master. They moved like well-trained foot soldiers.

From a coat pocket, the mongrel removed a small, diamond-shaped object. The uppermost point of the object was far too sharp for Nicolau's tastes, especially if it was he on whom it was to be used.

"Say good night, blue eyes . . ." Again the mouth moved out of synch with the words.

Grigori struggled, but was held fast. The brutish figure jabbed Grigori's neck with the needlelike point. The world suddenly grew murky, but not completely black.

"He looks dead," came a second voice from what seemed a thousand miles away. The voice was a low rumble and only barely comprehensible.

"No, he's awake." Through the haze, the mongrel's ugly visage leered at his prisoner. The artifact was no longer in his hand, but Grigori could not recall when the man had disposed of it. "The master'll really be interested in this one."

"What makes him so different?"

Mongrel looked up at his unseen companion. "He didn't ask about the house. That's enough, don't ya think?"

"Maybe he's not one."

"With those eyes?"

"Yeah, well, I don't know . . . he under yet?"

"Must be by now." A beefy hand waved back and forth in front of Grigori's face. Although the ability was still there, Grigori chose not to follow the movement with his eyes. "Yeah, he's under."

Although he felt as if his body was floating in syrup, Grigori was not the helpless slave his captors evidently thought him to be. He had no explanation for their failure, but had he wanted to, Grigori could have struck out at them physically. Two things prevented him from doing so. The first was the need to understand the reasons behind his assault. His visit to Teresa had garnered someone's interest. Grigori cursed himself for not being more adamant about searching for the source of the mental intrusion he had sensed. These men had a connection to that.

His second reason for cooperating was more practical. Grigori doubted that he yet had the will and strength to slip his bonds, much less take on both men with his bare hands. Under normal circumstances, he could have attacked them using the power. The same ability that enabled him to make a cup float worked on objects as large as men. In times past, Grigori had put men to sleep with but a touch of the power on their minds. These two, though, were evidently shielded from his power, which meant that all he could do was bide his time and hope for the best.

The mongrel reached out and slapped Grigori hard. "You can hear me. I know that. You're going to answer a few questions. Then we're going to take you to see someone very important. It's not like you've got a lot of choice. You can't do anything but obey now, right? That's all you *want* to do, isn't it?"

It was not. The compulsion had not taken. Still, it behooved him to play along with his captors. "Yes."

"What's your name?"

"Grigori Nicolau."

"That's really his name?" muttered the other man. "He doesn't talk like no Russian."

"Talks better English than you," snarled the first hood, mouth moving even after the words had ceased. "Are you Russian?"

"No."

"Where, then?"

I don't know. Grigori chose the most obvious place he could think of. His name would back his reply. "Rumania."

That brought a predatory smile to the mongrel's distorted features. The expression revealed to Nicolau what was wrong with the man's face. It was not real, but rather an illusion masking his true countenance. Whoever had tied the false features to his face had done so ineptly. Grigori felt safe in assuming that it had likely been the thug himself.

"He said *Rumania.* That was one of the places the master said to listen for."

"I heard. Get on with it."

Grigori's interrogator nodded. "Are you left-handed or right-handed?"

The question left Grigori perplexed, but he did not have time to consider its meaning. "Left-handed."

"Good."

What happened next proved so peculiar that it made the question of whether he was left-handed or right-handed irrelevant. His brutish companion whispered something in a tongue that Grigori was certain he had never heard before. However, the moment the other man ceased talking, Grigori's mouth moved of its own accord, responding in the same tongue.

"There!" snarled the man to his companion. "Do you see? He *is* one of them!"

"He looked at apartments . . ." countered the still-unseen man. "He didn't say nothing about no houses. They all ask about the house."

"*They* think he's one!"

Grigori could sense that this comment unnerved the other villain. The man stopped protesting. "Well, if he's one after all, let's get it over with."

"Yeah . . ." Rising, Grigori's inquisitor reached into a coat pocket. It was all Grigori could do to keep from reacting at the sight of the slim, curved object that the man revealed. It was a knife, a black, ugly blade that made him shiver. Fortunately, neither of his captors seemed to notice his reaction. "Yeah, let's do it."

The knife was no ordinary weapon. Grigori could see the tiny, faded runes etched into the handle and blade. He knew that he was to be brought somewhere else, so they could not be intending to kill him. However, there *were* rituals of binding that required blood.

They could not have killed him even had they tried. Yet how much pain would he go through before they discovered that his wounds healed even as the knife cut his flesh? Worse yet, where the first artifact had failed to control him, this one might succeed.

Grigori no longer saw any reason to feign cooperation and so began to struggle as hard as he could. There was some slack in the bonds, but Grigori quickly discovered that it would not be enough.

"He's moving!" hissed the unseen villain. Strong arms pushed down on Grigori.

Nicolau's strength failed him. The world grew murkier yet, threatening to become the blackness of unconsciousness. It was a struggle to keep his eyes open. The effort made Grigori dizzy—

"Shame, shame, little boys," crooned a very familiar, very sinister voice. "Not nice to play with another's toys, not without permission."

The dizziness should have warned him. It always heralded a dream state, always heralded the coming of Frostwing.

One of the thugs, Grigori could not tell which, muttered something in the strange tongue that he himself had spoken moments before. Frostwing only chuckled.

"You should watch your tongue . . . no, on second thought, let *me* do that."

There was a scream, then a horrific wrenching noise. A

fine spray splattered across the right side of Grigori's face. A second later, a heavy thud shook the room.

Grigori's vision began to clear. He saw the blurred form of the winged fury move across the hotel room toward him. Frostwing patted him on the head as he passed. The gunshot that rang out then nearly shattered his ears. He struggled harder to free himself.

The knife lay on the floor before his chair. Beyond the knife, the crumpled form of the mongrel resembled a mound of discarded clothing. Nicolau counted himself fortunate that he could not see the man's face and chest. The blood pooling over the carpeting and splattered all over the walls was enough to tell him what the gargoyle had done. Grigori reached out with his foot and dragged the knife to him. The blade was small enough to disappear under his shoe.

Behind him came another shot. The mongrel's companion screamed out in the unknown language. Frostwing laughed again.

Grigori heard the breaking of bone, accompanied by a brief gasp. A breath later, another heavy weight struck the floor nearby. A hand and part of a forearm rolled into the very edge of his vision.

Grigori leaned back in the chair, awaiting the inevitable. The fluttering of wings prepared him as Frostwing landed before him, eternal smile in place. The golem's sharp, stony claws were moist and red. The bi-colored wings folded as Frostwing eyed his eternal victim.

"Aaah, Grigori, Grigori . . . can I not leave you alone for a moment? What would you do without me to watch over you?"

"Live."

The gargoyle bent his head back and roared with laughter. Shaking his head, Frostwing bent over so that his visage loomed above Nicolau. "That is the gratitude I receive for all the care, all the comfort I give? That is the gratitude I receive for saving your hide time and time again, dear Grigori? I could have come later, after they were done with you.''

He met the gargoyle's shadowy gaze. ''But that would mean someone else had given me pain. That would mean someone else had trespassed upon your domain.''

One wet hand seized Grigori's chin. He tried to ignore the blood, reminding himself that this was a dream and that it *might* not be real in the waking world. The thought was small consolation, however.

''I do this for your own good, Grigori. If there is pain, it cannot be helped. Do you think that I like to cause you pain?'' Frostwing released his victim. ''I am wounded by your misconceptions. How many times in the past have I come to your aid and yet you still misperceive my intentions . . . or perhaps you have just forgotten those times. I know how faulty your memory can be.''

Without warning, Grigori's bonds unraveled. Grigori did not rise; he did not even move. Frostwing might choose to make something of his actions. It was best to sit and wait.

''Poor, poor Grigori.'' Frostwing was suddenly at his side, a taloned hand touching his forehead. ''If no words of gratitude, then I shall simply take my due and be gone.''

''Why do you keep doing this to me?'' Nicolau shouted. ''Why don't you end this once and for all?''

The malevolent gargoyle chuckled in his ear. ''All in good time, Grigori. All in good time.''

He woke with a start to find himself sitting on a chair in the center of the hotel room. Music was playing on the radio; Grigori's clearing mind identified it as the last strains of Modest Moussorgsky's *Night on Bald Mountain*. He did not recall switching on the radio and he most certainly did not recall sitting down in the chair.

''Frostwing,'' he whispered. As with the previous visitation, Grigori could not recall the details. Once more the gargoyle had done the unusual and stolen his memories of the dreamtime. That was twice in a row, and such a trend was not to be ignored.

Nicolau put his face in his hands and rubbed. Frostwing knew how he would react to this situation. The gargoyle knew that Grigori would fret about the lost events for hours or even days after. It was just another of the creature's cunning tortures.

It was not until he tried to stand that Grigori noticed the object underneath his foot. He lifted his shoe gently, never certain what Frostwing might have left behind. What he saw made his confusion only greater.

A knife. Small and dark, with runes etched into both blade and handle. For some time, Grigori eyed the sinister blade with fear and loathing. He recognized it enough to link it to something foul.

Grigori studied his room. There was no other sign that anything unusual had occurred, but then, much of what had happened would have been a part of the dreamtime.

He bent down and gingerly retrieved the blade.

As he touched it, the room became a nightmare in red.

Grigori dropped the knife and fell back against the chair, almost tipping it over.

There had been *blood* everywhere. Blood on the walls, blood on the floor, and even blood on himself. Something large lay crumpled on the floor, something half-soaked in crimson.

Remaining clear of the dagger, Grigori slowly rose from the chair. He walked hesitantly to where he had glimpsed the still form and ran his hand over the area. There was nothing there but empty space and slightly weathered carpeting. He put a hand on the carpeting and found it dry, even a bit dusty. There was no blood, no body.

What is happening here?

His eyes returned to the knife. Without it, he would have remained ignorant of whatever it was that had taken place, but somehow Frostwing had missed it under his foot. For once the winged terror had erred.

The small victory did not give Grigori Nicolau any comfort. He was too concerned with what his bloody vision meant. His only way to discover that was to pick up the knife again.

Steeling himself, he reached for the handle.

This time, Grigori forced his panic down when the room changed and he found himself awash in blood. What he saw was a memory linked to the blade, a last image that would soon fade. He glanced at the deadly artifact. There were a few drops of blood on it as well. That was why the memory remained so potent. It was a foul piece, the blade, created by those not satisfied with the powers that they had been granted. Such ritual pieces were unpredictable in their efficiency. Sometimes all that they did was maim or kill.

Despite his repulsion, Grigori kept the knife gripped tight in his hand as he studied the body nearest to him. The gargoyle's work, there was no denying that. What remained of the man's face was a rather nondescript countenance. For some reason, though, the man's features seemed wrong, as if a different face should have been there. The intruder had been wearing a cheap suit that was now blood-soaked. He had been ripped open quickly and efficiently.

Grigori shuddered as he backed away. He felt no sympathy for the dead man. It was simply that, despite all he had witnessed over the centuries, despite the wars and fighting he had known, a part of him had never become inured to violence. It was all Grigori could do to keep from fleeing his own room. Only the vision's unreal nature prevented him from running . . . that, and his need to know.

The other corpse was much like the first. Only now, however, did Grigori Nicolau realize that he had been sitting right next to the second body. This man had not suffered quite like his companion. Frostwing had simply broken his neck and tossed him away. A gun lay nearby. Grigori knew how useless the weapon would have been against the gargoyle.

There was not much else to see in the room. The images were already fading; such memories did not last long once they were woken. He surveyed the room one last time, making certain that he had missed nothing.

The blood began to dissipate. The bodies became dark lumps that melted into the floor. Within moments, the room had returned to normal. Only the knife remained.

Common sense dictated that he rid himself of the blade. No good could come of the artifact. Yet it was also the sole clue to the mysterious intruders who had penetrated his wards. Grigori did not recall entering the hotel room, but he suspected that the pair had been waiting within and not in the corridor outside.

Once more he recalled the brief intrusion into his mind. There must be a connection. Someone had been watching either him or the realty office, likely both. Perhaps this mystery was related to whatever secret Teresa had kept hidden from him. Something to do with a house.

Should I tell her I've changed my mind? Should I ask to see a house instead? Every indication she'd given made it clear that doing so would set her against him. Not only did he have personal reasons for wanting her companionship, but Grigori needed her as the one source of information he might have concerning the two hapless villains and whoever was behind them.

They could not have acted on their own. Grigori had gathered that from their appearances alone. Someone else was master, but why did he want Grigori?

It would be best to leave Chicago, to go far away. I should do it now. Take a plane tonight. There's always a plane leaving from O'Hare.

He knew that he would not. He would arrive at Sentinel

at the appointed time, regardless of the possible danger. Frostwing had watched over him this time, but who was to say that the gargoyle might not decide to wait a bit longer if his human pawn kept insisting on walking into danger? A little pain might be what Frostwing would consider a proper lesson.

A disconcerting notion occurred to Grigori. What if the villains' master proved to be stronger than the gargoyle? The thought seemed incredible, but not impossible.

With practiced skill, Grigori Nicolau threw the knife into the carpeted floor. In his mind, a pair of beautiful steel-blue eyes stared back at him.

Nothing else mattered. He would be there tomorrow.

V

IN THE NEARLY DARK CHAMBER, THE BOUND MAN'S EYES AND ears informed him of his servants' failure. As useful as his pets were, the information that they gave him was limited. He had always understood and accepted that . . . until now. At the moment, he would have given anything to question the shades of his men, to discover from them what had gone wrong.

Nothing had happened as it should have. This new one with his eyes, the eyes they *all* had, had arrived too soon after the last. Then he had broken form and asked about *apartments* of all things. Not one word about the house.

Now came the deaths of his servants. They had never been more than competent, but neither had there been any need for better. This assignment should have been straightforward—a ritual with blood to bind the new one to him so that the house could not call him. There was nothing demonic about the ritual; it simply would have laid a compulsion on the victim that nothing could counter.

The rite had obviously failed.

The bound man could find no trace of the pair. It was as if they had never existed. That could only mean power of a level he had not encountered in years . . . and never in one of *them*.

"What is so special about you?" he asked the empty air. A rat scurried across the narrow expanse of dim light. It paused briefly to look up in what might have been respect to the man tied to the ancient chair. Steel-blue eyes met steel-blue eyes. Then the rat scurried back into the shadows.

The bound man looked into the darkness. "You have something to report?"

There was some shuffling of feet. A nervous voice replied, "He has an appointment tomorrow, sir."

"With her?"

"Yes . . . I could take her place and—"

"That is not your purpose. Your purpose is to watch for those who come to her. She is the bait."

"Yes, sir."

The bound man considered something. "Step closer. Step into the light."

From out of the shadows emerged a nervous young man. Grigori would have recognized him as the novice real estate agent who worked with Teresa Dvorak. He eyed the figure in the chair fearfully.

"Open wide your left suit pocket."

Confused, but hardly in a position to question, the real estate agent pulled the pocket wide. A small form darted from the black and raced to his left leg. The young man started and almost backed away. A sharp look from his master prevented him from doing so.

With the fantastic dexterity of its kind, the rat climbed up the pants leg and snared the jacket with its teeth. It took hold with its front paws and pulled itself up onto the coat. As it slipped into the open pocket, it brushed briefly against the agent's hand. The moment the rat was safely inside, the realtor let go.

"Be early tomorrow. Drape your coat over your chair for five minutes, then do with it as you please. That is all you need to do. Is that clear?"

"Yes, sir."

"You are dismissed."

The real estate agent nearly scrambled away. He was a poor subordinate in comparison to the two lost, but his position at the office where the woman worked made him useful.

"Conrad."

From behind the chair materialized a stout, narrow-eyed man with a piggish face. He was clad in a suit almost as elegant as that of the bound man. His thick, black hair was tied back in a ponytail more reminiscent of another century than of modern fashion.

"Master?"

The bound man indicated his straps. "Ten minutes, Conrad. Not one second more. If I hesitate, you know what you must do."

"Yes, master." Concern crept over the piggish face. "You think that it will not be too long?"

"The call is weak tonight. No more than ten minutes, however. Remember."

"Very well, Mr. Frantisek." The man called Conrad began to remove his coat. Underneath was revealed a slim shoulder holster. In the holster rested a slender, white pistol designed to fire something other than bullets. The servant folded his coat very carefully and laid it on the floor next to him. He then began undoing the straps that held his master's left wrist.

The bound man watched with growing impatience, steely eyes almost aglow.

The next day, Grigori had the cab leave him the very same place the other taxi had the previous morning. If there was anyone observing, they would have no trouble noticing him, which was what Nicolau desired. In a sense, he now had some control over any unseen watchers; knowing that he might be observed, Grigori could adjust his schedule to make them work harder at their tasks. It gave him a perverse pleasure to control someone else for once.

It had been an arduous task waiting to return to the realty office. Grigori had forced himself to concentrate on necessities he had already ignored too long. A telephone call to a number in Great Britain had brought about the transfer of his remaining funds to an account accessible in the United States. The account was under another name, of course, and could never be traced directly to him. The money was less than he had calculated; the pound had risen against the dollar. He would have to earn a living again soon.

It would be something other than writing. Grigori never allowed himself to continue in the same profession when he moved; beginning anew created at least the impression of a fresh start. It allowed him to pretend to live.

His contemplations in no way hindered him as he surveyed the area around the office. Grigori's power reached out two to three blocks in every direction, seeking anything out of the ordinary. He felt nothing, however. Finding nothing today did not mean that he went unobserved. It was safer to assume that in some shape or form he was followed or watched at all times, perhaps even in the Sentinel office itself.

It had occurred to him that Teresa Dvorak might be one of them, but Grigori had finally dismissed that notion as utterly impossible. She was too open. The glimpse of surprise she had revealed when he had chosen renting an apartment over purchasing a house had been very real.

It was still several minutes too early when Grigori reached the office door, but he did not think that anyone would mind. If Teresa was busy with another client, he could wait. It would give him the opportunity to consider further his intentions.

To his surprise, she was not at her desk. Grigori paused, uncertain as to how to proceed. The slightly disarrayed look of her desktop seemed a good indication that the blonde woman had come in that morning. She might be in the back room again, but then why could he not sense her nearby? As he pondered it, Grigori came to realize that he could not sense her anywhere at all. He had been so consumed in searching out spies that he had not even noticed her absence.

"It's Mr. Nicolau, isn't it?"

The same young agent from the day before came up to greet him. Grigori removed his hat and shook the hand the novice realtor thrust at him. "Yes. I was looking for Miss Dvorak."

"She's showing a house to another client. She asked me to apologize for not being here and hopes that you can wait. If not, I can either take care of you myself or perhaps help you to reschedule your appointment."

"Thank you, Mr.—"

The young man looked sheepish. "I'm sorry! My name is Eric."

Grigori nodded slightly. For some reason that he could not pinpoint, the realtor made him uncomfortable. "Thank you, Eric, but I'll wait for Miss Dvorak. If there is a place where I could sit."

"Sure, right this way." Eric put a guiding hand on Grigori's arm, a hand which Nicolau had a great desire to peel away. "We have a small sitting area with fresh coffee and donuts. You can look through magazines or check out some of our housing guides."

The room was off a little to the side. On the walls hung several premier house listings. Someone waiting for an agent could not help but look at them.

"Can I pour you some coffee?"

"Thank you." Grigori did not really desire any coffee, but the sooner Eric felt his task was accomplished, the sooner he would leave Grigori alone.

"Teresa should be back real soon." With that, the young man finally departed.

Exhaling, Grigori put the cup on the table and sat down. He had come very close to exerting his influence on the agent. Normally, someone like Eric would not have annoyed him so, but his nerves were taut. That Teresa was showing a house to someone did not sit well with Grigori. He kept recalling her reaction of the other day.

The waiting soon became a trial. The insipid music playing over a speaker only made matters worse. Grigori attempted to focus inward, but the music cut through his concentration. Irritated, he decided to peruse some of the magazines instead. They held no interest for him, but Grigori hoped that perhaps he might come across something, even an image, to focus his thoughts upon. Anything to pass the time until Teresa returned.

As he reached for the assorted magazines and brochures, Nicolau glimpsed something scurrying behind the small cabinet on which the coffee maker stood. He forgot the magazines and walked over to inspect the area behind the cabinet. There was nothing there, especially nothing that even remotely resembled the form he had noticed. It had looked like a rat or a mouse . . .

· Rodent or imagination, Grigori found he really did not care. Rats and mice thrived in Chicago, just as they thrived in nearly every populated area of the world. He despised rats, recalling the plague years and the hundreds of people that he had watched die. Yet another memory that Frostwing refused to steal, no matter how much Nicolau would have desired such a theft.

Abandoning his search, Grigori returned to the magazines. He picked something at random from the table and sat back in one of the uncomfortable chairs. As he settled in, he found his eyes grazing the listings on the wall across from him. At first, he ignored them, but his gaze slowly returned, as if of its own accord, to the listings. Grigori impatiently returned to the magazine, but it was not long before his gaze again drifted to the opposite wall.

By the fifth time, he began to realize that it was not of his own doing.

Throwing the magazine down, Nicolau rose and crossed over to the wall. It was a subtle compulsion that made him look; he could sense that now. The listings drew him, almost like a siren's call.

Then Grigori Nicolau saw the house.

He nearly tore the picture from the wall in his haste to study it closer. Restraining himself, Grigori gently pried it loose. Hands shaking, he peered at the image.

It was not an old structure, not by Grigori's measure of time, but the details printed below the photograph indicated that it had been built near the end of the last century. The house sat atop a slight incline and, from the picture at least, seemed to loom over all else, save for a pair of tall yet thin oaks in the foreground. The photograph was black and white, but the house itself was listed as charcoal gray. Its central entrance and the curved trim reminded Grigori of older Italian styles that he could recall once being new. There were two great bay windows in front and several small windows above, indicating the house had at least three floors and numerous rooms. The house's most distinctive feature was a tower situated above the entranceway. The tower's windows looked to be stained glass, but it was difficult to see on the picture and no mention was made of stained glass in the text.

The sight of the old house sent shivers through Grigori. At the same time, it seemed to call to him. Grigori Nicolau knew that he must see the house itself. Even if it meant risking the ire of Teresa, he had to go there.

The top of a wall stood resolutely in the foreground. It appeared to circle the property, but that obstacle meant little to Grigori. Walls could be climbed or, in his case, bypassed through other methods.

Across the middle of the page, he found the address.

Listing in hand, Grigori abandoned the sitting room and headed toward the front door. Eric rose from his desk and started after him, but Nicolau paid him no heed.

"Mr. Nicolau! Is something the matter? Where are you—"

The remainder of the agent's words were cut off as Grigori slammed the door shut behind him.

There was no taxi in sight. Grigori swore in frustration. There were other methods by which he could travel, but for them to be of any use Grigori needed to know where his destination lay. An address listed on a piece of paper was insufficient.

At last a cab came into sight, but it carried a passenger. Grigori's eyes narrowed as he stared at the vehicle. This time, he cared little about abusing his power. All that was important was for the taxi to come to him.

The taxi passed by then suddenly swerved around, narrowly missing another vehicle going the opposite direction. Grigory quietly waited as the cab pulled up to the curb. The door opened, and a young man in a tailored suit climbed out, briefcase in one hand and coat in the other.

The disembarking passenger had a puzzled look on his face; he could not remember why he had insisted upon stopping here. The compulsion was a minor one: Once the taxi was safely on its way, the unfortunate man would retain no memory of the encounter.

The driver, too, was under a compulsion, so that he would not consider it strange that one fare should disembark so abruptly and another should be waiting. To further assuage his growing guilt, Grigori swore that he would tip the man generously when they reached his destination.

"Where to?"

Grigori thrust the sheet toward the driver. This way, there would be no chance of error. When the taxi driver nodded, the anxious immortal pulled back the listing and waited.

The cab reentered traffic. Grigori settled back as best he could and stared at the listing. What was it about the house . . . ?

From the corner of the block which housed Sentinel's office, Eric watched the cab depart. His face was pale and he was trembling. How would he explain this to the master? For some reason, this Grigori Nicolau had rushed out of the office, abandoning even his hat and coat. While Eric did not know the reason behind the dark man's abrupt escape, he knew that it boded nothing good. If something happened to Nicolau before the master could claim him, it would be Eric who was blamed for the failure.

He turned and started back to the office. He would have to make a telephone call. There was still a chance that the failure could be transformed into a success.

It did not occur to him to wonder what had happened to the rat he had brought with him to the office.

Only when he was well on his way did Grigori recall his hat and coat. It was a situation easily remedied; a single thought and the items rested on the seat next to him. He could have even been wearing them, but that would have required strengthening his influence on the driver, which Grigori did not want to do.

The trek took him into some of the older, yet still dignified neighborhoods of Chicago. He dated most of the houses from the early part of the century, which made them almost new to Grigori. This neighborhood was still well kept, which he suspected had something to do with the expensive, European tastes of the people living there.

On and on the cab traveled. At last, Grigori leaned forward and asked, "Are we almost there?"

It took a moment for the driver to respond. "Almost. I think that it—"

He did not have a chance to finish. At the edge of Grigori's field of vision, nearly hidden by other homes and tall oaks, there appeared the pinnacle of a tower. "Stop here!"

"But I can bring you—"

Nicolau glared at the driver. "*Stop* here!"

The other man's tone grew distant. The confusion left his face, to be replaced by a look of calm. "Sure."

Grigori silently cursed his rashness. He had lost his temper and strengthened his hold on the driver's mind. It was not like him. He was not one to abuse people.

His regrets faded, though, as the taxi came to a halt. The tower was still barely visible, but could not have been more than a block away. Reaching forward, he handed the be-spelled man twice the amount the ride should have cost. Had the driver not been mesmerized, he might have noted how his fare never reached into any pocket for the bills with which he paid.

Seizing his hat and coat, Grigori Nicolau bolted out of the cab.

He waited as the vehicle drove off, the listing in his hand. It was definitely the correct house. Even without the picture,

Grigori would have known that. This close, he could feel the unearthly presence of the place. The house both attracted and repelled him, but either sensation would have forced him to continue on. In some way, the house seemed as much a part of him as Teresa or any of the others like her.

What have I found here? Is this what Teresa was hiding? What does she know about this?

There was only one way to discover the answers to any of his questions. He had to risk a closer examination of the house.

Donning his hat and coat, Grigori started down the street. The block was longer than he had first assumed; huge lawns surrounded these stately old homes, each block almost a separate kingdom. The estate he now approached was an excellent example; an elaborate brick wall designed to resemble the wall of a castle shielded the property. The wall rose over him at least a foot and had been built with care. The only break that he saw proved to be the front entrance, which was barred by a sculpted iron gate next to which a speaker and button were located.

It would not do to stand too long outside the place. This was a neighborhood that was likely well-patrolled by the local police. They would find his presence of interest. He began to walk faster.

It was at the corner, just as he was turning, that Grigori first became aware of the watchers in the dark green car.

They were parked some distance away. He never would have noticed them at all if not for the incident in his hotel room.

How it was done, he did not know, but the men . . . and even their vehicle . . . were invisible to his senses. According to what his abilities revealed to him, neither the men nor the car should have been there at all. Whatever they had used to shield their presence from . . . from the *house?* . . . had made them so very obvious to him.

He also had the unsettling feeling that they knew why he was here.

There was no move to prevent Grigori from turning the corner and proceeding in the direction of the house. That struck him as odd and only added to his anxiety. Were they content simply to watch? After what had happened in his room, that hardly seemed likely.

In the back of his mind, he suddenly found himself again wondering how Teresa Dvorak fit into the puzzle.

At the end of the block, Grigori Nicolau got his first view of the house in its glory. The photograph had been an excellent one, but it was a shadow compared to the structure before him. The charcoal-gray house did indeed stand higher than its neighbors, which was fortunate since, like so many of them, a high, brick wall surrounded the grounds. Short iron spears thrust above the wall, spears that appeared sharper than decorative ironwork needed to be. Grigori could make out an arch farther on, an arch with some sort of sculpture, perhaps a bird, at the top. The arch overlooked the front gate.

His gaze returned to the house. Curtains covered each window, preventing anyone outside from prying. There appeared to be no lights within, but it was still bright enough outside that indoor illumination might not be visible. Still, there was someone within the walls. How Nicolau could be so certain was yet another question he could not answer at the moment.

A surreptitious glance informed him that the watchers had not yet moved from their previous positions. Curious but determined, Grigori started across the street.

As his foot came down, an invisible force pushed against it. His foot froze inches above the ground, unable to move further despite his best efforts. He nearly lost his balance. Grigori tried again and achieved the same results. Stepping slightly back onto the sidewalk, he reached out to the street with one hand. Once more, something pushed against him the moment his hand crossed the boundary between curb and street.

What is happening here? The house was not the source of the compulsion, but when Grigori sought to locate its exact location, he failed. Each time, he sensed only himself.

Grigori strained against the pressure, trying to move forward. He fought the barrier with both physical strength and his special gift of power. "I will *not* be turned away!"

To his surprise, his foot suddenly struck the pavement hard, sending small shockwaves through his leg. He barely noticed the pain; his pleasure at succeeding overwhelmed all else. Grigori stood in the street, the thrill of triumph— something he did not often feel—threatening to make him giddy. Then it occurred to him that a new danger loomed nearby. He had broken the spell. Now the riders in the dark green vehicle might try to stop him in a more direct fashion. With great trepidation, Grigori looked over his shoulder.

The car was gone. Grigori frowned. Surely he would have heard the engine starting, or the car itself moving.

Over the centuries, Grigori had suffered his share of encounters with others of power. He was certain that he had survived even more incidents than those remaining in his piece-meal memory. Still, Grigori could remember no encounter so . . . unsettling.

Eyes lingering on the location where the car had last crouched, he started again toward the arch. Grigori had made it this close to his goal; he had no intention of turning back.

As he walked, Grigori turned his attention to the house itself. The features that he had seen in the photograph came into closer view. One of the bay windows. The curved, Italian woodwork. The almost Gothic look of the tower. The house was in remarkable shape. It looked as if it had been built recently, but Grigori could sense that such was not the case. The house was every bit as old as the listing indicated. Indeed, to him it felt even older.

Grigori tried the gate. The tall iron bars rattled, but the gate itself was locked. He inspected the lock and was pleased to find it the more traditional sort. There was also, Nicolau noted briefly, no call box. Nothing appeared to have been added since the edifice had first been built. That too pleased Grigori. As one who changed little through time, he found it painful to watch everything either fade away or change so radically as to not even resemble its original form.

He sensed vague impressions of power around the lock and gate, but nothing he could not overcome. Grigori reached out with one hand and touched the lock at the keyhole.

There was a spark, but, somewhat to his surprise, the gate did not open.

Grigori tried again, with identical results.

He stepped back, both anxious and irritated. He had never thought much of his poor abilities, but they had always been sufficient to open a simple lock. He probed again, finding nothing more than he had the first time.

Growing more concerned by the moment, Grigori stepped farther back. His hand went to his chin as he contemplated what he should try next. If the gate would not admit him, it might be possible to go over the wall. Of course, he would have to be careful that no one saw him. There were other methods of entry available to him too, but using his power so freely made him edgy, especially here.

His eyes drifted upward as he searched for the most suitable place to climb. It was then that Grigori Nicolau first saw clearly the arch above the gate and what he had assumed some distance back was the sculpture of a bird.

It was *not* a bird.

He almost screamed. What held his tongue in the end, Grigori could not have said.

It was not a bird, but it *did* have wings. Wings of gray stone and white.

Perched over the gateway was *Frostwing*.

VI

THE SUN HAD ALREADY SET BY THE TIME TERESA DEPARTED the office. She was the last to leave, which both pleased and frustrated a waiting Grigori Nicolau. There would be fewer witnesses now, but his nerves would have been less frayed if he could have confronted her sooner.

From around the street corner he watched to see which direction she walked. Grigori shivered, due only in part to the brisk wind. The terrifying sight he had confronted only a few hours before still burned in his mind; the figure of Frostwing looming over him.

The gargoyle had been only two feet high, but even this diminutive horror had been capable of utterly unnerving Grigori. That the gargoyle had been a motionless statue perched atop a decorative arch made little difference. Seeing Frostwing while awake had been enough to make Grigori flee the house.

Yes, he admitted to himself, he had run away like a frightened child, racing block after block in an attempt to put as much distance between himself and the hated gargoyle as possible. Nicolau could almost hear the laughter in his head, laughter brought on by his shame and nothing else. The statue had done nothing to make him believe it was anything but what it was supposed to be—a lifeless chunk of stone.

When his senses had finally returned, many blocks from the house and the damnable arch, Grigori had realized that there was only one person who might be able to help him solve this mystery. He doubted that Teresa knew everything, but she certainly knew something. What that was he would find out one way or another, even if it meant drawing the information from her unwilling mind.

Teresa paused to lock the door. Two other employees walked a little ahead, conversing with one another. Grigori abandoned his post and started after her. Despite the hard pavement and the elegant dress shoes he wore, he made no sound as he hurried to catch her.

When he was within a few yards of her, Grigori called out. "Teresa! Please! I must speak with you."

She started, then whirled around. Her expression was not promising. "Mr. Nicolau. You missed your appointment."

That one sentence said a great deal . . . too much, in fact. Grigori pretended not to notice. "I'm sorry, Teresa. You must forgive me, please. Now, however, it is imperative that we talk." He hesitated. "About a house."

"About *the* house?" she snapped. "The one whose listing you tore off the wall and ran out of the office with. I'm sorry, Mr. Nicolau, but I don't have time for games. If you wish to discuss that place, find yourself another agent. I won't have anything more to do with it or you."

While she talked, she was careful to keep the distance between them constant. Try as he might, Grigori could not reach out to her. Each step he took she countered with one of her own. He did not want to chase after her; she might scream.

"Please!" He paused where he was. "I promise not to come any closer if you will just hear me out! You misunderstand me. Until I saw that photograph, I knew nothing about the house! Something obviously troubled you the other day, but it was not my concern and so I did not ask."

"I don't care to discuss this further," she insisted. Nonetheless, Teresa did not back away.

"Teresa . . . Miss Dvorak . . . I say again that when I came to you the other day, I knew *nothing* about any house. My first hint of it actually came from you, when you seemed stunned that I wanted to know about apartments." As he spoke, Grigori took a step toward her. He was relieved to see that she did not retreat. "Please, I'm telling you the truth when I say that I am in the dark at least as much as you concerning this abode . . . but I need to know more. There is something dangerous about that house."

"Dangerous . . ." Teresa's expression altered. She no longer looked so fearful of him; in fact, she almost seemed somewhat thankful. "You're the first person who's noticed that." She looked down. "Besides me."

Besides me? She's noticed something, too? It was almost too much for him to believe. Was there more to her than she had let on? "Miss Dvorak, forgive what might sound like an insane question, but how old are you?"

"Twenty-four."

She was not like him. For a moment he had hoped. "Do you often sense that things are . . . dangerous?"

This time she considered her answer. Her long hesitation made Grigori more anxious. He almost sighed in relief when she finally answered.

"No, no, I don't. It's . . . it's just that house. Strange things happen there, but no one seems to notice."

The wind was growing more brisk. Grigori looked around. "We must talk more, Miss Dvorak, but this is hardly the place. Please, allow me the courtesy of offering you dinner in exchange for what you know. Perhaps I can also shed some light on the situation. Then, if you so desire it, I shall depart your life forever."

He thought at first that she would refuse. Teresa had every reason to call for help or run from him. He had made quite a spectacle of himself in the office, and his intrusion now could not have aided his image. He held out one tentative hand in what was almost a gesture of pleading.

Teresa pointed in the direction that she had been walking. "My car is this way. I know a place if you like Italian. We can talk there."

She was choosing the place. Grigori could understand that. He simply appreciated the fact that she had not turned him away. He would have resorted to his power if she had done so. That would have been regrettable.

"Thank you," was all he could say. He started toward her, putting his hands in his coat pockets as he walked.

The fingers of his left hand touched something furred.

"What is it?" Teresa asked as he pulled his hand back out and stared at the offending pocket.

"I . . . I seem to have lost the key to my hotel room. I must have dropped it around the corner." He indicated the street corner that he had started from. Grigori was thankful that the darkness prevented his companion from noticing how his hand shook. He gave Teresa a look of chagrin. "Please, if you could wait here, I think I can find it quickly enough. It must have fallen out when I paid the taxi driver."

"I can help you."

"That is not necessary." He glanced in the direction they were heading. The edge of a pay parking lot was just visible. "Your car is in the lot? Then I will meet you there."

Grigori did not wait for her to reply. His story had been a poor one, but the unexpected shock of discovering something living in his coat pocket had almost been too much. He could only hope that Teresa would indeed wait for him. This latest strange behavior might be too much for her.

With speed comparable to his frightened flight from the

house, Grigori crossed the street and hurried around the corner. He walked just far enough to assure himself that Teresa could not see him. Then, gritting his teeth, he thrust his hand into the pocket.

His fingers closed around a soft, motionless form with legs and a tail. He realized that not once since abandoning the realty office had he put his hands in his coat pockets. That was peculiar enough in itself; like many people, he tended to do so.

Slowly, Grigori withdrew the thing from his coat.

When he saw what it was, he gasped. Fingers instinctively opened, dropping the horrible form to the sidewalk, where it struck hard and then lay motionless.

A rat. There had been a rat in his coat pocket all the time.

A *dead* rat. Grigori kicked the limp body. He had mistaken it for a living creature because of its warmth, but his coat pocket had probably preserved much of the rodent's body heat even after its demise. Still, the rat could not have died too long ago, perhaps only a couple hours.

Almost exactly when he had located the house.

Grigori prodded the rat one more time, but the creature was quite dead. Although it was cruel to think so, he felt satisfaction at the rodent's grim fate. Somehow, this creature was linked to his misfortunes. It was too peculiar to be a coincidence. The more Grigori mulled things over, the more certain he became that the rat had joined him somewhere nearby the office of Sentinel Realty.

Nearby? Why not within? Apparently he had seen something scurrying across the floor of the waiting room after all.

Grigori lost track of time as he stood and stared at the vile form. He was still gazing at the small corpse when the headlights of a car suddenly engulfed him.

He raised his arm in surprise as a dark sports car pulled over next to him. His first thought was that the watchers from earlier had returned with orders to take him. Then, the engine still running, the door of the sports car opened and a head of blonde hair rose above the hood.

"I waited, but you didn't come," remarked Teresa a little cautiously. "You headed in this direction so I thought I'd see if I could find you here. Did I startle you?"

"A little, yes." In fact he had been ready to use his power against the supposed attackers. Grigori was thankful now that he had hesitated, although such a hesitation might cost him in the future. Perhaps a part of his subconscious had recognized his ally. The link between Teresa and him went deeper than simply the conscious mind.

"Did you find your hotel key?"

He slipped his hand to his pocket. "Yes, I just did. Thank you."

One graceful hand indicated the door on his side of the vehicle. "If you don't mind, I'd like to get this over with."

"Of course." Grigori started toward the car, surreptitiously kicking the rat's corpse into the gutter. He glanced down at the rat as he opened the door, still not quite convinced that it was dead. The rat, however, remained on its back, paws curled inward like the legs of an equally dead beetle.

As he seated himself, Teresa looked at him with a penetrating gaze. "Did you lose something else?"

Grigori first shut the door. With an innocent expression on his countenance, he shook his head. "No, nothing."

She eyed him a moment more, then, with a shrug, began to pull out into the street. However, the moment they were on their way, Teresa glanced at him again and asked, "So what—?"

Grigori raised a hand. "Please, Miss Dvorak. Not until we are settled elsewhere."

"Why not now?"

"Because I would prefer for you to be able to concentrate on your driving as much as is still possible for you."

Her expression indicated that she thought he was joking, but when she started to protest, Grigori again silenced her. "Trust me, please, Miss Dvorak. I'm doing this for both of us."

It was clear from her expression that Teresa found this answer questionable, but she held her tongue. Grigori exhaled quietly as he settled into his seat. He would have to handle the conversation delicately. There were many things he would tell Teresa, but there were also many things he dared not tell her . . . especially about himself.

Teresa suddenly reached over and turned on the stereo. To Grigori's surprise and delight, Prokofiev's *Romeo and Juliet* began to play. It was one of his favorite modern pieces.

"You enjoy such music, Miss Dvorak?"

"I always have."

"Then may I say that you have excellent taste, as I already suspected, of course."

Her long-lost smile returned. "Thank you . . . and it's Teresa, Grigori."

This time, it was *his* smile that returned.

Chicago had a reputation for fine food, and Italian cuisine in particular, but circumstances prevented Grigori from enjoying the meal as much as he had hoped. The matter of the house poisoned everything. Grigori ate halfheartedly and fumbled toward the best way to begin the awkward conversation.

Teresa, too, only played with her food. At last she gave up the pretense of eating. Pushing her plate aside, she took a quick sip of water and eyed Grigori. After a moment of hesitation, the woman quietly spoke. "You said that you would explain some things to me. About the house."

Grigori pushed his own plate away. At least six hundred years old, and the situation still left him as tongue-tied as a child doing his first recital. "It would be good if you would tell me what you know. Then, I might better understand what it is that you desire of me."

Clearly she would have preferred him to begin, but she evidently saw the logic in his suggestion. Taking another sip from her water, Teresa cleared her throat. Her voice shook a little as she talked, and every now and then she would tap the table with the index finger of her left hand. "Have you seen the house itself?"

"I have," Grigori replied without elaborating.

A shudder. "I first learned of the house about a month after I began to work at Sentinel. That was nearly two years ago. I don't even recall exactly when it became *my* property to deal with, but it was soon after that." She looked down at the table before continuing. "I think that it was assigned to me after the previous agent quit."

Teresa grew silent. Grigori gave her a minute to settle herself, then leaned forward. "Please continue."

She looked up. The dimly lit restaurant would have been very romantic at another time. A long candle glowed at the center of the table. Its flame glittered in Teresa's eyes.

"I'd come to Sentinel from another company and wanted to prove myself, so when I inherited the listing along with a few others, I studied up on them. They all seemed fairly typical. A few were older listings that had been handled by other companies before Sentinel. That always happens. On the surface, that was what it appeared had happened with this house, too." Teresa smiled, but the smile was a bitter one. "At that time, the house had already been with Sentinel nearly a year. The previous realtor to handle it had closed down. Nothing remarkable, but it made me determined to sell the place." She put one hand flat against her chest. "I was going to sell every one of those places and prove that I was best."

A waiter came to remove their plates. Teresa and Grigori both leaned away as the man worked. The waiter looked at the two. "Can I interest you in some dessert?"

"No thank you," Grigori almost snapped. Across from him, Teresa shook her head. The man started to go, but Grigori signaled him back. "Wait." Pulling out his wallet, he gave the server enough money to cover not only the meal but a substantial tip as well. As the man thanked him, Nicolau added, "We will want nothing else, so there is *no* reason to return."

The waiter nodded, then departed.

Grigori returned his attention to the blonde woman, who smiled slightly and said, "Thank you for dinner."

"I regret that the circumstances are not as pleasant as they should be."

The smile vanished. Teresa tapped the table again, then resumed her tale. "I didn't pay any special attention to the first two people interested in the house, although they were both European."

Grigori Nicolau's eyes widened a bit, but he did not interrupt.

"It was only later, after the next few, that I began to notice the pattern. Each and every one of them knew of the house when I first spoke to them. Some of them walked in and asked where the house was and when they could see it. Others seemed almost in a daze or even a bit frightened, but they all knew the house at least as well as I did. That wasn't the only strange thing about them, either. When I saw you, I couldn't help but think that you were one of them. You look just like the others."

Grigori had been growing more disturbed by the moment, but now he stiffened in outright fear.

Teresa saw his expression and mistook it for confusion. "It's the eyes, Grigori. You all have the same color eyes."

It took him a moment to respond. When he did, it was only to ask, "How—how many others?"

"In the time since I've dealt with that place . . . more than two dozen, some of them couples." She reached for her drink and took a sip. Her hands shook. "One time, a *child*—I think that maybe she was ten, no more—just walked in and asked me where the house was. I thought she was just some kid from the neighborhood pulling a prank. I didn't tell her and she never came back, but . . . it's just eerie."

Over two dozen people, all with eyes the same as his. The same as hers. Grigori wondered whether Teresa had considered her own connection to the mystery? Perhaps she had or perhaps something inside denied the possibility of a connection.

"What happened to these people, Teresa?" He wanted her to say that they had chosen other houses or had moved on to other regions. He wanted her to say that, but he knew that she would not.

Her finger continued to tap. "I don't really know. I saw some of them only once, a few of them twice. Nobody came a third time. None of them called back." She looked up, a rueful smile briefly crossing her face. The candlelight continued to dance in her eyes. "You know, when I talk about it, it sounds like nothing. Maybe I ran into a lot of eccentrics who might have been related to one another. Maybe it's all my imagination."

Grigori vehemently shook his head. "No, not your imagination. No coincidence, either."

"Then what is it?"

He owed her explanations, but Grigori still needed to know more. "Have *you* ever seen the house, Teresa? I mean *truly* seen the house . . . and the gate, perhaps?"

This time, the pause was longer. "Yes."

"What do you think of the place? What does it make you feel?"

"I've told you quite a bit already," she returned, her tone becoming strident. "You've not told me anything in return."

"You fear the house." He leaned forward and took her hand. "You have good reason to, I promise that. You want me to give you something in return for your answers?" With his free hand, he indicated himself. "I visited the house a few hours ago. You had assumed that already, I know. Shall I tell you what *I* felt? I stood before the house and shivered. I looked up at the arch above the gate . . . then turned and ran in blind panic for several blocks! I ran in fear from the house, and that fear has not left me yet."

Talking about it caused the fear to flare anew. Now it was Grigori's hand that shook. He removed it self-consciously from Teresa's own. The blonde woman began tapping again.

"I was there . . . three times," she said. "The first time I went there with someone, I didn't notice anything. Maybe I just missed it. The second time was different, though. I began to notice little things, to feel sensations that were . . . I don't know . . . *cold* and *hungry*. Malicious, too." Her eyelids lowered. "After the third visit I refused to ever take anyone else there. If they wanted to go there, they were going to have to get one of the other agents. I always found excuses. It—"

Grigori took her hand again, his own fears and concerns suddenly overwhelmed by his desire to comfort her. "Breathe slowly, Teresa. Let the words come one at a time if you must."

Her hand squeezed his. "I felt as if the house *called* to me, as if it wanted me to come inside . . . and I knew somehow that if I *did* go in I would never come out!" Teresa was shaking. "If that isn't insane, I don't know what is!"

"Have you never been inside?"

"The first time. That's what makes it all so crazy. It's just a stately old house in immaculate shape. A little dark for my tastes. The furnishings looked as if they had been brought in when the house was new, only they were in perfect condition. It was as if I'd walked into another time.''

Another time. Grigori wondered how much truth there was in Teresa's last sentence. "What about the gate?"

"The gate?"

"Nothing about it disturbed you? The . . . design of it?"

"No. It's a bit odd-looking, but the gate didn't bother me at all. Just the house.''

"Who owns the house?"

"It's held in some sort of trust by a group in Europe. I can't pronounce the name, but I think they're located in Rumania or Hungary. We receive correspondences about twice a year. I contacted them once, but the only answer I received was a letter commending us for our fine efforts and noting their continued faith in our company. They indicated that they were in no hurry to sell the place.'' Her face hardened some. "I think I've told you enough, Grigori. If you know something that can make sense of this . . . this *thing* that's going on, I would appreciate hearing it.''

"I know many things, Teresa. Some of them you might believe. Others you will find so incredible that you might think me mad . . . providing that you do not already think that of me.''

"Not quite,'' she returned with a slight, nervous smile. "Not yet.''

"Then I hope that means that you will hear me out. You talked about how the house seemed to call to you. I felt something similar; it drew me to the listing on your office wall. It made me go there, frightened as I was, and confront the place.'' It was Grigori Nicolau's turn to shudder again. "Teresa, does the gargoyle above the gate mean anything at all to you?''

"Not really. Was that why you asked about the gate?"

"It was." He wondered how much he might safely say about Frostwing, even as an inanimate statue over an entranceway. Grigori desired no harm to come to his companion. "For some time, quite a long time, in fact, I have . . . I have had dreams about the creature. *Nightmares* would be more appropriate to say."

"The gargoyle that sits over the gate?"

"Yes. When I saw the monster leering down at me from the arch, I lost all reason. It was that as much as the house, that sent me fleeing shamelessly. It was as if my nightmares had become real."

Her hands clenched until the knuckles grew white from the effort. "This is like some bad horror movie, isn't it? A haunted house? Gargoyles? What next? Don't think I haven't thought a lot about the eyes. *I've* got the same eyes as you and all the others had. No one else in the office has ever noticed that. I commented on it to Eric after the last one. He said something to the effect that I just notice the ones with my eye color more. Of course I do—when *everyone* has that same color!"

"Teresa—"

"What are we, some missing tribe? Some ancient clan from Transylvania, the last descendants of Dracula, for God's sake?" Her voice rose toward the end, causing a pair of diners in one of the other booths to look in her direction.

Grigori succeeded in maintaining his poise. "Please, Teresa, we have to keep our voices down."

"Then tell me what's going on with this house! Better yet, tell me how to get myself free of it. I don't care what happens, as long as it doesn't involve me."

This was it, then. She seemed to accept the presence of the supernatural in the house. Could she be convinced of the existence of magic?

"You know what you felt when you entered the house. It was as if the place were alive and hungry. It was as if something *magical* lurked within, wasn't it?"

"I don't know if I'd use that word," the blonde woman returned, beginning to withdraw a little.

"Can you think of another word? Magic, sorcery, the power . . . different words for the same thing. Different words all apt for what you sensed. Would you prefer more modern terms, such as telekinesis? In the end, they all mean the same thing."

She pulled back into her chair and crossed her arms defensively. "This is crazy. There's no such thing as magic."

"What other explanation do you have, Teresa?"

"That I'm crazy. That would make more sense than what you're saying, Grigori. It can't be true."

He was disappointed, but not surprised by her reaction. In a world where ships flew and people spoke to one another over distances that a horseman could not cross in a month at full gallop, the concept of magic should have been as acceptable as the idea that nations could literally destroy the world with the weapons at their command. The blinders people wore continually astounded Grigori, but then he supposed that few folk had his lengthy perspective on the world.

For Grigori to convince her to listen to the rest of his tale, he would have to do something that he had forsworn long ago. To do so might draw the interest of Frostwing, and the last thing that Nicolau wanted was to place Teresa at risk from the wretched gargoyle.

Yet, what choice did he have? She was closing herself off from him even as he watched. Grigori rubbed his fingertips together in preparation for what was to come. "Before I can tell you anything else, Teresa, I must convince you that the power exists. I know this sounds mad—perhaps a little madness is necessary when dealing with such abilities . . . but if you bear with me, I will demonstrate that, even if the existence of a thing is denied by many, it may still be real.''

Teresa reached for her purse. ''I'm sorry, but this was a mistake. I have to go now. Thank you for dinner.''

He quickly raised a hand toward her. ''Please, sit down.''

She did, but with a startled look on her face. Grigori swore quietly. He had not wanted to compel her to stay, but she had forced his hand.

''You're a hypnotist.'' The way she spoke the word made it an insult.

''That ability is related to my power but I am much more than a stage conjurer, Teresa. Of your own free will I ask you to carefully pick up the candle and inspect it.''

''Do you do two shows a day?'' the young woman snapped. Nonetheless, Teresa did as he requested.

''Is there anything attached to the candle or its holder? Any way I might be able to manipulate it by strings or such?'' He smiled ruefully. ''I do sound like a showman.''

She put the candle down with much more force than was needed. ''Nothing. May I leave now?''

He turned his gaze from her eyes to the candle. ''Watch.''

The still-lit candle and holder rose several inches above the table. Grigori put one arm across the table to block the sight from any potential onlooker. The candle did not waver; even the flame burned steadily. Noting that his feat went unobserved, Grigori dared to make the candle float serenely toward his companion.

Teresa said nothing during the entire display. Her beautiful features were molded into an emotionless mask.

''Take hold of the handle on the base. Look again for any string.''

She obeyed, albeit with understandable reluctance. Teresa ran her hand over, under, and around the candle, searching for anything that might discredit its flight as only a stage magician's trick. When she was finished, she looked at Grigori again. Although her expression remained stern, her eyes revealed a number of conflicting emotions, chief among them confusion.

"Let go of the candle."

Her hand released the holder, but the candle did not drop. While Teresa stared at it, Grigori carefully brought the piece back to him. When it hovered over its original location, he let it slowly come to rest. Nicolau glanced around, but the rest of the diners appeared oblivious to what had just occurred. He turned his gaze back to the woman across the table.

"Have I convinced you of anything, Teresa?"

"I want to stand," she replied, her voice level. Her eyes bored into his. "I want to stand. I want to be able to leave this table, leave this restaurant, and never see you again."

"Teresa—"

She shook her head as he reached for her. "It was hypnotism, nothing else. It *has* to be. And I must have mistaken what I felt from that house. I'm sorry, Grigori, but I don't want to be a part of this."

"You are already part of this, Teresa. You became part of it when the house was passed on to you—maybe even before." He indicated his eyes. "If you will only listen to me, believe in me, there may be some hope."

"May I rise?"

She will not listen, though she knows I speak the truth! She thinks that by denying it all she will make herself safe!

"May I rise?" she repeated. Teresa held her purse like a shield.

He slumped back in his chair, defeated. Grigori could not bring himself to force her to remain. He could only hope that she would be all right. With a wave of his hand, he replied, "I will not stop you."

Her rise was slow and uncertain at first. When she had

finally straightened, Teresa looked down at the weary Grigori. He looked hopefully at her, but saw that she was still determined to leave.

"I'm sorry." The young woman's voice was almost a whisper. "I don't know if I'm making the right decision walking out, but I just can't stay and listen to this. It's too crazy. I can't let this be a part of my life; I just want to get on with things." She paused before adding, "I'm sorry, Grigori, I really am. I hope you overcome whatever it is that troubles you so."

As she turned away, Grigori tried one last time to reason with her. "Teresa . . . one thing."

"What?"

"Your third visit. You said it felt as if the house had been calling you, as if it wanted you to come inside."

"So?"

"All those people who came to you, talked of the house, and then disappeared. I am not certain, but the house might have called them, too. . . . and where you chose not to enter, perhaps they could not resist."

She faced him, her countenance pale. "What do you mean?"

It was all he could do to keep from leaping up and taking hold of her. She could not see the danger threatening her. "Should you ever feel the house calling to you again—you have my hotel number. *Please.* If *anything* happens that you do not understand, call me." In a slightly more subdued voice, Grigori added, "I do not want anything to happen to you."

Teresa almost smiled, but she suppressed the urge. "I'll keep that in mind. Thank you for the dinner, Grigori."

He sat there at the table, completely numb, as she walked away.

I have failed again . . . Had Frostwing been here, he would have laughed loud and long at his antics. "*She doesn't appear to have been impressed with your parlor tricks, dear Grigori! Perhaps you should try sawing her in half! Better yet, allow me the pleasure!''*

At least I have learned more about the house. It was small consolation. In fact he had gained more questions than answers. He had no desire to ponder any new puzzles, but then, there was no choice there.

He was still mulling over his failure when a sense of dread overcame him.

''Teresa!'' Grigori shouted. Ignoring the startled expressions of the other diners, he darted frantically around the tables and raced toward the door. A hostess tried to open the door for him, but she was not swift enough.

Grigori burst through, pausing only when he stood outside, in front of the restaurant. A couple just arriving eyed him with uncertainty. Grigori glanced their way, then turned left toward where Teresa had earlier parked her car.

He could not say where his dread originated, only that it concerned Teresa. She was in terrible, immediate danger. What that danger was, he did not know, but it hardly mattered. Grigori would not . . . *could not* . . . let anything happen to her.

He ran, searching for her car. A few of the vehicles looked familiar. Grigori finally recognized one larger car and breathed a sign of relief.

A moment later, he stopped. Not only was her vehicle not there, but the space was filled by another car, a dark green one. He studied the vaguely familiar auto, trying to recall where he'd seen it.

By then it was too late.

Grigori could not sense his attacker until an arm wrapped around his throat, almost choking him. There was no one else within sight who might help Grigori.

Still, he was not entirely helpless. Swinging his elbow back, he caught his assailant in the stomach. The man grunted in pain and loosened his hold. Grigori gasped in a breath. With air in his lungs again, he recovered enough to counterattack in earnest.

Grigori's assailant yelped as a black shadow spread across his hand. He released his captive. Grigori turned around, for the first time getting a look at his attacker. The night obscured some details, even with the moon and the parking lot lights illuminating the area, but Nicolau found himself confronting a bearded man likely in his thirties. Except for the beard, he could have been a brother to the two men whom Frostwing had killed.

Where *was* Frostwing, for that matter? He had rescued Grigori the last time; why not now?

There was no more time to consider that; the attacker muttered words in a tongue vaguely familiar to Grigori. The shadow receded.

At the same time, there came a sound from behind him.

Grigori turned, but as he did, something sharp and searing caught him in the side.

The first attacker snarled, "About time you did something! Did you see what he almost did to me?"

"Yeah. The master'll be *really* interested in this baby."

Things grew blurry, but Grigori could make out a thinner variation of the generic thug he had encountered so far. This man had no beard, and the expression on his rather vulpine face gave the impression of a greater capacity for thought than his companion. But even had the two men not mentioned a master, Grigori would have known that this was yet another soldier, not a general.

Grigori felt his consciousness slipping away. Groggy, he touched the area from where the initial pain—and now the present numbness—flared. One of Grigori's fingers fumbled over a small shaft sticking into his side. He had been shot with some sort of tranquilizing potion. That was odd, though. Such potions should not have affected him.

He never had the chance to consider the puzzle further. With his next breath, he collapsed onto the harsh parking lot pavement.

VII

HE HAD SLEPT, BUT HE HAD NOT DREAMT. GRIGORI WAS aware of this peculiar fact the moment he awoke on the floor of the darkened room. Grigori always remembered dreams, whether Frostwing plagued them or not. That he could recall nothing so astonished him that for a moment he forgot his predicament.

The squeaking returned his thoughts to the situation at hand.

"You are awake," announced a voice. Its tone implied that Grigori had the speaker to thank for that simple fact. He considered the notion briefly and decided that, perhaps, it was true. One who could give him his first dreamless slumber—the first that he could recall, Grigori corrected—was one to be respected.

"I will warn you once, Mr. Grigori Nicolau, and only once. You would be best served by *not* utilizing your . . . skills . . . in any attempt to flee." The speaker sometimes had an accent, but it was impossible for Grigori to say exactly what sort. First it sounded German, then Russian, then perhaps even British. There were others he could not identify.

Grigori had not gotten around to contemplating escape. It was all he could do to concentrate on his captor's words. It was an almost herculean task, made all the more difficult by the throbbing headache he—

No, it was hardly a headache. Only grogginess had prevented Nicolau from recognizing the sensation earlier. When he did, Grigori froze. A link, just like the one that had drawn him to Teresa.

He looked around, but his eyes could not adjust enough to see. Grigori could not recall ever being in so dark a room before. "Who are you?"

More squeaks, as if an army of rodents surrounded him. The calls of the rats almost hid the sound of more than one man breathing.

"I am someone close to you, Mr. Nicolau, as you are close to me. I've never come across another like us, and you may rest assured that I have looked hard."

Grigori cared neither for riddles nor speeches and this was both. He started to rise, only to discover that something held him in a kneeling position. It took him a breath or two to discover that his bonds were phantasmal, immaterial. Power kept Grigori prisoner, more power than he had encountered in at least two hundred years . . . unless, of course, he had forgotten it.

This had to be the master of the men who had perished in his hotel room. He could be no other. "I'll ask again, who are you?"

A light flickered on, a poor one that illuminated only a patch of floor a few feet wide. Grigori Nicolau knelt, very much a prisoner, on the edge of that patch.

In the center, seated in a tall chair made of what Grigori guessed to be silver and iron, two metals naturally attuned in different ways to the power, was an elegant figure. The backrest was covered in archaic runes that left Grigori unsettled; the chair served some dark purpose. He looked closely at his captor and finally noticed the glittering cloth bonds that prevented the other from rising. The cloth bonds looked thin, positively useless for the task, but Grigori assumed that, like the chair, they were much more than they appeared.

The bound man smiled slightly and inclined his head toward his prisoner. "I am Peter Frantisek, my dear Grigori, but you may call me *brother* if you wish."

The man's eyes were steel blue.

The drug had masked the link with this Peter Frantisek. Like Teresa, the bound man touched Grigori differently than those he had met before. He had never felt a force like Frantisek's, yet he *was* as familiar as a brother. Nicolau could muster no explanation. There was a darkness to the whole affair which made Grigori uneasy.

"What have you done with Miss Dvorak?"

Peter Frantisek smiled slightly again. "Your concern is commendable. It may mean that we can work together after all. As to your question, the young woman rests safely at home by this time. You were asleep for three hours."

Three hours! Remarkable! The bound man had held him captive for that long, yet Frostwing had still not come to free him.

"You are the one who concerns me at the moment, Grigori." The bound man studied his expression. "Rest assured, I want no harm to come to Teresa."

Frantisek's use of her first name made Grigori Nicolau bridle. It was as if the man in the chair was laying claim to her. True, Grigori had no right to consider Teresa his, but he doubted that she would have found the figure seated in the light attractive. Frantisek had an imperious manner about him. He obviously believed the world existed to fulfill his desires.

"What do you want from me?" Grigori finally asked his host. "I have nothing you want. I am simply a visitor to your country."

"An unusual visitor. Few wield so much power."

It was futile to deny his abilities, but Frantisek's claim that Grigori was a person of *much* power was enough to make the prisoner smile grimly. "So much power? I have *nothing*, Mr. Frantisek. If I did, would I have been so easily subdued by your two . . . associates? I claim some small ability, but that meager power is nothing worth disturbing yourself over. I pose no threat to you."

His host tapped a finger against the arm of the chair. Peter Frantisek's eyes seemed to glow with a light all their own. His expression remained unreadable.

A small form broke from the darkness to scurry to the side of the chair. It was a rat almost identical to the one Grigori had discovered in his pocket. At least he now knew who had caused it to be there.

The rat peered at Grigori, who gasped as he caught sight of the creature's eyes.

Like those of its master, the rat's eyes were steel blue.

"At first," began the bound man, seemingly oblivious to his tiny companion, "I was inclined to dismiss you, but my eyes and my people have created doubts in my heart." The rodent turned and scurried back into the shadows. "You are something more, my dear Grigori. Much, much more."

Grigori winced at the way the bound man spoke his name. It reminded him too much of the way Frostwing spoke to him. There were many similarities between the two, even the two names.

"I know nothing. I am nothing. I am one who yearns to live a peaceful existence, Mr. Frantisek."

"Then we are indeed brothers under the skin, dear Grigori, for I, too, yearn for a peaceful existence." The moment the words left his mouth, the bound man's voice tightened. The accents became more pronounced. "Yet, I *cannot*." Peter Frantisek indicated the straps that held him in the chair. "You *see* the ties that bind, my dear sir? You see this chair? This is my home for all but brief periods each day. I am as much a prisoner as you believe yourself to be.''

A prisoner whose arms have a very long reach, Grigori wanted to say. Even if the man before him could not leave the chair for more than a few minutes at a time, he still had great influence upon the world.

"What do you know about the house?"

The question caught Grigori by surprise, although it should not have. Of course, the bound man was interested in the house. His steel-blue eyes linked him to the place. Grigori realized then that his present circumstances might prove advantageous.

Frantisek obviously knew something about the house. He might even share those truths. If only Grigori was able to make use of the information after this audience. Even the bound man's power would not be enough to kill Grigori. That did not mean Frantisek might not try to slay him several times before finally giving up. The images that formed in his head made Nicolau shiver.

That was a mistake. The elegant figure strapped into the chair took Grigori's shivering as a response to his earlier question. Frantisek leaned forward as much as his bonds would permit and nearly hissed, "You *do* know something about the house.''

"I know only that I want to stay as far away from it as I can.''

Frantisek leaned back, a frown on his lips. "Understandable, but I think there's more to your story than that. Perhaps you will be kind enough to explain what happened to my people who visited your hotel room. They have vanished. There is no trace of them anywhere, not even an afterpattern."

"I did nothing to your men," protested Grigori, wondering at the same time what an afterpattern might be.

Something hard and heavy battered Grigori's ribs. He grunted and nearly fell over.

"That will be *enough* of that!" Through tearful eyes, Grigori noted that his host glared past him at something in the darkness. Nicolau had forgotten that there were others here, that he could not sense them unless they acted. Only their breathing revealed their presence, and one had to listen for it to notice the sound. Now, however, the thug who had kicked Grigori shuffled back into the dark.

"You have my apologies, Grigori. That was uncalled for."

As strange as it seemed, he actually believed Frantisek's apology. That did not excuse the man for everything else, of course. "I did nothing to your men. I don't know what's happened to them."

That was stretching the truth a bit. Grigori knew they were dead, but what Frostwing had done with the corpses afterward, he could not say. He did not *want* to know.

The bound man turned his head to one side, as if trying to see behind the chair. "Conrad."

"Yes, Mr. Frantisek." From the shadows behind Grigori's host, a piggish-looking man emerged. His appearance did not fool Nicolau; Conrad was obviously a very dangerous man. Frantisek's taint was on him, too, which meant that the servant was more than he seemed. Grigori noticed a slight bulge under Conrad's jacket, which did not at all surprise him. The weapon underneath the jacket was likely no ordinary gun.

The brutish Conrad now stood before him. Grigori braced for the worst; in the past, this was generally where his enemies had begun torture. The man before him looked quite adept at such work, too.

The ponytailed servant reached into a coat pocket and brought out a knife. It was a moment before Grigori Nicolau recognized the blade. Smiling, Conrad thrust it close to the captive's face.

"If you don't know what happened to them, then how is it that this blade was found upon you?" The bound man did not seem angry with Grigori; rather, he sounded curious.

"Who are you, my friend? My people indicate that you injured yourself falling when the drug took over. Yet, your injuries healed even as they brought you to me. You also broke through the wall that had been placed, for your own protection I might add, in front of you during your sojourn to the house." Here Frantisek seemed slightly annoyed with him. "Your stubbornness caused the death of one of my children."

In the shadows, the squeaking renewed with more vigor. The man in the chair silenced the hidden rodents with a glance. Conrad, meanwhile, looked more and more inclined to further wield the blade. Grigori did not desire to discover just how much pain and damage he could suffer from a knife thrust into the face. It was one wound he had happily avoided . . . as far as he knew . . . during his long life.

Frantisek suddenly straightened in his chair. "Conrad, I would like a drink."

"Yes, Mr. Frantisek." There was no hesitation, no hint of disappointment on the servant's piggish countenance as he returned the knife to his pocket and departed again for the shadows. Conrad clearly lived to serve his master in whatever manner demanded of him. Grigori had met his type before and respected their dedication. He also avoided such people whenever possible.

The manservant returned with an elaborate silver chalice and positioned himself so that Frantisek could drink from it. The bound man took two short sips from the container, then indicated to his minion that he could remove the chalice. Conrad stepped to the side of the chair and stood at attention, chalice in one hand, eyes focused straight ahead.

Peter Frantisek returned his attention to Grigori. "And what is the gargoyle to *you*, Mr. Nicolau?"

The question stunned Grigori. He had expected to be interrogated about the house and the people who had disappeared, but after his conversation with Teresa he had come to think that only he knew of the connection between the house and Frostwing.

"You said that you dreamed of the gargoyle." There was an edge to the man's voice that had not been there earlier. Different accents still highlighted his speech at irregular intervals. "What did you dream? What do you know about him?"

Grigori said nothing.

"My eyes and ears are everywhere, friend Grigori. A restaurant is certainly no haven from my pets."

It took all of his willpower to enable Grigori Nicolau to utter, "I don't know anything."

"That is really a shame, my dear Grigori . . ."

With those words, Peter Frantisek ceased to be.

Frostwing sat in the chair . . . and he was by no means bound.

The gargoyle laughed. "Such a shame indeed, dear, dear Grigori! I expected better entertainment from you!"

The shock finally wore off. Grigori Nicolau struggled to rise, all the while cursing the taunting golem. "Damn you, Frostwing! What kind of game are you playing n—?"

His voice died as the gargoyle faded, to be replaced by Peter Frantisek, still bound. "Frostwing, is it? How very apt a name."

An illusion. I fell for an illusion. His captor was astute; he recognized his guest's weaknesses quickly. Yet, Frantisek also knew something about the gargoyle, apart from his appearance. For the first time, Grigori discovered himself fearing someone nearly as much as he feared his winged persecutor. Who *was* this Peter Frantisek?

"Frostwing," the bound man continued to muse. His eyes glittered in the light as he matched gazes with his captive. "I could not have named him better myself." He smiled at Grigori. "I think, my dear friend, that we have a mutual enemy to discuss. If you know the gargoyle as I do, you realize that it is not enemies we should be, but *allies*.'' One hand moved in a peculiar gesture. ''As a token of my faith, I will remove the power that held you in so uncomfortable a position. You may rise.''

Grigori cautiously tested his host's claim and found it to be truth. He straightened with little difficulty, his stiff muscles and bones the only hindrances.

''Conrad, another glass for my friend.''

The servant nodded and stepped back into the blackness. Grigori nervously surveyed the dark chamber.

''Is something amiss? You look as if you're expecting someone, Grigori.''

''You might say that.'' What sort of game was Frostwing playing now? He had never left his hapless plaything in another's hands for so long. Never.

''Aaah, you're expecting the gargoyle . . . pardon . . . *Frostwing* to appear.'' Frantisek shook his head in mock sadness. ''There will be no show. Your friend will not appear for the simple reason that he is *prevented* from doing so.''

''Prevented?'' Grigori was certain that he could not have heard correctly.

''Prevented.''

Conrad returned with a second chalice, but did not approach Grigori until his master indicated that he should. The brutish servant held out the chalice to the captive. The moment Grigori took the cup, Conrad backed away until he stood once more at Frantisek's side.

''A chair for Mr. Nicolau, please. A comfortable one.''

A chair appeared next to Grigori. He knew that there had not been one there earlier. Grigori eyed his host with respect and heightened fear.

''Sit, please.'' Frantisek signaled for another sip from his own chalice. When he was done, he nodded at Grigori, who, after some trepidation, had finally seated himself. "Much better. It was Frostwing who took my two men, wasn't it?" He did not wait for an answer. "You may know something about that or you may not. Actually, I suppose it does not matter. It was their error, anyway. They went to your hotel room without my permission. I wanted them to observe you. Kidnapping was not part of their orders."

Grigori had not yet taken a drink, and had no intention of doing so. He rested the chalice on one knee, keeping his grip on it tight should he require the heavy cup as a weapon. "Mr. Frantisek, what is it you think I can do for you? I cannot deny that I know Frostwing, but if you know him, too, your knowledge likely exceeds mine. No doubt you know what I told Miss Dvorak. I can add nothing more to what I said to her."

His answer clearly disappointed his host. "Perhaps you do not truly understand our situation. We are *alone*, Grigori. We are alone among our fellows, those with our eyes. Before you came here, I thought that I was unique. No one else is aware of our friend the gargoyle, neither are they aware of his link to the house, a link that extends beyond the arch he haunts. The others are sheep. They do not possess the wherewithal to resist; they don't even have a notion of what is happening to them."

"And what is that?"

"You refer to what is going on in the house? For that knowledge, I would have to enter the place, and I dare not do that. You, too, must avoid the place. Teresa told you about the others who asked about the house. I think you suspect what happened to them . . . don't you, Grigori? I can tell you that they gained access to the house." Peter Frantisek tapped the arm of his chair. The veins in his neck throbbed. His voice, however, was surprisingly soft as he leaned forward again and commanded, "Tell me what happened to them, Mr. Nicolau, so that you can hear it from your own lips. The words are simple ones; all you have to do is say them.''

The bound man cast no spell, but his aura of authority demanded an answer. Grigori, still overwhelmed by his predicament, could not help but obey. ''They never . . . never came out . . . but . . .''

Silence briefly filled the chamber as Grigori found himself unable to go on.

''It's too terrible to believe—isn't that what you want to say? Even knowing it as the truth, you still want to deny it, don't you?''

''Yes.''

Frantisek calmed, as if forcing Grigori to speak his suspicions had relieved him of a great burden. ''The gargoyle has resided there since the house was built. Who built it does not matter. A pawn, that's all. The arch and the monster himself, however, are older than the house. I know that to be true, although I have never been able to discover from where the arch was shipped. Somewhere in Europe. That's all my efforts yielded on that subject. Ownership of the house has also been a perplexing, shadowed thing, the papers switching from one trust to another with no direct contacts.''

''There is a—''

''Yes, I am aware of the group that claims to hold the house in trust. The address they use does not exist, but somehow they receive their post. No, the only constant about the house is your—*our*—friend. Frostwing.''

Despite the earlier assurances, each time the bound man spoke the demonic golem's name, Grigori expected to see the stone fury materialize in the chamber. Frantisek's promise could not wipe away centuries of being haunted by his winged nemesis.

''Let me tell you a little about the gargoyle as *I* know him.

He is nightmare itself. He is a malicious, sadistic creature from the darkest pits of Hell. His power is great, yet he rarely ventures from the house—save when it is time to call another.'' Frantisek signaled for yet another sip. Conrad was there immediately. Across from them, Grigori continued to cradle the chalice. The bound man appeared not to notice his unwilling guest's lack of thirst, his concentration on the terrible tale he was relating. ''I first encountered him when he made the rare mistake of calling me.''

Grigori said nothing. Had someone offered him his freedom at this very moment, he would have been hardpressed to accept it. Here at last was someone else who had confronted Frostwing . . . and had lived to speak of it.

''He called some fifteen years ago,'' began the bound man in a low, steady voice. ''He came to me in my dreams, a figure of monumental horror. Only you can imagine what that was like. I knew it was a dream, yet I also knew that it was not. He came to me, a nameless dread in stone, and told me that my time had arrived; I was to come to the house.'' Frantisek shifted as best as his bonds would permit him. ''I did not even have to *ask* him what house he meant. It did not seem important. I only knew that I had to come to Chicago and fulfill my part in the grand scheme.'' He shook his head and smiled in self-mockery. ''I did not even know what that grand scheme was, only that I needed to complete it as soon as I could. That I was in mortal fear of the creature meant nothing to me; I intended to obey with all my heart.'' The bound man nodded to himself. ''But as you can plainly see, my dear Grigori Nicolau, I did not fulfill the gargoyle's command. That shocked him as much as it did me.''

''*How?*'' Grigori blurted, spilling some of his drink on the floor in the process. ''How were you able to defy him?''

Raising one hand as best he could, Peter Frantisek pointed

at him. Grigori felt his skin crawl as a subtle force, dark and hungry, began to creep over him. He tried to back away. As he did, the force dwindled, leaving him a little dazed.

"Let us simply say that I had the knowledge and power to do so," returned his host, "but even so, it was an effort. I have possessed such power since I grew into manhood. Why I am different from the gargoyle's other victims, I cannot say. You are also different; perhaps there are others."

Frantisek continued his grim narrative.

Not content with what he feared might be a temporary victory, he had researched further. He wasted no scrap of information. His power grew, but so did Frostwing's call. After a time, he began to realize that his own efforts undermined him by weakening him a little at crucial moments. Yet he was not a man to surrender.

At last, he found the ultimate use of his abilities, a way to protect himself from the siren call.

The bound man gestured at the chair he sat in. "It is over three hundred years old . . . perhaps more. Designed by a man of power, Italian, I believe. I will spare you the story of its original function, but suffice to say that now it acts as a shield against the call. The chair deflects it, so to speak. In its embrace, I need concentrate less on fighting the summons. It also acts as a focus for my own power, enabling me to do things that would be much more difficult otherwise."

Frantisek grimaced. "Sometimes, though, my dear Grigori, the strain is still too much. That is why I must remain bound. I can never predict when the summons will strike. Sitting in the chair will not alone save me." His eyes fixed on the straps keeping him in the chair. "These are a painful necessity. Each day, I allow myself only the most urgent times away, the necessary times."

Grigori tried to imagine what it would be like to live such an existence. Difficult, yes; but given the choice between his own life and that of his host, Grigori was almost tempted to offer a trade. The man before him clearly controlled events more often than not, something he could only dream of doing. "You even sleep in it?"

"I have no *choice*." Frantisek's steel-blue eyes blazed. "There is something happening in the house, my dear Mr. Nicolau, and that something will culminate very soon. I need all the strength that I can muster. Only one action can save us from at last falling prey to our gargoyle friend, and that is to make him bow to us first."

Frostwing bowing at my feet . . . It was, admittedly, a dream that Grigori Nicolau had once fostered, but one he had abandoned long ago. Now, however, the slight man could not help but wonder. Was Peter Frantisek truly capable of bringing down his eternal tormentor?

As if reading his mind, the bound man said, "I *can* stop him, but I need your help, Grigori Nicolau. Alone, I have fought the damnable beast to a standstill. I have never been able to take the battle to *him*." The figure in the chair leaned forward again. "I have never had a capable ally before."

Perhaps it was the way that the bound man looked at him, or perhaps it was Grigori's memory of his abduction that made him, almost without thinking, replace the word *ally* with *pawn*. Grigori Nicolau was a fair enough judge of character to know where he ranked in the schemes of the man seated before him. Still, it behooved him for the time being to pretend he believed the bound man.

The elegantly dressed Frantisek tapped the arm of his chair again. The tone in his voice altered at the same time, once more becoming subdued. The confused mixture of accents remained, but Grigori found himself growing accustomed to the peculiarity. "How long have you dreamed of him?"

"As far back as I can remember," responded Grigori quite truthfully. He did not want to offer his captor dates. "I thought he only existed in my dreams. When I saw the house—''

Frantisek waved a weary hand at him. "This much I know. Tell me what you did *not* tell the woman. Sadly you know little about the house itself, but you know the gargoyle better . . . perhaps even better than myself.''

For what Frantisek had already told him, Grigori was willing to supply some bits of the truth. Not enough, of course, to reveal the entire truth about himself, but something that would at least satisfy his host. He would not lie. Unlike so many in this century, he was bound by a code of honor. It was a mangled, beaten code, but Grigori still cherished it. Besides, he suspected that Frantisek was adept at sensing lies and not at all forgiving to those who spoke them.

Nodding, Grigori Nicolau began his carefully pared account. His best chance lay in omitting facts, as he had done with Teresa, albeit for different reasons. "I have known Frostwing for so long I cannot even recall the first time he visited me . . ."

Both the bound man and his servant listened with avid, growing interest as Grigori told them what they wanted to hear. He described the coming of the dreams in detail, knowing that Peter Frantisek likely knew enough about them to recognize their truth. Grigori talked about moving about from place to place. He did not mention anything specific before London, merely hinting that his roots were in the eastern half of Europe.

At that, the bound man nodded, but did not otherwise interrupt. Conrad took his hints from his master. Seeing that Frantisek was satisfied so far, a little of the darkness left his eyes. Only a little, however. He was definitely not a man that Grigori desired to cross, power or no.

Grigori made no mention of his stolen memories. That would lead to questions he dared not answer. The bound man had made no mention of any similar experiences, which convinced Nicolau that his host did not suffer as he did.

He finished with his assumptions concerning the deaths of the two men who had entered his hotel room. It came as no surprise to Frantisek that Frostwing could touch the real world through dreams, which made Grigori wonder about the man's own experiences in that respect.

Both men listened intently to the very end. "I have never known why I was chosen—I should say *condemned*—to this existence."

The final words were the most truthful words Grigori Nicolau had spoken so far. He spoke them with such conviction that it seemed impossible Frantisek might not believe them. When the bound man nodded thoughtfully, Grigori almost sighed in relief, but that would have looked too suspicious. He contented himself with swallowing and waiting. His mouth was dry after the lengthy tale, but he still avoided the contents of his chalice.

"Not as much as I had hoped for, but more than I knew before. My gratitude, Grigori, for your thoroughness and your trust." The accents became less evident; Frantisek's voice became monotonous. Yet he was not indifferent to what he had just learned. "I must now think upon this."

"What about me?" The question was blurted out before Grigori could stop himself. He cursed silently. Six hundred or so years had not taught him to keep his mouth shut when it was wisest to do so.

"It has been a pleasure making your acquaintance, my dear Grigori. When we first began this talk I foresaw great things for our alliance—I at work here and you out there. However, the gargoyle is a reader of minds, as you very well know. Before I can proceed with my plans, I must make certain that he knows nothing of our conversation. I trust you understand the need for that."

Grigori's grip tightened on the chalice. He had heard that tone before, the last time from a uniformed officer in Berlin during the 1930s. He had no doubt that it meant the same thing now. The officer could not have known that the man before him was immortal—and also had the power to make him regret the intense pain he had caused.

Grigori knew he had to defend himself. He tensed, thinking that perhaps his chances would be better if he surprised his captors with a physical attack. The chalice made for a hard and deadly weapon in the hands of one who knew how to throw it.

Grigori estimated the distance between Frantisek and himself. Even as his grip tightened on the chalice, Conrad's hand snaked under his own coat. Grigori attempted to call his power into play but as he cocked his arm to throw, a sudden buzzing in his head prevented him from concentrating.

The manservant pulled free a slim, tapering gun with a peculiar trigger mechanism. It did not shoot bullets, but rather needles.

"I am sorry, my dear Grigori, but surely you can see that this must be done." The bound man pursed his lips in annoyance and concluded, "This is not the proper way to treat an ally, but circumstances call for it."

Conrad fired. The gun was almost silent, the only sound a slight *hiss*.

Pain wracked the slight man's arm.

The manservant fired again, this time striking Grigori's left leg.

Grigori collapsed into dreamless sleep or possibly even death. He knew not which and found, in that last second, he honestly did not care.

VIII

IT WAS A DREAM . . . AND YET IT WAS NOT. GRIGORI Nicolau stood across the street from the house.

He was not alone. Only a few feet from him, yet seemingly ignorant of his presence, was a man of about forty. He wore a bushy mustache which failed to give his features any distinction. The top of his head, in contrast to his upper lip, was devoid of hair, save for a few brown strands. He was stocky, slightly taller than Grigori, and dressed in clothes suitable for a leisurely walk—a blue sports jacket, weathered black jeans, and running shoes. When the stranger reached up to scratch his cheek, the sun reflected off of a large, glittering, diamond ring with one lavender stone and two smaller white ones positioned to each side.

Grigori attempted to say something, but no sound escaped his mouth. Nonetheless, the man suddenly looked his way.

His eyes were steel blue.

Grigori's initial elation gave way to frustration when he realized that the other looked not at him, but rather past him to the street. A moment later, the man turned away and glanced down the other end. Satisfied that there was no traffic coming, he started across the street in the direction of the house.

Stretching forth a hand, Grigori tried to stop the stranger. To his horror, his hand slipped *through* the other man. He tried calling out again, but still no sound emerged. In desperation, Grigori followed, hoping some plan would come to him before it was too late.

Only when the two of them had crossed onto the sidewalk did he recall the gate. Despite his desire not to, Grigori glanced up at the arch.

The gargoyle leered down at him. Frostwing stood frozen, a true statue. Yet Grigori needed every ounce of willpower to keep himself from once more fleeing in blind panic.

His companion moved close to the gate. Grigori stepped aside, then waited to see what would happen.

The man looked up at the image of Frostwing and spoke. To Grigori's surprise he could hear the man. The voice was sluggish, but also determined. "I'm here."

It was then that Frostwing began to move.

Grigori Nicolau gaped as wings spread and the two-foot-tall gargoyle crouched forward to inspect the newcomer. Frostwing chuckled, which again almost sent Grigori running. Then the sinister golem said, "You may enter, Matthew Emrich."

No snide comment to Grigori, no mocking laughter. Frostwing seemed only to see the man named Emrich. Nevertheless, Grigori did his best to remain still, fearing that he might draw attention to himself.

A harsh, grating sound made him jump. He tore his gaze from the gargoyle and saw that the gate was opening of its own accord. Matthew Emrich had not moved yet, apparently waiting until the entrance had swung wide enough to receive him.

When the gate was half-open, the balding man started forward. Despite his fear of the winged terror perched above, Grigori attempted to seize Emrich by the arm. Once again his hand went through the other as if Emrich did not exist . . . or perhaps it was *Grigori* who did not exist. He shook away the chilling thought; what mattered now was that Matthew Emrich had passed through the gate and was walking toward the house, his pace increasing with every step.

Nicolau took one last look at Frostwing, who was turned so as to gaze at the back of the balding man, then forced himself to cross beneath the gateway.

The gargoyle did not react.

Grigori allowed himself to breathe again. But by now Emrich was a good way to the front of the house. Mouthing a cry, the dark man ran after him. If Matthew Emrich crossed the threshold, Grigori would have no hope of saving him. Even if he did catch him, what could he do?

Listen to me! he tried to shout. He managed to come up beside Emrich. *You must turn back!*

His warnings went unheard. The determined figure continued up the sloping walk. Grigori leapt before Emrich, but jumped out of the way when it became apparent that the man would have walked through him.

Only a few more yards and Emrich would reach the house.

Grigori felt the presence within the edifice and knew it to be a thing much older than the house itself. There was a darkness to it that reminded him of many things at once, including both Peter Frantisek and the gargoyle. Had it concerned him alone, Grigori would have stepped no closer to the foul abode, but another's life was at stake. Emrich continued blindly on, eager to reach the front door and whatever waited behind it.

Pointing at the man, Grigori attempted to use his power. Nothing happened. He tried several times, but only succeeded in falling behind the relentless figure.

Matthew Emrich put one foot on the step.

The door creaked open. The scene would have almost been ludicrous to Grigori, looking as it did like something out of one of the more atrocious moving pictures of this century, save that he was a part of it. He ran, but stumbled to a halt at the stairs. Grigori looked down at the wooden step and could not bring himself to put a foot upon it.

His silent companion had by this time reached the top. Emrich continued toward the now-open doorway without pause.

Grigori, caught between two terrible choices, could not move. He stared past the figure walking through the doorway. At first, there was nothing distinct within, but then, as Emrich reached the entrance, a shape coalesced from the empty air.

It was . . . a face. Shrouded, Protean, it was still most definitely a face. Nicolau shivered. The face was familiar.

The mouth opened wide, until it encompassed the width and length of the doorframe. Huge teeth hung over the head of the oncoming man. A massive, writhing tongue spread forth like a carpet. Oddly, the gullet faded into darkness rather than the back of the mouth.

Matthew Emrich walked toward the gaping maw with no sign that he even noticed it.

Shouting futilely, Grigori started up the steps.

It was too late. Emrich walked onto the waiting tongue and into the open jaws.

There was no hesitation.

The mouth snapped shut.

The face smiled at Grigori . . .

"Noooo!"

Like a mousetrap sprung, Grigori Nicolau shot up in bed. His breath came in short, painful gasps as he not only wrestled with the nightmare, but attempted to comprehend where he was now. As his breathing grew more relaxed, Grigori focused on his surroundings. A room.

His room.

Sunlight shone through a crack in the curtains of one window. Grigori Nicolau looked down and saw that he was lying atop an unrumpled bed, his clothes from the evening before still on him. Peter Frantisek's men had returned him to his hotel. Apparently no one had noticed what must have been a strange sight.

With the question of where he was now settled, he tried to comprehend the dream . . . or whatever it had been. Grigori had never suffered anything like the scene that had played out in his mind; it did not look or feel like either his normal dreams or the ones that Frostwing forced upon him.

The dream was certainly not of his own creation. That left Frantisek. It seemed reasonable to assume that the bound man had forced Grigori to experience the disappearance of Matthew Emrich. But *why*? Had he wanted his reluctant ally to see what had befallen all those others like them? Was the vision meant to convert him to Peter Frantisek's cause? Were that true, the bound man likely had some task in mind for him. The thought did not sit well with the centuries-old outcast.

The last notion explained why Grigori had been brought safely back to his room. Frantisek had talked of them being allies. Nicolau wanted no part of that. He knew very well that to the bound man he was a pawn, pure and simple. Perhaps he was even bait, a way to draw Frostwing into danger at a time of the bound man's own choosing.

Grigori Nicolau had been the pawn of one creature of power for as far back as he could remember; he had no desire to chain himself to a second lord, especially when the two were locked in a deadly struggle for supremacy. Moreover, Peter Frantisek had not revealed the entire truth of his struggle; there was more to it than simply the need to end the gargoyle's reign of terror. The bound man desired something more, perhaps control of the house—or the force that lurked within.

The final part of the vision flared in his memory. What had the face in the doorway represented? Even thinking about the thing sent a strange jolt through his body. A part of him feared and loathed it, yet it drew him like a flame draws a moth. Why was that?

He shook his head, which proved to be a mistake. The sudden pounding in his skull sent him falling back onto the pillows. Grigori stared up at the ceiling.

His life no longer followed the long, consistent pattern it had for the past centuries. He was used to living in one place for a while, avoiding as best he could contact with other power wielders and trying to find some way to rid himself of the gargoyle. Sometimes men like Frantisek tried to hunt him down for various and sundry reasons, but they had always departed his life quickly. At some point after, it always proved necessary to depart for another place . . . where the pattern simply repeated itself again without end. While there were always changes on the part of the game Frostwing played with him, there had still always been a sense of continuity. That sense of continuity was now lost. The house, the man strapped into the peculiar metal chair, Teresa . . . none of this was consistent with the past. It was almost as if events were actually leading up to something.

Teresa . . . Ignoring the anvil chorus playing in his head, Grigori rolled over and seized the telephone. Frantisek had claimed that she was unharmed, but Grigori could hardly take his word for that. He had to know that she was safe, even if she only hung up on him.

As he began to dial, his eyes grew heavy and dizziness joined forces with his headache. The telephone receiver slipped from his shaking hand.

"No! Not now!" An image of Frostwing perched atop the arch flashed through Grigori's mind. He could not face the demonic golem, not after his encounter with the bound man. The gargoyle would immediately realize the truth. There were no hiding places in Nicolau's mind. Frostwing had access to every thought and dream.

Grigori forced his eyes open and rubbed his forehead. To his surprise, the dizziness began to recede and it became easier to keep his eyes open. Grigori stayed still, fearful that any movement would bring back the dizziness tenfold.

Things slowly reverted to normal. When Grigori finally realized the symptoms had passed, his eyes widened. Throughout his existence, he had sought to keep Frostwing at bay, to block the gargoyle's access to him. Now he had at last done so.

No, he corrected himself. *It may be that I have simply defeated a headache.* It could hardly be possible that he had rejected the malicious gargoyle's attempt to come to him. What Grigori had felt was nothing but the aftereffects from whatever potion the manservant had injected him with.

Yet, he could not help but wonder . . .

A harsh, electronic whine reminded him of the telephone. He pressed a button in order to restore the dial tone, then punched in Teresa's number. As the call went through, Grigori's eyes drifted to the clock.

Three in the afternoon. The realization almost made him drop the receiver again. The loss of so much of the day disturbed him.

The telephone rang and rang. He was about to hang up when, finally, someone answered.

"Sentinel Realty. Teresa speaking."

He hesitated, pleased that she was safe after all. "Teresa, this is Grigori Nicolau."

The line clicked again. For a moment there was silence, then the dial tone returned.

She had hung up on him. Grigori had expected it. Nevertheless, he knew that he had to try again. She was safe, but for how long? If Frantisek allowed her to follow her daily routine, it was only because he was best served by having her do so. As with Grigori, however, there would come a point when the bound man, or even Frostwing, would find it advantageous to make other use of the young woman.

He pictured her entering the house. The vision was enough to make him immediately dial again. Grigori paused after the first three digits, however, suddenly thinking of something. With his free hand he burrowed into his coat pocket, searching. When at first he did not find what he was looking for, the slight man grew anxious. Then, in an inner pocket, he finally located the object of his search.

It was more than likely that Teresa would not answer her telephone or, even if she did, that she would hang up again. If he hoped to talk to her at all, Grigori had to contact her through a different route.

As he hoped, her business card listed not only her personal line, but the main office telephone number as well. Looking it over, Grigori quickly redialed. The telephone rang four times before someone answered.

"Sentinel. This is Eric speaking."

For once Grigori was pleased to talk to the novice agent. Teresa would be less likely to refuse the call if someone else in the office knew of it, especially someone who had met Grigori face-to-face. Granted, the young man had witnessed Nicolau's abrupt departure from the office, but Grigori still hoped that Eric would not be so willing to lose a possible buyer.

"Eric. Good. This is Mr. Nicolau. I was speaking with Teresa when I was cut off. It was only a moment ago, so I know she's still there." He pushed a little with his power, seeking to turn away any objections or uncertainties in Eric's mind. "Would you please connect me with her again?"

"Sure! Just a minute." He was put on hold before he could say anything else.

An eternity passed. Then—

"I want you to leave me alone," whispered a voice on the telephone.

"I am sorry about last night, Teresa. You must believe me when I say that."

"I don't want to talk about this insanity." Her voice remained a whisper, but he could sense the rising anxiety in her tone.

In desperation, Nicolau blurted out, "Where is Matthew Emrich, Teresa? How long ago has it been since he last came to you?"

The silence that followed made him at first wonder whether she had hung up on him again, but then Teresa, her voice even quieter, asked, "How do you know him?"

"I do not know him . . . I know of him, if that makes a difference."

Again she paused. "What do you know?"

"He came to you to ask about the house and later disappeared. I can describe him for you." He thought back to the balding man and began to list as many details as he could. Teresa was silent throughout, although now and then Grigori could hear her breath catch.

"Where did you see him?" she asked when he was through. "I thought he was gone, like all the others but if he—"

"*Teresa.*" Grigori waited until he was certain that she was listening again. "Teresa . . . I think he entered the house." Before she could ask how he could know that for certain, Nicolau quickly added, "This is not something I would like to discuss over the telephone. Teresa, I *implore* you. Let me meet you again someplace where you feel secure. We must talk about this, but it needs to be in person."

"I can't . . . I . . . your story . . ."

Running a hand over his face, Grigori desperately sought some way to force a meeting without using his power to coerce Teresa. He could think of nothing short of threatening to come directly to the office.

Then, in a resigned tone, Teresa said, "All right."

At first Grigori did not understand her meaning. When the words registered in his mind, the stunned man had to ask, "Are you certain?"

Another pause, then, "No . . . no, I'm not, Grigori, but . . . I couldn't stop thinking about it all last night. Truthfully, I waited for you to call. When you didn't, I thought I might be able to put it behind me. Then of course you had to call, didn't you?" The strain in her voice was more evident. When she spoke again, her voice trembled. "I don't know what to do."

"I understand, Teresa." He did, more than she would probably ever know. "I will come to the office. Is that all right with you? Would you prefer we meet elsewhere?"

"No. The office is fine."

He worried about her stability, but there was nothing he could do to aid her until they met again. It was easy for Grigori to understand her plight. Teresa Dvorak had been drawn into a horrific, improbable situation. All she had were suspicions and the fears her imagination generated from those suspicions.

"I will be there just before you close the office."

"All right."

Feeling the need to add something, *anything*, that might encourage her, Grigori concluded, "You are not alone in this, Teresa. I am here for you, if you wish."

"Thank you," she said in the same strained voice.

Teresa hung up.

Grigori replaced the receiver, his gaze lingering on the device for some time. Her voice, her entire attitude, revealed far more desperation than should have been reasonable. Perhaps something else had occurred while he had been an unwilling guest of Peter Frantisek.

He hoped he was not too late already. He hoped that the house had not already called her for the final time.

* * *

Grigori arrived at the Sentinel offices half an hour early, but he chose not to enter immediately. Instead, he started from a point roughly a block from the realtor and paced a crude, surrounding loop about the area where the building was located. The task took him almost twenty minutes, but by the time he was finished, Grigori knew that *something* was watching Teresa's place of work. He was also fairly certain that those watchers wore the shape of one or more rats.

It had occurred to him soon after his conversation with Teresa that the bound man would expect him to contact her. Yet, despite that, Frantisek had done nothing to prevent Grigori Nicolau from arranging a rendezvous.

He is waiting for Frostwing to make his move. That has to be the reason! Peter Frantisek was much like the gargoyle; the more Grigori compared the two, the more he saw the truth of that.

Reaching the front door, Grigori Nicolau found his pulse racing. It was due in part to the nerve-wracking situation, but also to simply seeing Teresa again. Grigori tried to reason with himself, but the desire would not cool. Never had he been so besotted. That could prove dangerous to both of them, especially if his concentration slipped at a crucial time.

He smiled rather grimly. When had he come to think that he had some chance against the damnable gargoyle?

There were mostly employees in the office this late in the day. Two of the agents supervised clients and some of the others talked animatedly on the telephone. Few noticed when Grigori entered. One of those who did was Eric, who seemed a little surprised to see him. Wasting no time on the young agent, Grigori walked directly toward Teresa's desk.

She looked up from her work and her expression became

a mixture of relief and uncertainty. He could read no fear of him on her face, for which he was thankful.

He took off his hat. "Have I come too early?"

The young woman closed a folder that she had been perusing and added it to a short pile just to her left. "No. I was just rereading something." Teresa shook her head. "I haven't been any good to anybody all day. I don't know why I even bothered to come in. I might as well go now."

She rose from her chair and gathered her things together. Grigori remained where he was, feeling slightly conspicuous, but no one paid any attention to him—save Eric, who glanced his way once or twice. The dark man paid the glances little mind; perhaps the other realtor was jealous of him, suspecting that Teresa was dating one of her clients.

That notion almost made him laugh out loud. Now he was *fantasizing*. Grigori had not thought it possible of himself anymore. It was amazing what Teresa could inspire in him without even trying. The attraction he felt for her went beyond the link between them; he realized that now.

Teresa put the small pile of folders on the center of the desk and laid her purse next to it. Donning her coat, she started to reach for the papers again, but Grigori reached forward and seized them before she could. "If you will allow me. It's the least I can do."

"Thank you." She gave him a slight smile, but it lacked warmth. He did not take it personally, recognizing her obvious preoccupation with other things. The files were not very heavy, anyway. Grigori only wondered why she needed to bring them along. Perhaps they involved clients she was supposed to meet tomorrow. Judging by her present condition, he doubted that she would accomplish much work this evening. Grigori almost suggested leaving the files, but his companion had already walked past him and was heading toward the door. He followed, again hoping that no one in the office would take special notice of their departure together. It *was* late in the day to be showing houses.

Only when the two of them were outside did Teresa, walking in the direction of her automobile, speak again. "I brought something . . . something that . . . that you might want to look at."

"What is it?"

She indicated the burden in his arms. "Those files. I don't know if they'll be of any use, but those are the files I kept on . . . on everyone who asked me about the house."

Grigori was half-tempted to open the files right there and then, but he forced himself to be patient. For Teresa to have thought of the files while under so much stress was admirable. "You did very well. I should have thought to ask you about such files. Thank you very much, Teresa. This may be of great aid to us."

Her expression lightened a little and a spark of hope glimmered in her eyes. Grigori, not desiring to quench that spark, did not add that it was also possible they might find no trace of any of the people in the files. He was frankly surprised that the files even existed.

Teresa was just about to say something when a movement ahead caught Grigori's eye. In the growing darkness of early evening, it was impossible to see what it was, but Grigori estimated it to be too small for all but the youngest cats or dogs. It also ran with a different gait.

"Is something the matter?" Teresa's voice was tense. He glanced her way and saw that she seemed almost to be expecting some monstrous horror to leap out at them. Grigori freed one hand and put it on her own.

With his power, he searched the darkened region where the tiny form had disappeared. There was no indication of another power nearby, but that meant little. Although his time in Frantisek's care had afforded Nicolau a better understanding of the bound man's abilities, that did not mean that he could always sense the presence of one of Frantisek's minions, especially if that servant was not human.

Grigori decided that the rat . . . or maybe even *rats* . . . lurked nearby, watching, but he saw no point in wasting more time in searching. There were ways to blind prying eyes that he was certain would be effective even against the bound man's pets.

"It was nothing," he finally informed his companion, trying to act unconcerned. "A cat or some other animal."

They finally reached her car. As she unlocked it and they climbed inside, Grigori finally dared ask, "Where are we going?"

She stared straight ahead for several seconds before turning to him. "I don't know whether I'm crazy to do this, but I feel somehow that I can trust you. I'm driving us to the only place I feel safe any more. We're going to my apartment." She tried to smile playfully and almost succeeded. "Don't get any funny ideas now, okay? I'm not trying to seduce you."

"A pity," he replied, giving her an open smile in return. "If you change your mind, let me know?"

"I'll think about it." Her attempt to build a more pleasant mood withered in the awkward silence that followed. Teresa finally started the car and turned on the radio.

A piece that Grigori recognized as by Sibelius was already underway. After a moment of listening, he was able to identify it as *Finlandia*. The centuries-old man would have preferred something more romantic at the moment. Sighing quietly, Grigori leaned back and simply listened.

Eric waited until Teresa and the European were gone before reaching for the telephone. He made only the pretense of dialing, knowing that with the master that was unnecessary.

"Well?" asked a gruff voice.

Conrad. The young agent feared the manservant almost as much as he feared the master. After failing to quell the quaver in his voice, he reported, "They just left. She took some files with her."

"What were they?"

"I think they might be about the people."

There was a pause, which could only mean that Conrad was relaying the information to the master. After a time, the manservant returned. "Everything is proceeding as it should, then. Mr. Frantisek says that you may go home now. Be ready to be summoned, though."

"I . . . I understand."

"Good." An insistent dial tone suddenly blared from the receiver.

Eric held back a sigh of relief. Unlike most of those who served the master, he did not consider himself a good field agent. Eric valued himself above such tasks; he hoped to apprentice with the bound man and learn how to use the power he was certain he possessed. Had not the master, upon first bringing him into the fold, said that he showed promise?

Still pondering his potential future, Eric gathered his things together. The others were almost all gone now. Only a few of the more obsessive types still huddled at their desks. He looked forward to the day when he could leave Sentinel behind and begin the journey toward his true destiny.

Eric departed the office and headed for the local parking lot that most of the employees used. A few of the others walked ahead of him, and one or two strangers traveled in the opposite direction. The day was almost a memory.

His aspirations lightening his mood, he tossed his car keys up in the air as he walked. It was a habit Eric had when he was exceedingly pleased with himself. He whistled a little, too, ignoring the occasional glance of an amused passerby.

As he neared the far side of the building that housed the realty office, he once more tossed the keys.

Seconds passed.

The keys did not drop back into his outstretched hand.

Eric looked straight up. He could see no place above him where the keys might have lodged.

"What the hell?" The agent turned in a circle, his gaze still skyward.

A tree rose to one side, the type that cities all over the country plant in an attempt to beautify a neighborhood, but this one was too far away to have snagged his keys. Eric dismissed the possibility with a shake of his head and continued to search. He even looked down on the sidewalk.

Behind him, he suddenly heard the repeated clink of metal against metal . . . the sound of someone shaking a ring of keys. The novice agent turned around, but saw no one.

He heard the clinking again, but this time Eric realized that not only was it behind him, but it was also *above*.

He looked up.

Perched precariously on a ledge of the building was a large winged form. Eric could not make out the thing's features, but in one hand it dangled something. From the sounds the object was making, it had to be his key ring.

But what was—

"Oh my *God*," he whispered in disbelief. Eric backed away as quickly as he could.

Wings—wide, massive wings—spread. A shadow-masked head looked down at him. Although he could not see the eyes, the agent could feel them burning into his mind.

"Someone's been very, very *naughty*," the thing mocked.

Eric took a panicked glance around, seeking any sort of help. To his dismay, those people nearby walked on as if they had noticed neither his shaken state nor the huge winged figure above.

"Very naughty, indeed."

The creature tossed his keys down to him, then leapt after them.

Wings hid the sky. Long, taloned hands reached for the gaping man.

Eric screamed as death swooped down on him, but no one, not even the elderly businessman walking right past him, noticed.

IX

"**WE'RE HERE.**"

Grigori jerked straight in his seat. Through bleary eyes he peered out of the windshield at a tall apartment building, then at his anxious companion. Belatedly, he realized how he must look to her.

"What happened?"

"You fell asleep shortly after we left the parking lot."

"I fell asleep?" Consternation overwhelmed him. Grigori had not been the least bit tired when they had departed. He thought back. He remembered looking out the window, still searching for any of the bound man's watchers. That was his last memory before now.

No, not his last. There had been just the briefest sense of sudden disorientation . . .

"Frostwing," he whispered, hands trembling.

"Frostwing? What is that?"

Grigori quickly collected himself. "Nothing to concern yourself about at the moment. Something . . . a personal matter."

Teresa eyed him suspiciously, but did not pursue the matter. She wished only the information required to resolve her own predicament. It was not that she was selfish; the young woman was just human. Her own troubles were bizarre enough without adding Grigori's to the teetering stack.

She turned her attention back to her driving. "There's an underground garage. I have a parking space down there. It'll be only a few more minutes before we're in my apartment."

"Good." Staring ahead, Grigori pondered what had happened to him. It was the same sort of deep slumber that the gargoyle inflicted upon him, but this time the macabre golem had not visited him. Grigori could only recall a handful of times when he might have suffered something akin to this. There had been the time in Oslo, shortly after he had departed Sweden after . . . after . . . after *some* tragic event he could no longer recall. Even now the lost tragedy made him twitch with vague regret. That had been three centuries ago, yet fragments of the incident remained clear in his mind.

A pair of power wielders had been hunting him. Two men working in concert. Grigori had never seen them, but he could sense their presence and, from past experience, suspected their intent. They had proven his suspicions when a tall, healthy tree collapsed, nearly falling on him.

Frostwing had been strangely absent during the hunt, so Grigori had been forced to rely on his own abilities. He had found a place to stay just outside of Oslo, with a recently settled family named Lyshol. The harried Nicolau knew that he could safely stay two, perhaps three days, thanks to his ability to shield his presence, but that was all. At least that would be enough time to plot his next move.

There was not much more to it. One night Grigori had sat down after helping the father, Kjetill, with the chores. The next thing he had known, it had been morning. The mother, Heidi, had informed him that he had dozed off and no one had been able to wake him. The children had even made a game of poking him in the stomach until their parents had discovered what they were doing and warned them away.

Assuring them that he was all right, Grigori departed their company that very day. He had recognized the signs of the nightmare-sleep upon waking, but the gargoyle had not appeared. Nonetheless, he had no desire to endanger folk who had been kind to him.

From Oslo he had fled west to rain-soaked Bergen, but pursuit had never materialized. Grigori had never discovered whether the hunters had simply given up or their attention had been turned elsewhere.

He tried to make sense of what had happened, either in Norway or now in Teresa's car, but could not. By the time they had parked and walked to the garage elevator, Grigori abandoned the topic. He could only assume that for the second time he had succeeded in preventing Frostwing from coming to him. How he had been able to do that, Grigori could not say, but he was more than willing to accept such an ability. If he now had the will to turn back the demon, then perhaps there truly *was* hope of ending his curse.

As they entered the elevator, Teresa took only enough time to press the button for her floor before looking at Grigori. "You've been pretty silent since you woke up. Anything that I should know about?"

He could not deflect her interest much longer, especially since Frostwing was somehow linked to the house and her vanishing clients. However, the malicious gargoyle was a difficult topic to discuss. First Grigori had to convince her of the magic all around her and how it related to the odd disappearances. That in itself would take some careful explaining.

She probably already regretted bringing him to her home, but Grigori did not want to fuel those misgivings. He could bring himself to tell her nothing. "I was thinking about the house." It was not a complete lie; after all, the gargoyle did perch over the front gate of the ungodly place. "And I was thinking about the files."

They reached her floor a moment later. The trek to her apartment was short, for which Grigori was grateful. He was growing more and more anxious to study the files concerning Emrich and the others who had preceded the balding man to seeming oblivion.

"It's not much," Teresa tried to joke as she unlocked and opened the door. "And the maid's not been in for a year or two, but I hope you'll like it."

He did. The apartment was small but elegantly decorated. The style blended old and new, with the latter just barely dominating. Most people could not have made such a combination work to such a stunning effect. The modern couches and the widescreen television should have clashed with the old-fashioned coffee table and end stands. The painting hanging on the far wall, a mountain scene that touched something within Grigori, should not have fit so well with the stereo system and computer desk.

Traditional and yet modern. He suspected it was a good description of the young, blonde woman beside him.

Closing the door, Teresa took a deep breath and said, "Why don't you sit down while I go and change? I need to put on something more relaxing."

"Very well." He was seated before she could even move, his eagerness to begin overwhelming all other thought. Only after he had seized the topmost folder did he realize that she still stood nearby.

"There's some soda in the refrigerator. Not much else. If you want some, please feel free to help yourself." Then, without waiting for a response, she hurried off in the direction of a tiny hallway, which undoubtedly led to her bedroom. Each movement she made proclaimed her great anxiety. Grigori hoped that he was no longer the cause of that anxiety, but suspected that such *was* the case. Simply being involved in her nightmare made the dark man suspect in her eyes. Desperation had prompted her to turn to him for help.

At the same time, Grigori knew that she liked him. Perhaps not as much as he might hope, but enough for the time being. Still, the conflicting sides of her mind surely complicated things for her. He hoped that, if nothing else, he could help free her from the situation.

Grigori turned his attention to the topmost file. It was sparse in detail. The client's name was Maria Petruska. An ordinary name by most any standard. Maria's file indicated that she had come from the east coast, near New York. A box next to the words *Job Transfer* had been marked, presumably by Teresa. Maria had come asking about homes.

The file gave no local address, but did list a telephone number. It was a local number that probably belonged to a hotel. Grigori memorized it, then put aside the abbreviated history of Maria Petruska. The woman was a blank to him; Grigori could not create any mental picture. He doubted there was much hope in tracing her. The date on the page was more than a year old.

Grigori picked out another file and found much the same. The information was even older than on the previous sheet. This time, however, the file concerned a couple. He wondered briefly if both of them had steel-blue eyes. If not, what could have happened to the spouse? Would the house take that one, too?

Again the sheet cited a local number, but again it was a number that Grigori was fairly certain would lead him to a hotel. Even had they left something behind, he doubted whether it would still be there now. Nicolau tossed the folder on top of the previous file. He might search out the hotel rooms the people had occupied, but any emanations would be faded almost to nonexistence by now. None of the missing people could have been living at the hotels for very long and too many other guests had likely stayed in the rooms since, further fouling his chances of sensing the right traces. Grigori's earlier hopes began to fade. He hated to think that he might have to dash Teresa's hopes concerning the files, but so far they had revealed little of use.

Then he saw the file with Matthew Emrich's name on it.

Seizing the thin folder, Grigori almost tore it in his haste to open it. He scanned the part of the page that listed the date that Teresa had first conducted business with the missing man.

It was recent. *Very* recent. Matthew Emrich had come to Sentinel only a month and a half ago and had revisited the office three days later. Those were the only dates listed.

As with the other people, the information on Emrich was sketchy at best. Grigori glanced at the address and telephone number listed and noticed that only the number was given. Again it was local. He glanced once more at the other two reports.

Neither of the two cited an address. Like Matthew Emrich, only a local number had been written down.

Emrich's file still interested him, despite the lack of obvious evidence. Less than two months. Perhaps not quite enough time for the traces to have dissipated beyond his abilities to recall them.

"You found something?"

He glanced up to find Teresa looking down at him. She was clad in a simple white blouse and black designer jeans. Comfortable but elegant. Her hair hung loose and somewhat disarrayed; the style gave her a more formidable look.

Grigori had not heard her return. That did not sit well with him. If his attention to his surroundings was that poor, he risked leading them both blindly into the maw of the thing in the house.

"What do you recall about this man?"

She looked at the file he was holding. "Mr. Emrich? That's the one you asked about earlier. He seemed nice. Ordinary, except that he was anxious to know more about the house than I could tell him. He kept looking around, as if . . . as if . . .''

"As if what?"

"As if expecting something to happen." Teresa shuddered. She returned the file to Grigori, then sat down beside him.

Grigori's brow furrowed. "Did you take him to the house?"

"No. I made an excuse."

"Was he never shown the house, then?"

"Of course he was. I asked Eric to take him."

Eric. The young man seems to be everywhere. "Nothing happened that time? Eric noticed nothing?"

"As far as I know, he didn't. Never has, which is why I've always thought that I was just crazy."

The path of questioning surprised Grigori Nicolau. "*Never* has? Has Eric taken your clients to the house before?"

She was obviously uncertain as to what Grigori had in mind. "Not all of them. Some of them didn't make appointments to see the place. A few only came back to ask a question or two." Teresa paused, the frown on her attractive face growing more pronounced. "Eric did offer to take some of them, but they refused."

It seemed the house affected no two people the same way. Grigori wondered if the call was stronger to some. Perhaps those who had not been so attuned to it needed help in locating the dark edifice.

He fell back against the couch, thinking, *There are too many questions and not nearly enough answers!* Grigori rubbed his eyes and thought again about the other realty agent. It could be that *agent* correctly described helpful Eric . . . and yet, it seemed unlikely that the novice realtor served the house. Eric was too willing, too animated, to be the thing's slave. Grigori knew his kind; some bait had been dangled over the boy, some prize.

Grigori realized then that, if he had identified Eric's motivation correctly, the agent did not serve the house, but rather *Peter Frantisek.*

It made perfect sense to him. The bound man needed a human watchdog to observe the proceedings between Teresa and her special clients, someone who might also take over the account if the possibility presented itself. Then Eric could—

But no! That cannot be right! Nicolau closed his eyes. Teresa was neither one of the bound man's servants nor his slave. Grigori could sense that. Yet it could be no accident that she had been burdened with the house and its peculiar chain of would-be purchasers. Her eyes alone precluded such a possibility. She might be bait of sorts, bait placed on the hook by whatever power the gargoyle served.

"You know something. I want to know what it is."

Grigori opened his eyes and studied her. He could not possibly reveal his suspicions. Nicolau finally looked away and searched his thoughts for something else he could tell her. His eyes alighted on the open folder before him.

"Emrich," he replied cryptically.

"What about him?"

"Did you try calling after his last visit?"

Teresa glanced at the sheet. She pointed to a line at the bottom that Grigori had not noticed during his previous inspection. "I called two days after his last visit. Twice. I left messages with the hotel both times."

"It is a hotel, then?" What Grigori had in mind was a long shot, but Matthew Emrich had only been missing for about two months. That, added to the fact that no one had come searching for the man, gave him hope.

"Yes, he was staying at—let me see that." She looked at the telephone number. "He was staying at the Hyatt Chicago. It's on Wacker and Michigan."

Grigori's own hotel was not that far from the towering Hyatt. "Did you have a room number?"

"I thought I did." Teresa peered at the sheet again. "I guess I was wrong. Sorry."

"No matter." Now that Grigori had steered them toward this course of action, his mind began to work on the details. "May I use your telephone?"

A bit puzzled, she nonetheless handed him a portable telephone.

"Thank you." Grigori dialed the number and waited. The phone rang several times before someone at last answered: "Hyatt Chicago. May I direct your call?"

He took a deep breath and prepared himself to use his power, should the need arise. "Yes, I am trying to verify a business expense report. It was from a man who stayed at your hotel approximately two months ago. Is there someone who could look up the record of his stay?"

"One moment and I'll connect you."

Grigori nodded at Teresa. She smiled uncertainly and waited.

The next employee he spoke to, a young woman in the hotel's accounting office, did not seem as agreeable as the operator. After Grigori had repeated his request, she hesitated before answering in an officious voice, "I don't know if I can do that. We generally have to have authorization to release that information."

Grigori concentrated on her as he spoke. "The dates and the total bill, that's all I need."

There was a pause, then, "All right . . . I'll make an exception this once. What was the name and the approximate date?"

He gave her Emrich's name and the date one day before the missing man's visit to Sentinel. The woman repeated the information, then put him on hold.

Teresa signaled to him. "What happens when she finds out he disappeared? Won't she ask why he didn't pay his bill?"

"I'll be ready for that." With Teresa's uncertainty about magic, Grigori was not about to tell her that he could guarantee the hotel employee's cooperation simply by willing it. For now, she would just have to think him persuasive.

"Sir?"

Grigori put the telephone back to his ear. "Yes?"

"I have the information here. Mister Emrich checked in the day you mentioned and checked out three days later. His total bill was—"

The numbers buzzed meaninglessly in Grigori's mind. Matthew Emrich had not only checked into the hotel; he had also checked *out*. The house . . . or perhaps Frostwing . . . had been very thorough. He should have foreseen that possibility.

"Will there be anything else?"

He stirred. Now came the chance for the information he was really after. "Yes. Just for the record, do you have the number of his hotel room? Our bookkeepers seem to want every little bit of data."

"I think so. It should be on the card." A pause. "Here it is. 2213."

"Thank you. I'm sorry to have bothered you. I'll make certain that this does not happen again."

Once he had said goodbye, Grigori hung up. Teresa squirmed with impatience. "What happened? She didn't say anything about him disappearing?"

"Matthew Emrich checked out three days after he checked in. He paid his bill."

She slumped. "Oh. He didn't leave anything behind?"

"What do you mean?"

"I assumed that you wanted to see if he'd left a suitcase or something behind. Something to tell us about him, maybe."

Grigori had not really considered that, assuming that whatever power was involved would leave no obvious clues to Emrich's disappearance. That was why it made sense for them to pay the bill for the missing man's stay.

"If anything had been left behind, I would have welcomed the knowledge it offered. Nothing was, not if he checked out. However, what I did want—and did receive—was his room number."

"Why do you want that? There can't be anything in there to see, not after two months and who knows how many other guests. The cleaning people would have cleared everything away by now."

He clenched his fists and vaguely wished that some Mahler was playing in the background. The silence only made him edgier. "Teresa . . . it is time, I think, that we discuss a topic I know troubles you. If we are to proceed, you *must* believe what I am going to tell you."

Her entire body stiffened. "What do you mean?"

"I am talking about the candle and the centerpiece at the restaurant. I am talking about forces that most people consider legendary—the thing that most people these days refer to simply as *magic*."

Grigori braced for a new torrent of denials. He even considered it likely that he would be thrown out of the apartment. From Teresa's perspective, it would certainly seem the thing to do.

To his surprise, she nodded. "All right. Tell me."

"Tell you? Are you certain?"

Her eyes held a haunted look. "I'm probably crazy, but if I am, then maybe it'll help to believe in magic. That candle. The things I've felt . . . the dreams about that place . . . magic doesn't seem an impossibility after what I've been through."

It was all he could do to keep from hugging her. She was stronger than Grigori had imagined, which made her even more appealing. He had to save her somehow. "You do not know how pleased I am to hear that . . . and you are not insane, dear Teresa. These fantastic powers are still very much a part of the natural fabric of things. A few men and women are aware of those powers, and fewer still understand how to manipulate them with varied success.''

''How can you call whatever is inside the house *natural*?''

Grigori frowned. ''The powers are natural. This can be abused. You may rest assured that there is someone behind the house.''

He mentioned neither Frostwing nor the fact that there were elemental forces with intelligence of their own. The demons and spirits of legend. The world held many, many things that the majority of mankind would never understand.

''What do you hope to do at the hotel?''

He felt it necessary to remind her of the kind of things they might face. If she chose to back down, then so be it.

He held up his hand before her. As he did, a glowing sphere materialized above it. Teresa's eyes widened, but she remained otherwise unmoved. That was a good sign. Still, a ball of light was nothing.

Quenching the ball, he showed her his open hand. ''That is just a minor sample of my poor abilities. There are others with so much more power at their command, my dear Teresa. The power of the house is greater still.'' He closed his hand into a fist. ''But where the power is used, there is often a residue, a trace. Sometimes the past, the memory, can be drawn up. Think of it as images burned into reality. The images cannot be seen by the naked eye, but can, in my case, be summoned by use of the power.''

''You want to see if there are any images in Emrich's hotel room?''

''Exactly.'' He was pleased by her understanding.

''Won't the presences of so many other people in the room since then affect it? Can you summon particular memories?''

Again, Grigori was amazed at her understanding. ''Yes,

the more recent lodgers could present problems. If there is some trace of Emrich's power remaining, that will make uncovering the correct images easier. Of course, the less time that passes before I begin, the better . . ."

"Do you want to go now?"

The centuries-old wanderer would have been quite satisfied with rushing to the hotel, but he did not want to pull Teresa away from the security of her home before she was ready. "We can wait until—"

"We'll go *now*. I want to resolve this." She paused. "I just need to eat something. What about you? I can make us each a sandwich. Will that be good enough?"

So much use of his abilities would certainly leave him drained of energy. "Yes. A sandwich will be fine. Anything you wish to put on it. Also, if you have something with sugar in it?"

"I think that I could probably rustle up a soda and about a hundred pounds of chocolate," she replied in slightly better humor. "I *always* have chocolate."

"Chocolate will do nicely. The soda even more."

"You know that you'll rot your teeth out eating like that."

Grigori smiled wide, revealing perfect white teeth. Sweets did not affect him at all, but he was not about to tell her so. "I will need the energy."

"All right. I'll be right back." She rose and turned in the direction of the kitchen. Grigori could not help admiring her form again. He imagined her in one of the gowns popular among the aristocracy in the courts of King Louis just before the French Revolution. Many of his memories of that era had been long stolen, but he still recalled one of the ladies at court. He could only watch her, since it would have been scandalous for one of his lowly station to approach, much less speak with her. At the time, Nicolau had been in the employ of a duke who was fighting against the odds for better treatment of the peasants. Grigori had influenced the man greatly, but without the use of his powers.

The lady had been Marie Antoinette, legendary for her supposed comment concerning peasants eating cake. She had also earned renown for her beauty, but clad in such a gown, Teresa would have put the grand queen to shame.

Grigori had not felt sympathy for Marie's plight when she was dragged to the guillotine. He only regretted that the duke he had come to admire perished in the same way, a victim of the very folk he sought to aid. Grigori had been away when the mob had taken the aristocrat; by the time he had discovered his master's plight, the man had lost his head.

Grigori could not even remember his name.

He rubbed his eyes, trying to clear his muddled thoughts. Fragmented recollections of long-dead friends had no place in his present situation. *Perhaps I am at last going senile.*

Senile or not, Grigori intended to proceed with his plans. He was uncertain exactly what he sought at the hotel, yet he had the premonition that it was important he go. Such premonitions, the centuries-old wanderer had discovered, were generally worth following . . . even if that meant walking into danger.

THEY HAD HAD NO TROUBLE ENTERING THE HYATT AND taking the elevator up to the proper floor. This was, after all, a hotel with many guests. It was not until they reached the twenty-second floor and stepped out of the elevator that Grigori's concerns forced him to speak. He glanced around in order to make certain nobody was watching, then said, "Teresa, you should wait downstairs or even in your automobile. It would be safer.''

She was adamant in her reply. ''I'm staying with you. It's the only way I'll ever get any answers . . . and the only way I'll feel safe.''

The compliment warmed him, even if the logic seemed a little askew. Danger followed Grigori. Still, he knew that nothing he could say would deter her. *Better to finish this and be gone as soon as possible, then.*

It did not take long to find 2213. Grigori and Teresa paused at the door. They had not asked the front desk whether anyone was staying in the room; Grigori didn't want to chance someone recalling the two visitors too well. Besides, a lodger would present a minor obstacle in comparison to what else might be waiting for them.

''Do we knock?'' Teresa asked. She had trusted her companion in this expedition, but at the moment her tone indicated that that trust was wavering a little.

''Give me a moment.'' Grigori closed his eyes. Seconds later he opened them and smiled. ''There is no one inside.''

''How did you—''

Her voice faded as Grigori seized the knob and opened the door without the use of any key. She eyed him with some suspicion, but said nothing.

They slipped inside, Grigori closing the door behind them. He then reached for the light switch and flicked it on.

The room was neat and attractive. The bed was made, and the carpet had recently been vacuumed. Across the room, the open curtains revealed a high, wide window.

Grigori stalked to the other side and closed the curtains. He turned to see the real estate agent studying the room intently.

''It looks perfectly normal. What do you hope to find?''

''Something that cannot be seen by the naked eye.'' He joined her near the room's center. ''I have never tried this before, but it might be possible to enable you to see whatever I see. Do you want to try that or would you prefer I describe things to you?''

She did not even hesitate. ''I want to see everything.''

''Very well, then. Sit down with me here on the floor.''

''On the floor?''

He guided her down as he explained. ''The sheets on the bed have been changed many times since Emrich stayed here; even the bed itself may be different. Matthew Emrich might not have used the desk or any of the other furnishings, but he had to use the floor.''

Teresa shrugged. ''That makes sense, I guess. Seems funny somehow.''

''You'll have to hold my hand throughout this. I hope you will not mind. We must touch for you to share my eyes.''

''I understand. I don't mind at all.''

He gave her a smile. ''I am gratified to hear that. Please ready yourself. All you have to do is relax and watch me.''

''Seems simple enough.''

''Let us hope so.''

His right hand in her left, Grigori concentrated. Unlike the incident with the knife, the images would not simply materialize when he touched his other hand to the carpet. The memories he sought now were more complex. They were also older and, unlike the other vision, not strengthened by a powerful artifact like the deadly blade.

After several moments, Grigori blinked and wondered if the memories of Matthew Emrich's visit had already faded or had perhaps even been purposely eradicated. He had no idea whether the latter was possible, but it was something to consider. Grigori wished that he had some music, especially Bruckner, to help his concentration.

Teresa, who had been sitting patiently, suddenly stared over his shoulder. Her voice was a whisper. ''*Oh my God!*''

Grigori's first thought was that Frostwing had materialized

in the room. He almost rose, which would have broken the link with the memories, but when Teresa continued to stare past him, he knew that it could not be the gargoyle. His companion would not have been sitting so still, so calmly if the demonic golem had appeared, although perhaps *calm* was not the correct word to describe her reaction.

Fascination, perhaps.

She pointed with her free hand. "It's him!"

Grigori twisted around. His efforts had succeeded far beyond his expectations. Matthew Emrich did indeed stand before them, more solid than the dead villains who had broken into Nicolau's room.

He was also moving. The balding man, clad in the same outfit that he had worn in Nicolau's peculiar dream, folded clothes with the intention of packing them into a plain, brown suitcase that lay on the bed. An anxious look hung in the spectral figure's eyes, as if he were late for some appointment. Grigori tried not to think about where that appointment had taken place.

As best as he could recall, he had never managed such a feat before. Matthew Emrich looked real; only close examination revealed that one could see through him. More amazing still, he moved about normally. They were witnessing a replay of some part of the missing man's stay.

"I . . . I didn't think . . . deep down . . . that you could really do something like this."

"I never *have*," he replied, eyes still on Emrich. "I never have. All I have ever conjured is a still image, sometimes nearly real, but always frozen in time."

"Then how—"

Eyes wide, Grigori swung his gaze to her. "*You*. I did not want to tell you this, Teresa, fearing that it would frighten you away, but I first came to you because I felt your presence from afar, felt as if a part of me was waiting to be reclaimed." He looked down. "I could not resist that call." His hand began to shake. "If you desire to break contact and leave, I will not stop you. I know that what I have said sounds insane."

"No . . . no it doesn't. Not any more."

The ghost of Matthew Emrich continued to perform nearby, still packing. Despite his interest in what might happen next, Grigori could not help but focus his attention on the woman at his side. "What do you mean?"

She raised their clasped hands so that he would look at them. "Ever since you began summoning Emrich's ghost, this sensation has coursed through me, getting stronger and stronger by the moment." Teresa hesitated, embarrassed. "What you just said helped me define it. It's the same sensation you described, Grigori. I . . . I almost feel as if, somehow, you and I . . . you and I are . . . supposed to be together."

He could hardly believe what he was hearing. His heart nearly leapt into his throat. "Teresa, I—"

The wall beyond Teresa suddenly swelled, pulsating like a huge heart. Grigori almost broke contact with his companion, but at the last moment, he realized that, like Emrich, he could see *through* the fantastic sight.

Teresa, seeing his near-panic, twisted her neck to see what was happening. When she saw the wall, the blonde woman let out a gasp and started to rise. Grigori pulled her back down, shaking his head as he did. In a controlled voice, he whispered, "Please sit down, Teresa. We are seeing a memory. It cannot harm us. Look. You can even see the true wall through it."

She returned to the floor, but positioned herself closer to him. The hand Grigori held in his own shook . . . or perhaps it was *his* that did. The sight would have given the strongest men pause.

Then a piece of the wall broke away, forming into the outline of a man. It had no human features. Instead, the same trim and paper covered the figure as it did the wall from which the thing had emerged.

There was something especially disturbing about that, but Nicolau could not say what. He felt as if he had witnessed this scene before, but *where* he could not say. At the moment, the question was moot. What was important now was to make some sense of what had happened.

"Emrich's seen it!" whispered Teresa.

Grigori swiveled so as to see Emrich. The balding man gaped at the macabre figure, which was moving around the bed to intercept him. Emrich shouted silently and backed away. His bizarre assailant seemed unconcerned, which made sense since his victim had no place to go. He could only hide in the corner or flatten himself against the window.

It was the latter that Matthew Emrich chose. Arms flailing in a desperate attempt to ward away the living wall, he leaned against the covered window.

Arms of glass and metal reached out and seized him from behind. One transparent hand slid upward to cover Emrich's mouth.

"Can't we do something?" pleaded Teresa.

Grigori knew how helpless she felt. This was the second time he had been forced to watch as Matthew Emrich was taken . . . and *that* made no sense. Emrich had vanished into the house; Grigori had been there. Yet, here he was now, struggling for his life against creatures as horrifying as the house itself. "We can do nothing. This has already happened, I'm afraid."

The window creature began to turn opaque. At the same time, the thing from the wall took on distinctive features. All traces of the wall faded from it . . . *him*. The wall creature transformed into a brutish man with an extremely canine face. Grigori turned to the other attacker, and saw that he, too, had become human. Like the first, he wore a dark outfit and had a face more resembling a dog's than a man's.

"Who are they?"

"I have no idea," he replied, unable to tear his eyes from the confusing and frightening tableau. "I have no idea."

He had *suspicions*, however. With Grigori Nicolau, there was a distinct difference.

That suspicion was confirmed when the man from the wall reached into his coat and withdrew something. At first what it was remained a question, for the two watchers' views were partially blocked by the first assailant. Then the man raised his hand slightly, revealing just enough of the item for Grigori to see. It was a knife.

It was *the* knife, the one that Grigori had discovered in his own hotel room.

The men's countenances were different than the ones he remembered, but they could only be Peter Frantisek's missing servants. His fears concerning the bound man had been proven true, but he had not been prepared for this. The house did not have Matthew Emrich. Frantisek's men had taken him.

For what reason, though?

The first man raised the knife over the struggling prisoner.

Teresa let out a muffled cry and tore her hand free from Grigori's. The moment she did, the scene faded away.

"No!" Nicolau seized her hand again, but it was too late.

"I'm sorry . . . I just couldn't . . . I just couldn't watch them murder him!"

"I understand," he replied in soothing tones. "They were not going to kill him, I think. I cannot be certain, but I believe instead that they were going to bind him to their will somehow using the knife."

"What do you mean?" Teresa looked at Grigori as if he had just grown fangs. " 'Bind him'?"

"There are ways, various ways, that one can bind another to their will. In some circles, it would be called 'black magic,' although the only blackness is in the soul of the one casting the spell. I am fairly certain something of that sort was about to take place." He squeezed her hand in reassurance. "I have fallen prey to that temptation myself, pushing someone's thoughts to the conclusion I desire, but I would never do something this abominable."

"The telephone. When you called the hotel."

"Yes. When it was urgent, I used it to find a taxi cab."

She did not pull her hand away, but neither did she tighten her grip. "And *me*?"

Grigori colored. "The restaurant was a mistake. I feared for you and wanted to convince you of the truth, but you would not listen. I swear to you that I will not do anything of the sort again, Teresa. If you can forgive me for this one error . . ."

"All right . . . just behave from now on, or *else*."

"I promise." He took a deep breath. "Teresa, I would like to recall the memory, if that is possible. I need your cooperation again. Would you consent to that? I will break the link if things turn for the worse."

"I'll just turn away. I know this is important."

"You have my gratitude." Grigori began the spell immediately. His free hand again touched the carpeting.

Several seconds passed before Teresa quietly noted, "I don't think anything's happening."

Grigori did not respond for another breath or two, attempting to increase his concentration. Despite his best attempts, however, he soon had to concur; not even the slightest shadow of memory remained. Neither Matthew Emrich nor his sinister attackers reformed. The link between Grigori and Teresa was still as strong as ever. It was as if the memory had faded away.

"Let me try something on my own." They released hands, after which Grigori attempted to recall the images without her aid. He did not expect to see the moving ghosts again, but even a still image would be welcome. Gritting his teeth,

Grigori concentrated long and hard on the vision of Emrich as prisoner.

Still nothing happened. There was no trace at all of Emrich. As with the image Grigori had accidentally summoned with the dark blade, the memory had faded away.

"It's my fault!" Teresa folded her arms, looking upset with herself. "I destroyed it when I broke the link, didn't I?"

"It happens. You could not know, and I, who should understand, did not think to warn you. Your reaction was very human, my dear."

"We've failed, haven't we?" she asked, standing.

"Failed?" Grigori was stunned at first, then realized that she did not understand all that they had accomplished. "No, that is not at all true." He rose and took her by the arms. "I have seen more than I ever hoped to see! I expected a vague, motionless image, a shadow reflection of what had happened. Thanks to you, I have learned volumes. Not, of course, everything we need to know, but enough to enable me to understand a few things that have been pressing on my mind."

"What sort of things?" Her voice began loud, then quieted as she remembered that they were not supposed to be here.

"I have learned, for instance, to question my dreams." Her puzzled look made him shake his head. "Tell me, have you ever communicated with a man named Peter Frantisek?"

"No. I think that I'd remember a name like that." Unless she was a superb actress, the blonde woman was telling the truth.

Grigori described the man, omitting the fact that Frantisek was usually found strapped to a tall, ancient chair. When Teresa again replied that she had never met him, he was satisfied.

"Who is he?"

"Someone who knows more about this business than I. Someone who, in his own way, is as great an evil as the house. Those men who attacked your Mr. Emrich, they were his.''

''How do you know him?''

''I was his unwilling guest the other night. His men captured me in the parking lot.'' He described his visit with the bound man, omitting certain details that Teresa was not yet ready for, such as the rats and, of course, Frostwing. ''A strange man whose game I cannot yet fathom, but who deals a deadly and confusing hand.''

''This is crazy, Grigori! When does it all stop?'' Teresa shrilled. ''There's always something else, something even more unbelievable! I'd almost rather be mad than accept all this. I wanted some answers to some odd, frightening puzzles, but this—''

''Teresa, you must keep your voice down. I understand what you're saying. I wish that most of these fantastic tales were not true, but they are.''

She took a step away from Grigori, not so much in fear but as if to study him. ''Just who are you, Grigori? You're not like me and you're not like the others.''

''I can't tell you. Trust me in this matter, please. I want to help you. That is all that matters.''

''Is it? One minute I trust you completely, the next you say or do something that makes me question your sanity.'' She sighed in frustration. ''I really don't know what to think.''

He moved toward her, but then thought better of it. She was again on the edge. ''Teresa, you are better not knowing. You are a strong and reasonable woman, but this knowledge could endanger you in ways you could never believe possible.''

''I want to know.'' The young woman's tone left no doubt as to her determination. ''Tell me.''

Grigori could have easily dismissed her objections by the use of his power, but he could not bring himself to invade her mind. He knew her too well, especially after linking with her. He would rather she hate him forever for not revealing the truth.

"I'm sorry, Teresa. There are some things I cannot tell you. That should not matter, though! What matters is—" He swayed suddenly. "What matters is—"

It became impossible to stand. Grigori sat down on the bed and held his head.

"Are you all right?" Teresa rushed to his side.

"Yes . . . please . . . a moment is all I need." It was a lie, of course. He knew what was happening. He knew that it was Frostwing. *No! he screamed silently. I kept you away once and I can do it again!*

His head pounded. Grigori desired nothing more than to close his eyes, but he did not dare do that. Once, they shut for a moment, but Nicolau forced them open again.

Then, the assault on his mind ceased.

He looked up to see Teresa, her face pale, staring at him as if he had risen from the dead. "Grigori! What happened to you?"

"A moment of weakness. Nothing more." How could he tell her about Frostwing? He knew that before long he would have to, but, until no other choice remained, Grigori intended to make no mention of his ancient tormentor. Teresa's ignorance protected her from the gargoyle.

Even as he struggled with this latest chaos, a peculiar sound made Grigori looked around. It was a *tap-tap* sound, as if someone rapped a finger against a sheet of metal. It ceased the moment he tried to concentrate on it, but Grigori already knew where it came from.

He rose from the bed and started toward the door. After a moment of bewilderment, Teresa asked, "Where are you going?"

Grigori gestured for her to be silent. He did not walk to the door itself, but rather paused before a ventilation grate nearby.

He stood there in silence, well aware of his companion shifting impatiently behind him. Nonetheless, Grigori Nicolau remained quiet, waiting. He could be a patient man if he put his mind to it.

His patience was rewarded. After more than three tense minutes of waiting, Grigori again heard the *tap-tap*. It came from the vent—and it *was* the sound he had thought it might be.

The sound of a small, furred form moving through the hotel ventilation system.

Grigori heard more tapping, but from farther away. He listened closely and, after a few moments, heard the patter of even more tiny feet. The noise grew louder the longer Grigori listened. They were coming closer.

By this time, even Teresa heard them. "Grigori, what is that? It sounds like—"

Grigori spun about and grabbed her by the hand. He almost dragged her to the door. Even as he opened it, he heard a new sound coming from the vent. Although it was muffled, he recognized it as the sound of a rat calling to its own.

"Grigori," Teresa whispered. "Where are we going?"

"Away from here. Out of the hotel. Quickly!"

While Teresa opened the door, he used his abilities to learn what he could of the creatures in the vent. They had to be Frantisek's pets, but what mission had he sent them on? Were they guardians or watchers?

It was difficult to say how many there were and where they all were located, but Grigori's power told him enough. He practically pushed Teresa through the open doorway in his desire to get them both far from this place. Once in the hallway, Grigori shut the door and relocked it.

From one of the hallway air vents came the now familiar *tap-tap*.

He pulled the young woman toward the elevator. Teresa lagged behind, caught by anxious fascination with the things moving through the ventilation system. Grigori was thankful that she did not ask any more questions. Once they were in her automobile, they might have a moment to discuss things. Here, however, a conversation would slow them down.

One of the elevators opened as they neared it. This was not fortunate happenstance; concentrating as best as he could, Grigori had brought the nearest elevator to them. Combined with all else, the effort had been draining. He was thankful that Teresa had suggested food prior to their coming here. He had already depleted a good portion of the energy he had stockpiled, and they had yet to escape the hotel.

The elevator was empty, which he had known. Grigori and Teresa leapt inside. A harried Nicolau pushed the button for the lobby, then warily eyed the hallway until the doors closed.

When they were at last on their way down, Teresa dared to speak. "There was something in the vents, wasn't there, Grigori? I heard—like an animal—no . . . there was more than one—running through the ducts. They seemed to be closing on us. Were they?"

He nodded, only in part aware of her words. It had just occurred to him that climbing into an elevator shaft was nothing to rodents. Now Grigori had to use his overworked powers to guard against the possibility that the creatures would sabotage the lift. Grigori had no idea whether the bound man desired him dead or even injured, but the timing of the rats' appearance convinced Nicolau not to take any chances.

Teresa repeated her question.

"Yes, they were coming toward us."

"What were they? Rats?"

"Rats. Exactly so." He sighed. Here was yet another bit of information he would have to tell her and hope that she would be able to accept. "I mentioned a man . . . Peter Frantisek."

"I remember."

"Peter Frantisek is like me, but far more skillful than I at wielding this gift—or better yet *curse*—that you would call magic. He has a fondness for using rats to observe those in whom he is interested."

"You're joking." Her eyes pleaded with him to say that he was.

"I am not."

She turned her gaze to the door. "There are rats near the office. I've seen them . . ."

Grigori did not tell her that her suspicions were not so far off the mark. He would then have to explain that he had known about the rats around and even in the office for some time without sharing that knowledge.

Fortunately, the elevator stopped and the door began to open. The pair stepped forward, only to realize that this was not the lobby. Grigori glanced at the numbers and saw that they had paused on the sixth floor.

No one was waiting for the elevator, yet the door did not slide closed again. Both Teresa and Grigori stepped back. Teresa pressed the button for the lobby again.

Still the door did not close.

Grigori heard something small land on the top of the elevator.

"Maybe we should take the stairs the rest of the way down. It's only a few floors," Teresa offered.

He shook his head. "I do not think that would be wise. The emergency stairway is more the rats' domain than here." He braced himself. "Give me a moment."

His mind sought out and located the cause of the elevator's sudden halt. The control system had been damaged by a great electrical charge. The timing was too precise for it to have been accidental, but anyone else inspecting it later would not suspect the truth. By that time, Grigori and his companion would be gone . . . one way or the other.

Grigori was thankful that it was the rats, and not Frantisek himself, who had confounded them. Operating through the rats, the bound man's abilities were greatly limited. The rats were still rats. Grigori was determined to prove that he could defeat even such insidious rodents as these.

"Teresa, hold my hand tight."

She obeyed. Grigori was pleased by her quick acceptance of things so far. Too many others, both men and women, could not have coped with the bizarre crisis. He only hoped that he could justify her faith in him.

His assumption was based on how her contact had magnified his own abilities. He had not exactly drawn strength from her; it was just that the two of them together somehow amplified his results. Grigori was not a philosopher, but he did know that when something worked better, one made use of it if possible.

The door slid closed, and the elevator resumed its descent. Grigori might have achieved both feats on his own, but with Teresa holding his hand, Nicolau had been certain their combined power would bring quick and accurate results.

His feeling of triumph was shattered by Teresa's startled cry.

A rat crouched on her shoulder. The rodent and the woman stared into one another's eyes. Steel-blue matched steel-blue.

Grigori reached out with his free hand and snatched up the huge rodent. Realizing its peril, the beast twisted around and tried to bite him. Grigori ignored the attack; he had suffered worse than rat bites in the past.

Throwing the rat to the floor, he kicked it hard into the wall. The beast squealed but was by no means slowed. It whirled on him, staring with those eyes that were so much like his own, yet also inhuman.

The heel of Teresa's shoe came down on the bound man's furred minion, crushing the life from it. The rat did not even have a chance to cry out.

Unfortunately, the victory was short-lived. From above them came more squeaking. Grigori looked up and saw a second rat trying to work its way through the newly cracked elevator ceiling.

Unconcerned about the danger, he reached up and pulled the monstrosity through. The rat squeaked in pain, but its suffering was cut short as it suddenly burst into a miniature inferno. Grigori dropped the burning creature; only his own power saved him from being injured by the flames. By the time the rat struck the elevator floor, it was nothing but ash. The tiny inferno had not been his doing. Evidently Frantisek was unwilling to allow his pets to be captured.

"Stand by the door!" Grigori ordered Teresa.

She followed his lead, but not before taking a pair of gloves from her coat and stuffing them in the crack. A rat protested and received, for its complaints, a mouthful of wool.

The door slid open again, this time revealing the lobby. Grigori and Teresa backed out of the elevator, turning around the moment they were in the open. Grigori glanced over his shoulder, but there was no sign of the persistent rodents. Nonetheless, neither he nor his companion slowed until they reached the hotel entrance. The night staff paid them little mind, for which both were grateful.

"Where do we go now?" Teresa asked under her breath.

"Back to your apartment . . . if you do not mind."

That brought on a smile. "Actually, I was going to ask you if you wouldn't mind staying over tonight . . . on the couch."

Grigori had touched her prior to the night's events, but linking power with her had afforded them greater intimacy than two people who had known each other for years. It was not love—at least, he assumed, not from her perspective— but it might someday become that . . . if there *was* a someday. Still, her request did not have anything to do with the link and the emotions it engendered. Teresa was frightened. Grigori knew that because he was frightened as well.

For himself, he was not certain that he could do anything. For the woman at his side . . . Grigori Nicolau would do everything possible, even if it meant confronting both Frantisek and the gargoyle.

He hoped, however, it would not come to that.

The pair of rats scurried swiftly through the parked cars, seeking the one they knew belonged to the prey. No order had been given, but they were intelligent enough, thanks to the master, to know that they should follow the intruders. There were places in and under an automobile where a clever rat could hide, and other places a little gnawing would serve to make just as useful.

The rats followed two trails. One was the combined scent left by the two humans, an almost certain track back to the vehicle they had taken. The other trail was more subtle, but mingled with the first assured that there would be no mistake. The male of the intruders carried much power, and power had a scent all its own.

One of the large rodents paused. It sniffed the air, peering into the darkness with its distinctive blue eyes. The other saw its companion's actions and followed suit.

Both rats grew agitated. A warning by those within the vast catacomb of vents the humans called a hotel informed them that the intruders had departed the building. Time was of the essence.

They scurried along at a faster clip. The scent of the female human grew especially stronger. The rats knew that they were close to their goal, but did not voice their anticipation. Silence was important. Already a few of them had perished in the performance of their duty. While willing to die for the master, the rats did not like to give up their lives so easily.

Their objective came into sight. Both knew that this was

the proper vehicle; the mixed scents were strong. The humans could not be far behind, but now that danger no longer mattered. A few moments more and the watchers would be able to secrete themselves in the car.

Then a winged form swooped down between the parked vehicles and seized both rats before they sensed the danger. The furred minions of the bound man struggled, but the grip on them tightened . . . and continued to tighten even when it became impossible for the rats to breathe.

The last thing either rat heard was a quiet, taunting chuckle.

XI

SOMETHING WAS TERRIBLY AMISS.

The gargoyle had finally made his next move, removing one of the bound man's pawns. Not only that, but something had happened to his pets again, something that was not quite clear save that it involved Grigori Nicolau.

Peter Frantisek shifted in the chair. Conrad stood at his side, as always. Frantisek stared into the darkness, contemplating the ramifications and wondering just how the cursed piece of mobile marble had managed the attack in the first place. Frostwing—an apt name, as he had informed that hopelessly naive Nicolau—had never spread his massive wings so far afield before.

The bound man would have liked to have thoroughly studied his pawn's remains, but Frostwing had left nothing to examine. As with the two previous, the body had vanished. One minute the pawn had been on his way to his automobile, little suspecting that Frantisek would soon sacrifice him, anyway. The next, he had simply ceased to be. *To think that the idiot had believed himself worthy to become a full acolyte. I lost more when the gargoyle took those two mentally deficient fools in Nicolau's hotel room.*

Peter Frantisek had learned something, however. Ever since the narrow, dark-complexioned man with the eastern European features had come to Chicago, Frostwing had begun to behave strangely. He had broken from his typical ways, becoming more daring, more unpredictable.

It's something to do with you, my dear Grigori Nicolau. You've upset the pattern. Everything is askew.

"I was correct in letting Mr. Nicolau go, I think, Conrad. I was also correct in making the adjustments I did in his mind."

"Yes, Mr. Frantisek. It seems to be working out for the best."

"We cannot be certain of that yet, Conrad." He cocked his head and considered. "Still, this incident with the boy provides some illumination. To all outward appearances, he was walking along when, suddenly, he screamed and disappeared. So, at least, my eyes said. None of the people nearby noticed a thing."

Peter Frantisek wished that the rats hiding by the walls of the office building and among the weeds near the parking lot could see beyond the mortal plane. It would have been educational to know just how thorough the winged nightmare had been at his work. How long in the half-imaginary world of Frostwing had it taken the fool to die? Had it been a slow, methodical killing or had the gargoyle slaughtered him with wanton abandon?

Grigori Nicolau was the real key. The man provided the focus for the winged golem's activities. He was capable of things that Frantisek did not understand. The images he had received from the hotel confused him: both Nicolau and the woman, hand-in-hand, had stared at something with avid interest, but identifying what they saw was beyond the abilities of his watchers.

Then, just after the two had finished their odd vigil, the link between himself and the rats slipped to nearly nothing. Again, although he had no proof, the bound man suspected Frostwing at work. Until some of the rats returned, however, he could verify nothing. He wondered what had happened after the severing. There was some hint that the rats might have overstepped their commands and attacked Nicolau. If only there had been some way to strengthen the link again . . .

The dream about the house should have led him to the most logical conclusion, the bound man thought, still staring into the darkness. *What was Nicolau doing in the room? More than he should have been capable of doing. Perhaps I should bring him in. He might give me more sustenance than the few crumbs I received from Emrich!*

Caught up in his speculations, the bound man did not notice his hands beginning to twitch. Conrad did; one of his most important tasks was to watch his master and wait for such signs.

"Mr. Frantisek . . ."

"Hmmm?" Peter Frantisek saw the expression on his man-servant's ugly features and immediately glanced down at his hands. His gaze fixed on the twitching. "I think that you should prepare yourself, Conrad."

"Yes, sir." Calmly, the brutish figure reached into his jacket and removed the long, strange needle gun he had used on Grigori Nicolau. With his other hand he retrieved a trio of cartridges from one jacket pocket. "Weak or strong, Mr. Frantisek?"

His master was paying him scant attention. Something else had come to mind. *The house . . . if I just went to the house, just walked in and looked around, everything would finally make sense. All I have to do is go to the house. No one would stop me, and—*

And I would never come out again! The bound man shook his head, causing the notion to recede but not entirely dissipate. He had no true desire to step inside the house, not at least until he became its master instead of its slave. For that to happen, Frantisek needed control of the gargoyle. With the gargoyle under his command, the house would soon follow. He was certain of that.

"Strong," he finally responded, gritting his teeth. The call came to him in waves, each one building in intensity. "The strongest dose you have, Conrad."

All the answers lie in the house . . . the house is where it can all be found . . .

"The strongest?" For the first time, the manservant looked uneasy.

"Do as I say."

In some ways, it all seemed so reasonable. If he went to the house and looked inside for a few minutes, he would find what he had been seeking. Perhaps he was being overcautious. Perhaps the chair and the straps were not necessary.

"*No, damn you!*" the bound man snarled. "I'll stay right here!"

Conrad was quiet, his attention shifting back and forth between the pistol and his master. He inserted one cartridge in the weapon and slipped the two extras back into the pocket. "I'm ready, Mr. Frantisek. I apologize for the delay."

The second attack had already receded, but Peter Frantisek knew that the next was on its way, ten times as powerful as the last. The one after, if he permitted it to come, would be ten times stronger than its predecessor.

Already his arms and legs strained at the bindings. He had hoped that adding Emrich's contribution to what he had already gathered would give him the strength he needed, but the summonses were too strong. He could not yet defeat the attacks without the chair and the potion, *especially* the potion. Perhaps he would have to take Nicolau sooner than he had anticipated.

"Shall I shoot you now, Mr. Frantisek?"

He only nodded, for he was steeling himself for the newest assault. Once more the subtle, siren voice of the house called to him.

The house probably holds the key to the gargoyle . . . a quick search would provide the advantage I need to put the gargoyle under control . . . The answer lies in the house . . .

There was a slight hissing sound, like that of a snake readying to strike. A sharp pain jolted the bound man momentarily from the call.

Oblivion rescued him.

To Grigori's surprise and relief, Teresa asked very few questions during the drive back. Her growing acceptance of Grigori's world pleased him, but he hoped that she was not trying too hard to adjust to a realm where the powers of legend were so very real.

She did ask about Peter Frantisek.

"He kidnapped you, is what you're saying," she retorted when Grigori described again how he had met the mysterious figure. Grigori did not mention the chair; it was enough to know the man himself. "But why did he let you go?"

"Because I was aware of the house's secret. None of the others knew what was happening. They only heard the call. I was different."

"And me?"

Grigori struggled hard to concoct an answer. At last, he said, "He had no interest in you. What he wants is the house."

"He can have the damned thing."

Grigori shook his head. "He isn't ready to take it yet. I do not know how he intends to prepare, but I gather that he plans to build up his power."

To say more would risk being forced to reveal some of the more unsavory methods by which those who wielded power could increase their abilities. Fortunately, Teresa asked no more about that. In fact, from that point on, she said little at all.

True to Teresa's word, Grigori slept on the couch. He had expected nothing else and, to his own surprise, realized he would have rejected an advance if it had been offered to him. He could not take advantage of her. Perhaps such thinking was outmoded these days, but Grigori did not care.

Teresa walked back into the living room just as he was attempting to arrange the decorative pillows on the couch into something comfortable to sleep on. In one hand she held a large sleeping pillow, in the other a neatly folded blanket.

"I thought you might need these. Those other pillows are worthless to sleep on. I know; I've tried to more than once."

"Thank you."

"There's food in the refrigerator and in the cabinets above the sink. Eat whenever you like. You can have the bathroom when I'm done with it. I put a brown towel and washcloth on one of the hangers. You can use those."

He put the pillow and blanket on the couch. "Thank you, but I think that I shall wait until morning, if that is all right."

"Sure." She gave him a slight smile. "Good night."

As she turned away, Grigori thought of something. "Teresa, do you plan to return to the office tomorrow?"

The agent looked at him, her brow furrowed. "I hadn't decided. I don't want to . . . but I don't really know what to do. After tonight, it really wouldn't make sense, would it?"

What would happen if she did return to Sentinel? Grigori was too tired to think.

"Make an excuse for tomorrow," he finally replied. "Tell them that you should be able to return the next day. Tomorrow, we will be able to think more clearly."

"That sounds good." Her smile returned, this time stronger. "I think I'll be able to sleep a little better. Thanks."

He watched her depart, then sat down on the couch. Now that she was gone, there was one more thing for Grigori to do before he dared risk sleep. Teresa, for all she had come to accept so far, still considered things in mortal terms. To her, the danger of the rats was past; she had not considered that there might be more of their ilk in her building. In fact, there might be other things besides the rats . . .

He had laid the groundwork for the wards while she had been in her bedroom. Now that he knew she had gone to bed, the wary Nicolau could complete his task.

Closing his eyes, he linked himself to the five points he had chosen throughout the apartment. Bound by his power, the points would form a pentagon encompassing most of Teresa's home. What little lay outside could be protected by the intensity of his casting. There would be no rats in her apartment this night. Frantisek's human servants would also find their way barred. He could not keep everything out, but he would be warned if something intruded.

Shifting the pillow and blanket, Grigori laid down. His mind ever at work, he thought about the coming day. Teresa would want answers, but he was at a loss as to what to tell her. He had lived his life knowing no escape; it was now extremely difficult for him to imagine such a possibility for another. Yet, if he could save her, then Grigori could focus on his own trials later.

He fell asleep with no answer in sight.

It was still dark when a tingle in his mind awoke Grigori. His eyes took some time adjusting to the darkness, but by then he had already made a thorough mental probe of the apartment. Curiously, there was no sign of any intruder, not even a trace of power.

Not entirely satisfied, Grigori rose from the couch. He raised one hand, palm upward, to chest level, then concentrated.

A small yellow flame burst into life only an inch or two from his palm. It lit the living room just enough to enable him to see everything, but not enough to disturb Teresa in the bedroom. With the flame in hand, Grigori searched the room, inspecting with both his eyes and his power.

The living room seemed clear of threat. Nicolau entered the kitchen, a small room off to the side. Grigori, who had lived in London and Europe for so long, marveled at the size of the apartment, though he found its costs astonishing. He could still recall when a house large enough to hold a family of ten cost a man only a few days hard labor to build.

Next came the bathroom. There the mirror caught his eye, and he could not help staring at the face he had known for so long.

It was the face he had always possessed, as far as he knew, yet it was also different. Everything he had experienced, whether recalled or not, was reflected in his countenance . . . and especially in the eyes. For all the similarities between his eyes and those of Teresa, Frantisek, or any of the others he had met throughout the centuries, none of them had eyes that hinted at so much brutal experience, so many years of travel and hardship. Their eyes—save perhaps Frantisek's— were young. There was a spark in them that Grigori felt was merely a dying ember in his own.

Grigori Nicolau blinked, then turned away from the revealing mirror. He despised mirrors and only used them out of necessity. Besides, there were more important things at hand than self-pity. He had all the time in the world for that.

Only Teresa's bedroom remained. Grigori was leery of

entering, in part for fear that she might wake and think ill of his motives, but it was the only place he had yet to physically search. Surely she would understand.

With but a touch of his finger, the knob of her door turned. The door slowly swung open without a squeak. The need for quiet was twofold; he hoped to complete his search without waking her, and if there was anything amiss in her bedroom, silence might give him a slight advantage.

When the door had opened enough to admit him, he made it stop. Grigori raised the flame to eye level, then released it from his hand. The flame drifted back behind him, then hovered in the air. From that angle, some light would still shine in, but not enough to wake Teresa. Grigori had not yet sensed anything out of the ordinary in the bedroom, but he could not rest until he had searched it thoroughly.

Her bedroom contrasted so radically with the rest of her apartment that it made him feel all the more guilty that he had intruded. The room gave him the impression of the private sanctum of a much younger woman, almost a child. There were stuffed animals on one chest and paintings of animals on the wall. The furniture in general, while stylish, fit into the mold of a young lady's room, not that of a fairly successful real estate agent.

Teresa lay asleep on the right edge of her bed, thick, soft blankets wrapped around her. Her face was buried in the pillow. From her breathing, Grigori knew that she was deep into slumber. His eyes lingered on her for longer than necessary, then he managed to turn his attention to the wide, curtained window.

A flick of his finger made the curtains part long enough to reveal that nothing hid either behind them or outside the window. His power verified this. He did the same with the closet, then the drawers of a chest on the far wall. It quickly became clear that the room was free of danger.

Feeling ashamed for having remained as long as he had,
Nicolau retreated from the room and quietly closed the door.
He then reached up and took renewed control over the flame.

"Naughty, naughty, Grigori! Sneaking into a helpless
maiden's chambers."

The flame fluttered out of his grasp as he spun around to
face the living room.

From the dimly lit room, Frostwing stared back at him.

The gargoyle perched atop the back of the couch, his
wings outspread. His weight did not mar the piece of furniture in the least, but then, this was the dream world. Only
when the gargoyle chose to do so did he leave any mark
on reality.

"One would think that you do not desire my company,
dear Grigori. One would think that you have been delving
into knowledge not intended for your poor little mind and
making bad use of it."

"I do not know what you mean." Although he was loathe
to approach the sinister golem, Nicolau nevertheless did.
The farther he was from Teresa's bedroom, the less likely
Frostwing was to include her in the confrontation.

"Indeed." The single word was drenched in sarcasm.
Then, as if forgetting their conversation, the winged terror
reached down into the shadows behind him and retrieved a
form roughly the size of a small cat. Frostwing dangled the
limp shape before him. "I cannot say I care for some of the
company you've kept of late."

It was a large rat. Grigori did not have to ask if it was one
of Frantisek's; that much was obvious.

Frostwing chuckled. "Generally I prefer my meat a little
more lively, but it was necessary to put this one out of its
misery."

The stone gargoyle opened wide his maw and tossed the
corpse in. Despite having no gullet, the monster swallowed

his meal whole. The moment the rodent vanished, Frostwing produced another.

Again, he glanced at Grigori Nicolau. "He had a friend. The two of them thought to join you for a ride, but I was certain that you and the lady would prefer to be alone. So very kind of me, and yet I still hear no thanks from you. Tsk."

The second rat followed the first to oblivion. Frostwing pretended to wipe his toothy maw. When he was done, he contemplated the figure before him.

Grigori tried to think of some way out of this confrontation. He had grown lax; the success of his earlier battle to turn the monster away had made him overconfident.

"You're so far away, my friend. Why don't you come closer, hmmm?"

Nicolau's left foot rose and stepped forward. His right followed. He struggled, but, as ever, his efforts were wasted. Grigori could only watch as his body moved him closer and closer to the shadow-enshrouded monstrosity perched on the couch.

Frostwing did not allow him to stop until he was within arm's reach. Still unable to move of his own accord, Grigori could do nothing to prevent the gargoyle from reaching up and taking hold of his chin.

"Dear, dear Grigori. You should be careful. I worry so much about you, you know. I think about you all the time, in fact. I do not think that you appreciate that sometimes."

Grigori said nothing.

Frostwing sighed. "You have no idea how often I have guided you back to your proper path after you strayed. You have no idea how *long* I have worked to bring you to this point. All I ask in return is a little cooperation on your part, and you cannot even give me that."

The gargoyle's taloned hand snared Grigori by the collar.

The demon dragged him forward until their faces were no more than an inch apart. Not for the first time the fearful man noted that he could not make out his tormentor's eyes. They were still only shadows.

"Let me tell you a story . . ."

The words unnerved Grigori almost as much as the gargoyle's presence. When Frostwing told a story, it was certain to be one integral to the human's existence . . . and never for the good. Every story that the horrific golem had told to him was etched into Grigori's mind. Frostwing had made certain that he would never forget them.

"Once there was a man. This man nursed great ambitions, ambitions far above his station, yet he could not see that. In his mind, he was the *power*." The gargoyle snorted in disdain. "Not that he understood anything about the power. Oh, he could perform a few good tricks and could raise a few pets, but he was greatly mistaken to believe himself more than a fortunate fool."

Frantisek, Nicolau thought. *He talks of Frantisek.*

"I see you know the story," the winged monstrosity remarked. "Very good, dear Grigori, but I do not think you know the ending yet. I think that you have confused the tale with another . . . in which there is a grain of hope. Understand me when I say that there is no hope in this story. In the final scene, the fool perishes and with him perish the fools that followed him . . . oh, and also a man who is an even bigger fool, for he knew more truth than all the others, yet still did not see the danger until it swallowed him along with the rest."

Frostwing abruptly released Grigori, who nearly fell before he realized that the gargoyle no longer held him in thrall. He stumbled back a few steps before righting himself, moving at the same time out of arm's reach.

"The moral of the story is quite clear, I think." The gargoyle flexed his wings, then raised a taloned hand in his victim's direction. "But just in case it is not—" At first Grigori thought that the demonic golem was gesturing for his human toy to come back to him. Then he realized that Frostwing was not reaching toward him, but rather beyond.

"No!" The word escaped even as Nicolau twisted around to see what the gargoyle pointed at.

Teresa.

She stood just beyond her bedroom door, arms slack at her side, her expression one of sleepy contentment. Light surrounded her, light that appeared to come from within. A thin, fluttering nightgown of lace barely concealed the details of her body. As Grigori watched in growing dread, she walked toward Frostwing like a child joining her beloved father. Grigori reached out to stop her, but as in his nightmare about the house and Matthew Emrich, his hand passed through her.

She walked on until she stood next to the perched monster, then turned so that she faced Grigori. Frostwing put a companionable arm around her shoulder, but the hand pretended greater intimacy by playing with the fabric near her breast. The other hand stroked her cheek.

"You have always had an eye for beauty. I must concede that, dear Grigori . . . And it is all in the *eyes*, isn't it?" The gargoyle's talons roamed near Teresa's eyes. "Such a pretty color, too. Reminds me of someone—"

"Frostwing, please. She has no part in this."

His nemesis tilted his head. "Oh but she *does*, Grigori, she does. We all have parts to play! We are all of us puppets to a master with strings reaching through time! Have you so soon forgotten?" Frostwing chuckled, but there was an edge to his voice, an edge that, to Grigori Nicolau, possibly hinted of bitterness. "But of course you have."

The talons traced lazily around Teresa's eye for a moment, then rose to toy with Teresa's hair. The eternal smile etched into Frostwing's vague face widened.

The gargoyle's talons slashed down Teresa's cheek.

Blood dripped over the creature's hand. A trio of scars glistened wetly in the dim light of Grigori's magical flame. They were not deep, but the attack sent Nicolau into a frenzy. Somehow he broke free of the spell that held him. Words spouted from his mouth, words of the same nonsensical tongue he had used earlier. Grigori did not understand the words he spoke, but he knew that they were ones he needed now.

Frostwing cringed away from the motionless Teresa. It was not fear, but rather pain that forced him back. Grigori could sense that. Even still, the demonic golem remained confident. He receded into the dark shadows of night, chuckling despite the blow struck against him.

"Very good, my dear Grigori. Very good, indeed! You are coming along just fine, but always remember that I am the one who guides you and no other! Ally yourself with fools and you suffer the fate of fools!"

Again the outraged man spoke the words, but the gargoyle shook his head and spread his wings as if to depart. As was his wont, however, Frostwing insisted that the last words be his. "I do what I do because you ask it of me, dear Grigori, and for no other reason! Hate me, but learn also to hate yourself. It is the only chance you have, if you have one at all . . ."

No memory was stolen, no piece of soul taken. The gargoyle was there and then he was not.

A scream shattered the brief silence.

Grigori woke and found himself once more on the couch. He blinked, trying to orient himself.

A second scream stirred the still-groggy man to life. The scream had come from Teresa's bedroom.

He vaulted over the back of the couch and rushed across the room even as she screamed again. Grigori burst through

the door of the bedroom. As he moved, he summoned up a
blazing light to force away the darkness.

Teresa sat up in her bed.

Blood covered her face, her hands, her gown, and the
pillow. Not much, but too much. On her cheek, three scars
ran a short, ragged course.

Teresa stared wild-eyed at him. "*A gargoyle* . . . it was
you and a gargoyle called *Frostwing* . . ."

XII

THUS IT WAS THAT GRIGORI NICOLAU TOLD TERESA DVORAK
everything.

He spoke of the centuries of wandering, of recreating a
life building fortunes, making investments based on experience, and sometimes simply working as a hired hand. Then
he told her about the gargoyle and the power.

They were not disturbed by fearful or angry neighbors.
The shield that Grigori Nicolau had forged blocked any unusual sounds from being heard by anyone outside the apartment. There had been no screams, no shouts . . . and no
malevolent laughter.

"He steals your memory?" Teresa asked, surprisingly
calm after her initial fear. She was like that, he had come to
realize. Once the first shock passed, Teresa somehow always
pulled herself together.

"Just portions . . . but he has taken so many that my
memory is like a huge puzzle with half the pieces gone."

Grigori sat on the edge of the couch. With his power he had healed the scars, and a long, very long shower had washed away most of her panic. When she had returned to him, still a little damp but freshly clad, she managed a smile of gratitude. Scars remained on the inside, but there was nothing he could do about that. "Time has buried much of the other memories so deep that he might as well have stolen those, too."

"And you don't recall when he first came to you?"

"That was one of the first memories I believe he stole from me. You must understand, Teresa, that Frostwing delights in leaving me confused and wondering." It suddenly occurred to him that something had changed with this visit. "This was the first time he did not take anything from me . . . although I could be wrong, I suppose." He knew that he was not. The gargoyle had taken nothing. All his memories seemed to be intact. There was no doubt this time.

"God!" she whispered, not for the first time. Teresa sat tucked into a corner of the couch, her arms and legs folded in tightly. "Centuries of not knowing why he was doing it, never knowing when he would take what you had built, never knowing how it would end . . . I'd have gone insane."

Grigori's mouth was a straight gash. "He will not let me go insane. That is one of the grandest parts of his game; I will always be cognizant of what is happening to me."

He recalled unbidden a small town near Berlin—Zechlin?—but did not know why. No other memory of the place occurred to him. Grigori did not even know in what century he had visited the place. Many of his memories were like that, but Zechlin meant more for some reason. Whenever the dark man thought of insanity, Zechlin came to mind. "He can prevent me from ever escaping him using that path. Madness for me remains a hopeless wish."

"And you have no idea how it all began . . ."

Her words reminded him of the end of this last visitation.

"That is not quite true any longer. I must know something about the power behind the house . . . and Frostwing. I think that his master, the force that guides all this, must have once been known to me."

She straightened. "Are you trying to tell me that there might be a centuries-old sorcerer in the house? It was only built around the turn of the century."

"Appearances can be deceiving . . . but, yes, the house is probably only as old as you say. The gargoyle's master might have moved everything here from elsewhere." A sigh. "I learned much from this night's encounter with Frostwing, but I gained so many more questions, too."

The questions filled his head, making it hard for him to think. What were the words he had spoken that had driven away his nemesis? Why did they feel so natural on his lips? How were he and those others with eyes like his own linked to the thing in the house? What did steel-blue eyes mark him and Teresa as?

"Could you make me forget all of this?" Teresa abruptly asked.

He froze for a heartbeat. "I could make you forget anything, if that is your desire."

The blonde woman thought about it, her hand caressing the place where the scars had been. Then at last she shook her head. "No. I couldn't run away like that. Besides, I wouldn't even know if it would help me. He might still come after me . . . and then there's the house."

Yes, the house would call to her sooner or later. Both she and Grigori knew that. And Frostwing had marked her. The physical signs might be gone, but the taint of the gargoyle would forever remain.

Grigori happened to glance at the clock as he considered this, and the hour made his eyes widen. The night was more than half over. He could survive with no sleep for a day or two, but Teresa did not have his abilities. After such a horrifying introduction to the evil golem, she needed rest more than ever.

"You should go to bed, Teresa. You will need your strength."

"No." Her entire body shook. "I can't think of going back to sleep . . . not yet. I feel like he still might be there."

The fear was a reasonable one, but Grigori did not want her collapsing from exhaustion at some point when it might threaten her life. Teresa *had* to sleep.

He reached over and put an arm around her. She did not resist, sliding closer to him and resting her head against his shoulder. "I understand how you feel. I've felt the same so many times. The best thing to do then is simply to relax. He will not return, I promise you. At the very least, even if you cannot sleep, you can rest . . . allow your muscles to loosen."

"I won't sleep," she mumbled, looking down.

"If you do not, then so be it," Grigori responded, staring resolutely in her direction. "If you do—"

Teresa's head sank. Grigori waited for a short time, then shifted so that he could see her face. As he had expected, the woman's eyes were closed. Her soft, steady breathing verified that she was sleeping.

"I know I am betraying you now," he whispered, kissing the top of her head. "But sleep is the only way the memory of the fiend will lessen. When you wake up in the morning, the nightmare will be less vivid. I will not steal the memory. I only make you sleep."

Grigori covered Teresa with the blanket and made himself comfortable in a nearby chair. One night of sleeplessness was nothing to him if it meant that she could rest easier.

"What happened to me?"

The sun shone through the cracks between the curtains. Grigori, still seated in the chair, casually replied, "You fell asleep. I moved aside so that you could better rest."

Teresa rose to a sitting position. "I fell asleep?" She yawned despite her consternation. "That was silly to say; of course I did. I just can't believe it."

"You were exhausted. It's not so surprising."

"I guess." She rose and stretched. Grigori politely turned his gaze elsewhere, not wishing to be thought of as a voyeur. "Oh my God!"

His gaze snapped back to her. The woman stared at the wall clock. It was nearly ten.

"Why'd you let me sleep so long?"

"You needed it. Especially after last night, you needed it."

She paused to consider that, finally nodding. "I suppose, but we've wasted so much time. You said we would talk things over in the morning."

Grigori steepled his hands in his lap. "Time has not been wasted. I've thought over many things."

"You were awake all night."

"It does not bother me to do so now and then. Please do not be concerned about it, Teresa."

The conversation stalled when her stomach rumbled. Looking slightly embarrassed, Teresa put a hand on her stomach. "I think I need to eat something. Maybe take another shower after that; I still feel a little funny. How about you, Grigori?"

He finally rose from the chair. "Food would be fine."

Teresa had coffee and toast; Grigori chose fruit and some sugared products. He ate heartily, drinking a Coke to wash everything down.

Teresa laughed lightly at the sight. "There are people who would kill to be able to eat like you and look so good! God! Coke in the morning?"

"I prefer it over coffee most of the time."

"There are people at work like you, but—" She broke off, eyes widening. "Work! What should I do about that?"

That had been the least of his concerns during the night.

After the gargoyle's intrusion, only one sensible course of action remained. "Call them and tell them that you are not feeling well."

The agent rose from the table, wiping her hands on a piece of paper towel. "I'd better call now."

He watched her go to the kitchen telephone. Once more she had overcome her fears enough to function. In so many ways, Teresa Dvorak reminded Grigori of himself, which was probably not that strange. One thing he had considered during the night was that he, Teresa, and all of the others must somehow be related to one another. The links went far back, centuries, but they were there. That did not smother his interest in her. After all, the blood link must be so distant that they could hardly be called cousins or, at worse case, grandsire and granddaughter. He did not know if he had fathered any children, but generations lay between him and the attractive young woman standing nearby.

"Hi, Laurell?" Teresa took a deep breath before continuing. "Yeah, I know I'm late. I'm sorry. I'm not feeling right today. I don't think I can come in at all." A pause. "He won't mind. I have plenty of sick days. Listen, I had some clients scheduled for today: Can you get Eric to take care of them?"

Grigori grew suddenly alert. He had told her of his suspicions concerning the novice realtor and was surprised that she would bring him into the situation again. He tried to signal to her, but Teresa was listening with avid interest to something the other woman said.

"He's not in either? Is he sick?" Another pause. "He hasn't called in? Maybe he's still sleeping." She gave Grigori a look that asked if he had heard everything.

He nodded. She had wanted to check on her co-worker for him. He appreciated her effort, but knew that it would have been better if she had left Eric out of the conversation. Still, the news that the boy had not come to work this day was indeed interesting.

"Thanks, Laurell. I know it's too late to cancel those appointments. Tell Gary I appreciate his taking them. I think that's—what?"

The tone of her voice changed again, becoming strained. Her face paled, and her hand shook a little. She fumbled for a notepad and pen nearby. "Let me jot this down. If I feel any better by this afternoon, I want to try to give this one a call." Teresa waited while the other woman spoke again. "I know, but I'd like to do something to get rid of that place. I don't want to pass this up, sick or not."

Teresa leaned over and wrote on the pad. Every other moment, she would mutter "okay" or something similar, as she scribbled down the information.

Dropping the pen next to the paper, Teresa straightened. "Thanks, Laurell. I'll get on it soon, so tell Gary not to bother with it. I've got all the information right here." Another pause. "Right. See you tomorrow, I hope. 'Bye."

Teresa tore the piece of paper off the pad and turned to Grigori. Her face was pale and her hands clenched into tight fists.

"You won't believe this!" She held out the crumpled paper and shook it. "There was a call this morning."

He stiffened. "A call? Tell me."

"His name is William Abernathy. Laurell, a friend of mine who works in the office, took the call and the information. He said that he was looking for a certain type of house and thought that he might find it in Chicago. He didn't even wait for her to transfer him to somebody else. He just started to describe the sort of place that he was looking for—"

Grigori finished for her. "And what he described could only be the house."

"Exactly. Laurell mentioned that she thought we had such

a listing but that the agent wasn't in. Abernathy left her his address and telephone number." Teresa passed the paper to Grigori. "I took it down. I thought you might want it."

"You did the right thing," he assured her. Grigori Nicolau read the name and address. Another hotel. Not as elegant as the Hyatt, but still a reputable place. He tried to sense something from the information, but drew a blank. His abilities, while enhanced of late, were still quite limited. Frantisek might have been able to learn something by probing where Grigori could not.

"We should call him, shouldn't we?"

"Yes, and now, if you are up to it. If you are not, then perhaps I should call."

"No, he's expecting me to call. I'll do it." She crossed her arms, nearly hugging herself. "Do you think he's one of them?"

One of us, you mean, Grigori wanted to say, but did not. He looked at the paper again. "Perhaps. I cannot tell from this. It is possible that this Mr. Abernathy simply wishes to purchase a home that happens to match the one we are interested in."

"That's some coincidence. I don't believe that."

"Coincidence happens. However, I am inclined to agree with you." He rose, handing the paper back to her. "It appears that the day has chosen our path for us, saving us at least that chore."

"Hooray," she returned, not even a spark of enthusiasm in her voice. Once more she scanned the information. "What should I say to him?"

"The same things that you would say to any client, only make an appointment for today. If he is like the others, he should agree to that."

"All right. Just give me a moment to prepare myself." The agent sat down by the telephone. She stared at the note for some time, then finally picked up the receiver. As she pushed the number, her demeanor changed. The anxious woman vanished. In her place was the Teresa Dvorak of Sentinel Realty, the professional.

Teresa pushed another button on the telephone and the room resounded with ringing. Grigori was not used to speaker phones, even after the past few decades, but he was pleased that Teresa had thought to use hers.

Someone answered just as she was about to hang up. An operator for the hotel. Teresa gave the woman William Abernathy's name and room number. There was a short silence as she was connected with the room.

"Hello?" The deep voice sounded vaguely English to Grigori. He was not familiar with the accent, but he guessed that, if the man was not from the British Isles, he might be from New England.

"Hello, this is Teresa Dvorak calling for Sentinel. Is this William Abernathy?"

"Yes, I'm William Abernathy." The man tried to remain nonchalant, but he sounded uncertain.

"Mr. Abernathy, you called earlier today, but I was unavailable at the time. I understand that you were curious about some houses." Teresa looked at Grigori for reassurance. He nodded encouragingly. "Particular styles, I believe."

"Yes, that's correct, Ms. Dvorak." The tension had increased. Abernathy was having trouble remaining calm. "I was told that you might have exactly what I was looking for—an older place, something like a Victorian, but not precisely . . ."

Teresa shuddered, but kept her distaste from interfering with the conversation. "I may have something like that. We should meet so that I can talk things over with you. Would that be agreeable?"

Abernathy hesitated for a moment, then said, "That'd be

fine. I'd like to do it soon. I—I'd like to do it today if possible."

Grigori and Teresa exchanged glances. Grigori nodded, then pointed at his watch. He raised two fingers.

His message was clear. Returning to the conversation, Teresa replied, "That would be just fine with me, Mr. Abernathy. Could I meet you at your hotel . . . say at two? I'm not in the office today, but I have some information at hand. At the very least, I think that I should be able to get a clearer picture of what you want by spending some time with you in person."

"Two's good." Abernathy hesitated again. "The young lady said that there was one place that she thought sounded just like what I want—"

"I'll look into that before I meet with you. Would you like me to come to your room—" She stopped in mid-sentence as Grigori furiously signaled her. He pointed down and mouthed the word *lobby*. After a moment, Teresa acknowledged the suggestion. "Or perhaps the lobby would be better."

The man considered her suggestions. "Lobby's fine, Ms. Dvorak. That would be better, in fact."

Better? Grigori wondered. He would have expected Abernathy to desire privacy. Of course, meeting in the lobby would provide privacy of sorts if the man wanted to keep the contents of his room a secret. Possibly it was just Abernathy's way, but now Nicolau had a desire to see just what the other's hotel room looked like.

"Very well. I'll see you at two, then. Thank you."

William Abernathy bid her goodbye. Only after she had turned off the speaker did Teresa blurt, "I forgot to ask him what he looked like! What was I thinking?"

"Under the circumstances, it was an understandable oversight." Grigori leaned back. "Still, if we are correct, and the conversation leads me to believe that we are, then it will be simple for you to identify Mr. William Abernathy."

"How?"

"Look at his eyes."

It had not been a pleasant night for Peter Frantisek. The call had been at its strongest yet, and the strain on him had been tremendous.

He found himself blaming Grigori Nicolau. Ever since the man had arrived in Chicago, things had accelerated. All of his carefully crafted plans were coming apart, and his predictions no longer ran true. He had lost servants, both rodent and human, and the gargoyle was now flying far afield.

Yes, somehow it was Nicolau's fault, but the bound man intended to change that. The stress of last night had convinced him that he needed to use the dark man, just as he had used the rest. Whatever secrets, whatever knowledge Grigori Nicolau had withheld from him would be his when the transference took place. Peter Frantisek was fairly certain that with this one he would at last gain the edge he sought in his battle for control of the house.

"Conrad." The manservant appeared at his side, moving silently as always. Frantisek looked up at him. "Conrad, I want Mr. Nicolau brought to me. I've learned more than a few things thanks to him, but necessity demands that we now make the *fullest* use of him, so to speak. Do you agree?"

The piggish features screwed up into an expression of satisfaction. "Yes, Mr. Frantisek. I thought about doing just that last night while you were under, but you had given orders, so I could only hope."

"Loyal Conrad." Of all of his servants, only Conrad deserved the bound man's instruction. So long as future circumstances did not demand the man's sacrifice, Frantisek would see to it that Conrad was well-rewarded when he seized the power of the house. "As usual, you precede me in my desires."

"I do what I can."

He had chosen well when he had rescued the young Conrad from the streets. Conrad had been a terror among the youth gangs, but a few more years would have seen him dead. Sensing the force within him, Peter Frantisek, not then so bound, had introduced the younger man to the power and the use of it. He had been correct in his first assessment; Conrad had respected force throughout his life. He had sworn himself to the bound man and had served with dedication ever since.

I will mourn him well if it proves necessary to sacrifice him. Dear Conrad deserves that. He discarded that line of thinking and returned to the subject at hand. "You are the only one I can trust to follow my orders to the letter. Therefore, it is up to you to locate Mr. Nicolau and bring him back here. Take however many of the others you'll need to accomplish this."

"You no longer desire to observe him, then, sir?"

Frantisek exhaled slowly. "More time to study him would have been nice, but we must make do as we are permitted, Conrad. I need our dear friend Grigori in a different way now. He possesses the strength I have been lacking; I see that now. With him, I shall control the might I need to force that blasted pile of marble to bend a stony knee to me. I will be the one reborn, not the thing in the house." He suddenly felt a great need to be free of his chair, but knew that such would not be wise at this time. Fighting down the urge, Peter Frantisek stared into the darkness. "Go out now and find him. I see him with the woman. Her home, I think . . . the children will know."

"What about the other matter? The man Abernathy?"

"Send two to take him. He will be a bonus. You have the address." The children had noted the blue-eyed seeker and relayed the information. The bound man had intended to wait a little longer to deal with Abernathy, but the man's worth was minuscule compared to Nicolau's. No point now in allowing the newcomer to wander, possibly to be added to the house's already much-too-swollen ranks. Better that he take Abernathy's contribution at the same time he took Grigori's. Peter Frantisek knew that the culmination of everything approached with great speed; it could be only a matter of days now. Every fragment strengthened him for the coming battle.

The conflict would probably demand the sacrifice of Conrad and the others, he realized. The children, too. Sad, but they would be replaced.

"You have your orders."

Conrad bowed and slipped into the darkness. He would succeed, of that the bound man was certain. It would be a tragedy to lose him after such efficiency, but he would undoubtedly understand.

Frantisek returned his gaze to the darkness. The culmination of the gargoyle's centuries-long task was coming at last . . . and *he* intended to reap its benefits.

XIII

GRIGORI ENTERED THE HOTEL FIRST. THE TIME WAS NOT YET two, but he wanted to position himself. Crossing the lobby, he made his way to a row of pay telephones.

Standing there, Grigori considered his mortality for the first time in centuries.

A number of people milled in the lobby, but none of them paid him any mind. Not wanting to draw suspicion to himself, Grigori refrained from staring too intently at anyone. Watching for Abernathy would be Teresa's task.

She walked in but a minute after he had stationed himself. Clad in a blue business suit and made up, she was even more stunning. Teresa, case in hand, walked through the lobby and surveyed those gathered there. More than one man gazed back, but none of these was Mr. Abernathy. She turned to her left and studied the men nearby, then glanced at those in the restaurant. Still no success.

Her gaze drifted to Grigori. He could see the frustration in her eyes, frustration no doubt mirrored in his own. Then, Teresa's eyes shifted to the elevators. From where he stood, Nicolau could not see the elevator doors, but he guessed that one of the lifts must have just released passengers.

Teresa blinked and started toward the elevator, a professional smile spreading across her face. She disappeared from his field of vision, but he could just make out the sound of her voice. Her words were unintelligible from where he stood, but the tone gave every indication that she had found their quarry. A moment later, she walked back into view, headed toward the lobby with a tall, sandy-haired, and fairly muscular figure in a dark business suit.

There was something wrong, something Grigori could not put his finger on. He muttered to himself as he searched with his power for anything out of the ordinary. His probing covered the entire lobby and beyond, but revealed nothing to him, save that some patron possessed slight, *very* slight, latent abilities. Grigori had run across the type before and was not concerned. Generally these were people who had more than their share of good luck, who never realized that they brought the luck upon themselves. He forgot the potential power wielder and expanded his probe.

Then he realized what it was.

He had not *sensed* Abernathy, not even after the man had entered the lobby. If Abernathy was like Teresa and the rest, Grigori should have been able to sense him the moment he entered the hotel, possibly even before.

Yet, if the man was not one of them, how had Teresa recognized him so quickly?

Unable to contain his curiosity, he walked toward the lobby seats, paying no obvious attention to the two as they talked. Teresa, he was pleased to see, neither hesitated nor glanced his way as he passed by. Grigori continued on until he found a plush chair not too far from the pair and sat down. He reached for a copy of the *Tribune* someone had left behind.

"And have you set a price range?" she was asking.

"Yes—no. It would depend on the house."

Glancing over the edge of the newspaper, Grigori Nicolau caught his first glimpse of Abernathy's countenance. The man had a face to match his build—broad, muscular, very much like that of a dashing football hero. He wore a slightly shaggy mustache the same color as the hair on his head.

His eyes were steel-blue.

Grigori could not help staring. Why was Abernathy different? The few others that he had met had all been to some degree or another like Teresa. He could sense the others from a distance. Teresa was the strongest, the weakest a man in Budapest who Nicolau had not noticed until they were across a courtyard from one another. Yet with Abernathy he sensed *nothing*.

Then the other man's eyes shifted to him . . . and widened.

Silently cursing his own stupidity, Grigori Nicolau tried to look away, but found he could not. His eyes bore into Abernathy's, which in turn bore into his own. He felt an intrusive touch and suddenly realized that it came from Abernathy.

Ignoring Teresa's questions, Abernathy continued to stare. Now Grigori sensed the link between them, a link that the other man had somehow *shielded* from him.

William Abernathy was a power wielder. And one who now sought to invade Grigori's mind.

To an onlooker, it would seem that the two men simply

glared at one another. However, Grigori read a hungry look in those other eyes, an unsettling hunger for what he began to believe was his very soul.

Teresa stopped talking, realizing at last that something was occuring between the two men. Grigori wished he could spare the energy to say something, for her help would have been sorely appreciated at the moment, but the effort would have weakened his counterattack. Abernathy had surprised him with the power; Nicolau could not recall ever crossing paths with anyone of similar abilities. He was certain that even Frantisek would have underestimated the man's talents.

Out of the corner of one eye, Grigori saw Teresa shifting her gaze frantically from one man to the other. Then she turned toward the large figure of Abernathy, who had completely forgotten her, and quite soundly kicked him in the shin. The blow was not enough to hurt a solidly built man like Grigori's adversary, but it caused his concentration to slip. That was all Grigori Nicolau needed.

William Abernathy had just enough time to gasp before his eyes glazed over. He did not fall, for Grigori's power held him in a casual sitting position. Grigori put aside the newspaper, rose, and joined Teresa.

"What happened?" she whispered.

"He's like me," replied Grigori with a friendly smile toward the frozen form. "A wielder of the power. A sorcerer, if you like."

"Like Frantisek?"

"Similar, but as Frantisek and I apparently have varied talents, our Mr. Abernathy differs from both of us. He can shield his abilities and his link almost perfectly; I walked past here earlier because I could not sense the link, even from as close as the telephones."

"I wondered why you did that." The agent looked around. No one was paying the trio any attention . . . yet. "We can't just sit here with him like that."

"I agree." Grigori felt no compunction against using his power on William Abernathy; the man had made clear what sort he was. "I think that Mr. Abernathy wants to show us his hotel room after all."

Grigori stared at the man, who then slowly nodded his head. Teresa eyed her companion open-mouthed. He felt a slight pang of regret. What must she think of him now that she knew he could control another person so completely?

However, her expression gradually changed to one of acceptance. "I really can't feel too sorry for him I guess. Let's get this over quickly, though."

The three of them rose, Abernathy at Grigori's silent command, and headed for the elevators. Grigori scanned the hotel staff, but no one looked at them for more than a moment. They reached the elevators unhindered and were fortunate to find one that they could have to themselves.

They arrived in the larger man's room only a minute or two later. As the door closed behind them, Grigori commanded William Abernathy to sit in one of the chairs. The man did, staying ramrod straight and staring ahead at the blank wall.

"God, can you make him relax a little, or at least not look so zombielike?" Teresa stood as far away from the seated figure as she could. "I'm sorry, Grigori, but he gives me the creeps."

Nicolau made the man lean back and cross his legs, but that was the best he could do. As for the eyes, he finally gave up and commanded Abernathy to close them. There was no danger of his hold being broken; he and the other man were linked mind to mind.

"What now?" asked Teresa, relaxing now that Abernathy did not look so much like a creature just raised from the dead. "Should we search the room?"

"That is an excellent idea, but first let me do something."

With a man like the menacing Mr. Abernathy, Grigori wanted to be prepared for traps. A skilled wielder could leave

some unsavory surprises for those who intruded upon their
domains. Therefore, before they could physically search his
room, Grigori searched it with his mind.

The probe was swift, the results even swifter. There was
nothing in the hotel room that registered as anything but
normal, nothing, that is, save the black suitcase nearly hidden
in the far corner.

He pointed at the closet. "Start with his coat, if you do
not mind, then search the dresser drawers. I will search the
suitcase."

"Is there something in that thing? What did you sense?"

She knew him well enough now to read his interest in the
piece of luggage as significant. "I don't know what the contents are yet. It is protected by his power. It is the only thing
in this room other than our friend himself that is so tainted.
It would be best left to me to open it, if I can."

"Why should I bother to search anywhere else if that's the
only thing in this place worth looking at?" Annoyance flavored her words. "You don't have to try to convince me that
I'm any help, you know. If there's nothing I can do, just say
so."

"You misunderstand. This is the only item surrounded by
his power, but that does not mean he hasn't hidden other
clues of a more *normal* nature. A scrap of paper with notes
on it. An address. Something. I would not ask if I did not
think the task important, Teresa."

"All right," she returned. A slight but encouraging smile
played briefly on her lips. "I'm sorry if I was wrong."

"We are in this together . . . always."

She turned to the closet and Abernathy's coat. Meanwhile,
Grigori walked over and knelt by the suitcase, not yet ready
to touch it. Using a more subtle probe, he tested the field of
power that surrounded it. It was, as he had first suspected, a
safety system. On the surface, it did not seem designed to

harm someone. Perhaps a bit too curious for his own sake, Grigori reached for the handle and touched it.

He released it immediately, wondering suddenly if perhaps he should search the coat instead of having Teresa do so. The suitcase could wait. There was nothing worthwhile inside; no doubt Abernathy was using his power to keep hotel thieves from rifling through his belongings, that was all.

What am I thinking? Grigori looked at the suitcase again. *How can I put aside searching the case's contents for such absurd reasons?* Strengthening his will, Grigori once more touched the black luggage.

Again an impulse urged him to forget the suitcase, which would only reveal his counterpart's taste in clothes if opened.

I will open you! Grigori fought the urge to abandon the search. He knew now what Abernathy had done to the suitcase. A spell, for lack of a better word, had been wrapped around the bag, a spell that convinced the curious that investigating the contents was pointless. Now, however, the spell had backfired, for Grigori wanted more than ever to see the contents.

"Nothing in the coat," Teresa said, slipping around the still figure of William Abernathy. "What's the matter? Is the bag locked?"

"In a matter of speaking. It will take me a bit longer, that is all."

Teresa nodded, then indicated their silent companion. "Is it safe to leave him like that? He won't wake up while we're searching, will he?"

"I doubt it." His mind returned to the problem of the case. He dearly wanted it open now. Teresa turned to the dresser and began searching the drawers.

Abernathy had designed a complicated barrier. It could take some time to unlock the spell that protected the suitcase's contents. He either had to take the suitcase away and study it or find some quicker method by which to open it now.

The solution to his quandary was so obvious that he almost felt embarrassed at not thinking of it immediately. Rising, he turned toward the seated figure and stared. William Abernathy slowly stood up.

Teresa whirled around. "He's awake! Grigori—"

He raised a warning hand. "He is *not* awake, Teresa. I control him."

She continued to watch, her breath coming in short gasps. "What are you going to do?"

With a flick of his hand, he indicated the suitcase. "The easiest way to open this case will be to ask the one with the key to do so."

Staring into Abernathy's unfocused eyes, Grigori pointed at the suitcase. The other man looked at the luggage, then raised one hand toward it. Abernathy shifted his index finger in a short but complicated series of gestures that Nicolau likened to untying a knot. The process was so swift that he was not certain he could have repeated the steps. Grigori was thankful that he had not tried to puzzle out the method himself. He would have wasted far too much time.

Abernathy lowered his hand and waited for his next command. Grigori sent him back to this seat, then turned to the suitcase.

Now that the barrier had been removed, he could sense something else within that also spoke of power, power with a dark touch to it. He turned the luggage toward the wall, just in case there was something within primed for a thief, then carefully flicked open the mundane metal locks.

He opened up the suitcase . . . and nearly shut it tight again as a sense of evil pervaded his very being. Grigori glanced up at Teresa, but she had discovered a notebook and had begun perusing it.

It was all Grigori could do to force himself to even touch

the case, much less open it again. Slowly, ever so slowly, Grigori placed his hands on opposite sides of the lid. The unease grew, but he willed himself to continue. Up went the top, but inch by inch. Grigori felt himself fighting what he was doing; yet it was no spell that made him hesitate, only the knowledge that something within the case radiated a foulness he had rarely experienced in all his years.

Then at last the case was wide open, and Grigori Nicolau stared at . . . *clothing.*

Everyday clothing. Shirts. A pair of slacks. Some men's socks and ties.

These could not be the source of his horror. Reluctantly, he used his power to probe below the obvious layer of clothing. Beneath the top two shirts he found another, just as ordinary. Beneath the slacks lay another pair, also of no interest.

Under the socks—

Under the socks rested a container whose spell-protected contents both called to and repelled his very soul. Grigori thrust his hand beneath the clothing and forced his fingers around what felt akin to a jar. Unconsciously holding his breath, the dark man removed the object from the case and held it at eye-level.

It was indeed a jar. Grigori had seen its like often, generally in stores that sold fruit preserves. The lid was a little fancier than most, having a smaller, circular tab in the center that looked like a tiny bottle cap. A very ordinary jar in all ways . . . save that, while the container was most definitely made of clear glass, he could not see the contents. Instead, a fog swirled around inside, a fog that, if studied long enough, almost appeared to move with intelligence.

But that was absurd . . .

His hand was shaking so hard that he nearly dropped the jar. Grigori placed the jar on the bed, far enough from the edge so that there would be no danger of it falling off. Then, both reluctant and relieved to be rid of it, Nicolau continued his search. There was something else in the case, something linked to the container and its contents.

He found it just as Teresa called out, "Take a look at this notebook, Grigori."

He did not answer. Grigori Nicolau had lost all touch with the world around him. The new center of his universe was the object in his hand. It was not a jar, nothing so innocent as that. Rather, what he held now was clearly an instrument of darkness and death, akin to an object he had once had in his possession before Peter Frantisek's servant had taken it from him.

It was not a knife, though it was also black and covered with runes. Grigori turned it round and round, eyeing the cone shape distastefully and pondering the hollow center. The tip had a small hole at the end; he thought of it more as a funnel than a cone.

His gaze returned to the jar and the tiny cap at the lid's center. Grigori held the funnel point over the cap. If one *removed* the cap, which simply screwed off, this jar's mouth made a perfect receptacle for the funnel.

What *was* this?

A reddish shape within the jar pressed against the glass, then was gone the next instant.

Grigori dropped the funnel and stared. What he had seen had resembled a piece of red cloth—red cloth moving of its own volition.

In Germany during the winter of 1944, he had come across a power wielder attempting something that required items similar to these. In Muscovy, during his second stay there . . . or maybe it had been his third . . . he had come across writings by a mad monk who proposed a theory requiring the use of a container sealed by the power and a pipe.

"Grigori?" called Teresa again. She walked up to him, still reading the notebook. "I've tried to make sense of these, but I don't know what they might—'' Her mouth closed as she stared at his pale, sweating face.

Almost desperate to find something else to take his mind off of his suspicions, he abandoned the funnel and jar and rose to see what the young woman had located. It was indeed a notebook, one that Abernathy had made use of extensively, if the worn appearance was any indication.

Grigori's emotions shifted from horror to curiosity as he read line after line of notes concerning a woman named Julianna DeVoorst. The date on the top of the left page marked the text as ten years old, but three years' worth of notes on the woman filled the book. William Abernathy had kept track of where the woman, fifty-five years of age at the time of the first entry, moved and what she did. The last note on the woman, whose final address was listed as Groningen, Netherlands, concerned the sudden sale of her home and her equally abrupt plans to come to the United States . . . specifically Chicago.

Underneath the destination, Abernathy had written and then circled the date of her planned departure.

Grigori Nicolau turned his gaze heavenward. "And did she take that flight I wonder?"

"I don't know what to make of it," Teresa remarked, "but I'm pretty certain that she was one of us."

"Very likely." He turned to the next page. It concerned a couple and was dated more recently.

Before he could read it, Teresa blurted, "I knew those two."

"What did you say?"

She pointed at the names. "These two. One of my files is on them."

Grigori had only studied a few of the files, but he recalled at least two couples mentioned. He glanced at the last notes Abernathy had made on them.

4/11—House abandoned. Neighbor says they were home last night. Chicago?

Why Chicago? Second time now.

Abernathy had also circled the city's name.

Nicolau turned the page and found nothing. The rest of the notebook was blank save for a few scribbles of an inconsequential nature. He closed it and stared at the back of the man whose handiwork was more and more condemning him in Grigori's mind. Everything pointed to one abominable conclusion. "I think it's time to question our friend."

"Can we make it quick?" asked his companion, shivering again. "I don't think I want to be here much longer."

William Abernathy sat complacently in the chair. Grigori dragged another chair over and sat down before the bespelled man. He held the notebook in front of his counterpart and concentrated his will. "Look at the thing I have in my hand and tell me about its contents."

It took the larger man some time to turn and focus his eyes on the notebook, but as soon as he had, Abernathy replied to the command. "My notebook. To keep watch on the others."

Not very eloquent, but then Nicolau had not specified how precise he had wanted the answer to be. He tried again. "Tell me about the people listed within, William Abernathy. Did they all have eyes like yours?"

The other man's face cracked into a twisted smile. "All of them. After the third one, it became easier to sense them. The Dutch woman was tricky. She knew me, too. Had to wait a few years to get her."

"What does he mean by that?" Teresa, arms folded tight, studied Abernathy as if he were an adder that had crawled out from under the bed.

Grigori Nicolau had a fair notion of what his captive meant. "How old are you, William Abernathy?"

The question generated a curious glance from Teresa, but

Grigori forestalled her questions by raising a hand. He wanted to hear the answer the first time.

"Ninety-seven."

"He *can't* be—"

"Teresa!" Grigori hissed. She quieted, but still looked disbelieving. This despite knowing that the man with whom she was trusting her life was centuries old. What was ninety-seven years compared to that? Power wielders could live longer than most, although they could only hope to last two, perhaps in a few rare cases, three hundred years. There were tales of some who had lived longer, but Grigori could not recall ever having uncovered any truth in them . . . which, of course, did not mean anything. He himself was proof that it was possible.

Grigori Nicolau realized that he had not yet asked the other man one of the most important questions on his mind. "Do you know about Frostwing?"

Abernathy's brow actually furrowed before he answered. "No."

Of course he would not know about Frostwing! Grigori cursed himself for his own idiocy. He had named the gargoyle himself. No one else would recognize the name. "Do you know of a gargoyle?"

This time Abernathy didn't hesitate. "No."

So Abernathy was ignorant of Frostwing. He only knew about the house, and then not even that much.

"Is this the only notebook or do you have others?"

He both feared and hoped that William Abernathy might have a history of those he had tracked going back some seventy years, but to his relief the man replied in the negative. Abernathy's mysterious, but very likely dark work had only begun a decade or two back, which was still far too long a time. Rising, Grigori handed the notebook back to Teresa. "We take this with us."

"What now?" she asked, but he was already walking back to the bed. Grigori stared down at the small jar and funnel. The fog within still swirled about, but he could see no sign of the bit of cloth.

Hands trembling, Nicolau reached for the two items. However, his fingers came up short as he contemplated having to touch either object with his bare hands. Grigori then recalled the other contents of Abernathy's case. He turned to the open bag and rummaged through the clothing. After a few moments, he found what he was searching for.

The handkerchiefs were silk and skillfully monogrammed with the letter *A*. Scrollwork surrounded the letter, scrollwork that looked vaguely familiar to Grigori. Although he could not identify the design, it would not have surprised him to discover that it had played a part of his own past. After all, he and Abernathy were linked in so many ways.

With the handkerchiefs wrapped around his hands, he picked up the two artifacts and brought them back to the captive. Sitting down again, Grigori held the objects before the man's eyes. To his surprise, Abernathy focused on them of his own will. A light ignited within the eyes. Strengthening his control, Nicolau held the funnel close. "Tell me what this is."

Abernathy only stared. Grigori repeated his question.

After a time, the bespelled figure replied, "It is the . . ."

Try as he might, Grigori could not pronounce the mad word that slipped so easily off the other man's tongue. The word did not even sound like a word but rather more like noise one made when ill. "Repeat that."

The second time was no better than the first. Grigori gave up and said, "Now tell me what you do with it."

Again, Abernathy hesitated. Grigori Nicolau began to grow impatient. The other power wielder should have been able to answer such questions, especially where it concerned his own property. In frustration, he pulled back the funnel and brought forth the jar. As he did, Grigori noticed that the fog swirled yet faster.

The tiny piece of red cloth materialized out of the fog, only now it was not alone. As all of them watched, a blue cloth joined the first, then those two were joined by a green one. More bits of cloth revealed themselves. There were different materials and different colors, but all were cut into tiny squares.

Abernathy's eyes widened, and the hunger that Grigori had noticed in the lobby suddenly returned.

"Get ba—" His warning to Teresa came too late, but the larger man did not lunge at her. As the other power wielder fell upon him, Grigori Nicolau lost his grip on both the ebony funnel and the jar. The two objects bounced to the side.

Abernathy tore his hungry gaze from his adversary and searched frantically for the jar. Grigori, utilizing his sudden advantage, brought the heel of his palm up into the man's throat, striking the Adam's apple.

Choking, the other man clutched his throat and fell back. Grigori attempted to rise, but an unseen force threw him back to the floor. A crimson-faced Abernathy, still attempting to regain his breath, glared at the smaller man. Grigori's breath grew short and ragged.

It was very possible that William Abernathy was capable of accomplishing what no one else could . . . the death of Grigori Nicolau.

Now that death seemed possible for him, Grigori found that he did not desire to greet it. He wanted to live. He wanted to be there for Teresa. He wanted to be there for himself.

In the past, against a opponent such as the man before him, Grigori Nicolau would have been helpless. His meager powers would have only annoyed his adversary, nothing more. Grigori's only aid would come from Frostwing, but that had meant he suffered greatly first. After the last visitation, however, he did not know whether the malicious gargoyle would return at all.

But oddly enough Grigori felt stronger than ever. It was as if he drew power not only from within, but also *around*. He continued to grow stronger—or perhaps his adversary grew weaker. Whatever the case, Grigori knew that Abernathy could not stop him. Abernathy was a mite, a tiny fragment compared to Grigori.

"Damn you, little man! Fall!" Abernathy's face grew a deeper red by the moment. His attack faltered, then collapsed.

The redness on the large man's face faded away, leaving him almost as pale as the dead. Abernathy mouthed what looked like a denial. Then a desperate gleam came into his eyes and he reached for the ebony funnel. Grigori tried to grab the artifact first, but the sudden move had caught him by surprise.

The funnel raised like a dagger, William Abernathy roared, "I am the host, not *you*! I am the receptacle! I know the truth! I am the whole; you are only a fragment!"

The deadly artifact lent him a madman's strength. Despite the relative bluntness of the tip, Grigori had no doubt that the funnel would sink into his chest as easily as a knife into warm butter. It was the way of such foul devices to make easier the course of their darker masters.

He caught Abernathy's wrist and tried to use his power to weaken the man from within. A little more time and Abernathy would be his, but there was no such time available. Abernathy was literally burning himself out in his attempt to overcome the now-superior strength of Grigori, and the desperate measure was paying off.

The other power wielder was aging rapidly before Grigori's eyes, but still he pushed and still the funnel tip came closer to Grigori. It mattered not where it touched, Nicolau knew. Any touch would seal his fate.

Abernathy suddenly grunted and slumped forward as if pushed. His hands were wrinkled and spotted and he had lost some mass.

It was as if a part of Grigori's soul that had long gone astray had suddenly been returned to him. No, soul was not quite correct; perhaps *life essence* was closer to the truth. The link's purpose became clearer. It went beyond simply identifying those who were like him; he was now absorbing that piece of Abernathy that was somehow responsible for the bond between the two in the first place.

Realizing what that would mean, the slight man tried to cut the link, but it was like building a wall of straw to fight a flooding river. What he drew from William Abernathy, be it soul or life force, so belonged to Grigori that even the latter had no say in the decision. He could not have stopped the flow to save the other man's life even if he had wanted to do so.

Just before it ended, before Abernathy fell face-first onto the carpeting, Grigori experienced memories. They were not, however, the memories of the man before him nor, thankfully, were they the memories of anyone who had been listed in the notebook. He knew that because the memories, the images that flashed through his mind, were of a time so very distant, eight, maybe nine centuries.

Grigori saw a keep of sorts, the home of someone proud and feared, but prevented by his enemies from fulfilling his obvious destiny. That was the most persistent memory, but there were others, many simply jumbled fragments, that hinted at a darkness within the man, a darkness that repelled Grigori. None of them were very clear, but the picture that they painted filled Grigori with a loathing for the keep's master.

Mixed with those bits of memory were others concerning an uprising against that evil by others of might . . . other *wielders of power*.

Then the memories at last vanished deep into his mind. They would always be there, but he would have to concentrate to recall them, just like normal memories.

"Grigori?" Teresa was shouting. He blinked and looked her way. She stood next to Abernathy, an up-turned table lamp in her hands. There was blood on the lamp's base.

"I remember—" he began to say, then paused. What exactly it was he remembered, he could not say. Instead, he glanced down at the bloodied form of Abernathy, then back at the shaking woman who had quite possibly saved his life. "Thank you."

"Is he . . .?" Teresa could not finish the terrible question. She simply pointed at the fallen man, all the while pleading with her eyes.

"He . . . he is dead, Teresa, you didn't do it. *I* killed him. I didn't mean to, but something happened that I could not stop."

In truth, he could not mourn for William Abernathy. The man had been a devil, a butcher.

"Are you sure he's dead?"

"Very certain." Grigori, bracing himself, reached for the corpse. He had planned to make Abernathy empty his own pockets, but now he was forced to rifle through the clothing of a dead man. Not something he liked, but it would not be the first time in his long life that necessity had demanded it of him. Necessity seemed to feel it could demand *anything* from him.

"How can you touch him?"

"With distaste, I assure you." His mind was too muddled for a proper probe, and Grigori knew that he and Teresa had already spent too much time here. Now they also had a body on their hands, the body of a man who had obviously not succumbed to natural causes.

The back pockets were empty. Grigori found himself forced to turn Abernathy's body over onto its back. As he rose and shifted position in preparation for the horrific task, his eyes fell upon the jar. It lay on its side, still unbroken, but it had changed. The fog was gone, replaced by a transparent liquid. Floating in that liquid were more than half a dozen limp pieces of cloth. They did not move at all and seemed faded.

He picked it up, but in his mind he felt nothing. There was no trace of any power. Grigori recalled feeling as if he had been drawing strength from all around him and now he recognized the actual source. The thought so distressed him that he lost his grip on the jar. It struck the carpet and cracked. The fluid spilled out on the carpet, but Grigori did not care.

Something else occurred to him. "Teresa, how do you feel?"

"Upset, scared, angry, tired . . . should I go on?"

He tried to hide his worry. "But physically you feel fair? You do not feel as if the very life has been drained from you?"

"No more than I would after a busy day at work." She looked concerned. "Did he do something?"

She had not been affected. He said a silent prayer of gratitude to whatever god might be watching over them. Perhaps he had simply been imagining everything. "No, apparently not." Grigori leaned down and took hold of Abernathy. "You may wish to turn away."

"I'll. . . . I'll be okay."

Dead, the larger man seemed even heavier than he had been when he had fallen on top of Grigori at the beginning of the struggle. Grigori still berated himself for not thinking that the jar and the funnel might stir Abernathy to waking. He had not desired to kill the man, although Nicolau had wondered what he would do with Abernathy after he had finished questioning him.

William Abernathy stared up at the ceiling with dead eyes. He looked almost his true age now, only his hair remaining unchanged. Abernathy was a shriveled thing. Had Grigori not seen him alive, he would have been inclined to think the man many years dead.

"Grigori?"

His hand was near the man's upper coat pocket. He let it hover there as he looked up. "It is no shame if you feel you need to turn away or even flee to the bathroom. I care for this as little as you."

Teresa, however, shook her head. "That's not why I interrupted you." Despite her present pale complexion, she did not even so much as flinch. "I just want you to look at his eyes and tell me what you see."

He did and noticed nothing. The sight was, to be sure, disconcerting, but he had seen dead men staring heavenward many times prior to this. Teresa had not shared in his good fortune, though, so it was more than reasonable that she might find this all a bit much.

"Don't you see anything?" she asked. Teresa pointed at Abernathy. "Look at his eyes!"

The longer they remained in the room with Abernathy, the more chance they had of being discovered by someone. Grigori decided to allow himself one more glance at the dead man's eyes, but then he would have to continue with his search of the pockets. The two of them had to leave soon.

Grigori Nicolau gave the open eyes a cursory glance, then reached into Abernathy's pocket. His fingers closed around a pen, what was likely a handkerchief, and a piece of paper. He withdrew them quickly, eager to see what information, if any, the paper might reveal.

Then his gaze darted back to Abernathy's countenance.

He knew now why Teresa had been so adamant. Grigori could hardly believe that he, of all people, had not noticed the change.

Abernathy's eyes were now *brown*.

XIV

THE CHANGING OF ABERNATHY'S EYE COLOR TROUBLED Grigori much. That it was the result of what he had done to the murderous man he was certain. No link remained between the two of them. The force that had tied Abernathy to Grigori now resided in the latter alone. A different man lay sprawled at his feet. It was as if in drawing from his adversary, Nicolau had removed a layer of skin, revealing another person below. He felt nothing toward William Abernathy save revulsion and remorse for what he had been forced to do.

Whatever it was he had taken from Abernathy, the man had been unable to live without it. In the end, that was what mattered most. Grigori was disgusted with himself; he felt little better than the dead man. Only the fact that Abernathy had been a willing murderer while Nicolau had been forced to do it kept Grigori from utterly hating himself.

He shared his conclusions with Teresa, who could not truly understand but took his word. He did not press the subject for fear that she would think about the others who had come to Sentinel. Emrich, for instance. From what Grigori Nicolau had uncovered here, William Abernathy had been capable of an abomination a hundredfold worse than his own fate. He had drawn, or attempted to draw, the same force from the people on his list.

That was the purpose of the funnel, a foul item created by dark power. It seized the unwilling prize and ripped it from the victim.

Grigori glanced at the jar. If he was correct, Abernathy had been able to draw those essences from his victims, but not fully absorb them. Had he possessed such an ability, he would have been too powerful for Grigori to battle.

The jar held what remained of his victims. He stored them in the hope that he would discover a method by which he could take those essences and make them a part of himself. There were tales of such monsters throughout history, even among power wielders. Soul takers. Vampires. Succubi and incubi. Whatever the title, the legends were far less terrible than the truth.

He feared he knew what had really happened to Emrich and possibly others. The bound man surely had at least the skill of the late Mr. Abernathy, and the force lurking within the house was likely just as powerful and just as heinous. He suspected that the disappearances were tied to both parties . . . and Grigori was trapped in the middle.

Thinking of Frantisek goaded Grigori anew. They had to leave here quickly and without anyone seeing them. Grigori also had to deal with the body. All trace of William Abernathy had to be obliterated. Prior to the encounter, such a task would have been monumental to him; now he was capable of doing what was necessary. That did not mean that he had the will to waste. Exhaustion was an everpresent danger.

His hands clenched. A crinkling noise reminded him that he had not yet studied the paper he had retrieved from the body. It was likely nothing, but he dared not take that risk.

Scribbled notes in shorthand and an address in one of the city neighborhoods. The notes filled most of the tiny piece of paper. He wondered if Abernathy had forgotten his notebook. The paper itself appeared to have been torn from a desk notepad or something similar. The address meant nothing to him and the marks were incomprehensible, although Grigori recognized what they were supposed to be. He handed the note to Teresa and asked, "Do you know shorthand?"

"I'm a little rusty, but I think I can remember it." She looked the scrap of paper over. "It's notes on someone. Where they live. Movements by . . . by more than one person." The blonde woman looked up. "Some of this sounds familiar, Grigori."

"What do you mean?" It would have been better if they had waited until they were elsewhere to discuss this, but Grigori needed to know. If the large man had located another potential victim, then they had to find that person before either Frantisek or the house claimed another victim.

"Listen. 'Never leaves. Eyes around all sides of house. Three men today. Man with ponytail—his acolyte? House shielded still. Try Paris trick next. Gun under coat, not ordinary one . . . find out what it is?' " Teresa looked at her companion for confirmation of her suspicions. "This sounds like something you told me about. This wouldn't concern that man Peter Frantisek, would it?"

Grigori nearly tore the note from her hand. He stared at the marks, then fixed his gaze on the address. William Abernathy had been an exceptional tracker, it seemed, a man of many talents. More and more Grigori found himself amazed that he had overcome the other. It had been only his unexpected absorption of Abernathy's essence that had saved him from becoming part of the man's collection.

The address might not be Frantisek's. It might bear no relation to the other notes. Yet, from what Teresa had read, Grigori was certain that it *did*. Abernathy had indeed discovered the bound man's shadowy abode . . . but what was Grigori supposed to do with that information now?

Glancing at the late Mr. Abernathy, Grigori decided that the address could wait. What was more important now was to do something about the dead man. Abernathy had to disappear, but in a way that would not make the hotel or anyone else trace his disappearance to Teresa and Grigori. He would also have to help Teresa make up an excuse about the man's

abrupt departure from the office, just in case the story of
the dead man's mysterious absence reached them somehow.
Fortunately, the house had a long legacy of potential clients
suddenly losing interest and departing; it would not seem so
strange that yet another had abandoned the forlorn property.

Stuffing the address in his pocket, he prepared himself for
the distasteful task. Teresa eyed him uncertainly.

"We have to do something with Mr. Abernathy, Teresa,"
he explained. "but I can do it without your assistance. Why
don't you return to your vehicle and wait for me there? This
way, you stand less of a chance of becoming involved should
something go amiss."

"I can't leave you alone with this."

Grigori appreciated the sentiment, however misplaced at
the moment. What he had to do would best be done without
her presence, lest she come to see him as no better than his
late counterpart. Necessity demanded he make a cleansing of
this room, a cleansing that would require some brutality and
indifference to the sensibilities of this era. Teresa might not
understand that circumstances left him little choice.

"It would be better if you did not remain. This will not
be pleasant, Teresa. I must do what I can to guarantee that
no trace will be left to tie him to us."

She glanced again at the body and at last nodded. "All
right." The blonde woman's expression was one of fear, but
surprisingly enough, he realized that it was fear for him.
"You will be okay?"

"I will."

He guided her to the door, making certain that she would
not have time for second thoughts. Her concern almost made
the endless years seem worthwhile; he would have never met
her had he lived an ordinary existence. Even though it was
doubtful that their relationship could survive, Grigori already
cherished the few days he had known her.

At the door, Teresa turned to him. Catching Grigori com-

pletely off guard, she kissed him soundly on the lips. Her
voice was a whisper as she added, "Good luck."

The door closed behind her, leaving him standing dazed.
He put a hand to his lips, then, shaking his head to clear it,
Grigori faced his other, not-so-entrancing companion. He
knelt beside Abernathy and stared at the man's features. There
was something familiar about Abernathy, something he had
not noticed before. Grigori Nicolau could not put his finger
on it exactly, but he was almost certain he had either known
the other man or someone much like him.

That was neither here nor there, however. The time had
come to eliminate the presence of William Abernathy. Grigori
shuddered at the thought. While he would not be physically
doing the foul work himself, that made him no less responsible. By his doing the man would cease to exist in the eyes
of all.

With much disgust, he retrieved the funnel. Abernathy's
horrific tool of death would now serve to eradicate its master's
presence. When Grigori was finished, there would be no
body. The personal effects would need to be disposed of, but
that was simple in comparison.

May you be judged as need be, he thought, staring at the
emotionless features of the dead man. The funnel he placed
point up on William Abernathy's chest. When he released
his grip on the foul device, it did not fall. Rather, it *sank*,
slipping nearly an inch deep.

Grigori shuddered. How many times had Abernathy performed a similar ceremony on others, but with less regret.
And some of those victims had been living.

Not for the first time Grigori damned the power that was
so much a part of him.

Raising his hand over the open tip, Nicolau slowly let the
force flow through him. He needed to guide the tool for a
few brief seconds, then the foul artifact, understanding its
new function, would proceed with the rest. After that, Grigori

would only need to watch and wait, which would be a terrible enough thing to do. Already his repulsion with the act was growing strong.

He passed his other hand over the funnel. Abernathy's body shimmered.

Outside, someone tried turning the doorknob.

Spinning around, Grigori stared at the knob. It jerked clockwise, then counterclockwise, as someone attempted to open the door. The door would not open, however, not while Grigori's will kept it sealed. Whether that would eventually dissuade the person in the hall, he could not know. The would-be intruder might be a bellman or housekeeper come to perform some minor task. It was possible, too, that one of Frantisek's villains sought entry. Perhaps they had been following Mr. Abernathy.

He had sent *Teresa* out there.

The enormity of his folly struck him full-blown. He had sent her out to her vehicle, never even considering the obvious danger that might be waiting there. What had he been thinking?

He had *not* been thinking; that seemed too often to be his chief deficiency. If not for the curse, Grigori Nicolau would have been long dead . . . and not from old age.

William Abernathy forgotten, Grigori rose and stepped behind the door. He stared briefly at the knob. The tab in the center twisted, locking the door. Grigori removed the invisible barrier that he had created and waited.

The knob wiggled again, then stopped. He waited, not daring to use his power any more, even to see who stood on the other side. If they were the bound man's servants, it was possible that further use of his abilities would alert them to his presence . . . providing that they did not already know.

Somewhat to his surprise, there suddenly came a knock. It was tentative, hesitant.

From without came a muffled "Grigori?"

Teresa? He had every reason to believe that it was indeed her, but Grigori was not so trusting. He sensed her nearness, but that could simply be because she was still in the vicinity. The closer he and Teresa grew to one another, the stronger her presence was to him. She could be down in the lobby, but he would still sense her.

Grigori gave in despite his anxieties, finally probing the hallway just on the other side of the door. His abilities informed him that it was her. Still not quite willing to trust, the wary Nicolau stepped to the door and peered through the tiny glass peephole.

Teresa, glancing furtively to her left, stood in the center of the hall.

Unlocking the door, he almost dragged her inside, but at the last second recalled Abernathy's body and the funnel sunk deep into the dead man's chest. Grigori paused in the doorway, effectively blocking her view of the room's interior.

"What's wrong?" he asked.

Once more she glanced down the hall. Nicolau followed her gaze but could see nothing that might explain either her return or her expression.

"I think they're here!" she finally whispered.

He looked down the hallway in both directions, but still there was nothing. Grigori probed, only to achieve the same results. "*Who* is here?"

She tried to step inside, but he was unyielding. There was no protest from her; instead, Teresa answered his question, all the while her eyes darting to and fro. "I think they must work for that man . . . Frantisek. I saw them when I reached the lobby. Something about them . . . ." Her eyes were round. "Somehow they reminded me of the men from that ghost image we saw in Emrich's room."

"You are certain of that?" As he spoke, Grigori Nicolau

extended the range of his search. He still detected nothing; neither Frantisek's human minions nor his four-legged pets appeared to be in the hotel.

"I don't know how I know, but I do." Her eyes drifted to what little of the room that she could see. "Is that—"

A piece of the wall only two doors down might have rippled. Grigori was not certain, but he chose to not take the risk. He seized his companion and pulled her inside.

He tried to, anyway. Halfway through the door, Teresa stopped short. It was not through any choice of her own, as her expression readily revealed. She stared at her feet and gasped, "I can't move them! I'm stuck!"

"Slip out of your shoes," he hissed, staring past her in an attempt to pinpoint the false wall. Why he did not detect the camouflaged figures, Grigori could not say, save that it was obviously well within Peter Frantisek's power to shield his minions from the second sight of those like himself. Such shields would be costly, however, which was probably why he lavished them only on his hunters. The men themselves could not have the ability to create the shields.

Teresa struggled to slip out of her heeled shoes, but her feet might as well have been glued to them. In desperation, she took hold of one ankle and pulled.

Still Grigori could not sense the stalker's presence, but he knew the man—or men—had to be nearby. That would have to be enough. Slipping around Teresa, he stared at the seemingly innocent corridor.

The air crackled. The hair on both their heads rose. Teresa turned to see what was happening.

To an ordinary onlooker, the only sign of Grigori's attack would have been the flickering of the lights in the hall. Teresa Dvorak, however, had been touched by his world and now she saw as he did.

It was as if a lightning bolt had been loosed in the narrow passage. A shock of electricity coursed through the hall, outlining everything it touched. Doorways blazed with brilliant blue light. Every bulb flickered madly.

Against one wall, the blue lightning formed the outline of a tall figure. The agonized figure shook wildly, yet no scream assailed their ears. The form grew more solid, more real.

Then the figure became a dog-faced man in a rumpled brown suit, a man who slumped forward onto the corridor floor and lay still.

At the same time, the unseen force abruptly released Teresa's feet. She stumbled into Grigori, and the two of them floundered for a moment, then regained their balances. Grigori looked around, searching for another threat. The stalker could not be alone. Frantisek did not work that way. There were always at least two . . . sometimes three, as in the kidnapping in the restaurant parking lot.

"He fell out of the wall, just like in the image!"

Nicolau took hold of her shoulders. "And there will be others. We have to leave."

"What about . . ." she said nothing further, simply indicated the still half-open door.

He reached out and shut the door. Grigori could not face her directly as he replied, "In a few minutes, it will not matter. We shall have to leave some mystery as to his departure, though. There is no time to deal with that." There was still no sign of a second attacker. "Our concern now is to avoid that one's companions."

"What are you going to do with him?"

"Nothing. That is his master's concern." He read something in her eyes and quickly added, "He is not dead, Teresa, merely incapacitated."

She nodded, then gave him a fleeting smile that was also half apology. Grigori flushed. He had been tempted to kill the man. Only her presence had kept him from doing so. He hoped that his decision would not return to haunt them. The bound man had plans for both of them, plans that would conclude with their deaths—or worse. Grigori saw no reason to assist Frantisek with those ambitions, but eliminating villains such as the one in the hall risked Teresa's opinion of him. She accepted deaths if there was no other choice, but killing the stalker would have seemed too much like murder to her.

Even if he survived this century, Grigori Nicolau knew he would never understand such tender-hearted thinking. To escape from a deadly enemy meant removing that enemy. He would have preferred it otherwise, but history—fragmented as it was—had taught him so time and time again.

With Grigori leading, the two of them moved toward one of the emergency stairwells. The risk of rats existed, but Grigori doubted more than a few of Frantisek's children lurked in the hotel. Why he was so certain of that made no more sense to him than Teresa's earlier and obviously well-justified belief that Frantisek's hunters had discovered them. Something had felt different ever since he had absorbed Abernathy's power, but did that explain his certainty . . . or Teresa's?

The stairs appeared empty and a quick scan of the floors above and below revealed no presence save their own. Of course, Grigori knew how much he could trust such results. He took hold of his companion's hand and whispered, "Keep close. We must not be separated." His commands did not merely have to do with his concern for her. As long as the two of them continued to touch, Teresa would be able to amplify his power much the way she had in Emrich's room. "Allow nothing to distract you."

They descended the first two levels without incident, although each creak made them search the shadows for furred forms or walls that seemed to move.

"How—how much farther?" Teresa asked after they had descended two more floors at dangerous speeds. Her heeled shoes were not designed for such use. Now and then she had come close to stumbling.

"Only a few more floors," he assured her, sounding more confident than he felt. "Not long."

To his surprise, they reached the lobby level unchallenged. He opened the door and led Teresa out.

The lobby was much as the two had left it only minutes prior. Some of the people who stood or sat nearby were new and others from before had departed, but things remained more or less unchanged. Grigori saw no one who struck him as out of place, but nonetheless he probed the area, seeking even the most minute clue. Despite his amplified abilities, however, he discovered nothing. Perhaps the other stalker was above, trying to revive the first man.

"Maybe we should just walk out hand-in-hand," suggested Teresa. "You know, like we belong here."

He could find no real fault with her suggestion and acquiesced. The two of them strolled away from the doorway and the stairs, talking to each other about the weather and sights to see in the city. They reached the front entrance and, still not quite willing to believe their good fortune, attempted to exit through one of the glass doors. It proved to be locked. Foregoing the urge to unlock it himself, Grigori went to the next door, only to find that it too was locked.

Belatedly he saw that people were now entering and exiting through the revolving doors in the center. Grigori also saw that the design of the door made it difficult for two people to stand together as they pushed through. He paused and turned to Teresa.

"We will have to separate for a few moments. I will go first to ensure that nothing awaits us outside. As you go through, though, keep your eyes on me."

"Do you think there's still danger?"

With his eyes he indicated the lobby. "Do you see either

of the men that you noticed earlier? The ones you are certain were not simply guests?''

''No. I looked around while we walked. I didn't see them anywhere.''

''Then we are still in danger. Assuming one of them was the stalker near Abernathy's room, then there remains at least one more.''

They continued to the revolving doors. Grigori released her hand and, with one last, surreptitious scan of the hotel's interior, stepped between two of the sliding glass panels. He looked ahead to ascertain whether the way was clear, then glanced back to make certain that Teresa had entered behind him. When he saw that she had, Grigori relaxed and turned his attention to the outside.

He exited the revolving doors and, stepping aside to avoid a woman entering the hotel, made a quick study of the vicinity. The soft scraping of the turning doors and the sounds of steps coming up behind him drew Grigori's attention. Putting a confident smile on his face, he turned and began, ''It should be fairly safe from—''

A woman stared at him . . . but it was not Teresa.

They eyed one another, Grigori in stunned silence and the woman, a well-dressed dowager with silver-blue hair, in growing uncertainty. Then the woman stepped around him and continued on. Nicolau, still dazed with disbelief, followed her progress for several steps before recovering his senses. Whirling around, he focused on the turning doors and waited. Two more people exited, a young man in a business suit and a middle-aged woman carrying a small suitcase. Still no sign of Teresa, who should have departed the hotel only seconds behind him.

Grigori Nicolau ran back to the revolving doors and entered. As he pushed, he sought some trace of Teresa. She was still nearby, that much he could tell, but where was impossible to determine. Some force was interfering with his probe.

Midway through, the doors stopped and trapped Grigori. He pushed, but the doors refused to give. He glanced at the opposing side, but saw no one. He was alone in the doorway. Grigori realized that the unearthly stalkers had trapped him. They might even now be standing directly in front of him.

Grigori closed his eyes . . .

. . . And when he opened them, he stood once more at the bottom of the hotel's emergency stairway. Wasting no time, Grigori sought out Teresa. It was a strain to concentrate, his previous conjurations beginning to wear on him. Even with the added strength Abernathy had relinquished to him, Grigori had been forced to make excessive demands upon himself over a very short period of time. Maintaining a continuous probe of his surroundings was most taxing.

Grigori had barely begun probing the area when he sensed her. Teresa was near the back of the hotel. She was, as he had expected, not alone. There were two figures with her, two figures who weaved in and out of existence, at least as far as his probe was concerned.

Frantisek's stalkers. Grigori Nicolau grimaced and found himself almost wishing the gargoyle would make one of his violent manifestations. He was not certain that he had the wherewithal to take both men himself.

That did not mean that he would not try. Grigori inhaled, closed his eyes . . .

. . . And opened them to find himself now standing near the back of the hotel.

A long, sleek car of hunter green idled several yards to his left. A dog-faced man, identical to the stalker in the hallway, stood watch next to it, while another attempted to force Teresa inside.

The sentry noticed Grigori. The man did not pull out a weapon, but rather stared at the intruder.

Grigori's chest began to tighten. He knew instantly that it was not overexertion and that if he did not strike quickly, his heart would quite literally burst.

Focused as he was on Grigori, his opponent did not see the empty bottles that rose from a garbage bin behind him. One, two, then three of them—the bottles floated briefly above the trash receptacle, then flew as if shot from a gun at the figure beside the automobile.

Grigori's first missile narrowly missed the back of his adversary's head. The bottle crashed against the roof of the vehicle, causing the sentry to turn to see what was happening—and lose some of his own concentration.

The pressure in Grigori's chest abruptly eased, and his next missile struck with unerring accuracy. The bottle smashed against the attacker's temple, leaving in the wake of its own destruction a battered and bloody countenance. Howling, the stalker brought his hands to his ruined features, his fingers clawing at the glass shards in his eyes. The third bottle struck him alongside his head, ending his futile struggle. He collapsed to the ground, there to lay twitching.

The man holding Teresa turned at the sound of the struggle. His features were akin to his partner's. Grigori was growing tired of the nearly canine faces Frantisek's villains wore to hide their own. Yet, *dog soldiers* they truly were and, as such, they received no mercy from Grigori.

Teresa tried to slip out of the vehicle behind her captor, but the man pushed her back inside. Grigori snarled and hurried forward, already preparing his next attack. He was even less inclined to hold back against this man and his only hesitation now concerned striking at his adversary without harming Teresa.

The dog soldier raised his hand, then suddenly lowered it.

Grigori prepared a defense, but felt no attack. He slowed. Only then did he notice that the man peered past him.

A warning flashed through his mind, a belated sensing of danger behind him. Nicolau twisted around in mid-run, already aware that he was likely too late. As he dodged to the side, a sharp and familiar pain coursed through his leg. Grigori put a hand to the wound and felt a needle sticking out of his calf.

Down at the opposite end of the alley, the bound man's servant, the piggish Conrad, reloaded his long, narrow pistol. Around his neck he wore a medallion inscribed with runes and imbued with his master's energy. It would be the reason the man had gone undetected for so long.

Conrad finished loading his weapon. He walked toward the half-crouched figure of Grigori, leveling the gun as he came. Despite all the commotion, no one had yet come to see what was happening and Grigori knew that no one would. The power of Peter Frantisek was in its own way more terrible than the gargoyle's.

Grigori could not help Teresa, and in another moment, he would not even be able to help himself. His thoughts crumbled. Somewhere far away, he heard the sound of an automobile, but his eyes could see only the barrel of the gun.

Grigori shut his eyes tight, trying to will himself away.

Conrad fired.

A second shock of pain coursed through Grigori's system.

XV

ALL AROUND HER WAS DARKNESS. TERESA DVORAK TURNED in a complete circle, seeking some sliver of light, but could find none. Darkness was absolute here.

She knew that the man Grigori called Peter Frantisek had her.

Her kidnapping was still a jumble of confusing and terrifying moments, the worst being near the end, when she had watched with unbelieving eyes as Grigori had been shot down by the dire figure standing behind him. What had happened after the first shot Teresa did not know; her captor had driven off with her even as the grotesque man with the ponytail had raised his gun for a second shot.

How had they separated her from Grigori in the first place? She recalled stepping into the revolving doors, her eyes fixed on his back, when suddenly there had been a stomach-turning sense of dislocation . . . and she had found herself standing in a different room. There, two men with the same cartoonlike features seized her and dragged her out of the back of the hotel. There had been other people around, most of them employees, but not one had noticed her kidnapping, much less lifted a hand to stop it. It was unthinkable that such things could go on without anyone noticing them, but she realized now that the world of Grigori and his kind was an arrogant place where those of power did as they pleased with little fear of discovery. Frantisek and his like went blithely along, preying on the unsuspecting as they desired.

But not Grigori . . . not him. He had his moments when he frightened her, but she recognized the pain and fear behind his sometimes cold mask.

Something furred and swift ran across the toe of her shoe, scattering her thoughts and forcing her to smother a sudden scream.

"Turn to your right, Miss Dvorak."

"Where are you?" she demanded. It awed her that anger, not fear colored her reply. Her captor's audacity infuriated her.

"Turn to your right."

Frustrated, she obeyed. "How far do—"

"That will be sufficient, my dear."

A light blazed into existence. It was not a strong light, but after such absolute darkness it left Teresa first blind, then blinking to clear the spots from her vision.

When she could see well enough, she found the center of the small, dimly lit area occupied by a tall, narrow man some years older than she who sat upon a high-backed chair made of metal. The man's arms, legs, and even his waist were bound by some material that Teresa could not identify.

"Yes, I am Peter Frantisek. I know that our mutual friend Grigori Nicolau has spoken of me, although not very kindly I suppose."

She could believe that this man was a power to be reckoned with, despite his seeming helplessness. Even had she not been so familiar with his methods and resources, Teresa would have sensed the commanding force that was Frantisek. The bound man was not completely confined here, regardless of appearances. He probably knew more about what was going on in the city than the government and media combined.

Which meant that he should know one thing of great importance to her. "Where's Grigori? What've you done to him?"

A tired smile briefly escaped the dour figure. " 'Where's Grigori? What've you done with him?' . . . Very predictable, my dear Teresa. Cliches are of no importance to me at the moment. *You* are. This is a somewhat unexpected visit, I must say. My thinking must have been muddled, for I had intended them to leave you be.'' He shook his head, actually looking weary for a moment. ''My thoughts have been disjointed the past few days. The call grows stronger.'' The weariness vanished as he dismissed the last thought. ''Yes, I was hoping to leave you in the position the gargoyle had chosen for you, the better to observe, but you become too involved with Grigori's business. I thought it a shame at first, but since circumstances have brought you to me, I will make the best of things and perhaps have you finally answer some questions that have plagued my mind since you first took on custodianship of the house.''

''I don't know anything,'' Teresa snapped. She started to back into the darkness, but struck a solid wall. The solid wall had hands, strong hands. She was thrust forward to the edge of the lighted area. Teresa peered over her shoulder and recognized with horror the porcine man who had shot Grigori. Unlike the other men, he was not wearing a magical mask.

Her heart fell. If he was here, that meant that Grigori was either a prisoner like herself . . . or dead.

The bound man went on as if nothing had transpired. ''You may not know anything on the conscious level, my dear, but your subconscious holds secrets aplenty. I have always wondered why a select few were chosen to act as . . . shall we say *intermediaries* . . . between those who were called and the power behind that damnable pile of mobile stone Grigori dubbed so fittingly Frostwing. What is different about you? I have made conjectures, but have no proof to support any of them. You shall solve that dilemma.''

''I'm *not* different! I don't know anything that could help you!'' She paused, thinking. She had to offer him something. It was not that she wanted to; if she followed her impulses she would hit the man in the chair again and again until he brought Grigori back. But that was a mad, impossible hope. Her only real chance lay in making some sort of deal. Peter Frantisek was so powerful that he might release her and Grigori—*if Grigori still lived*, Teresa thought with a shudder—simply because she posed no threat to him. "I can give you all of my notes about the people who came to look at the house."

"I possess that information already, thanks to a minor servant no longer with us."

Eric. Teresa flinched. Even knowing that her coworker had willingly spied on, and then betrayed her, Teresa could not help feeling some shock and horror at word of his death. It should not have surprised her, however. Everything she had witnessed illustrated how ruthless was the world of the power. As Grigori said, the power was not to blame, but rather the men who wielded it.

She had to offer him something else. It was so damned frustrating to have to bend to Frantisek, but she did not have even the meager abilities Grigori had more than once lamented. Had she any power at all, Teresa would have tried her best to make Frantisek regret what he had done to the dark-haired stranger whom she had come to care for so much in so short a time.

There was only one prize she could yet offer. "What about William Abernathy?"

The bound man pursed his lips. He glanced past the woman in the direction of his manservant, then returned his penetrating gaze to her. "Yes, Mr. Abernathy is a point of concern. There have been contradictory and even outlandish reports concerning your unexpected meeting with him."

"I can tell you what happened." Hope flared within Teresa. What she could tell Frantisek would be of little value overall, but it would certainly interest him. "I can tell you everything I know."

"Of that I am certain." The man nodded, but the action was a signal, not an acknowledgement.

Hands seized her from behind. They did not belong to the servant, however, but rather two bright-eyed but brutish men in suits like those worn by her kidnappers. These men had true faces, not canine caricatures of humanity. Teresa preferred the masks.

She struggled, but as fit as she was, she was hardly a match for one of the men, let alone two.

"Do you know much about your bloodline, Teresa Dvorak?" asked Peter Frantisek. "Have you ever traced your roots?"

The question seemed so out of place that the captive woman could only gape in dismay and confusion.

"The tracing of one's ancestry is a passion of mine, you see. I can trace my bloodline back nearly eight hundred years. Would you believe it? Eastern Europe, in what is now Rumania. I would not be surprised to find that your roots stretch back there as well."

She still had no idea what he was talking about and so she kept silent.

"I think that it's time I learned something about *your* bloodline, my dear Teresa." He signaled to the men holding her. They dragged her even closer. For the first time, she made a detailed study of the bound man's features. Up close, Peter Frantisek was even more unsettling. Lines creased his face, age lines etched deep. He was older than she had first assumed. The skin was wrapped tight, dried out like cloth left out in the sun too long. Images of Boris Karloff in *The Mummy* came to mind.

Then, recalling how old both William Abernathy and Grigori claimed to be, she wondered if the image was that far from the truth.

The manservant came around so that he stood almost, but not quite in front of her. In one hand he held a small pendulum bearing a brilliant gemstone, perhaps an emerald. The stone had a mesmerizing effect when she stared at it, so much so that Teresa had to will herself not to even glance in its direction.

In his other hand the piggish man held a blunt, ebony blade with tiny marks etched into it from pommel to point. The sight of the knife caused her to renew her struggles, but the thugs held her tight.

"It will not hurt, I assure you. You may even find it interesting." A smile crept across the dry features, a smile that in no way softened Teresa Dvorak's fears. "We may discover that we are related—a distinct possibility, I might add."

The pendulum started to swing without any aid from the figure holding it. The moving gemstone drew her gaze. Once snared, she could not look away.

"You will tell me all, dear Teresa . . . even things you never realized you knew." The bound man's voice echoed in her head. "I must know who and what you are, and how you fit into the game."

As she drifted into unconsciousness, Teresa thought she heard laughter. It did not sound like the sort of laugh Peter Frantisek would utter, if he was even one to laugh.

For some reason, it reminded her of the gargoyle.

He was alive.

The realization both thrilled and daunted Grigori Nicolau. Although he had come to appreciate life of late, he assumed at first that his being alive also meant that he was in the hands of the bound man, who certainly did not intend to let him go a second time.

One eye opened, then the other.

Grigori stared at his surroundings. He had never seen the place before, yet knew instantly it could not be part of the sanctum of Peter Frantisek. The room was a blur, but the whiteness of it provoked some image, some splintered memory. Grigori tried to rise, but his arms and legs resisted, as if something held them down. His ears detected the quiet strains of music, some bland piece of modernistic misconceptions that would put him back to sleep if he listened too long.

His eyes began to focus and as they did, both the memory and the knowledge of what this white room represented became clear. It was a hospital room, not that different from one he had occupied in Berlin just after the rise of the Reich. An automobile accident had put him in jeopardy; the gaping crowds and watching officials had forced him to accept the offer of medical treatment from the man who had struck him, a mid-level SS officer. He received the best treatment possible, for his health would reflect on the reputation of the officer. But his injury healed itself at its usual fantastic rate, which brought on the scrutiny of the Reich doctors and scientists.

It had cost Grigori every bit of power to remove himself from the hospital and erase the knowledge from their minds. He had been forced to damage the memories of six men. Although most had been unworthy of sympathy, he had despised himself for his actions for some time to come.

That had been the beginning of the end of his stay in the Fatherland. It was not that he had feared death; how could he, after all? There were things worse than death, however, and there was no trusting Frostwing to step in before things grew too terrible. The dark side of the power had been growing strong even then. The power wielders left in the Reich after his departure were either those with an interest in the madness or fools. Grigori Nicolau had desired contact with neither group.

He tried to rise, but again his body would not respond properly. He gazed down at himself and saw that he had been strapped down to the bed. There was also a peculiar tingling coursing through his extremities, which Nicolau belatedly recognized as lingering aftereffects of the needles Conrad had shot him with.

As the malaise cleared, Grigori pieced together what must have happened. The brutish manservant had shot him not once but twice, yet Grigori had retained just enough sense and will to remove himself from the area. He had not been thinking clearly enough to choose a specific direction and so the power had cast him down somewhere at random.

He was fortunate to be in one piece . . . or perhaps he had only recently mended. He might have been in the hospital for quite some time . . . but that was not very likely, for Frantisek would have located him long before. No, no more than a day could have passed, which was still entirely too much. If Frantisek did not know where he was yet, he certainly would before long. His system of eyes and ears was far too extensive. Grigori had to leave immediately.

The bonds were no trouble. A glance in their direction and they were undone. He had no idea why he had been bound to the bed, but he hoped he had not revealed his power to whoever had found him. With Frostwing's intervention no longer a given, Grigori could not be certain as to what might have happened.

Rising proved to be far more of a battle than freeing himself. His reactions were still sluggish and unpredictable. Twice he tried to grip the safety rail surrounding the bed and failed. The third attempt succeeded, but then his left leg proved reluctant to follow the right over the edge. With effort, Nicolau finally got it over. He had to pause for several minutes before he dared trust the legs for standing. Nicolau also dealt with the small monitoring device someone had attached to him. A quick touch of the power caused the device to send routine information even after he detached the leads and placed them on the bed.

His concentration was strong enough that he was able to

monitor the halls outside. No guard stood at the door, which probably meant that his appearance had not been overly dramatic. Most likely he had landed in some alley or even in one of the parks, perhaps Lincoln. Fortune had smiled upon him, at least in this matter.

Grigori rubbed the leg that had been shot. Standing on it, he was now better reminded of the pain he had felt. One needle should have proven sufficient, but had not. Was it because he had taken in Abernathy's essence, that part of the man that had seemed a part of him as well? That was possible. If so, he had something of an advantage now, but at the very most it was a slim one. Frantisek might already know about Abernathy and what had happened. There would be little enough for his men to discover in the dead power wielder's room, but the bound man was thorough.

Frantisek also had Teresa. Grigori hoped that she would not be foolish and refuse to tell her captor what she knew; Frantisek was certain to get the information from her one way or another.

A closet to one side of the room held his clothing and personal effects. To his mild surprise, everything was there. Had his money or watch been stolen, Grigori would not have been surprised. He replaced the items in their proper places, then reached into one particular pocket.

He found nothing. The scrap of paper that he had thrust into the pocket while still in Abernathy's room was gone.

He had lost Peter Frantisek's address.

Grigori could only conclude that the note had fallen out of his pocket, either behind the hotel or near where he had materialized. If the latter, then the unknown Samaritan or Samaritans had probably not noticed it during his rescue. Why should they? What was a piece of paper compared to a life in danger?

Grigori knew the answer to that: it was invaluable if its loss meant the life of someone far more deserving than him.

A second, more thorough search of each pocket failed. The note was most definitely gone. How was he to find Teresa?

Teresa! This is my doing! Gods, I'm so sorry!

The exertion combined with his anxiety, overwhelming him for the moment. Grigori grew dizzy. Closing his eyes briefly, he leaned against the edge of the bed, trying to regain his senses.

"You know, old friend, you always get lost when I'm not there to guide you . . ."

Grigori stumbled away from the bed. As he backed against the closet, Nicolau saw who had spoken to him from the direction of the bed.

Frostwing perched on the narrow rail, clinging to it with little care. His wings stretched, somehow missing the equipment nearby. The grin was there, of course. The grin was always there, but this time it seemed more . . . expressive. This time, Frostwing was truly smiling.

Which informed Grigori Nicolau that his tormentor knew what had happened.

"I have no time for you now, demon." Grigori purposely looked away, pretending to adjust the fit of his coat.

"You had best make time, my pretty friend," hissed the stone figure. When Grigori glared at him, Frostwing ducked down a bit, as if afraid of being struck. His demeanor, however, was anything but subservient. "Not that you need worry about the time we spend chatting, dear, dear Grigori. Here, in my realm, a thousand years could pass by while, in yours, not even a second dies."

What did the gargoyle want of him? This was leading to something, but even with his newfound mastery of the creature, Grigori doubted that he could force the truth out.

"Let me tell you a story," began the gray form.

Nicolau started to speak, then clamped his mouth shut.

"Once there was a man of great power," continued

Frostwing without missing a beat. His shadowy eyes, though, noted the human's aborted objections; a touch of wry amusement tainted the first words. "This man had many ambitions, some of which the less continental might have termed *evil*. Oh, he did not gain all his power immediately. First, like any young boy, he had to be taught to use what gifts he already had."

Grigori found himself fidgeting. Was this story going to include the entire life history of the character? He wanted the damned gargoyle to get to the point. Unbidden, words began to tumble into his mind, words whose meaning he still did not understand but whose power was something even the dreaded gargoyle could not deny. Nicolau swallowed hard and forced them back. Something told him that Teresa would best be served by his listening, however much the storytelling grated on him.

Seemingly oblivious to the battle raging within his audience, Frostwing went on. "As any good lad should do, he found himself one who could tutor him." Frostwing cocked his head to one side, his tone mocking. "A fine sterling elder with some touch of the power, a man who could 'show him the ropes,' as they say these days. The lad learned much, so much in fact, that his skills and will soon outstripped his teacher's. Of course, only one path lay open to him at that point." The gargoyle leaned toward Grigori. "The lad killed his teacher and seized the elder's knowledge for himself."

"What does this have to do with anything?"

"Over the years, he continued to seek out knowledge from others," rambled the winged monster, ignoring the question. "He disposed of his tutors and those others who interfered with his quest for knowledge. For some reason this caused a stirring among others. They resented his draconian, but undeniably successful method of bettering himself. Can you imagine that?"

"How narrow-minded of them," snarled Grigori. Once more the temptation to use the mysterious words rose. Again, something urged him to hold back.

"I certainly agree." A rasping chuckle escaped the creature. Frostwing paused to preen. It was a ridiculous sight, but now the wanderer knew that his tormentor was baiting him, waiting to see if Grigori could hold his temper long enough to hear the end of the tale.

At last, the stone gargoyle returned to his story. "It is said that with great power comes great responsibility. That maxim certainly held true with the lad, now a man of truly great power. He was very responsible. From the lessers around his domain, he usurped their undeniably chaotic attempt to control their own lives and reorganized their existences under his own iron guidelines. That most of them failed to appreciate the effort this cost was their own fault, I assure you. In order to prevent a much more deadly danger, he experimented often with his power. He discovered its limitations and critical points. After all, too many wielders of the power did not understand it, which had often led to disaster. The man was so determined to understand the power that it became necessary for him to volunteer test subjects. They, being lessers, did not comprehend the reason for their trials, but I can assure you, my dear Grigori, that the man was certain that it was all quite necessary to further his research."

No longer did Grigori Nicolau think to stop the tale. He had met several who had sought to follow in this character's footsteps. Was this something to do with Frantisek? Was that what the gargoyle was trying to relay? Why not simply tell Grigori, then?

Perhaps that was not possible. Perhaps something prevented Frostwing from being straightforward.

For the first time, Grigori recognized the many tales his tormentor had spun as something more than fiction. He was almost willing to swear that in some ways, Frostwing was trying to warn him. Yet, there was no denying that the gargoyle was also the bane of his endless existence.

Frostwing knew that he had finally won over his audience, for he spoke with more relish now. "Some who wielded power, unfortunately, did not comprehend the scope or importance of the man's work. They decided—can you believe it, dear Grigori?—that his thirst for knowledge was an abomination. They gathered together, afraid, no doubt, to challenge him one on one." Despite the last statement, the gargoyle's tone of contempt sounded forced. "Then, when they deemed their number sufficient to take *one* man, they journeyed to the mountains where his sanctum lay, a place he chose, no doubt, for its serenity and beauty. A place of quiet contemplation."

From the way Frostwing spoke, Grigori knew that the mountain stronghold had been anything but a place of quiet contemplation. He shuddered, thinking of the cries of those chosen for the man's experiments. He imagined walking through the dark, foreboding passages, and recalled the evil tower that jutted up on the eastern—

The images and emotions flashing through his mind were not the creations of fancy.

They were memories.

Grigori tried to focus on them, to make sense of them, but a sudden movement of the dread golem's wings broke his concentration and drew his attention back to the winged figure perched on the bed.

Frostwing had stopped talking and was watching the human with what was possibly mild amusement.

Nicolau waited for the monster to continue the tale, but Frostwing continued to simply stare. Grigori finally asked, "What happened when they confronted him? Did they defeat him?"

The gargoyle looked down and ran his claws lightly across

the pillow on the bed, shredding it with almost no effort. At last he responded, "Oh, they won the battle, if that's what you're asking."

Grigori knew that Frostwing was not telling him everything. He was used to such evasions from his tormentor, but this time he pressed for the truth. "What happened to the man?"

A momentary glitter might have flashed in Frostwing's shadowy eyes. Certainly Grigori saw *something* there. As for an answer, the gargoyle replied, "He appeared to have died at his enemies' hands. A tale of morality, wouldn't you say, Grigori?"

That was it? That was the end of the story? Grigori frowned. Too many holes. Frostwing was hinting at something. Grigori assumed the story to be true more or less. It also related to his present situation somehow. But how?

He appeared to have died at his enemies' hands. The statement pointed in too many directions for Grigori's liking. If the man had only *appeared* to have died, did that mean that he had not?

"You must hate yourself." The words were uttered by the gargoyle not as a comment, but as a command. He had said something similar before. The words still meant nothing to Grigori and only served to further confuse his already jumbled thoughts.

Grigori took a step toward his adversary. "I'm tired of riddles, Frostwing. Tired of the game you keep playing with me. I want answers that I can understand—"

"You don't know what it is like to be truly *tired*, dear, dear, Grigori!" the creature rumbled. Wings spread full as the gargoyle hissed. Then, just as abruptly as the outburst had come, it ended. Frostwing was once more a parody of pleasantness and concern. "But if you are so very tired, then permit me to see you on your way."

"You are not going to leave yet!" It was the first time that

Grigori had ever desired his nemesis to stay. The gargoyle knew where Peter Frantisek's sanctum was hidden. With that knowledge, Nicolau would be able to save time and strength, both of which had become almost priceless commodities.

This time Grigori spoke the mysterious words consciously, but before he could utter more than the first, the gargoyle interrupted with a sharp, sardonic laugh that made Grigori pause and stare. The laugh did not mock Grigori Nicolau, but rather the winged devil himself.

A huge clock materialized in the midst of the room. It resembled an old pocket watch, save that the face moved and not the hands, which were pointed at four o'clock.

Frostwing pointed at the timepiece. "You're late, my old friend! The game is almost over! Just time for one last move before the finale, hmmm?" The smile was there. "Time to wake up and see things as they are, don't you think?"

Grigori *did* wake up, then.

He blinked away sleep. He was not in a hospital room. He was not even indoors.

A house, old but still elegant, stood before him, two similar ones to each side. Narrow yards and high metal fences divided the structures. The quality of care indicated that this was an affluent neighborhood, on par with the one containing the house over whose gate the gargoyle perched. Yet this neighborhood definitely lay closer to the heart of the city.

Grigori leaned against a lamppost, looking as if he were waiting for a bus. A few other people walked along the street, but evidently none of them had noticed a grown man suddenly materialize among them.

He looked left and right, trying to understand why he now stood here. Only when his gaze returned to the houses did he realize just what Frostwing had done for him.

Grigori stood in front of Peter Frantisek's citadel.

XVI

From where Grigori stood, the house looked innocuous. He could sense neither the presence of the bound man
nor that of Teresa, but he knew that they had to be inside.

As if to confirm his thoughts, the front door opened. A
figure emerged, a man who bore a great resemblance to the
dog-faced hunters. Grigori wondered what Frantisek's neighbors made of the reclusive figure next door. Perhaps they
were oblivious to the peculiar things occurring just on the
other side of the fence. Perhaps the bound man exerted his
influence over the nearest houses. It made sense to do so.

There was no indication that Grigori's presence had been
noted by those within. Whether or not Frantisek knew he
was there, Grigori did not care. His rival would know
before long.

He positioned himself near a tall tree. He was thankful
that this was one of the older neighborhoods where time
had allowed the trees to grow into titans; it enabled him to
shield himself from sight without wasting more energy
than was necessary. It was doubtful that the underling
would have noticed him, anyway, his attention fixed on a
familiar automobile parked in the driveway. It was the same
vehicle that Grigori had seen near the house the gargoyle
protected.

He watched the villain climb inside. As with the stalker
in the hall and Frantisek's manservant in the back of the
hotel, Nicolau could not sense the presence of the figure in

the vehicle. If what Grigori suspected were true, there might be a way for him to enter the house surreptitiously. That would be worth some time and effort . . . so he hoped.

As the automobile backed up, the front gate swung open. Grigori was puzzled by Frantisek's flaunting of his power, but then he realized that it was only an automated gate. No doubt Frantisek could afford many luxuries.

The vehicle pulled out onto the street, the gate closing behind it. Grigori watched as the minion drove away from the house. He waited patiently as the automobile dwindled from sight. Only when the car signaled to turn a distant corner did he finally act.

It took the driver a moment to realize that the seat next to him was no longer empty. His features shifted to the familiar doglike face Grigori had come to know far too well.

"Who the hell—?" was as far as Nicolau allowed the man to get. The next instant, the driver groaned and passed out, a victim of the full fury of Grigori's power. Uncertain as to how Frantisek shielded his men, he had no choice but to strike hard. Fortunately, his attack had proved more than adequate, a fact which boosted his confidence. Grigori could have succeeded using only a fraction of the power he had spent on the man. That would be good to know when dealing with the others.

Despite being driverless, the vehicle continued to travel smoothly. It was a small matter for Grigori to keep the machine on its proper course while he dealt with more important things. Reaching over, he searched the villain for the source of his shield. That proved simple enough; it was a medallion similar to what the manservant had worn. Grigori removed it, studied its design, then slipped it over his head. The medallion was a basic device, which did not surprise him. Why waste precious energy protecting underlings? The man Conrad was a different story. He wore a more complex item, one that bestowed benefits Grigori had only barely been able to

sense. The piggish manservant would be a problem almost
as great as Peter Frantisek himself.

Reaching forward, he touched the unconscious man's face.
The cartoonish features faded away to be replaced by the
rather bland ones that were truly the driver's own. Grigori
then touched his own face.

When he looked in the mirror, the other man's face stared
back. It was only an illusion and not a difficult one at that,
but it had been many years since Grigori had used this ability.
The illusion would not long fool someone like Frantisek, but
it would prove sufficient for tricking his minions.

That left only the disposal of the driver. Grigori contemplated sending the man to the hospital, but decided that might
place the employees and patients at too much risk. No, there
were other places he could send this one. He glanced out the
window and spotted a closed business that would do quite
nicely.

The limp form vanished, and Grigori slid into his seat. He
took a deep breath. The Chicago police would have many
questions for an unconscious man discovered in a bank vault.
The open vault door would further pique their curiosity. Grigori suspected that the police department was already familiar
with the driver, which would make any explanation the man
could muster even less plausible.

The driver had been fortunate. A hundred years ago, Grigori Nicolau might have contemplated a more permanent way
of dealing with him. Time and Teresa Dvorak had changed
Grigori.

He turned the vehicle around and returned to Frantisek's
house. It was still impossible to sense anything within, but
Nicolau refused to back off now. Teresa had to be inside.

There was a moment of worry when the gate did not open,
but then Grigori noted the speaker and button to the side. He
opened the window and pressed the button. No one responded, but the gate began to swing aside.

The automobile he parked in the same spot from which it had been taken. Grigori tried not to tense as he neared the bound man's sanctum. To calm himself, he conjured Vivaldi's *Four Seasons* in his mind. The music would not distract him; he had trained himself long ago to function on more than one level.

A large figure who could have been the driver's twin opened the door and eyed him dispassionately. "Why're you back?"

"Something I need." Grigori coughed. At the same time, he sent a very gentle probe to influence the man's thoughts. Grigori wanted the guard to hear the voice of the driver and to accept what was being said.

The sentry nodded and stepped aside. Grigori walked past him, hoping that the other underling would not tell him that he was going in the wrong direction.

Fortunately, that was not the case. The sentry closed the door, then took up a position near it. He no longer paid any attention to Grigori.

It took Grigori only a short time to realize that there was something wrong with his perspective. The house twisted at peculiar angles and, although he could not verify it, Grigori suspected that the building's interior was much too large compared to its exterior. The hallway still stretched before him, yet he had already covered a distance that should have brought him to the back door.

He decided that the dimensions of the interior were of no concern now. Teresa was his reason for daring entry. Despite a probe, Grigori Nicolau could still neither sense her nor the presence of his adversary, Peter Frantisek. *Have they departed his sanctum?* That was doubtful. Frantisek could not travel much. Perhaps, the protective spells the bound man had woven prevented thorough scrutiny.

He did not even bother with the upper floors. There was only one place in the house that could have held the dank, dark chamber that Nicolau had occupied during his brief stay as the bound man's guest. That was the basement. All he had to do was find the door.

That task proved easier than he expected, so much so that Grigori wondered if he was entering a trap. He reached for the knob, then paused just before his fingers touched the brass. Something did not feel right. For the first time since he had entered, Grigori sensed some tracing of the power . . . and all of that was centered on the door frame.

With careful precision, he inspected what lay behind the door.

A solid wall? Grigori probed again, just to be certain, and found exactly the same thing. There was indeed a wall behind the door. As best he could estimate, it was several feet thick. Someone had taken a great amount of care in filling up the stairway. What lay beyond the wall was unclear. Grigori sensed flickers of activity and the presence of several living creatures, but he could not identify them as human. They might even be Frantisek's rats.

That did not explain the door frame. Why place such power into and around the door when the stairway had been blocked? The entrance was useless.

Or was it? Grigori studied the medallion he had stolen from the driver. Perhaps there were more uses to this talisman than he had first assumed.

On a hunch, he opened the door. His first view brought him nothing but disappointment. The wall was indeed solid and, in fact, looked to be made from concrete. Then the dark man looked closer at the medallion. A very dim glow radiated from the artifact, a glow that pulsed in sync with the power emanating from the door frame.

Grigori reached out with his left hand and touched the wall.

His hand went through.

He walked closer, allowing the rest of his hand, then his forearm to sink into the wall.

There was a door after all . . . and Grigori had the key. He was grateful now that he had taken the medallion. Without it he might not have gained entry.

Taking a deep breath, Grigori pushed through.

There was no stairway. Grigori Nicolau plunged into utter darkness, but the experience lasted only a few brief moments before he noticed a dim, blue thread of light that led from the medallion into the darkness. *A guide rope, Frantisek? Is this how your dog soldiers find their way to you?*

Or did Frantisek know that Grigori was coming?

There was only one way to find out. He followed the blue thread. Grigori glanced briefly back and saw that the thread extended for several yards before disappearing. There was a way back then, at least for the moment.

The path continued on for much farther than should have been possible for the basement of the house, but Grigori was becoming accustomed to such things where his foe was concerned. Those who wielded power sometimes had the skill to play with reality, to make a mockery of the natural laws that dictated finite space. He was not surprised that Frantisek had such abilities.

"I did not summon you."

A light came on.

Peter Frantisek stared back at Grigori from the confines of his chair. Though bound from hand to foot, he still sent chills up and down Grigori's spine.

"Well? Speak up, man. Why are you disturbing my ruminations at this time?"

He does not recognize me! He cannot see through my poor illusion! Of course, not only was Grigori stronger this time, he had Frantisek's talisman to aid him. The irony was not lost on the disguised intruder.

What could he say to prolong the facade and still learn something about Teresa? Trying to sound like one of the bound man's gruff minions, Grigori finally replied, "I think I saw the woman's companion, master."

His comment brought no sudden accusation concerning his false identity. In fact, the figure strapped to the metal chair seemed quite pleased to hear his answer.

"At last! Where has he been? How has he managed to conceal himself from me?"

Frantisek's frustration intrigued Grigori. They had had no luck in their search for him, then. He had somehow evaded human agents, rodent watchers, and no doubt the probes of Frantisek himself. How could that be?

How else save through the intervention of the gargoyle? What sort of game was Frostwing playing?

"He was by the Art Institute," Nicolau answered at last, picking a location at random.

This perturbed his adversary. "The Art Institute? So public a place as that? He is either more clever and adaptable than I assumed or completely mad." The piercing blue eyes, so like and yet unlike Grigori's own, focused on the false acolyte. "You are certain of this?"

It was not difficult to pretend nervousness under that stare. "It looked like him. I tried to follow, but he disappeared."

"That might explain something," Peter Frantisek mused, looking into the darkness to his side. "He must be hopping from location to location one step ahead of me. I didn't think he had the strength in him. Curious, though."

Grigori said nothing, although the temptation was there to ask just what it was that his rival found so curious.

He was fortunate; Frantisek answered his question with his next words. "I am surprised that he has not come for the woman by now. I thought he cared for her."

At the mention of Teresa, Nicolau decided to risk speaking. "It may be that he'll still come, master. If he is able to evade your eyes and ears, he might even be with her now."

The bound man eyed Grigori in such a way that he felt certain he had overstepped the bounds of his role. Then Frantisek glanced away again, this time to his right. His eyes narrowed. Grigori sensed the other's power.

Something flashed into existence. Grigori almost blurted out Teresa's name when he realized that it was she. A fortunate thing that he did not; for the woman he saw was only a conjured image.

She sat in a dimly lit area, shaken but otherwise seeming unharmed. Her face showed signs of weariness, but nothing to indicate that she had been mistreated . . . at least physically.

"A reasonable suggestion on the surface, but, no, she is still mi—"

Grigori tore his gaze away from the image to see why Frantisek had stopped speaking. The bound man was not looking at him, but rather at some point skyward. Frantisek's hands shook.

At the same time, in his own mind, a voice began to speak. It sounded like his own, but there was something beguiling about it.

There is nothing I can do here, nothing at all. My only hope is the house. There I can find the power to deal with Frantisek. I should go there now. I have nothing to fear. The house will solve all my problems . . .

The bound man's strained voice cut through the fog in Grigori's mind. "Conrad! I need you!"

Grigori Nicolau struggled to regain his composure. Perhaps Frantisek might be too preoccupied now, but his manservant would be alert enough to wonder who this underling was who suffered as his master did. Conrad surely understood about the house and how it summoned its victims.

He had to act fast. With Frantisek caught up in his struggle, Grigori dared use his power to seek out Teresa. She was nearby. Very close.

In the back of Grigori's mind, the voice continued. The

words did not affect him so much as the tone. There was something insistent about the tone . . .

He found her before the call could seize control of him again. Grigori wasted no time. Conrad could only be seconds away. He teleported, dropping the illusion at the same time so that Teresa would recognize him immediately.

The darkness became a dimly lit chamber, a tiny room furnished with bed and table, but nothing more. One weak bulb offered the only illumination.

Teresa sat curled on the bed, her eyes closed and her arms wrapped tightly around her torso. She was not asleep. Her eyes opened a moment after Grigori appeared.

She gasped before either of them could muffle the sound. Grigori cursed himself for not giving her some sort of warning. What sort of response had he expected? She could hardly have known he was coming. For all she knew, he might have been—

"Dead!" she whispered, leaping from the bed and rushing into his arms. "I thought you were dead!"

Grigori could only stand there as she held him, his emotions a mixture of pleasure, sorrow, and embarrassment.

Teresa lifted her gaze to his face. A wan smile played at her lips. "He wouldn't say what had happened to you so . . . I expected the worst. I hoped that you were alive!"

"I escaped by accident." He quickly explained about the shots and how he managed somehow to transport himself away. Then, before Teresa could say or ask anything else, Grigori quickly concluded, "We have to leave *now*. Frantisek is being summoned by the house. While he is fighting that call we have the opportunity to slip away unnoticed."

Her expression was such that Nicolau paused.

"This call," she began, her eyes a bit wild. "Is it like a voice in your head, a voice that sounds like your own?"

As she asked, the sinister voice in Grigori's own mind grew more adamant. It tried to convince him that the only place the two of them would be safe was the house. There was a hypnotic quality to it, one that—

He blinked and forced himself to focus on the present. Grigori started to answer Teresa's question, then saw with horror that her eyes had taken on a distant look. He knew without a doubt she was hearing the call of the house.

"Teresa!" The fearful power wielder shook her hard.

Teresa stared at Grigori, renewed terror in her eyes. "That was it, wasn't it? That was what you were talking about. It *wanted* me, Grigori. It *had* me."

"It is all right, Teresa," he replied in a quieter voice. "As long as we are together, we are stronger than it is."

He hoped that was true.

Her confidence in him was astonishing. She nodded and managed a smile. Then she looked around her prison cell and asked, "How do we get out of here? Can you just spirit us away?"

"It will be difficult, but that is what I intend." The voice continued to whisper in his mind, making it difficult to think, much less perform such a strenuous deed.

Nonetheless, he tried.

It was like buffeting his head against a wall. Grigori nearly gave up after the first few moments, so great was the strain. He felt as if he were being pulled slowly in every direction, then twisted around and around just for good measure. It was all he could do to keep from screaming in pain. Yet still Grigori fought. There was no choice, he told himself, regardless of what the voice in his head insisted.

Teresa took his hand, offering her support. Suddenly, strength poured into Grigori. He could not understand this new energy until he recalled that he was once more actively linked with Teresa. Her touch amplified his abilities.

The wall began to peel away. Nicolau felt a tug. The room grew murky.

The cell became an elegant sitting room. Shelves of books

covered every wall. A rich leather chair was positioned next to a mahogany table, and on one side of the room stood a massive roll-top desk.

A man sat at the desk. He had been scribbling in a book, but turned as if somehow sensing the intrusion. The man, a very short, bespectacled figure of elder years, opened his mouth with the obvious intention of giving alarm.

A large wad of paper, propelled by Grigori's power, thrust itself into the man's mouth, stifling the sound. Stunned, he tried to pull the page free.

Grigori did not give him the opportunity. A heavy tome flew from one of the shelves and struck the man hard on the forehead. Groaning, he slumped back in the chair, causing it to spin in a half circle.

"Where are we?" Teresa finally dared whisper.

Grigori did not answer her, instead stepping just far enough away from her to study the unconscious form. The man would live, suffering only a bruise for his troubles. From his appearance and the number of accounting sheets scattered around the desk, Grigori assumed the man was Frantisek's bookkeeper. Someone had to do the mundane work involved in keeping the bound man's activities lucrative.

He eyed the huge desk. Grigori needed to hide the unconscious man, but there were no closets in this room. However, the bookkeeper was a tiny man and the desk was one of the huge ones from the earlier part of the century. There were no shelves on top, which meant that the roll top stretched over a very large, empty area. It was just possible that there would be space enough to do what he planned.

"Give me your hand again, please, Teresa."

She did. He stared at the body, imposing his will on it.

The body disappeared . . . to reform atop the desk. The rolling panel slid down, sealing the unconscious man inside. It was fortunate that his victim had not been a taller man.

"He will be all right," the power wielder informed his

companion. His thoughts then returned to her earlier question. "As to where we are, I am afraid that we have only journeyed as far as the upper floors of Peter Frantisek's house."

He did not need verification to know that what he said was true. The design of the room was too similar to what Grigori recalled from the hallway.

"Can't we get out?"

"I will try again. Hold my hand tight and let yourself follow my will."

She moved closer, putting her other hand on their clasped ones. Grigori repeated the gesture, then smiled at her.

Once more he battered at the wall of power that Frantisek had wrapped around his house. It was weaker, but then so was he, even with Teresa to aid him.

Grigori felt the barrier begin to collapse. He closed his eyes and pushed harder. The time for slowly peeling away things was over; they had to escape.

The barrier fell.

The familiar sensation of displacement that marked a successful attempt washed over Grigori.

They were almost away when something reached out and snared the two of them, dragging them from the ether and tossing them blindly to another destination.

Their surroundings became a dark chamber in which the only light source hung before them. The bulb was close enough to momentarily blind them.

"My dear Mr. Nicolau. You're more enterprising than I would have expected." The statement was punctuated by the squeals of many agitated rats.

Peter Frantisek, hands still shaking, glared at them from his chair. The manservant Conrad had a pair of guns pointed at them, one of which fired bullets.

The bound man leaned back. He looked pale but satisfied. "I hope that you weren't thinking of leaving just yet."

Conrad raised the needle gun and aimed.

XVII

"No, Conrad, that will not be necessary. You may lower the guns."

The ponytailed acolyte frowned but obeyed. All the while, his eyes remained fixed on Grigori's. The dark man had seen hunting dogs with similar looks in their eyes.

"As for you, Grigori, you may remove that trinket you appropriated from my man. It will do you no good any more."

Nicolau did, only briefly contemplating using it as a projectile. He held out the medallion to the manservant, but Conrad did not so much as move a finger.

"It will suffice to drop it," remarked the bound man.

Grigori did. However, before the medallion had a chance to strike the floor, it burned to ashes. The ash dissolved, leaving no trace.

"You are more than I first imagined, Grigori, more than I could have ever imagined. Dear Teresa here," he nodded politely to her, ignoring her glare, "told me much about you. Her perspective was, of course, a little limited, but I gained quite a picture of you. A surprising man you are." Again he glanced at Teresa. "But then she, too, has her surprises."

Grigori's look of puzzlement was matched by Teresa's. He turned on Frantisek, the edge in his voice growing sharp as he spoke. "What did you do to her?"

"Merely dredged up the past—something that I am eager to do with you. I am especially interested in two things: your background and the fate of a certain Mr. William Abernathy,

who *also* appears to have been a bit more than I thought him
to be.'' A sudden scowl darkened the tired but triumphant
features of the bound man. ''My concentration is not what
it once was. The house and that damned gargoyle call to me
as they never have before. Part of the blame for that can be
attributed to you, my dear Grigori. Your arrival in Chicago
started something. You may even know what that something
is.''

''I do not.''

''You'll pardon me if I verify that for myself. I've learned
enough fascinating things from Miss Dvorak to know that
nothing should be taken at face value any more.''

''I don't know what you're talking about!'' she snapped.
Her hand clutched Grigori's tighter.

Conrad actually smiled briefly. For some reason, the smile
reminded Grigori of a hungry bear's. Everything about the
manservant seemed to relate to animals, Grigori noted. Under
other conditions, the captive power wielder would have been
most interested in the forces that had formed such a creature
as this.

The bound man also smiled. ''You were a little out of it
during our chat, my dear. You know, you have the most
fascinating bloodline. Now that I've seen it, your part in this
macabre, centuries-long game makes a great deal more sense.
Did you know that her father was a police officer in this
city, Grigori? A patrol officer. His route took him near the
neighborhood of the house.''

Teresa said nothing, too anxious and confused to argue,
but Grigori began to understand what Frantisek was hinting.
Teresa dealt with the house now. Her father had done the
same during his prime. There were probably others, all blue-
eyed like her and her parent, who had connections to that
foul place.

Guardians. Perhaps not an exact description, but the closest one that Grigori could derive. Unwilling and unknowing guardians. They were linked with the ones who came in search of the house, yet were also isolated. A police officer familiar with the area. A real estate agent marketing the oddly unmarketable house. Perhaps a mailman before that.

But why? For what ultimate purpose?

Fascination nearly overwhelmed Grigori's other emotions. He wanted Peter Frantisek to continue. A few things finally made some sense, and it was clear that the bound man seated in the high-backed chair likely knew far more than he had revealed.

It also seemed that Frantisek *wanted* to tell him more. Perhaps because Grigori was the only other person who could understand much of the strange business.

"After so long, everything is coming together, dear Grigori. Do you know how many years I have waited for this conjunction? I watched the riots of the '60s. I followed the rise and fall of Colisimo, Torrio, and then Capone." His eyes grew bright. "As a young man freshly into his power, I watched as Chicago, my city, burned to the ground."

"You *can't* be that old," interrupted Teresa, but then she glanced at Grigori and quieted.

The Chicago Fire. Grigori recalled from one of his books that the fire had taken place some time in the 1870s. That meant that Peter Frantisek was a century and a half old, perhaps a little more. An infant when compared with Nicolau, but Frantisek had quite obviously dedicated himself to his craft much of that time.

"I can be that old, as you truly know, Miss Dvorak." The bound man tilted his head as he studied his other captive. "A strange thing happened when I began to question the lady about you. She answered the first and most superficial questions readily enough, but then, as the questions probed deeper into your past, Teresa found herself unable to answer.

Even under a compulsion." A dangerous glint appeared in Frantisek's eyes. "A fog so thoroughly enshrouded her mind that even *I* could not penetrate it. I have also discovered, through various other sources, that you are a man with a very short trail behind you. You appear not to exist before arriving in the States. Even that meager evidence required my greatest resources. The strange thing is, you don't appear to really attempt to hide yourself. You just do not exist."

"I am a private man."

"I understand your sort of privacy, I think. Abernathy was a fool, you know, despite his flair for certain things."

The shift in topic caught Grigori offguard for a moment, but he was able to keep the surprise from showing.

"He was like the two of us, wasn't he?" Frantisek went on. "He knew more than the others. I was able to conclude that from what little your companion was able to relay to me about your meeting. He knew about the house. Knew about the gargoyle, too, most likely."

Grigori was pleased to see that Frantisek could make wrong assumptions. It was an indication that the bound man was not so infallible after all. Let him think what he wanted to about Abernathy. His probing was giving Grigori a chance to learn a little, too.

His captor did not seem put out by Grigori's failure to respond. Frantisek leaned forward as best he could. "How much do you remember? Whose line are you?"

This time Nicolau let slip a hint of uncertainty. Frantisek noted the fleeting look and smiled wider. Grigori could not decide whose smile was more disconcerting, the master's or his acolyte's.

"You don't know everything after all, do you? You know the gargoyle well enough, and that says something. Do you have dreams, Grigori? When we talked with one another the first time we met, I thought you as insignificant as the others, but now I feel I did us both a discourtesy." Frantisek sank back in his chair. "Do you dream of a mountain sanctum? Do you dream of the man who lived within? I dream of him often, you know. More, I dream of how he foresaw his betrayal and how he sought to cheat his enemies of his death."

The story that Frostwing told me? How true was it? Peter Frantisek obviously wanted to tell his own version, and Grigori was not about to stop him.

Yet, the narrow figure did not continue. He collected himself, acting almost embarrassed for how much weakness he had already revealed.

"I am growing maudlin in my old age. Conrad, if I should conduct myself so again, you are commanded to reprimand me."

Eyes and weapons still on the two prisoners, the porcine figure replied, "Yes, Mr. Frantisek."

Returning his attention to the two, the bound man said, "I am wasting time. The house is nearing the culmination of the spell, and the gargoyle's master is preparing to receive the centuries' reward his stone lackey has toiled to create. He has made a mistake, however. He could not realize that there would come one with enough memory intact to foil his scheme. I know what the master planned and how he used his own enemies, in the midst of his death struggle, to guarantee himself victory."

Little of what Peter Frantisek said made any sense to Grigori—and yet it did. It sounded familiar. Were the memories to which Frantisek so cryptically referred among those he had garnered from Abernathy? It would make some sense and yet . . .

The bound man was staring intently at Teresa now. "I thank the gods that I didn't take you into the fold sooner. Had I known your place in this, had I known the place of any of the guardians, I would have recognized your value."

"I still don't know what you're talking about!" Teresa tried to push herself closer to Grigori. She was not a timid woman, Nicolau knew, but this was far beyond anything her life experience had prepared her for. He wondered what had befallen her during her captivity, then decided that it did not matter. Frantisek would be made to pay for everything.

"Like and like," returned the power wielder. "The Law of Similarity. You carry his bloodline. You play a part in the gargoyle's method of gathering. He is the catalyst. I have always known I must master the gargoyle, but I didn't realize he had an unwitting pawn of his own." He inclined his head toward Grigori in what was clearly a gesture of mock gratitude. "I have *you* to thank for uncovering the truth. If you had not involved her, I would never have understood her role. Now . . . now I have the elements I need to make the gargoyle—and thus the contents of the house—*mine*."

In the darkness, the sounds of hundreds of tiny forms stirring caused the two to start. Some time during Frantisek's insane ramblings, the rats had returned.

Steel-blue eyes met steel-blue eyes as the two power wielders locked gazes. "You will give of yourself to me, my dear Grigori Nicolau. You will become a part of me like the others before you. Then, with your essence to add to mine, I will at last control Frostwing and, through him, the gifts of his former master."

"Listen to yourself, Peter Frantisek," Grigori said. "Do you know what you are saying? I have known Frostwing for more years than you would be able to believe, and I tell you that all you have done will avail you nothing. I do not know what takes place in that house, but I will have no more part of it. If you wish to live, you will do the same!"

"We have no choice. We were born into this game, Mr. Nicolau. The spell follows the bloodlines of his enemies. We have kept the spell alive simply by being born, but the years have taken some toll on that spell, altered it in ways its originator did not intend. *I* recall his own memories. You do also—but with lesser clarity, I imagine.''

The bound man could not know how old his captive was, but his words had given Grigori food for thought. The spell—whatever it was—followed the bloodlines of his enemies. Might Grigori be tied to those other wielders of power, the ones who had toppled this mysterious master, but had left his animated servant to perform some act of vengeance taking centuries to unfold?

The thought staggered Grigori, yet it also suggested an explanation for his longevity and the gargoyle's particular interest in him. Perhaps he had been singled out for a special reason. Perhaps Grigori Nicolau, under some other name, had led those who had brought down Frostwing's master.

That still left the house unexplained. What sort of legacy had been left behind, to come to fruition so many generations later?

He was given no more time for thought. Frantisek's eyes had grown more and more intense. Something about them forced Grigori to stare, to become lost in them . . .

The vision of William Abernathy and the foul deeds he had performed was enough to help Grigori break free of the bound man's will only a few seconds later.

"Do not defy me, Grigori Nicolau. Time is short. The house will be summoning you before long. What I offer is a quicker, sweeter oblivion and a chance in your own little way to cheat the gargoyle. Through me, you will also be his master. Think of it!''

Grigori could only think that he did *not* want to suffer the fate of Abernathy. There was no rune-inscribed funnel, no bottle to collect his essence, but it was the same horror that the lesser power wielder had been attempting throughout the years. The difference was Frantisek had succeeded where his counterpart had not.

Peter Frantisek intended to swallow his essence as readily

as Grigori had that of Abernathy . . . except that the bound man was happy to do so, where Grigori had been dismayed and disgusted.

He doesn't understand the truth half as much as he thinks! He doesn't know it's all a dead-end!

Grigori almost succumbed to Frantisek as the thoughts pushed through his mind. They were and were not his own. It was almost as if some little bit of Abernathy still existed within him, still had voice enough to cry out.

The thought was enough to make him even more repelled at what his adversary sought to do. Grigori found the will to defy the man in the silver and iron chair.

Grunting, Peter Frantisek straightened, his eyes looking upon his prisoner as if for the first time. "Your will is not enough."

Grigori added his physical strength to his defense, but when he tried to raise his hands, he found himself still motionless. Frantisek was not completely mad. He knew what a danger his opponent could be.

"My right to the legacy is greater than anyone else's! I am much more him than any of you others!"

More babbling. Nicolau did not care about any legacy left behind by a long-deceased sorcerer. He only cared about his life and Teresa's. It was a thrilling notion in some ways, to realize how important life had become to him now that he finally risked losing it. Teresa had been responsible for much of that.

Teresa? Grigori cursed himself for a fool even as Peter Frantisek's will bore him down. Once again, he had not made use of his link to her. They held one another, but he had to make an effort to cause the link to activate.

He did . . . and barely in time. Frantisek drew power from beyond himself in an attempt to quash Grigori's will quickly and with finality. It nearly worked. Nicolau could sense death around him, the deaths of small forms. He knew then that his foe's strength originated in the deaths of his pets. Only a part of it emanated from the figure in the chair. Frantisek was conserving himself for other things. His arrogance let him think Grigori unworthy of his full attention, even in battle. The disdain also revealed both the strength and ruthlessness of the other wielder.

Grigori began to wonder whether he and Teresa together stood any chance.

"You are stronger, but that . . . that will prove naught."

There were squeals from the darkness. Several large rats skittered across the lit region in madcap dances of death. One tiny corpse within Nicolau's range of vision shriveled. The eyes dimmed and changed color, becoming a milky brown.

Just like Abernathy . . .

The strain was already so great that Grigori thought his mind was going to swell and then burst. He could not counterattack. It was all he could do to shield both of them from the bound man's hunger. Frantisek might desire Teresa alive, but if he realized the truth behind the clasped hands, then she, too, might come under attack.

Still, Grigori could sense that his foe was utilizing more of his own strength. Frantisek had discovered that victory would not be so easy. He would have to expend more than the life forces of a few rats.

Conrad hung back, but both his weapons were still trained on them. He was clearly awaiting word from his master. Grigori had known many men like Peter Frantisek: the bound man would not call for aid anytime soon. Frantisek wanted to see his foe fall to him without any outside aid. That arrogance might just be what Grigori Nicolau needed to win.

The pain tore Grigori apart and put him back together time and time again, but he did not give in. He wanted to scream, but refused to give his captor even that victory. It had come to the point where he almost believed it impossible to surrender even had he so desired. The power, the essence that was him and had also been Abernathy, refused to waver, almost as if it wished to preserve the completeness that had been achieved in Grigori. To be drawn to Frantisek was to shatter that completeness.

Grigori did not care about completeness; he only cared about survival. Shaking from agony, he gritted his teeth and glared defiantly at his counterpart.

Then, in the midst of the silent, nearly invisible struggle, the siren call of the house once more touched his mind.

The house . . . the house is the only sanctuary . . . the only savior. If I give myself to the house, the power to free myself from Frantisek will come.

Utter nonsense, but the seductive tone made him want to believe. The call's timing could not have been worse. Between the summoning and the battle of wills with the other power wielder, Grigori knew that he was all but lost.

He felt Teresa shiver. She, too, felt the summoning. Grigori had never felt so helpless.

Then Peter Frantisek *screamed.*

The bound man tore one arm free. The bonds that had held that arm fluttered to the floor.

Come, whispered the voice. *Come and see the truth . . .*

Behind the voice, Grigori thought he heard a laugh.

It sounded exactly like the gargoyle.

Frostwing had brought Grigori to Peter Frantisek's sanctum not because of any desire to assist him against the bound man, but rather because the deadly creature had evidently calculated that Frantisek could not both battle Grigori and withstand the call. After so long defying the house, the bound man was at last its victim.

The gargoyle had calculated correctly where Frantisek was concerned, but then why not take all three of them?

The rumbling that rolled throughout the chamber made any such question moot. Both Teresa and Grigori fell to the floor.

Their ability to move returned, but neither was eager to rise. Grigori looked up at his adversary, but Frantisek was no longer concerned with him. The bound man was escaping his bonds. His acolyte had dropped one of the pistols and was trying to keep Frantisek's arm still long enough to shoot him with the needle gun. At such close range he risked harming his master, but Conrad was probably aware of that.

The piggish villain had the gun nearly pressed against his master's thigh when a blue haze covered him.

Conrad let out a startled cry before he was thrown bodily into the darkness. There was a crash and the sound of a heavy form striking the floor. Then the shrieks of the rats began anew.

Wide-eyed and sweating, Frantisek tore at his remaining bonds. The straps burned away under glowing fingertips. The power wielder himself fairly blazed. Grigori had not seen so much raw energy in all his centuries.

It was a sight he wished he could forget even now.

More and more rats now raced across the small lit region. Teresa gasped as a pair sought to climb over her body. The gasp caught the attention of the crazed Frantisek, who had just freed himself of the straps across his torso. He looked at Grigori's companion, then at Grigori himself. A bit of reason returned to the man's narrow eyes.

"Give me your hand, Nicolau!"

Grigori wondered if Frantisek believed him that much a fool.

Evidently he did, for he repeated his demand, stretching one hand toward his counterpart. When he saw that Grigori had no intention of obeying, he glanced again at Teresa, then looked beyond her at the darkness.

A horde of frightened, dying forms swarmed out of the shadows and raced toward Teresa Dvorak.

Her reaction was instinctive. She tore her hand free from

Grigori's and tried to roll away from the furred flood. Nicolau tried to seize her arm, but she was out of reach before he could react.

"Teresa! No!"

Her movements sent her toward Frantisek. At the last moment, she realized her mistake and tried to change direction. Bereft of Grigori's protection, Teresa proved no match for the still-powerful will of the figure in the chair.

Frantisek stood, proving himself to be even taller than Grigori Nicolau had imagined, and reached for her.

Grigori shouted again, already moving forward. The tips of Frantisek's fingers made contact with Teresa's arm.

Summoning his strength, Nicolau found the wherewithal to seize the rats with his power and begin flinging them into the tall figure's visage.

The living bombardment proved as effective as he had hoped. Frantisek broke contact with Teresa in order to protect his face. Grigori did not stop even when Teresa began to crawl back to him. If he stopped or even slowed, Peter Frantisek might regain control of her. Until Teresa was once more linked to him, he had to keep the other man at bay.

Nevertheless, his assault withered as his strength waned. Teresa was nearly to him, but the mad run was still in progress. Scores of rats raced around and over her.

A hundred cannons went off in his skull. Grigori half-collapsed, but Teresa caught him before he could fall. A large rat clambered onto his knee, but then fell to the floor, dead. More and more of the rats were now collapsing.

Peter Frantisek let loose a cry that was half anger and half fear. His body blazed, yet he did not burn.

One more time the two power wielders matched gazes. Hatred smoldered in Frantisek's eyes, hatred and hunger.

Then his body seemed to turn to smoke. Frantisek twisted and turned like a rising tornado, yet all details of his face and form remained distinct. Steel-blue eyes looked skyward . . .

. . . And the power wielder faded away.

Grigori was granted but a few moments to drink in the horrific sight he had just witnessed before the room itself began to crumble. The evidence was invisible to the naked eye, but he could sense Frantisek's handiwork collapsing around him. How like the bound man, Grigori thought, to make his works live and die with him. Whatever spell kept this chamber larger than it should have been was failing, and that meant that soon the dimensions would collapse inward.

He did not want to be here when that happened.

"Teresa! Hold me tight!"

She seemed dazed, but nonetheless obeyed. A few rats still stumbled around. Grigori ignored them. Already he could feel the walls pressing in. The irony was that no one outside would notice that anything out of the ordinary had occurred.

The cannons roaring in his mind, Grigori summoned what will he had and, with Teresa to amplify it, attempted to send them away.

They faded away even as the walls rushed toward them.

— XVIII —

HAVING LIVED MUCH OF HIS LIFE IN ERAS WHEN AIR TRAVEL was only a dream of a few far seers, Grigori never considered sending them to either of Chicago's major airports. He had arrived in O'Hare International and knew of Midway, but it was travel by land that came to mind first. Carriages and horses were familiar to him, but he had become accustomed to travel by train . . . And train stations were easy to locate these days.

They were fortunate. In the press of bodies flowing through Union Station, no one noticed the two that joined the crowd as if out of thin air.

Grigori pushed through the throng and found them a seat off to the side of the hall. It was fortunate that he had earlier noted the station's location; it was even more fortunate that, in his present condition, he had not thrown the pair of them into the Chicago River instead. After what had happened to him during his earlier escape from Conrad, Nicolau was paranoid about transporting himself any more than was necessary.

Once seated, he turned his attention to Teresa. She still appeared somewhat muddled, which worried him. "Are you feeling any better?"

"Some . . . not much . . ." The blonde woman looked up at him. "Is it over?"

"For our former host, I would say so. I think the house finally has him." Even the chair and the bonds had not been enough in the end. Grigori regretted the fate of Frantisek, but reminded himself that the man had intended a similar end for him.

"It wasn't an accident that the voice came at that time, was it? He was set up, wasn't he?" she added.

"Yes." He told her about his awakening in the hospital and the visit by the gargoyle. "When Frostwing departed, I found myself just across the street from Frantisek's house. I knew I was being used even then, but it did not matter."

"Because of me?" Her smile was weak, but it still managed to light up her face.

"Because of you."

"I kept thinking about you and what—" She broke off, the dazed look returning to her expression.

Grigori moved so that his face was inches from her own. "Teresa!" he hissed. "What is it? What is the matter?"

"The keep . . . He's so dark . . . But they're coming and the spell isn't complete. . . . Where's that foul piece of rock?" Her voice took on an imperious tone. "You are the flesh of my flesh, all of you! Be grateful I send you away . . . away now . . ." The dreaming woman's arm rose, but Grigori quickly pushed it down. "I have given you a task, my children, a task which you were bred for, my *dear* ones . . ."

"Teresa!" Grigori whispered as loudly as he dared.

"The winged one . . . bones of earth and bones of men . . ." She blinked. Her eyes focused. "Grigori?"

He had her face cupped between his hands. The fear he felt for her was so great it threatened to overwhelm him. "Teresa, what happened to you?"

"I . . . I don't know. I saw this . . . this castle or something; it was in some hills or maybe even mountains. Then, the memories flooded in." A pause. "I can still feel the house calling to me, Grigori. I can't fight it, damnit! Look what happened to Frantisek and he was so strong!"

Nicolau, too, could still feel the siren song of the house, and now and then memories akin to what Teresa must have suffered touched his mind. Still, hers seemed so much more vivid. Frantisek had mentioned some connection. *Bloodlines* . . .

All of this only strengthened his resolve. He had not chosen the train station completely at random, after all. Looking his companion in the eye, the dark man said quietly, "Listen to me closely, Teresa. The choice will be yours. We should leave this place, if only for now, and put as much distance as possible between Chicago and ourselves. That is why I have brought us here."

"Take a train?" She looked around, watching the commuters as they made their way to various platforms. "Just leave like that?"

"Yes. I know it is much to ask. I would understand if you preferred some other solution, but flight is the only one that I know. We will be safer on the ground than in the air."

Her gaze returned to his. "I can't take any more of this. I'll go anywhere if it means an end to this."

"I cannot promise that, but I think that we will definitely be stronger if we are farther away. I can better protect us."

"But the summoning reaches all over the world. You know how far away some of them came from."

"What other choice have we?" he asked bluntly.

She saw his point. "Where will we go?"

He was pleased with her quick decision, although deep inside he regretted the disruption of her life. It was unfair. She was an innocent compared to him.

As for a destination, he already had one in mind. "I believe we should head south. I have heard that New Orleans is an interesting city to visit."

"I always wanted to see the French Quarter," she remarked with a rueful tone. "We'll need tickets, though, and a few things to bring along." The blonde woman looked down at her disheveled outfit. "Some clothing would be nice, but I guess that'll have to wait."

"Yes, I am sorry but it *will* have to wait. I may be able to do something about that once I have rested. We, however, must not delay any longer."

The two of them rose and hurried to the Amtrak ticket counter. There was a train that would eventually get them to New Orleans, and Grigori was pleased to discover that it had private compartments. They paid for two tickets, then hurried to one of the tiny stores in the station to pick up supplies. They had little more than half an hour before boarding.

While they shopped, the normalcy of the act put Teresa at least partly at ease. Not Grigori. He scanned the crowds around him. Peter Frantisek was gone, but that did not mean that his minions might not still be hunting the pair. Granted, it had been only a few minutes since their escape, but that was time enough. Once away, there might be less chance of pursuit. Frantisek was not there to goad his servants on. Given time, the acolytes would likely go their separate ways. Life and justice would catch up with them soon enough after that.

As Teresa prepared to pay for their purchases, Grigori's eyes settled on the rolls of instant lottery tickets behind the counter. Peering at the various games, he asked the clerk for two specific game cards, one from each of two different lotteries. Inured to the eccentricities of lottery players, the clerk complied.

The two cards were both winners, combining for just over a hundred dollars. Because they were both small winning amounts, the store was required to give Grigori the money. Going through the state itself would have taken days.

As the two departed for the train, Teresa eyed the power wielder with suspicion and not a little humor. "You knew which ones to choose, didn't you?"

"I did. I apologize. I only do this when necessity demands it of me."

"Could you pick the six numbers for the grand game? That would be millions."

He shook his head. "I could not, although I could probably make a better guess than most. Besides, with those millions come notoriety."

Grigori did not have to say anything more. The last thing a centuries-old wanderer needed was publicity.

It was with great relief that they watched Union Station recede behind them. The private compartment was small, but it offered them their first opportunity to relax. Grigori studied Teresa as she stared out the window, once more admiring her ability to adjust to new situations. It was an adaptability that he had learned only through suffering, but to her it was natural.

"I love this city," she said, turning toward him.

Grigori nodded. "It is a wonderful city. I would have liked to have known it better. There are many great cities in the world, many that I have seen, and this would have been a fine addition to my travels."

"Where've you been?" she asked with growing interest.

"Everywhere." Grigori could not hide some of the weariness in his tone. "Everywhere." When she continued to wait, he amended, "Berlin, London, Vienna, Cairo, Muscovy . . . I have been everywhere, just as I said."

"How much of your travels do you remember?" As soon as she had finished asking, Teresa looked upset with herself. "I'm sorry, Grigori! I shouldn't remind you—"

"It is all right. As I mentioned to you, I remember fragments of different places and times. Some portions of my life I recall more clearly than others. Frostwing is not the only threat to my memory, though. Time has stolen, or at least hidden, almost as much as he has."

"But the memories are all yours?"

He was about to answer *yes*, when he remembered William Abernathy. "No. Since the hotel room there have been new memories floating in my head. They do not belong to me . . . I think."

After a minute or two of contemplation, Teresa asked, "Why do you think that I'm recalling the castle?"

Now he understood her line of questioning. She was trying to comprehend what Frantisek had dredged up from within her. The memories could not be hers, after all, for she was mortal. At the same time, their former captor had hinted that Teresa Dvorak was not like the others who bore eyes so blue. She was of *the* bloodline, a comment whose meaning was lost to Grigori. Many things unsettled him about what Frantisek had said. Grigori needed more facts.

Sighing, he finally answered, "I cannot say for certain. It may be that when he touched you just prior to his vanishing, Frantisek planted those images. I could be mistaken, but . . . but if you are willing, I can try to uncover those secrets. Unfortunately, it would require doing something similar to what he did to—"

"No!" Then, visibly calming herself, Teresa recanted. "I take that back. Do it. It might help us." Her eyes narrowed in deep thought. "We're not out of this yet. I don't dare hold back anything. You haven't."

Her resolve was admirable, but Grigori wanted her to understand what he had to do. "It will be like hypnosis, Teresa, but there is a risk, a slight one, of delving too deep. Peter Frantisek opened the path and quite obviously did not close it completely, else you would not recall all that you did in the station. I can retrace his path, but I may succeed in doing nothing for you save opening the way for even more vivid recollections. Do you want to risk *that*?"

His companion was not swayed. "Do it, please."

"As you wish." Grigori reached into an inner pocket. As he fumbled, he noted the rumpled appearances of both Teresa and him. The temptation to clean and tailor both of them was great, but that must wait. Delving into her memories would drain him further.

"Could you please open up one of the cans of soda and unwrap two of the candy bars?"

Now familiar with his need for processed sugar, she did not comment on his choice of food. By the time Grigori had untangled the chain in his hands, Teresa had the items ready.

"You're going to use that?"

Grigori, already devouring the first of the candy bars, nodded. He swallowed and added, "The stone is an excellent focus. I have found a number of uses for it over the years."

It took him only a minute or two more to devour the second bar and drink most of the soda. Putting down the can, he raised the pendant that he had utilized to search the city maps and held it at eye level.

"Stare at the pendant, Teresa." As he talked, the power wielder slowly swung the stone back and forth. His words echoed the motion of the pendant. "It will be easy. The power will help you slip under . . ."

It took but a few more words of encouragement to lead her into the trance. Grigori was pleased; he had feared that Frantisek's earlier, uninvited entrance would make Teresa more resistant. Her trust in him was astounding at times. He certainly did not have such faith in himself.

The next part of his task was the more difficult, for now Grigori had to place himself in a state halfway to hers. That was the only way he could be fully receptive to what she had to convey.

"Give me your hand, please." She obeyed instantly. The link would both strengthen him and facilitate the transfer of knowledge.

Grigori stared at the swinging pendant.

The room blurred around the edges, then slowly seeped away like some peculiar liquid. Soon, there was only Teresa and him.

Will you let me in? he asked her. *Will you show me what you were forced to show him?*

Teresa did not answer, but the fog around them transformed, becoming mountains and hills. Trees and other vegetation dotted those giants, but what snared his attention was the dark structure sitting high above them. It was not a large structure, but its air of darkness was almost palpable. Grigori wondered if he had stepped into a memory of some terrible horror film Teresa had seen. Yet, that could not be, because he recognized the castle from the memories that once had belonged to Abernathy.

There was an odd perspective to everything. It was as if Teresa saw things through more than one pair of eyes. More than one pair, but all those eyes somehow belonged to one being.

Ancestral memory. The words came of their own accord and seemed flavored with the spirit of Peter Frantisek. It was merely an echo of the man, however, words that he had spoken in her presence during his own search. Nicolau was grateful, for the clue clarified things.

The resident of the dark keep, he who had been cast down by his enemies, who had worked his vengeance despite that— he was the direct ancestor of Teresa Dvorak.

The other perspectives could only be other ancestors in the same line. Children or grandchildren, most likely. Some of the descendants of various children had intermarried generations or even centuries later. Teresa inherited the vision from both of them, strengthening her link to the past. It made some sense. If the originator had hoped to succeed, he needed his descendants to keep the line strong.

To guide such a plan spoke of more power than Grigori could have ever dreamed was possible. Even in his dream state he could not help but shiver.

What was the legacy that Frantisek had spoken about? Who was supposed to receive it? Could it be—?

He refused to press further. What he had been about to surmise could not be possible.

The image faded. After so long, the memories would be as fragmented as his own. It was amazing that what remained was so clear. That was also a sign of the vast power of Teresa's ancestor, the master of the keep.

Another memory. A statue carved from the rock of the very mount upon which the sanctum rested. Someone was adding highlights with a white stone, grinding it into the statue's shoulders—no, *wings*—melding the two stones together.

It was Frostwing. It was the gargoyle when he had been but a piece of stone.

The making of Frostwing. Grigori studied the memory closely. Perhaps he could learn something about his age-old adversary.

Bathed in a sickly light, the two pieces of rock became one . . . and as Grigori continued to stare, he saw that the white stone was not stone at all. It was *bone*. What had Teresa said in Union Station? The bones of the earth and the bones of men . . .

The hitherto unliving statue, only two feet high, suddenly screamed to the world, announcing its birth. Nicolau recoiled at the sound. There was so much pain in that howl that he felt some sorrow for the gargoyle, a creature who he now saw for the first time had truly had no choice in existing.

Then the gargoyle opened his eyes, revealing the evil within. The eyes were steel blue and filled with hate. Then the blue began to fade, the *eyes* began to fade, to be replaced by the more familiar shadowed brow. What sorrow Grigori had felt for the creature faded . . .

As, suddenly, did the memory.

In the next moment he was swept up in battle. The keep shook. Magical forces that he could only imagine moved unhindered, destroying all in their wake. Grigori caught glimpses of Frostwing and other creatures. He saw men and women encroaching. They were the enemies, the lessers who feared the true master. There were so many of them; he could not combat them all. Words were spoken, words Grigori understood even though they were spoken in that same unknown language he had spouted to banish Frostwing.

The words did not matter so much as the identity of those who spoke them. The enemy moved ever closer, crushing one defense after another. Nothing could stop them. It would not be long. The outcome had never been in doubt. The master of the keep could only lose the battle.

That, though, had already been considered. There was a way to foil the inevitable victory. Most of the children, children begat on chosen women, were spread throughout the world. Only the most gifted remained at the keep, for they had been needed to aid in the final steps. Now, those preparations were complete. The attackers would not harm children and when they took him, the die would be cast. He would see to it that each laid their hands upon him or touched him with their power. Either would be enough. *Their descendants would be marked.*

Marked? What did that mean, Grigori wondered.

In the next instant the keep came down. Frostwing fluttered off with a small bundle held tight in his arms. The power unleashed in the conflict tore the world asunder.

There was the memory of determined hands reaching for a figure in a dark cloak who could only be the master. Other hands, more gentle ones, reached toward Grigori . . . or rather the children whose eyes he saw through. Grigori realized that he had not really seen many faces, not even of those who now talked to the children. Only Frostwing's features had been defined. The enemies of the gargoyle's master were shadow folk, darting phantoms.

I see as the children saw. The master's children. Grigori was certain now that more than one of them had contributed to Teresa's ancestry.

Hands closed upon the master, who even in dying laughed. He knew that . . . that he would . . . would . . . his legacy . . .

Would what? Grigori demanded silently. *What is the legacy?*

This time, his demand was met. This time, the doors opened in Teresa's memories, freeing the truth.

Through his enemies and their descendants, he who had been Frostwing's creator would be reborn into the world. He would live again. He would cheat death.

Grigori Nicolau recoiled. It was true, then? What he could not believe was possible . . . *was?*

The life faded from the master. The others, his victorious

rivals, shifted away, weary shadows all. Grigori tried to get a better look at the dead figure.

The memory shattered. Pain and confusion assailed him.

He was left in darkness.

There was more, Grigori was certain, but unlike Peter Frantisek he did not have the tools or the power with which to better probe. In truth, he was not even certain that he wanted to uncover more. He had learned enough. In some ways, too much.

With that thought, the power wielder found himself back inside the compartment. Teresa sat across from him, still entranced. Nicolau shook his head in an effort to clear it. He had not learned everything, but he had learned enough for now. The so-called legacy was nothing of the sort; what Frostwing worked at was nothing less than the summoning of his ancient master back to the world of the living. How that was to be accomplished was still a puzzle, but it involved many people—descendants, it seemed—of those who had battled the dark master.

What had that ancient power wielder done when they had touched him? He had wanted to force as many of them as possible to actually lay hands upon him. What had he passed on to the unwary victors?

To return from the dead. Grigori could not help but admire the arrogance of the master power wielder, while at the same time rejecting his act. Men and women, both ordinary and otherwise, had sought to overturn death since the very beginning. Those who could use the power managed to stave death off for two or three centuries, but that was not the same. Even he would not have had the effrontery to believe that he was strong enough to battle death from the other side.

There was one other conclusion Grigori had drawn from the memory fragments. What little he had seen of those who had come for the master verified a notion he found almost as impossible as rising from the dead. He had never viewed the attackers' features clearly, but there was a consistency in the *type* of features each had that hinted of a similar background. People of the same land.

People with a background like his own. He might be their kinsmen. Or perhaps even something more startling still . . .

I was one of them. I was among those who defeated him. I was one of his enemies.

It made sense to him. This was why Frostwing took such a personal interest in tormenting Grigori. He had been one of the leaders, one chosen for special punishment. Perhaps the cloaked figure had wanted *one* of his less-than-worthy foes to witness his eventual triumph. Perhaps Grigori Nicolau, whose name had probably been something else then, had been kept alive so long just for the ancient one's pleasure.

It would also explain what Frostwing had done to his mind. With no memory of that time to call upon, he could hardly interfere with the grand spell. The rest of his suffering was likely simple, sweet torture. Vengeance against all of the master's foes, suffered upon him through the dark figure's agent, Frostwing.

Grigori returned his attention to his companion. Now that he shared Teresa's knowledge, or at least the essentials, he would do for her what Frantisek had not thought necessary. He would bury the memories deep in her mind, there to be summoned only if she willed it so.

He held the pendant before her eyes.

A shudder went through him. A sense of urgency.

Lowering his hand, Grigori stood up and carefully made his way to the compartment entrance. A search of the corridor revealed no threat, yet the feeling of impending danger would not leave him. He had learned long ago to trust such intuition. The incidents in Chicago had only strengthened that trust.

Grigori stepped out into the corridor. The movements of the train jostled him, but not enough to endanger his footing. Grigori put one hand against the door and peered down the length of the corridor. Still he saw nothing. Turning, he gave the other end a similar inspection. A probe in both directions revealed nothing.

Still leery, Grigori returned to Teresa. Regardless of whether there was danger or not, he could not very well leave her in so helpless a state. Raising the pendant again, Grigori went to work on burying the ancestral memories. The sooner he finished the better he would feel.

He had made it to the train. It was the first time that he had managed such a feat without the master, but he had made it.

Conrad smiled despite the dizziness that still plagued him. Mr. Frantisek would have been proud . . . if he had still been alive. That, though, was the fault of the foreigner and the woman. He was not certain what they had done, but the acolyte was positive that the blame could be traced to them.

He removed the dart pistol from inside his jacket. Following the man's trail had proved futile, but the runt had forgotten to mask her path. Conrad's master had taught him enough to follow so obvious a trail. It also helped that some of the master's field agents had recognized the fugitives in the train station. A few pointed questions revealed which train they had taken.

Conrad shrugged to himself as he placed a needle cartridge in the pistol. Even without the spies, he was certain that he would have found the girl's trail. The day would come when he would be as powerful, if not more so, than his teacher.

First things first. The manservant eyed the medallion lying against his chest. Even with the bound man gone, it still protected and hid him. No one on the train would notice anything he did unless he willed it.

He readied the pistol and started down the corridor, smiling in anticipation.

XIX

GRIGORI EYED TERESA WITH CONCERN AS SHE EMERGED FROM the trance. "Are you well? Do you feel any different?"

She blinked several times, then slowly focused on him. Her face was devoid of emotion at first, but gradually a tentative smile played across her face. "My head doesn't feel . . . I don't know how to describe it except to say that it doesn't feel so crowded any more." Teresa blinked. "What did you do?"

"I buried the memories deep. They will not return to plague you. You may summon them back, should you so desire, but otherwise they will never disturb you again." He could not be completely positive about that, but decided not to say so to her.

"I don't think I'd ever want to remember them again, but I appreciate having the choice." She brightened. "Did you find out anything of value?"

He started to tell her, but then the sense of dread returned. For some reason, Grigori was reminded of the taint of Peter Frantisek, but that was insane because Frantisek was no more, wasn't he?

Teresa picked up on his nervousness. "What is it? Did you find something terrible? What——?"

Rising, Grigori signaled for quiet. He glanced toward the corridor, then extended one hand toward her. She understood, reaching out and grasping the hand with her own.

His weariness, his weakness, slipped away. Utilizing his enhanced abilities, he probed the area outside of the compartment.

Frantisek's manservant Conrad stood only a few feet away. He wore a medallion that glowed with the power of his former master. In one hand the piggish figure carried the sinister needle gun.

Although caught between disbelief and dismay, Grigori retained enough composure to recognize that the pistol had been loaded with more than a simple sleeping potion. That the acolyte had chosen this particular weapon over a normal gun hinted at just how potent and likely fatal the potion was. Conrad's mind, while difficult to read, radiated hatred and vengeance. The medallion, his sole legacy from Frantisek, kept him partially hidden from Grigori's senses even this close.

Nicolau released his grip on Teresa's hand, then pushed her to the far side of the room. Ignoring her stunned expression, he snatched up one of the thick seat cushions.

In the next instant, Teresa's gaze darted past him and she shouted, "Grigori!"

He brought up the cushion and prayed he had timed this correctly.

Frantisek's acolyte was in the room, astonishingly silent and swift for so large a man. The pistol was already level. Conrad did not hesitate to fire.

The needle sank deep into the cushion. That Grigori had not utilized his abilities to defend himself was no coincidence. Quarters were too close and his energy level too low; Teresa might have been at risk, especially if Conrad, protected as he was by the medallion, fired a wild shot.

Conrad, unfazed, tried to fire around Grigori's makeshift shield, not caring who was hit. Peter Frantisek had chosen his servant well.

Throwing himself forward, Grigori Nicolau pushed both of them into the corridor. Conrad's pistol went off, but the shot struck the ceiling. The massive figure tried to push his lighter opponent back, but momentum was with Grigori. The two of them tumbled to the floor.

"Why do this?" hissed Grigori as he struggled atop the manservant. "Your master's disappearance was not my doing! The house took him, as it has taken so many others!"

Conrad said nothing. His free hand came up and nearly caught Nicolau by the throat. Grigori gave up trying to convince his foe to quit this vendetta. There was only one way to stop him.

Grigori tried a quick strike with his power, a simple thrust that would shut down Conrad's mind. The attack met a wall much like the barriers that had surrounded Frantisek's domain. The bound man's servant was far better protected than the dog soldiers had been . . . and had some ability of his own. Grigori discovered that almost too late, as a sudden counterattack nearly slipped past his own guard. He barely deflected the assault, so cunning and swift was Conrad.

No one had as yet come to see what the struggle was about, but Grigori had expected that. Another trick Frantisek had taught the would-be assassin.

The needle gun slowly turned in his direction. Grigori was not as physically strong as Conrad, and his power, already much overtaxed, was waning.

Conrad's gaze flickered from Grigori's face to something

just past the smaller man's shoulder. The acolyte grunted in fury and pressed harder in his effort to bring the gun into play.

Something nudged Grigori in the back . . . and suddenly he was stronger again. *Teresa!* he thought and was stunned to feel her acknowledgement. She was behind him, her hand on his back. Her conscious effort activated the link.

Conrad would never surrender. He was too much Peter Frantisek's hand. Grigori did not think he could breach the porcine man's defenses, especially the medallion, but now he had the power to affect the world *around* the deadly manservant.

It meant opening himself up to Conrad's own power, for he needed every bit of will to do what was needed. For Teresa's sake, Grigori chose to risk it.

Tearing one of his hands from the struggle, Nicolau touched the floor of the car.

Conrad sank into the floor. There was no warning, no preamble. Suddenly the floor below the villain was simply unable to hold the weight of the two.

The pistol went off again as the manservant, snarling still, slipped through the solid floor as if it had turned into water. Grigori snapped his head back just in time to save his nose and chin. The shot struck the ceiling of the railroad car even as Conrad's weapon followed its owner through. It was all Grigori could do to keep from slipping through himself. Only Teresa's hand clutching his clothing kept him from joining the would-be assassin. He finally lifted his hand from the floor, breaking the spell.

The scream that surely followed as Frantisek's man fell beneath the wheels of the train did not reach them, but Grigori could sense the psychic shock preceding his death. Conrad would not be returning to stalk them again.

Rising slowly, Grigori stared at a shaken Teresa. He reached out and took her in his arms, only belatedly realizing that she was comforting him as much as he was comforting her.

"You had to do that," she whispered. "He didn't give you any choice."

Her attempt to placate Grigori only served to make him realize what he had just done. Grigori had killed his share of men over the centuries—more than he could recall—but Teresa had made him recognize the value of lives other than his own. To pity an enemy so was new to him, though he had always considered himself a compassionate man.

"We should return to the compartment," he finally said.

She nodded. Neither of them looked back at the spot where Frantisek's man had disappeared. Grigori paused only long enough to retrieve the damaged cushion. When he had more rest, he would restore it to its original condition. Doing so now just did not seem that important.

"Are there any more, do you think?" Teresa asked. She was pale but otherwise well.

"I do not think so. He was Peter Frantisek's apprentice, his greatest acolyte. The others are nothing more than spies and soldiers. However, I will plant some safeguards, just in case."

They sat down, Teresa leaning against his side. She eyed the opposite wall as if hoping to find the answers to everything written there. "Are we fooling ourselves? I can still hear that voice in the back of my head, the one that keeps whispering about the house."

"Sleep will help vanquish that," he responded, side-stepping her question. "You should try to rest now."

"I can't sleep, not after this . . ."

The rest of her comment died as she collapsed against him. Grigori studied her for several minutes, filled with guilt at what he had just done. He had sworn after the first time that he would not use his power on her, not even for something as harmless as this, yet here he was again, breaking his silent word to her. Teresa needed rest, however, and Grigori needed the time for private contemplation.

Some of the troubling thoughts had been with Grigori since the gargoyle had toyed with Teresa back in her apartment. This last attack by the bound man's servant had only cemented matters. He could not hesitate any longer.

His own fate was tied to Frostwing. There was no escaping it. They might run for a time, but the gargoyle always knew where to find him. He was very important to Frostwing and therefore to the force within the house. Perhaps a trade could be made, his cooperation for Teresa's freedom. Surely he could fulfill his role as guardian especially if, as he suspected, he *was* the one surviving member of the band that had brought down the gargoyle's master. That Frostwing had tracked him through the centuries spoke volumes concerning Nicolau's importance. Surely his cooperation was worth the price of Teresa's freedom.

She was no threat to Frostwing or his mysterious master, no enemy that needed to be dealt with. There was really no reason why Teresa could not be left alone, especially if Grigori made certain that she in no way interfered. If it meant casting a compulsion on her to save her life, he would do even that. He would make her move far away, perhaps to the west coast. His own investments could be turned over to her; he would no longer need them.

More and more it made sense to him. A trade. Grigori could find ways to guarantee that she remained safe after he was gone. He did not relish surrendering himself to Frostwing, but for Teresa's sake, Grigori had to try to bargain with his age-old tormentor.

For the first time in his life, or at least the first time that he could remember, Grigori Nicolau chose to summon Frostwing.

He was unsure how to begin. He was not even certain that the decision was a good one. It seemed the only way, however. Sooner or later, the voices would ensnare Teresa the way they had finally captured Frantisek. That she still heard them now was a sign that she was already well on the way to becoming like Matthew Emrich and the others. Soon, Teresa would find the need to follow the voices back to Chicago . . . and she would have no trouble locating the house. He closed his eyes and pictured the stone creature in all its terrible glory. The image shifted, becoming the memory that he had viewed within Teresa's mind. Once more he saw the birth of his adversary. Once more he heard the cry, the cry that seemed to protest the shackles of existence.

Grigori shook the image away and recalled the first one. Once that was secure in his thoughts, he called out in his mind to Frostwing.

There was no response. After several minutes, Grigori opened his eyes. Nothing. The effort had worn him out. If he intended to continue, he needed more energy.

Carefully shifting Teresa, the power wielder reached toward the already diminished food supplies.

The dizziness that caught him then was so great he nearly toppled to the floor. It passed swiftly, but Grigori was all too aware of what the dizziness meant.

He looked up. Frostwing had not materialized.

There *was*, however a gilded stairway where the opposite wall and seats had once been. The passage stretched through both wall and ceiling. Grigori peered up through the hole, but saw only a dull grayness.

His summoning had been answered. Now it was time to follow through on his decision. He walked to the base of the steps. Grigori paused then, turning to look once more at his companion. Deep in power-induced sleep, she would not wake until either he woke her or several hours elapsed. By the time the latter had passed, he would be gone.

He stared at her a little longer. Abandoning the stairway, Grigori returned to her, going down on one knee. He took her hand, kissed it, then leaned forward. His lips brushed hers, but that was all. He was not one to take liberties, even though this might be the last time he saw her.

"I will always watch over you," he whispered. Then, feeling rather foolish, Grigori rose and returned to the stairway. This time, there was no pause. He ascended, his back straight and his mouth set in grim determination.

The world beyond the roof of the rail car nearly made Grigori retreat a step.

It was not the sight he had expected. There was no sign of the city. The sky hinted at sunset, but no sun hung in view. The train itself ran on and on at breakneck speed, with the tracks disappearing into oblivion. There was no landscape to speak of, just a vast sea of nothing. Wind tousled Grigori's hair as he pulled himself up.

In the background, adding both absurdity and foreboding to the situation, tense music played. The music was so compelling, Nicolau could feel himself tensing. The tension struck him as rather redundant, considering how nervous he had been *before* climbing to the top of the train.

This is all just a dream, he reminded himself.

"There is nothing like speed," mocked a familiar voice from behind him. "Aaah, how I love a fast train ride!"

Frostwing crouched at the end of the car. He seemed unaffected by the fierce gale created by the train's speed. The gargoyle even spread his wings.

"How do you like the little touches I added to the scene? I did it all for your pleasure, you know!"

The music, while in some ways beautiful, was disconcerting. The lack of landscape kept Grigori on edge. He almost expected the train to plummet into oblivion. "I have seen better works of art . . . and I prefer to enjoy such a ride from the train's interior."

"Poor Grigori! You have no idea what fun you miss that

way. But then, you've missed a lot of fun, haven't you? Always afraid that someone was watching you . . . and if they were, so what? The world could have been so much more your plaything than you made it.''

"Even if I had the power, I would never use it thus.''

The gargoyle preened. ''Yes, you are rather boring that way.''

Something huge flashed by the train, but whatever it was had disappeared by the time Grigori turned. He thought of asking his tormentor, but decided not to do so. Even if the living statue knew what the thing had been, Grigori could hardly expect a straight answer.

There was nothing to do but get straight to the point. ''I want to make a bargain with you.''

Despite the whipping wind and the unnerving music, their words carried perfectly. Frostwing widened his eternal grin and replied, ''A *bargain*? With me? How novel! Did you miss me so much that you want to see me more often?'' The taloned hands toyed with the car's metal roof, leaving runnels in the steel. ''Have you come to offer more of your tasty memories in exchange for your release?'' The gargoyle shifted, as if preparing to pounce. ''I've not had one of those treats in days, dear Grigori!''

The music accented the final words. Grigori was almost tempted to ask the demonic golem to put an end to the melody, but Frostwing was more likely to increase the volume.

The power wielder lifted his hand in warning. Frostwing subsided, then chuckled. ''It is unwise to grow too confident in the little tricks one picks up along the way.''

''You would know about tricks, would you not? You played one on Peter Frantisek. And there was the one you orchestrated during your first visitation in my hotel room.''

Frostwing shrugged, somehow looking smug. ''I warned you about fools . . . and our friend, Peter, was one of the biggest fools of all. Woe betide the man who believes in his own glory so much!'' The gargoyle leaned forward. ''A warning that *you* should heed, my old, so old, friend.''

There was an intensity in Frostwing's voice that caught Grigori's attention. It was almost as if Frostwing was trying to convey a warning. The gargoyle's creation came to mind again. How loyal *was* the monster to his master? Then again, how disloyal could he be? It should have been a simple task for Frostwing's creator to imprint upon his servant a magical yoke of loyalty that the gargoyle could not break.

''You had a bargain in mind?'' the subject of his deliberations asked slyly. ''I am always interested in hearing you beg.''

''My life for the woman's freedom.''

Frostwing laughed again. It was quite some time before the creature could bring himself to answer. ''You bargain with something you do not own for something that cannot exist. I thank you for such amusement, my dear friend!''

Although his words denied the possibility of a covenant, Grigori noted that the gargoyle did not simply end things there. An almost expectant air settled about Frostwing. It was as if he was waiting for the rash human to say something more. What could that be, though?

What?

The lengthening silence seemed to erase whatever sense of anticipation the winged golem had. He shook his head. ''You disappoint me so, dear Grigori.'' The edge that the dark man had noted once or twice in the recent past returned. ''Ever you do that. Just when I think that you might understand the joke, you fail me.''

''Perhaps you should remind me what the joke is again. Maybe I will appreciate it better if I hear it.''

''But the mystery is part of the joke! Still, I will give you another hint . . . as if you haven't had enough of them! Face yourself, Grigori. Know the man you are and deny the man you were. You are a new man, but you are an original! *That* right is yours . . ."

Grigori Nicolau had no idea what the gargoyle was talking about.

A momentary flash of frustration tinged the stone beast's next remark. "Hate yourself! In that lies your only strength! Hate yourself and be proud of what you've become!"

Still the words made no sense. Grigori waved them aside and took a step toward the winged monstrosity. "I ask again, will you bargain? I will go freely to the house. I will take whatever fate awaits me, but in return I want Teresa's freedom!"

Frostwing shook his head. Despite the eternal smile carved into his visage, he seemed somehow to frown. "Grigori, Grigori! Your fate was written away long ago."

The gargoyle stretched forth a hand. The power wielder almost spouted some of the foreign words that would repel his hated foe, but then he saw that Frostwing was only pointing.

"My stop is coming up. I'm afraid you've wasted your breath and time, old friend."

He did not want to look, if only because it was too likely that this was another trick, but look Grigori did.

In the distance, he saw landscape for the first time. Only a small point, but definitely landscape. It floated in the void next to the track.

Rather than slow down, the train picked up speed. The dot became a shape. Then the shape became a structure surrounded by land. Grigori watched as the unidentifiable structure took on detail. The outline grew familiar. It was a building he had seen before. It was—

It was the house.

He started to turn toward Frostwing, intent on casting out the gargoyle, when someone emerged from the stairway onto the train. It was Teresa. The look on her face recalled some other face familiar to him.

"You are just in time, my dear," announced Frostwing with a chuckle.

Teresa Dvorak smiled at the winged golem.

"Teresa!" Grigori blocked her view of Frostwing. She looked up at him with an unreadable expression as she climbed onto the roof. "You can't be here. I put you to sleep. You can't be awake yet."

"Then I must be dreaming," she remarked casually in a voice that was and was not hers.

Nicolau stumbled back. He had heard that voice before. He had heard it in her memories, memories he had supposedly buried deep but a few minutes before.

"It was all inevitable, Grigori," mocked the gargoyle. "It was all inevitable despite what either you or dear Peter thought! You wondered what I stole when I left you no memory of my first visit in the city? I warned you that I was waiting for you here, that the culmination of all was to take place here!"

He only half-heard the rantings. Grigori was more concerned with Teresa. He took her by the shoulders and stared her in the eyes. "Teresa, listen to me! You must see that you are being used! You must wake up!"

"But I'm more awake now then I've ever been, Grigori! I understand everything. I know what the destiny of my family has been all these centuries. Why, I even know that you—"

A massive form passed above them. Grigori Nicolau ducked as Frostwing darted to a place behind Teresa Dvorak. She, on the other hand, quietly watched the winged monster land.

"Enough talk!" snapped the gargoyle. "Enough prattle!"

Frostwing took the woman in his arms. Grigori started to shout the words of banishment, but then clamped his mouth shut, knowing that the banishing would harm Teresa as well. Instead, he began to summon up what little reserves of power he had left.

To his horror, the gargoyle had lifted Teresa in front of him, turning her into a shield. Grigori dared not attempt anything powerful.

"This is our stop, as you can see." Frostwing and his hostage rose several feet into the air. Somehow his beating wings kept him apace of the speeding train. "I am afraid that the train itself does not come to a halt here."

"Teresa!" Grigori tried to pull her back using his power, but it had no effect. Frostwing rose higher.

"You think too small, dear Grigori. You have failed me, I am afraid." The gargoyle's toothy smile widened again. "I shall see you in Hell."

Teresa secure in his arms, Frostwing flew away. The gargoyle turned once in the air, then, laughing, darted toward the house.

Grigori tried to follow, but although this was his dream, he had no strength whatsoever. None of his attempts at flight so much as lifted him from the roof.

The train turned sharply as the tracks altered their course, heading away from the house. Looking forward, Grigori saw that now the train had *nowhere* to go. The tracks simply ceased just ahead.

He did not want to be aboard when the train reached the terminus, but when he tried to rouse himself from the dream Grigori could not.

The engine had nearly reached the end. Beyond lay nothing but nothing.

Left and right revealed nowhere to leap. Behind him stretched other cars, but dashing along them would only prolong things a few seconds more.

Grigori turned toward the stairway, but the steps had vanished along with the hole. He was trapped on top of the car.

The engine reached the end . . . and plummeted. The car behind it followed suit. So did the next.

Then came Grigori's.

* * *

He woke with a gasp, the scream barely held in check by the realization that he had, in the end, escaped the dream.

Dream? No, *nightmare extreme*. Had he not woken up when he had, it was quite possible he would have never woken up again.

He put his hand on the seat to steady himself, then realized what the empty seat meant.

Eyes widening, Grigori twisted around to find Teresa gone. The dream and reality were the same. Frostwing had stolen her away . . . and with her help.

As Grigori Nicolau drank in the horror of his situation, the train slowed to a halt. He frowned. There was no stop scheduled yet. The first station should have been more than half an hour away. He looked out the window.

The train had entered a station, a station that, even in the dark, Grigori recognized. *Union Station*.

He was *back* in Chicago.

XX

GRIGORI DEPARTED THE TRAIN QUICKLY. AMIDST THE rumble of hundreds of commuters entering and leaving the station, he heard the banal sounds of modern music streaming from various speakers. He tried to shut it out, but the music pierced through. The dark man was tempted to use his already strained will to short-circuit whatever board linked the system to the speakers.

Then he paused. *Music*. He grimaced, realizing just how

worn down he must be to have missed it earlier. He had his
own music in his head, music which would also give him
the calm he needed to think properly.

Franz Liszt slowly pushed the foul tune from his mind,
replacing it with true, soothing melody. Grigori began to
calm down. It was impossible to completely dampen his anxiety and fears, but the music allowed him to think despite
them. He took a deep breath and resumed his trek toward the
nearest exit.

Outside, Grigori discovered it was nearly night. In the
nightmare, the sky had been only a little darker than it was
now. Whether that meant anything, he could not say, but
with Frostwing involved, Grigori was willing to bet that the
dream sky had offered a clue. If so, the clue indicated that
time was rapidly running out. The only way that he could
reach the house quickly would be to transport himself there,
something that was beyond him now.

You have not changed, Frostwing, he thought. *What is the
purpose of having me run around beforehand save to amuse
you? Why did you not take me at the same time you took
her?*

Why did the gargoyle not want him to reach the house
until later? What was the difference?

His mind still struggled with the questions as he started
toward the street in order to hail a taxi cab. A cab might take
too long, but it was the swiftest method of transportation that
he could obtain now. Grigori could only hope that he was
wrong about the sunset. If he was correct, then he would
arrive much too late to save Teresa.

That could not happen.

He had just raised his hand to signal a nearby taxi when
he noticed a candy store across the street. The lights were
still on, but it appeared that someone was locking up the
place. In this area of the city, most shops closed soon after
the end of the business day.

The cab he had hailed started to pull over, but Grigori Nicolau shook his head, sending it away again. He reached into his pocket and counted his winnings from the two lottery tickets. There should be enough not only to buy what he needed, but also to pay the manager something for her troubles . . . especially since time demanded that Grigori devour his purchases right there *in* the store.

Summoning his strength for one last short hop, Grigori transported himself across the street.

A middle-aged black woman wearing a neat but slightly worn coat opened the door without seeing him. In one hand she held a set of keys.

"Forgive . . . forgive me for coming so late, madam," said the voice from behind her. "But I have an urgent purchase to make."

"We're closed. C'mon back tomorrow, hon," the woman rumbled to the now-unkempt figure of Grigori. There was a touch of anxiety in her eyes, for which he could not blame her. His appearance was certainly not conducive to trust. He looked as if he had slept in an alley for two or three days.

Grigori pulled out his money. At the same time, he gently began to prod at her mind with his power. "Please. It is a very important purchase I need to make. I promise you that it will be worth your time . . ."

It was a different Grigori Nicolau who materialized some minutes later across the avenue from the house and the gate. The meal he had eaten would have made most people dreadfully ill, so full of processed sugar had it been. He had eaten nearly pure sugar, avoiding any candies that contained nuts or other things useless to him. The sugar was all he needed.

Grigori could not recall the last time he had felt so strong and ready to do battle, but the dark man restrained himself from charging through the gate. The one sugar side-effect that he shared with normal folk was the high feeling that made one reckless, something he could not risk at this time. Grigori normally paced his eating better than this, but time had demanded that he bolt everything down, much to the shock of the watching store manager.

She would not remember the incident, save that a customer had come in at the last moment to purchase a vast amount of chocolate. The register would sing the increased sales, and she would find a bit of money in her pocket to make up for the lateness of that customer's arrival.

Anton Bruckner's Eighth Symphony played in the back of Grigori's mind as he studied the accursed dwelling. The Eighth was a particular favorite of his during troubled times. Something heroic in it, perhaps, something that made him feel as if armies followed him. It could have just as easily been the Fourth or the Seventh, but it was not. Grigori only knew that, facing such adversity as he did now, the Eighth just seemed appropriate to ready him.

The sky had nearly darkened to its nightmare color. He could hesitate no longer. It was time to enter.

How he could do so without alerting the watching gargoyle, he still did not know, but if it was possible to find his way inside quietly, Grigori wanted to try. It was a tiny hope, but there was a chance that he still might be able to surprise his enemies.

Then, staring at the gate, Grigori Nicolau saw that one thing had changed since his last visitation.

Frostwing no longer perched atop the arch. The pedestal where he had been situated was now devoid of the gargoyle's foul presence. The way seemed clear.

It was a trap. It had to be. Yet, he could sense nothing but the same patterns that had been present before. The gateway was defended, but by nothing he could not bypass.

Grigori braced himself and shifted to the entrance.

The gate was locked. Recalling the last time he had attempted entry, Grigori did not even bother to try to open it. Instead, he stared at a location just before the steps of the house.

He teleported flawlessly. Grigori glanced back at the gate from his new vantage point, but there was no indication his entrance had set off any alarms. If they knew he was coming, then Grigori could do nothing about it. If they did not, then he would accept whatever advantage that gave him. He might be walking into a trap, but they would learn that he could still bite even from within a cage.

Grigori shook his head, the better to clear away such over-confidence. The vast intake of sugar was making him lightheaded, all right.

As he reached the top of the steps, the door swung open for him. Grigori peered inside, but all he saw was grayness. There was no sound, no movement, no light. It reminded him of the stairway in the train.

His augmented power awaiting his command, Grigori Nicolau crossed the threshold . . .

. . . And found himself standing in a vast hall that could not exist in even as large a house as this one. It belonged more to a stonework structure, a black castle or a—*a keep*.

A spiraling staircase made of the same stone rode up along the walls of the hall, climbing higher and higher until it eventually disappeared in the darkness above. The hall itself was lit by a mere handful of torches set higher than Grigori's head. A table sat against one wall, and an impossibly large fur rug covered the center of the floor, but other than that, the hall was naked of adornment.

There was a window, or more accurately an arrow loop for an able bowman to make use of, far to his left. Grigori carefully moved to the slitted window and peered outside. The sun was low, but he could see the hills surrounding the edifice well enough. It was the same landscape that he had seen in Teresa's ancestral memories.

Somehow he was in the very keep where Frostwing's creator had first spun his centuries-spanning web of horror.

He made his way from the arrow loop to the stairway. His destination had to lie above, for there seemed no other exit. The darkness seemed appropriate for the master of this place.

With great caution, Grigori Nicolau began his ascent. The first loop around the walls went quickly enough, but as he climbed, circling the hall again and again, Grigori wondered if the stairs were a defense, a way of tiring an opponent before the battle was joined. He could have transported himself above, but in this sanctum, that was the equivalent to putting a gun to his own head and playing Russian roulette.

The light of the torches dwindled away, leaving Grigori to climb in complete darkness. The situation was as absurd as it was precarious. He stood a good chance of ending things simply by taking a misstep, yet utilizing his power to create light added to the risk of discovery.

Grigori had been guiding himself by keeping one hand against the wall, but at that moment the wall disappeared— or at least became impossible for his groping hand to locate. The sudden loss of support made him slip. One foot slid to the far edge of the step.

In order to save himself, Nicolau dropped to the steps. He lay there for several breaths, until his heart began to beat more calmly again.

The choice was obvious now. Whatever risk he took summoning light was far less than the risk of moving without it.

Kneeling, he raised one hand to eye-level and concentrated. A dim sphere of light the size of a marble formed in the palm of his hand. A few seconds more and it swelled to the size of an apple.

Grigori held the sphere high and looked around. The results were not spectacular. Within the limited region of light, the power wielder saw only the wall and more steps. It was almost insane; the building was much too huge inside, at least based on what he could recall from Teresa's memories. For the interior to be so vast spoke again of the might of the master.

Small wonder it had taken an army to bring him down . . . and now Grigori was coming to challenge the master alone.

A dozen or so steps higher, Grigori heard the flutter of wings. His first thought was of the gargoyle, but these sounded too swift and there seemed to be more than one set. It had not occurred to him to wonder if Frostwing's creator had added other horrors to the ranks, creatures more primitive than the winged golem, but equally dangerous.

The fluttering grew more pronounced as he climbed, but nothing attacked him. Grigori held the light high and sought for an end to the stairway.

Without warning, his sphere winked out of existence. Utter darkness descended again, but before Grigori could react, the darkness instead became *torchlight*. The swift change from light to dark to light blinded him and made him stumble.

His eyesight soon adjusted. Grigori found himself in a vast workroom, a chamber reminiscent of the dark abodes of fictional wizards. The place fascinated him almost as much as it repelled him. Like the hall downstairs, it was sparsely furnished. Only a few tapestries, some tables covered with odds and ends, and a row of bookcases piled with scrolls decorated the room. In contrast, however, the floor was one vast design, the center of which was a pattern of symbols that he could not discern from where he presently stood.

He turned around to discover that the stairway had vanished. There was no sign of his entry anywhere, which meant that there was no turning back. With no other exit in sight, Grigori chose to investigate the symbols inscribed in the center of the floor. Perhaps they held the key.

They were not symbols, but words written in some peculiar

language. He looked them over carefully and as he did Grigori found himself giving voice to the strange words. It was the same language that he had used to banish Frostwing.

The inscription looped around in a circle roughly six feet in diameter. Grigori stepped over one row and moved to the center, the better to read. He followed the words, now creating sentences. There were several rows of words. It was not a circle after all, but a spiral. Grigori had to turn around five times to read the entire thing. While none of it made any sense, he felt as if he were closer to discovering the truth.

It was only when he tried to step out of the spiral that he discovered there was more to it than simply design.

White light bathed the entire chamber. It was *literally* white light, for everything save himself now seemed the color of sun-drenched snow. Once more his eyes were forced to adjust quickly. It took several anxious blinks before he was able to see.

He was no longer alone. A single figure stood only a few feet away, her back to him and her arms raised in what appeared to be supplication.

Teresa.

He rushed to her side, only belatedly noting that the spiral no longer held him prisoner. Grigori stopped himself from calling out, but it took great effort. As it was, he would have hugged her tight, if not for the fact that she gave no indication of being even the slightest bit aware of his arrival. The blonde woman continued to gaze heavenward. She breathed, but that was the only sign that she lived.

Grigori looked up to see what so fascinated her.

A gap marred the ceiling. It was circular in shape with a diameter at least as great as the height of a man. The source of the brilliant light lay beyond, but it took Grigori a moment to identify it.

The moon.

The *full* moon.

Light flooded the opening and a quick estimate told Grigori that in little more than a minute the moon would pass directly over the hole. The skylight had been carved at the proper angle to achieve that result.

The timing would fit exactly with the time indicated in the dream.

More and more it seemed as if the impossibly strong moonlight was focused upon the entranced woman. As the moon moved toward conjunction, Teresa grew more animated. She opened her arms to embrace the light and take it within her. A smile crossed her features. She resembled nothing less than a moon goddess, an image both arresting and frightening.

Grigori seized one of her wrists. He forced her around, away from the direct power of the light, and tried to make her eyes focus on him.

"Teresa! Follow the sound of my voice! Come to me! Come to me! We have to leave—"

His voice faltered as a new figure materialized in the chamber.

It was a man, rather ordinary save that his clothing was of a style that had seen its heyday four decades past. He was plump but sturdy and roughly Teresa's age. He stood completely still, arms against the sides of his body, and stared off to Grigori's far right.

When the man did not move, Nicolau glanced in the direction that the other was staring. He saw nothing but a wall, which in no way relieved him. Grigori turned back to the newcomer and, to his dismay, discovered that now a second figure had joined the young man.

This was an older woman wearing even more outdated clothes. She was perhaps fifty, Grigori surmised, but her dress reminded him of Paris in the late eighteenth century. She, too, stared off to his far right.

What was happening here?

Grigori abandoned his study of the two and shook Teresa. Nothing seemed to wake her. He tried probing her mind with his power, but a wall blocked his attempt.

Glancing back at the still figures, Nicolau was stunned to discover that there were now *six* of them. The new arrivals ranged from a man so elderly he should have been dead to a child perhaps five. Their clothing ranged across the centuries, the most recent only a few years out of style and the earliest from at least the time of Queen Elizabeth I of England.

The first figure that had materialized suddenly turned his way. The movements were slow, deliberate, and when he finally faced the power wielder, the young man froze again. His eyes remained fixed on Grigori.

The eyes were steel blue.

In the time it took the first figure to turn, three more materialized behind the others. Again they varied in age, gender, and apparent century of origin. As the last of the latest group solidified, the second and third figures to arrive joined the first in turning toward Grigori. They too had steel-blue eyes.

"Grigori?"

Hope swelled in his breast at the sound of Teresa's voice. Grigori tore his gaze from the unsettling horde, which added yet another to its ranks even as he turned. He found the woman blurry-eyed, but at least semi-conscious.

"Teresa! Prepare yourself! We are leaving now!"

"Leaving?" she muttered. "Are we going somewhere?"

He forbore to answering her, knowing her mind was not yet in a state to comprehend much. All else faded to the background as Grigori drew his full concentration into the task of transporting them away—*anywhere*—before something else happened.

A mocking chuckle that seemed to originate from his own

head shattered that concentration. Grigori Nicolau recognized that foul laugh and silently cursed the power wielder who had been so mad as to create a stony horror he had dubbed Frostwing.

Turning his gaze to the silent watchers, Grigori nearly stumbled back in astonishment. There now had to be nearly two dozen of the figures, and all of them had their eyes fixed on the centuries-old wanderer. In the back of his mind, the more analytical part of Grigori Nicolau noted that the two dozen sentinels nearly created a triangle or wedge, save that the point closest to him had not yet been filled.

He had no sooner thought that when a tall form did fill the last gap, solidifying into existence in the same way as his predecessors. The triangle now had its apex, its focus.

Steel-blue eyes wide, Peter Frantisek stared at Grigori.

"Well," said the tall, narrow figure. He was clad exactly as Grigori had last seen him, but his face was very pale. Ghostly pale, one might have said. As Frantisek spoke, each and every one of his companions opened their own mouths and said the exact same word, in the exact same voice. It was not Peter Frantisek's voice, despite the fact that the mannerisms *were* his. There was something familiar about it, though, very familiar.

"Well," the group began again. It was like watching some bizarre and shocking marionette show, only the puppeteer and the strings were invisible. "This is . . . a surprise. And what am *I* doing here?"

Grigori stood there, not at first comprehending what the question meant.

And what am I *doing here?*

He—*they*—were staring at him intently, as if he were the only one who could answer that question.

What am I *doing here? I?*

He means me. He means—

Staring back into the legion of identical eyes, Grigori felt as if he were gazing into some twisted mirror. He knew who stared back through all those eyes.

It was the only answer possible. He and they were the same. He *was* them . . . or rather, they were *him*.

The power behind the centuries-long spell, the power behind the house, the siren call, and the ever-grinning gargoyle was indeed the ancient sorcerer.

And that dark master was Grigori Nicolau himself.

XXI

"FROSTWING!" CALLED THE VOICES THAT WERE ONE. "I command you to appear!"

Through a haze of disbelief, Grigori noted the use of the name. He had thought that he had christened the gargoyle himself, but now he saw that his use of it had only been some latent memory . . . which, in a way, meant that he *had* named the gargoyle himself. The thought was too confusing and disturbing.

Grigori realized then that Frantisek and the others were not speaking English. If he watched closely, he could see their mouths shaping different words than what it appeared they were saying. He had the strong suspicion that the language they used was the same he had spouted when banishing his tormentor. Grigori wondered whether he, too, would be speaking the language if he opened his mouth.

There was flapping from above and then Frostwing joined them. Grigori Nicolau found it disconcerting to see the gargoyle in action outside of his dreams, even more so because of the incredible difference in the winged demon's size. Frostwing in the flesh, so to speak, stood little taller than Grigori's waist. It was hard to tell since the gargoyle was presently prostrating himself before the triangle, especially before the former Peter Frantisek.

"Explain this, my dear little tatterdemalion. Explain why I am both alive."

Each of Frantisek's movements, each inflection, was perfectly copied by those within the triangle. Somehow, the mind of the master occupied every single form. Even more frightening was that Grigori could sense countless other minds hidden elsewhere, minds all attuned to the group gathered here.

Frostwing's master had been reborn, but as a collective consciousness.

As the gargoyle rose, Teresa moaned in confusion. Grigori put a hand to her mouth. Too late, though. Each of the faces turned his way, eyes blinking once in perfect unison. Identical frowns spread across myriad faces.

"Also explain how he comes to know the woman." There were touches of Frantisek in the group's manner, possibly because he was the spearhead of the gathering, but Grigori wondered why the controlling mind did not recognize him. Surely Peter Frantisek's memories were open to the gargoyle's master. If, for some reason, they were not, Frostwing must have informed his master of Grigori's existence long ago.

The demonic creature's next words only strengthened Grigori's suspicion that there was a rift between lord and servant. "Glorious one, master of my creation," began Frostwing in a servile manner. "I must admit ignorance. It is a shock to me, my lord! I saw you die; therefore I began your grand and most glorious plan, never once turning to see if all was not as it should have been! I cannot begin to explain how you come to be here in both mind—'' he indicated the scowling group before him ''—and *body*.'' The gargoyle waved a negligent hand in Nicolau's direction. ''If you like, I can remove this useless one from your sight.''

Grigori was not certain which was the more unsettling, the outright lies of the supposedly loyal servant or the new glint in the eyes of each figure in the triangle as they studied the hapless power wielder.

''No, my dear Frostwing,'' they intoned. ''Not yet.''

The gargoyle bowed and backed away, but did not leave.

''I feel I should know you,'' the hosts began again. ''I feel that I should know your reason for being here, but this—'' the figures all pointed at Frantisek, including the man himself ''—while a most worthy form to adopt, is virtually devoid of memories.'' The triangle glanced at the grinning stone figure. ''Yet another question I would have an answer to.''

Frostwing only looked more servile, yet Grigori Nicolau knew other emotions lurked behind the mask the gargoyle presented. What was Frostwing trying to do?

The legion of eyes returned to Grigori. ''Do you know who we are, my dear body?''

Something about the way they regarded him dredged up defiance from him. Grigori shifted so that he stood before Teresa and met the gaze of Frantisek.

''I know who *I* am. I am Grigori Nicolau. I am *myself* and no other.''

There was simultaneous laughter. Even Frostwing dared a chuckle, which he immediately cut short when the eyes briefly turned his way.

''You are not you, but rather me, *Grigori Nicolau*. How I survived my death and became you is of mild interest to me, especially as the timing of the reappearance is so precise. I am interested to know also how it is you have survived all these years. Yes, my dear self, there is much to talk about.''

The Frantisek host rubbed his chin in contemplation, but surprisingly enough, the others did not follow suit. "There is much to consider."

Grigori suspected that he was about to be dismissed, but he had to ask something before that happened. "Who *are* you?"

"Who am I? You might as well forget your own name . . ." The chuckle that followed was reminiscent of Frostwing's. "I . . . the two of us . . . am and are *Mihas*. Surely you could not forget so grand and bold a name as our own?" The collective eyed him with disbelief.

"The name means nothing to me, nor do you."

"How very curious." Heads turned. "Frostwing, attend me!"

The gargoyle rushed to Frantisek. It was ironic to think that the bound man had finally gotten his wish; he was the winged golem's master. Of course, he was also no longer Peter Frantisek.

"I am your servant, great Mihas!" The gargoyle once more prostrated himself before the triangle.

"Of course you are," they returned. Frantisek actually reaching out and patting the creature's head. "You could not be anything else. You have no real choice, do you, but to serve your master. You have served loyally for all these centuries."

"The task is my joy, wondrous Mihas. I live but to fulfill your dream."

Frantisek removed his hand. The collective smiled at the fawning gargoyle. "You are a perfect servant, Frostwing. That is why I have a special task for you to perform."

"But name it and it shall be done." Was there a hint of bitterness behind the fawning tones?

"Remove my daughter of many generations to a place where she may be kept safe. Then remain with her until I call you." The triangle smiled at Grigori. "I would like to spend a little time with myself . . ."

The joke was lost upon the captive power wielder, for he was too concerned with protecting Teresa from the gargoyle. Frostwing seemed amused at Grigori's attempts. He stretched forth a taloned hand. For the first time, the eyes were more than dark pits. A baleful pair of yellow orbs glittered from within.

A gust of wind swirled around Grigori Nicolau.

Teresa, once more fully under the will of her captors, stood beside the short, winged figure, her hand in his own.

"Come, my dear," Frostwing crooned.

They vanished before Grigori could do anything further.

"Now it is time for I and I to talk."

The dark man knew he had to extricate himself from his own predicament before he could even hope to save Teresa. That meant dealing with the collective mind that was Mihas, a creature who seemed to be having trouble deciding whether or not it should consider Grigori a separate entity or still a significant part of itself.

"What do you remember?" asked the legion of figures, once again switching pronouns. It seemed a matter of whim. Grigori wished that his other self would decide, for it made the conversation even more confusing than it already was.

"I remember nothing. The story you claim to be true is nothing but fiction to me." That much was true and all thanks to Frostwing. Mihas obviously did not know of the centuries the gargoyle had spent tormenting Grigori and stealing his memories was yet another point of significance. If Frostwing was, by his very existence, compelled to be obedient to the will of his creator, then how was it he could hide secrets from that same being?

Grigori had no idea what the gargoyle wanted from his creator, but for now, Nicolau found himself allied to the winged demon. As astonishing as it was to believe, there *was* something worse than his age-old tormentor. That something was Mihas.

"You do not recall the final moments? You do not recall feeling your life force torn asunder and spread among your foes?" The faces twisted with the pain of memory. Grigori found his own lack of memory for once a benefit, for what the collective mind of Mihas recalled sounded horrifying.

"I knew that it would be terrible," the legion continued, a grim cast to each face. "Yet even I, Mihas the most powerful, did not realize the depths of suffering! How could I ever forget when they first laid hands on my valiantly struggling form? Each touch leeched a little more away. Each spell to bind or silence me stole still more. None of them ever suspected that they carried my legacy, my *lifeforce*, within them, that their descendants would inherit those hidden fragments and pass them down through the centuries. I did not even require all of those fragments to survive through the ages, only enough power to draw them all together when the time came. The knowledge that I had outwitted them made the suffering worthwhile." The Frantisek host took a step closer. "I—you—must recall the *spell*. My—our—*crowning* moment, our *vengeance assured*."

Grigori did not remember much at all and what he did recall were vague memories that had belonged to Abernathy. He was overwhelmed by what he heard. He recalled the ancient power wielder's fall, the hands grabbing him. Each of those who had touched him had been endowed with some tiny piece of the sinister figure's very life essence, what some might term the *soul*.

It was both a magnificent and horrible plan. The very ones who had destroyed him became his link to life. Like a parasite, the fragments had existed within, no doubt growing strong on the power of their hosts. Mihas had said that not all of them were necessary, but enough were passed on through the centuries . . . did that mean that the fragments divided *further* as they were passed on from generation to generation? Grigori thought that likely; it certainly explained how not only there would be sufficient fragments to recombine into the master wielder, but also why Grigori could sense so many others within the keep.

How many had it taken?

Was what he saw before him the end result? It could not be. No one, not even this Mihas who was also him, would want to live so. There had to be more to the grand design. Mihas needed to return to a single physical form. Perhaps that was the role Teresa was to fill. Perhaps Grigori had interrupted the rite with his arrival.

The triangle looked disappointed in his lack of response. ''I would have expected better of my flesh. You are my body but you are not me. That is clear now.'' The assembled throng rubbed their respective chins. You have kept from me the added power of the high moon. I must consider how this affects my plan.''

Something that Frostwing had said to him made Grigori suddenly straighten. The gargoyle had hinted that to save himself, Grigori Nicolau needed to hate himself. He had not understood the latter part, but then, he had not known of Mihas at that time. He could learn to hate the Mihas part of himself, oh yes. The more he listened to the collective figure's disdain and vanity, the more Grigori saw how little other lives meant to his other self, the greater was his own disgust.

Hate Mihas? It would be simple; but how did that aid Grigori at all?

''I shall decide upon a course to follow shortly,'' intoned the legion. The eyes turned away. ''You will return when I have need of you.''

Grigori strengthened the shield he had been building, but his efforts went for naught. In perfect unison, the hosts of Mihas casually waved a hand in his direction.

The chamber became a gray, endless fog.

He had been dismissed. His shield had not in the slightest protected him from the power of the ungodly thing that had once been him. Grigori's dismissal had been little more than an afterthought.

Searching revealed nothing. Grigori suspected that he could walk forever and never reach a destination. He attempted to transport himself away, but he had lost all use of his power. A curse escaped his lips, a curse upon a winged carrion-eater who had led him like the proverbial lamb to the slaughter.

"Flattery will get you nowhere," came the familiar, snide voice.

Frostwing perched behind him. Perched on *nothing*. The gargoyle squatted on empty space some four feet above Grigori's head. He was now as Grigori Nicolau remembered, a huge, arrogant creature with no concern save for himself.

"Truly I am amazed that you would simply walk into the mouth of the lion, my friend."

"There was no one at the gate. It seemed like a reasonable thing to do."

"You are mistaken. I was guarding the gate as I must always do. The gate and I are one."

"You were not there," insisted Grigori.

"Perhaps you did not see me."

The sly tone said all. Frostwing had known of his entry. Somehow he had made himself invisible to Grigori's eyes so that the human would blunder into the trap. The slight man felt like an ignorant fool for doing just that. He tried to bury the shame and frustration he felt by asking a question. "What is this place?"

"Welcome to my master's place of contemplation," Frostwing said, one arm stretched out as if to draw attention to the nonexistent wonders around them. "Called so, dear Grigori, because it only endures in the thoughts of Mihas."

"You are trying to tell me that this place is a product of his imagination?"

His dread nemesis allowed the question to pass unanswered. Instead, Frostwing scratched his chin in a manner very much akin to the way in which the hosts of Mihas had scratched their own. The eternal smile widened. "I want to tell you a story . . ."

"Damn you, Frostwing!" Grigori again attempted to use his power, but found that there was nothing to use. He had been stripped of his might.

"Yesss . . . a story." The leering gargoyle looked up into the fog. Now and then, a swirl of mist surrounded the stone golem, making the foul servant appear to fade away. "Let us imagine a place . . . much like home . . ."

Grigori tried to summon to his mind the words he had earlier used to cast out his adversary. However, the words would not come, no matter how hard Grigori tried. Instead, nonsense syllables spilled from his lips, causing Frostwing to chuckle at the depths of the human's plight.

"The words do not work well in this place, do they? Now then, where was I?"

The power wielder slumped. He had no other weapons at his command. His fate was in the talons of Frostwing, and the gargoyle quite obviously relished that fact. Still, Grigori remained defiant. "Are you here at your master's request, Frostwing? I thought you were supposed to be watching Teresa?"

A shrug. "As well to watch a rock grow, I think. She does not move of her own accord. Yet I monitor, just in case. I obey my master."

"But not always to the letter, do you?"

"Great and grand Mihas! Ah, how skillfully he chooses his new names. He knows that I am with you, but the knowing is of no consequence to him. He has your future, or lack

thereof, to keep himself occupied.'' Frostwing extended his
wings to their full glory. ''*Mihas* is only his latest title of
virtue; I do not even recall what his original and likely less
resplendent designation was. It means something like *God* in
what you would call modern Rumanian. He has always been
one to be honest regarding his talents. I believe he procured
the name from the otherwise very forgetful Peter Frantisek.''

There was something in his last statement that hinted at
more. Knowing how Frostwing liked to tease, Nicolau did
not rise to the tempting bait. Instead he asked a question to
which he already knew the answer, but needed to have verified. ''Am I really him?''

The gargoyle flew from his invisible perch. He rose above
Grigori, then fluttered to yet another invisible landing place
and settled down again. ''Let me tell you a story . . .''

There would be no answer. Frostwing was determined to
subject Grigori to one of his parables. This time the human
said nothing to interrupt. Perhaps the story *did* contain something. At least he knew that Teresa was safe for the time
being . . . probably safer than *he* was.

Frostwing saw that he finally held his audience captive.
The marble-gray and bone-white creature preened his wings
for a breath or two, then began: ''There was a tale once told,
to someone like you, about a good and powerful man who
was misunderstood by his lessers. He sought to cheat them
of his death, remember? Aaah, I see you recall it. And have
you also heard the tale of the man who was not dead, but
thought he was? I do not think so.''

Gazing around, Grigori Nicolau fully expected Mihas to
appear in all his multiple glory. This new story hinted at
some knowledge that the gargoyle's master might not have.
Yet Mihas neither appeared nor did he summon the two back
to him. Frostwing continued without pause, evidently unconcerned about his seemingly impossible betrayal. How *did* he
get around the compulsion of obedience? ''There was a great

and glorious man, so very much like the man of that other tale in all ways, who suffered a downfall. Those who came to him with their helping hands, believed that he had died. Assuredly saddened, they took his body and cast it out into the rugged lands surrounding his home. It was possible that their beliefs included the notion that his spirit would fly to the afterlife if his body was so treated, but his mortal form certainly lacked such a skill.''

Grigori shivered, thinking of the victorious foes tossing the remains of Mihas from his high keep. He could not help but look down at himself. If he was the original body of Frostwing's master, than what had prevented every bone from shattering and every bit of flesh from being scattered among the hills and mountains?

Frostwing provided an answer to just that question in the next part of his tale.

''Life is most precious, is it not, my dear Grigori? There are those who say life is the greatest and tenderest treasure imaginable, a thing that should not be twisted, a thing that should not be forced upon those that do not wish it.'' Here the gargoyle's tone grew bitter. ''Even in one who gives his life for a cause, is there not a slim possibility that some spark of defiance, some spark within that is unwilling to leave, might be just enough to keep him alive? Might that spark be enough to mend a shattered body?''

Frostwing saw Grigori's blank stare; he sighed and shook his head. The gargoyle looked around, as if seeking to determine whether or not they were truly alone, then returned his baleful gaze to the man before him. ''My stories no longer entertain? Your lack of artistry and your even greater inability to comprehend artistry have always appalled me, dear, dear Grigori. Very well, have it *your* way.''

The winged form was no more than a blur as he leapt at Grigori Nicolau. Reflex made the power wielder attempt some shield, some defense, but he still lacked the power.

The gargoyle landed upon his back, clutching him like a demonic child. Despite all the times that Frostwing had fallen upon him, Grigori could not help but tremble. The creature had never hurt him physically, his torments all of the mind, but it was difficult to remember that with the gargoyle on his back. "Do you recall that first encounter in your hotel room? The way I welcomed you to this vast and oh-so-enchanting kingdom of Chicago? No? Of course . . . you cannot recall because I took that memory, as I have taken so many, many more through the centuries."

Frostwing ran a talon down Grigori's cheek. The slight man knew better than to move.

"I have never thanked you properly for those delicious memories, my friend." Yet again, a trace of bitterness tinged the winged terror's next words. "To one created only to serve, to one given a task spanning centuries, even the freedom gained from another's memories is better than no freedom at all. The pain, the caring, the fear, the sadness . . . I have reveled in them as if they had been my own. I could not walk among men, I could not be as one of them, but I could live through your experiences . . . and I *did*."

A scream of protest at having been forced to live. The memory he had experienced while probing Teresa's mind gained new dimension as he considered what life had been like for Mihas's unwilling creation. Centuries of toiling for a master and being unable, by both compulsion and appearance, to deviate from that task. Frostwing could never live among men, that was certainly true enough.

He had taken Grigori's memories in order to experience the world. The human could sympathize with his plight, but not with his methods. As Frostwing gained some shadow of existence, Grigori lost his past. There had to have been other ways, not that Frostwing would have cared.

The gargoyle's head shifted so that he could now whisper in Grigori's other ear. "You want everything handed to you.

You even want the truth. I have taken and partaken of your memories, dear friend, and I understand how doing so might disturb you now and then. But come! This time, I do not feed! This time, it is I who will give the gift."

Reaching around and placing a taloned finger on his captive's forehead, the sinister golem leaned close. "Now it is *I* who shall give freely while you . . . while *you* simply need to *remember*."

Pictures flooded Grigori's mind.

His thoughts descended into a maelstrom. It was all Grigori Nicolau could do to keep from becoming lost within his own head.

Gradually, the images began to take order. He saw again the fall of the keep, but this time he witnessed the chaos first from atop a gate and then from an angle high, high in the air. The arch of the gate, Grigori noted, was the same as the arch in front of the house. Then, suddenly, the ground rushed up, nearly giving him vertigo. He found himself staring in both horror and nausea at the sight of a shattered, torn body. He remembered what Frostwing had said about Mihas's body, how the victors had flung it from the keep. It was amazing that the corpse could be this intact, considering the height from which it had plummeted.

Then he recalled that this was not a corpse, but rather a barely living man. This was *him*.

More memories leapt by. The body tended . . . by *Frostwing*? The same spark of life which had somehow protected the body during the fall, becoming stronger, more apparent. What had the gargoyle said—that perhaps this one bit of essence had refused to surrender because where there was life, as the saying went, there was hope? Better the tiny hope than the leap into the reckless unknown.

Thanks in part to the gargoyle, that hope had seen realization. That hope had thrived.

Memories again. The body was well, but the mind was

new, untutored. The spark had not been enough to maintain the personality of the power wielder. What existed now was an adult infant who possessed the potential to be once again a master of men, a *sorcerer*, as his kind were known in those days.

Cross-purposes. Frostwing had found a loophole in his orders. He was to work for the preservation of his master and his master's grand design, but was not this creature he had rescued also his lord?

There was no doubt that Frostwing hated Mihas and because of that, the infant that wore the body of the great power wielder. The winged terror saw little difference in the two, the spark having originally been a part of his despised creator, after all. However, the compulsion to protect his lord made it impossible to harm the body. Torment was the most that the gargoyle could inflict upon the innocent creature, but it was something that Frostwing soon excelled at. He had been, after all, patterned after Mihas himself.

However, there was more to the story than what had been so far revealed. Grigori could sense that. Frostwing was hiding something. Nicolau knew enough to guess that his tormentor had brought the body and essence of Mihas together with a purpose in mind, a purpose from which the gargoyle would benefit. Yet, at the same time, he was somehow fulfilling his mission for his creator.

Again came the rush of memories. Frostwing, so limited in movement, appearing in the young one's dreams and ushering him to a small village that had no knowledge of Mihas. The villagers had taken in the able, but supposedly addled young man. To their surprise, he had learned quickly, in two years his mental strength matching his physical. All the while, the gargoyle watched.

The dreams had started the moment the power began to manifest itself in the young man whose name, given to him by his foster parents, was a variation of what would eventually become Grigori Nicolau. As the power wielder had suspected, the region was in what was now Rumania, near Transylvania. And once his charge had learned to survive in the world of men, Frostwing put his theory of cruel protection into practice.

He caught scattered images of people forcing the confused young man out into the wilderness with shouts of "Demon" and "Evil." Thus had begun the centuries-long curse, as Frostwing molded by terror and defiance the personality of Grigori Nicolau to his liking. Keeping Grigori alive for so long had been a task as great as the one Mihas had originally set for the gargoyle, but such work was all that Frostwing had to entertain himself.

What was that gargoyle's purpose?

After seven centuries, the winged demon had failed to break his human toy's will. He had bent it, yes, and bent it far, but still Grigori defied him no matter how useless that seemed.

But if Nicolau had failed the gargoyle, then why was he here? Was this his punishment for not becoming what his nemesis had planned?

Too many questions still, but he felt as if the answers to all of them were buried in the recesses of his mind, just waiting to be rediscovered.

The next image puzzled him, so different was it from the others. A waking to the truth. The realization of who he was and the search to find a method by which that identity could be turned to his advantage. He had the opportunity to inherit the vast power the ancient sorcerer had left behind—

It was a memory from the mind of Peter Frantisek. Grigori was utterly confused, uncertain as to where that stray memory had originated. The only source was Frostwing, but that seemed impossible. The memories of the other power wielder now belonged to Mihas.

Did they not?

Frostwing suddenly burst into view. Unlike the other images, this memory had a life of its own. It flew closer and closer, like a dream within dreams.

"So disappointing, dear Grigori!" mocked the winged horror, growing ever nearer. "I had hoped you would wake up and see the truth before it was too late! I had such hopes! You must wake up, Grigori Nicolau! Wake up, old friend! Wake up!"

He *did* . . . to find himself back in the chamber where he had discovered Teresa, a legion of watchers with eyes the same dread color as his staring down upon him. This time they were formed into some shape other than a triangle, but from his vantage, Grigori could not say what that pattern was. All but one of the hosts were different from the last group. That one familiar form once more stood at the point, leading the rest.

Peter Frantisek shook his head, the others matching his movement. A mocking smile that somehow reminded Grigori of a certain winged creature spread across each face.

"Even if you are not me in mind, you still share one trait." All of them shook their heads in mild disbelief. "To sleep while you are a guest of mine, dear friend, takes much nerve . . . or perhaps *audacity* is the correct word. Still, I suppose after the first several hours, you were probably bored enough that sleep was the only thing to do."

The first several hours? How long had he been captive? Grigori looked for Frostwing, but the gargoyle was suspiciously absent.

Mihas clasped his many hands together. "You will be pleased to know that I have solved my dilemma concerning you. Originally the fragments needed to be gathered, a slow and tedious project, but the end result is as you see it. I exist, but I exist as this." Now the various components of the power wielder spread their hands to indicate themselves. "Not, I am certain you will agree, how one wants to spend one's return to the waiting world.''

Grigori only nodded, not certain what his captor was leading up to.

''Two options—'' The assembly raised one hand with two fingers extended. The insanely perfect choreography was beginning to get on Nicolau's nerves ''—were there for me. One was to find another such as myself, one of great power, and through the spell, gather all the fragments into that one.'' Here they indicated Frantisek, who, knowing him as Grigori had, would probably have been flattered. ''But while this Peter Frantisek, of the line of one of my more worthy foes, is strong, he is still an insufficient receptacle.''

Grigori did not understand, but again remained silent.

Mihas saw his expression, however. ''You know of the power, yet you frown. There is a limitation to how much power can be wielded by one of us. This shell is the strongest I have amongst my active hosts, but it cannot hold more than a fraction of my essence. The shell would burn away, leaving me nothing.''

The legion extended a hand to its right. Grigori looked— and saw with dismay that Teresa was now with them again. She stared at Mihas as if nothing else existed in the world. Before he could call to her, the ancient power wielder spoke again. ''Then, there was my original intention. Who would be nearer to my self than one of my children? They have interbred through the generations . . . never close enough to risk damage, but every now and then, when the blood needed to be strengthened, two were brought together.''

Teresa as the final host for the madman. Grigori, hands shaking, tried again to bring his power into play, but failed as he had before. Mihas did not even notice.

''She is my daughter of generations. Far removed from me, but retaining enough of the bloodline that she could bear

all that I am, become me. She has the will, the vibrancy.''
Despite the way he praised Teresa, Mihas sounded a bit
disappointed. ''She was the best choice I had.''

Grigori could stand it no longer. ''No! You cannot do that
to her! Not her!''

''I agree,'' the legion replied, turning their gaze back to
him. ''And after all, she is a woman. It would almost be
beneath me.''

Frantisek alone took a step forward. He eyed Grigori from
top to bottom, visibly appraising. ''You have kept me in
excellent condition. That will help.'' Steel-blue eyes met
steel-blue eyes. ''My crowning *triumph* . . . to cheat my
rivals of my death by returning through their very heirs . . .
and now I may even do it wearing my *own* flesh.''

XXII

''YES, IT IS SO SIMPLE . . . AND FOR THIS WE WILL NOT EVEN
need the high moon. Like draws to like, and there are no two
beings more alike than we, are there?''

Ignoring the desire to remind Mihas that his ancient self
was more than two people already, Grigori tried to back
away. Only the sight of Teresa's still form reminded him that
another's life, more important to him than his own, was also
in danger. Still, he was facing his doom. Either he would be
absorbed, as had Mihas's hosts, or he would be cast out,
which meant oblivion.

Although fear was certainly great among the emotions raging through his head, Grigori Nicolau found anger and hatred

rivaling it for dominance. The more he faced Mihas, the more he despised everything about the power wielder. If this was what he had been like before the fall of the tower, than Grigori was not sad that circumstances had changed him. His former self was an arrogant, pitiless creature who saw others only as pawns. Even his children had been nothing more to him than an extension of his will.

Hate yourself and be proud of what you've become. Now he understood Frostwing's words a little better, although he was at a loss as to how they could aid him.

"My daughter of generations will still play a part since, she, too, carries the blood, albeit in far less quantity and quality than you." Mihas scratched his collective chins. "Yes, she will play many roles. First, she will guide the transfer. Like to like, as I said. Then . . . then I think that when I am whole I will make her mine. It will be interesting to see what sort of children she will produce over the next few centuries. Being so much of my blood, they should prove quite useful and even entertaining."

Nothing Grigori could have said would have been sufficient to describe what he thought of the power wielder and his intentions. He strained hard, hoping that somehow his power would return, but he only succeeded in drawing the attention of Mihas to his efforts.

"I do not understand why you struggle so. The others came to me gladly, pleading in some cases to be taken in." The hosts smiled grandly. "I am nothing if not a willing benefactor to those in need. I happily gave them their desire, made them no longer alone and fearful."

Trying to stall for time, Grigori asked, "How long? How long since you became—"

"How long since I first returned in spirit? Since shortly after the first found his way to the gate and my most humble servant, Frostwing. Yet, I was and still am, captive to this place, a fragment of frozen time that exists only behind the gate and which has been moved from place to place through the efforts of my blood.'' Hands indicated Teresa. ''My children have worked for this day, too, and I cannot disappoint them.''

Even though they acted unwillingly or even unwittingly? Grigori was awed anew by the presumptuousness of his other self. The evil that was Mihas was a stain on him as well, despite their soul-wrenching parting those many centuries past. *All those lives . . . wasted for this monster. Frostwing is more human than he is!*

''You of all of them should wish to return, Grigori Nicolau. What a fanciful yet mundane name! You *are* me in body and spirit, even if the mind has wandered far afield. Do you not desire to become *whole* again? Do you not feel the rightness of the merging? Can you deny the *need* to see this done?''

The horrible thing was, Grigori *could* see it, *could* feel it. A part of him wanted more and more to be accepted into the whole, to know the completeness that he had always lacked. Even more terrifying, his desire was not due simply to the fact that he and Mihas were linked. It was also because of the centuries of loneliness that he had suffered because he was unable to live as other men.

''It is time, Frostwing,'' murmured the legion, evidently taking the prisoner's mournful expression as agreement.

''Yes, my lord.''

The sound of the gargoyle's voice broke the nearly hypnotic spell that had come over the captive power wielder. Grigori did not know when Frostwing had returned, but that was not why the gargoyle's speaking had stirred him. It was the tone of the creature's voice. Frostwing sounded *defeated*.

Grigori looked up. The gargoyle stood at one end of the vast design that covered most of the floor. Teresa stood opposite him. With Grigori and the collective hosts of Mihas, they formed a diamond with sides of equal length. The center of the diamond was the center of the pattern, the spiral of words.

"Soon you shall know the joy of unity, dear brother. I know that your hesitation is due to your lack of understanding of what you were and what you will be again. You are *Mihas*. You are the *power*. Not a wielder of power, but the ultimate *master* of that power. There has not been, nor will there ever be, another like you . . . me . . . us . . . and *I*."

Teresa raised her arms until they were parallel to the floor. Grigori thought at first that she had broken free of the mesmerizing influence of their captor, but the blank stare in her eyes revealed otherwise.

From the unholy host stepped Peter Frantisek. "Prepare to join the three of us as one, Frostwing."

"Yes, great and glorious Mihas." Was there again that edge that hinted at disappointment and defeat? What did the gargoyle still expect of Grigori?

Desperate, Nicolau called out to Teresa. To his surprise, her arms lowered slightly and she blinked once. Her gaze began to slide his way.

"My dear," called Mihas in soothing tones. Frantisek reached a hand out to her, as if beckoning, and the blonde woman's eyes glazed again. Her arms rose. Frantisek and the figures assembled behind him gave Grigori a look that, despite the absurdity of the image, made him feel like an errant child.

Frostwing, too, stepped forward. The gargoyle grew as he moved, grew until he stood as huge as he had in the wanderer's nightmares. When he was no more than a half-dozen paces from the others, the winged golem finally dropped into a squatting position. His gaze turned to the ceiling.

Little more than a heartbeat had passed before Frostwing, still staring heavenward, announced, "They are all prepared, most noble master. They hear and they wait."

Grigori glanced from beast to creator. Mihas looked at the trio before him. In many voices he intoned, "I will be complete. None shall be left out. Neither distance nor time shall prevent the full joining."

Grigori Nicolau sensed the minds of hundreds of people, perhaps even thousands, although such a number was too dreadful to contemplate long. The summons reached everyone who bore the taint of Mihas, whether already absorbed by the collective or living their lives ignorant of what was to be their fate. Mihas had needed many, but only so many before he could perform this rite. However, he had evidently not forgotten those still remaining. Of course he would demand nothing more than *every* fragment of his life essence be a part of him again. Mihas did not seem one to settle for anything less.

"We now join." As Frantisek walked toward Grigori and Teresa, the others in the throng behind him raised their hands toward the trio. The two captives began moving to join the tall figure, Grigori Nicolau struggling futilely all the while. Frostwing did not move, did not even look down, save that, as Mihas reached for Teresa's outstretched hand, the gargoyle casually made a tiny scratch in the floor.

At that moment, Teresa stumbled. She collided with a startled Grigori, who, unable to move his arms, could do nothing to prevent the impact.

The touch of her body against his was electric. He felt stronger, reunited with his power. Astonishment washed over him; the link was so strong that it needed no prompting to work.

Her eyes opened wide, the compulsion on her fading away the longer they held one another. She looked at him in surprise. "What are—"

Grigori no longer felt compelled to obey the commands of Mihas. He pulled a still-confused Teresa away from Peter Frantisek, who had started to reach out for her.

"Return to your proper place," commanded the legion.

Shaking his head, Grigori announced, "We are leaving."

Mihas laughed in a thousand voices, all of them equally harsh and unforgiving. "You have my sense of humor, to say the least! Now return to your proper places, both of you, and we shall conclude this."

Grigori continued to lead Teresa away. The expressions on the faces of the ancient power wielder's hosts turned first to disbelief, then to disappointment. The assembled figures raised their left hands toward the duo.

"Do not be absurd. You *will* return where you belong. You *will* return to me."

Even with Teresa holding him, it was all Grigori could do to resist the call of his counterpart. He grunted under the assault within his head, made all the worse by the fact that he was protecting his companion at the same time.

Frantisek lumbered forward, trying to grab Teresa from behind. Grigori twisted her away. It was hard to concentrate, so very hard.

"You are me. You will return to me. There is no other choice, my dear prodigal self." As Mihas talked, the rest of his hosts began, one by one, to vanish. They reappeared, forming in the matter of moments a circle around the spiral pattern and those within.

If he stepped back any farther, Grigori risked falling into the hands of one of the others. If he remained where he was, Mihas, through Frantisek, would claim the two of them. Frostwing offered no aid. The gargoyle simply watched the proceedings.

"You *will* come to me, willing or not."

The stone floor under Grigori Nicolau's feet rippled, throwing both Teresa and him forward.

Mihas, in the extension of Peter Frantisek, awaited them.

Grigori tried to prevent them from falling too close to his foe, but the suddenness of the cunning attack did not allow him to call upon his power until it was too late.

Frantisek seized Teresa by the arm and, with physical strength that shocked Grigori, nearly lifted her from the floor. Grigori, still gripping her hand, was pulled up as well. Teresa tried to tear Frantisek's offending hand from her arm, but the host body ignored her, stepping back from Grigori Nicolau and dragging her as if she weighed nothing.

The eyes of the two power wielders met even as they fought to win the macabre game of tug-of-war. Yet while Grigori battled with all his strength, his counterpart seemed calm and hardly strained at all. The tall figure even had the audacity to look to the waiting gargoyle and nod.

"You may begin, Frostwing," announced Mihas/Frantisek.

"Yes . . . my lord."

Too late did Grigori realize that he was now exactly where his other self wanted him.

Voices filled his head. No, *more* than voices, there were other *minds,* other presences, within him now, and more joined Grigori with each passing moment. The gathering voices made it hard to think, much less concentrate. Yet they also promised a sense of peace, of unity. He had felt something similar only once before. It was much the way it had been during his struggle with William Abernathy, save that these presences came willingly. They *knew* that this was their proper place. It was—

"Wrong!" snarled the assembled throng around him. They were not part of the flow. In fact, they seemed fearful of becoming a part of it. That fear, though, was concentrated into one mind, the mind of Mihas. "Wrong! Cease!"

The flow stopped instantly, but Grigori could sense others that seemed to float nearby, awaiting the command that would allow them to join their predecessors. He *wanted* them to join him, wanted them to be a part of him again, but he did not know how to make it so.

"What are you?" demanded the angry voices of those surrounding him. One outside voice in particular cut through his musings. "What did you do?"

Slowly, reality returned to Grigori. He blinked and found himself locked in a struggle with Mihas/Frantisek, Teresa desperately trying to add her own strength. Frantisek's face was a study in livid outrage, but that lasted only a breath longer. Calm returned, and with it the arrogant confidence that so well marked the personality of Mihas the great.

"Frostwing!" The head of each host turned to consider the gargoyle, who cringed and scraped and bowed and yet somehow still did not quite come across as servile as he might have hoped. Nonetheless, only Grigori appeared to notice that. Perhaps Mihas could not see anything but his own might. "Explain!"

"My lord, gracious and wonderful master, I cannot, save to suggest that perhaps because he is also you, there is some slight affinity. I brought to waking the fragments within each of your carriers and directed them here, but it seems that they need more. Because of her *interest* in this unworthy one, she is drawing them to him instead of you."

"Ridiculous! She is the blood of my blood!"

The gargoyle shrugged and spread his arms in a gesture of helplessness. "I suggest only what I can construe, my lord. The spell is your creation; I only perform a function."

"Indeed, my dear, dear piece of rock. Yet . . ." The hosts eyed the two prisoners. Despite Grigori's increased level of power, Mihas conducted this conversation while holding his opponent at bay. Worse, he also held Teresa's arm with no visible strain. "It could be true . . ."

Grigori Nicolau tried to use his newfound strength to free Teresa from the grip of Mihas/Frantisek. This time he was able to strike against the other power wielder, but Mihas shrugged off his attack and continued with his musings.

Frostwing suddenly interrupted his master's contemplations. "If I could be so bold, my lord. The problem is you, I think. How you were forced to . . . live again . . ."

"How I was—Yes . . ." The Frantisek host released Teresa and turned his attention to those forms surrounding them. "Yes, of course."

Neither seeing nor caring to see the answer, Grigori led Teresa from one part of the circle to the next, seeking some path of escape. There was none. Mihas had surrounded them.

"What can we do?" whispered Teresa, visibly struggling to keep fear in check.

"I will try to transport us from here. Hold tight."

She did as she was told, but in the end it did not matter. Even with what Grigori had gained, he evidently did not have enough will, enough of a hold on the power, to overcome whatever force kept them prisoner.

There was no time for a second attempt, for Mihas faced him again. The steel-blue eyes that had once belonged to Peter Frantisek were cold, so very cold that Grigori had to suppress a shudder.

"I have been doing this wrong. I have focused my efforts in the wrong direction."

"As you say, bountiful master." Frostwing's gaze shifted surreptitiously to the pair of prisoners. "As you say."

"I must concentrate myself and remove the blockage. The shell will remain, to be filled with my glory!" Smiles directed at Grigori spread across the chamber. Frantisek took a step toward the duo. "You must be removed, Grigori Nicolau. When the shell is empty, then I can use it properly. *That* was my error; I thought that I could keep you like all the others, but your fragment is of no use to me any longer. You would be a hindrance. The body, however, still fits my needs and so you shall simply have to go."

Grigori caught the gargoyle's eye. Frostwing's chiseled smile widened. He leaned forward and, with great relish, said, "He means to destroy the spirit, the personality that calls itself Grigori Nicolau, so that he can take your body without resistance."

Grigori wondered why the notion so entertained the winged golem, who had given every indication that nothing would please him more than his master's final downfall.

"Frostwing, we do not need the female for this," remarked Mihas, his Peter Frantisek host stepping forward. At the same time, the other figures moved too, tightening the circle. "We need only you and I, my shadow self. Both of me."

A thrust of power from Grigori was met and ignored. The Frantisek form stumbled slightly, but then continued on.

A taloned hand fell on Nicolau's shoulder. Frostwing no longer squatted where he had; the gargoyle had shifted behind him. "Time to face the inevitable, dear, dear Grigori! Allow me to remove the lady; she has her uses, you see, and you do not need to hold onto her any longer. You must accept who you are and embrace that fact. You are him and he is you, but you are the body and that, as you know, is the anchor of life. Just remember poor Peter."

"Take her and be gone, Frostwing," commanded Mihas from all around. "There is no time for taunting. I would have this done now. I grow impatient to live and breathe in one body. *My* body."

Teresa protested, but Grigori ignored her. He released her hand without a word and did not look when the gargoyle launched into the air, removing her from the circle. He was more interested in what he believed Frostwing had been hinting at. He was Mihas as much as Mihas was him. He knew that already. In some ways, he was Mihas more than the collective mind. He was not only the body, but also part of the life essence of the power wielder, no matter how changed by circumstance and time. All of that made sense, but what did that have to do with Peter Frantisek?

As if in answer to that question, his mind was flooded with

memories and knowledge . . . all of which had belonged, he
realized, to the selfsame man.

But how did they come to be in *his* head?

The visitation. Frostwing had not only given him his own
memories of his resurrection but the memories of Peter Frantisek as well . . . the same recollections that Mihas himself
had found inaccessible.

Frostwing must have stolen those memories before his master had claimed the other power wielder as one of his hosts.

What good did that do him, though? *Which* memories were
important? The summoning of Frantisek's recollections had
taken less than the blink of an eye, but Grigori had little more
than that left. Then Mihas would reclaim his body and draw
those lost fragments of himself into it, a process involving—

Grigori nearly shouted in surprise. Not only did he know
exactly what the summoning and reabsorbing of those bits of
life entailed, but also how he could perform the very same
rite. All Grigori Nicolau needed was sufficient power. If
only—

He got no further, for Mihas, using Peter Frantisek, reached
out abruptly and thrust his open palm onto Grigori's chest.
All thought scattered as the air burst from his lungs. Grigori
tried to pull away, but not only was Frantisek's hand stuck
to him as if glued, it felt as if a thousand needles had sprouted
from the palm and were sinking deeper into his flesh. He
knew vaguely that he might have resisted this attack if he
had kept his physical link with Teresa and not given her up
to the gargoyle. For some reason he had listened to his age-
old tormentor, despite centuries of Frostwing's treacheries.

Grigori had tried early on, after first discovering their link,
to draw from Teresa without touching. He could always sense
her, but never make use of her abilities. If that was what
Frostwing had been speaking of, what made him think that
it would be different this time? What made him think that
Grigori could reach out to her with only his mind?

His vision blurred. He could see Peter Frantisek before him, grinning merrily, but Grigori had to squint to make out any smaller detail. Helpless to do anything, again he silently cursed the gargoyle. He had not been strong enough that first time to link with Teresa over distance; did Frostwing think him stronger now?

He did. It came to him even as his head pounded and his heart shook madly within his chest. Grigori was stronger. Perhaps a better description would have been that the dark man was more *complete* than he had been during that first attempt. When Teresa had tripped, she had collided with Grigori and made him the temporary recipient of some of the lost fragments, some of those pieces of himself that had been separated from him for so long. An accident, to be sure, but through it, he had gained much.

It was no accident, was it? Frostwing knew that she would stumble! He must have known! His words, his actions, they make more sense now . . .

It was growing harder to remain conscious. Grigori decided to try again to link with her. That was all he could do. Try. If he was correct, he had a chance. If not . . .

He reached out with what will remained to him and tried to make the link come alive.

A surge of strength made him straighten so abruptly that both he and Mihas gasped in surprise.

I know how it is done, Grigori reminded himself as he stared at Peter Frantisek's uncomprehending visage. *I know how it is done, but can I really do it?*

The choice was either the death of Mihas . . . who had already used up one life wastefully . . . or his own.

Like to like. That was how it was all done. That was how Frantisek had taken his victims. That was how Abernathy had taken his victims. Whatever artifacts they had utilized, it all depended on the fact that each bore some fragment of the life essence of Mihas. But their own powerful wills had been all any of them had needed to draw forth their prize from the unsuspecting or ignorant victims. Matthew Emrich and so many others had been absorbed by Mihas and the other pair, but if the laws of similarity held so well, Grigori had the greatest advantage. He *was* Mihas in both mind and essence. If anyone could draw the fragments together, could ever achieve the unity that all of them either secretly or actively sought, then it was he.

The pressure and the pain in his chest dwindled, but Grigori Nicolau was not concerned with that. He knew everything that needed to be done, but one piece was still missing. One piece that had a name.

It came out as a whisper. "Frostwing."

In his mind, he heard the familiar chuckle, this time tinged with triumph. Frostwing, who Mihas himself had created as an integral part of the ritual, needed only open the way to let it all begin.

Grigori felt the gargoyle's great pleasure as he did just that.

The voices came again, first a few at a time, then several, then in a torrent. How many descendants had there been in all those centuries? How many had unknowingly carried his legacy within them?

They were coming too fast. He knew that if he allowed the flow to continue unchecked, every one who carried a fragment would die, their own life force torn from them in the process. Subtle. It had to be more subtle, more caring. Mihas, Frantisek, Abernathy . . . none of them had cared about the fact that they could have let their victims live. What was truly terrible was that much of the victims' own essence was wasted, lost. They died because their murderers had simply not cared to take the time.

A thousand thoughts could pass in the blink of an eye or the taking of a breath. Such was the way that Grigori came to understand. Unfortunately, Mihas, while taking longer to comprehend the sudden change in circumstance was not slow in reacting.

He tore his palm from Grigori's chest just as the first fragments transferred away from him. Mihas could sense them and he could also sense what was happening to Grigori.

Hands grasped Nicolau from all sides. Faces old and young, male and female, glared at him as they sought his death. For a moment, he lost his composure. Then Grigori recalled how the thing called Mihas had originally passed along his legacy and how these shells might be more susceptible to the summons than their distant, unsuspecting brethren around the world. More important, Grigori Nicolau could draw from those attacking him without fear of doing harm. They were already dead.

Relying on the knowledge that Frantisek and Abernathy had imparted to him, he reached out and touched one of his attackers.

The woman, clad in a costume from the French Revolution, *faded*. Just faded. He thought at first that he had failed, but then Grigori sensed the addition. She had been a shell so long that nothing really remained but shadow.

Despite the blows he suffered, Grigori touched three more. The others vanished as he summoned their fragments home.

So many deaths that one so undeserving of life could be reborn. Grigori was ashamed; he could not help but think that the sins of Mihas were his own. It almost made him falter, but then he considered the alternative. Stopping would only benefit the ancient power wielder.

Suddenly the remaining attackers stepped back and vanished. Mihas, he suspected, did not desire to waste any more of his hosts in an effort that was only weakening his power, not preserving it.

Grigori rose from where he had fallen during the assault.

Of all the hosts who had surrounded him earlier, only one remained. Peter Frantisek.

There was something different about Frantisek. He did not seem one shell among many, one appendage out of many.

He was also looking beyond Grigori.

"This is *your* doing, is it not? This is your betrayal, is it not?"

"Oh, *yes*, my grand and glorious master," came a voice from above and behind Grigori Nicolau. "Very much so . . ."

Despite the apprehension he felt at turning his back on Mihas even for a moment, Grigori did.

Frostwing perched on a ledge, the dark craters of his eyes now lit with that strange yellow glow that Grigori recalled from before. The eternal smile was wider than ever.

"You cannot betray me. That is impossible," declared Mihas.

The gargoyle spread his wings wide. "You gave the command. It was a compulsion that I have interpreted perhaps as you would not, but nevertheless, I remain true to my making. I have worked hard and long to ensure the continued existence of my master."

"I am your master."

Frostwing pointed at Grigori. "He is more my master than you, for he is both body and essence."

"Your logic fails you, faithless servant. I, too, am your master. How do you explain your thinking, then?"

Preening, the winged golem responded, "After this confrontation, there will be no need to worry about such gray areas, would you not agree? The conflict seemed the best solution to the quandary."

"You are a mistake, Frostwing, and when this is over, you shall be unmade . . . slowly."

The gargoyle came as close as he could to frowning. The tone in his voice was chilling as he glared at Mihas/Frantisek.

"I never asked to be created, wondrous lord of nothing! I never asked to be dragged to life, only to be condemned to putting you back together like some insipid puzzle! I would have preferred nonexistence to this!"

"And so you created this thing of your own." Mihas indicated Grigori, putting a sneer on Frantisek's visage at the same time.

"I saved my master." The wings flapped. "He *is* you, Mihas. More so than you are yourself. He has been tempered well for this day, a day that was fated to come eventually. I have seen to it that he prepared for the glory that is not *you*."

Tempered? Centuries of torment, rather, and not for Grigori's own sake. Frostwing had twisted the commands impressed upon him by Mihas to the point where they had been almost, but not quite snapped. All this for the sake of vengeance.

"This?" Mihas laughed. Oddly, Grigori could not sense the other hosts doing the same. He could not sense the others at all. It was as if Frantisek had become the one and only host, but that was not possible according to the knowledge the bound man himself had passed on to Nicolau. "He is nothing but a witless buffoon, a fool, my dear, mistaken servant. You know the story about fools and the fools who follow them, don't you? You should know it well."

All humor vanished from the gargoyle. "You are nothing, Mihas! Your day is—"

The words that emerged from Frantisek's mouth were nonsensical, no part of any language with which Grigori was familiar. Yet Mihas spoke them with confidence as he stared at the gargoyle.

Frostwing roared in anguish. He pawed at his chest, his wings, and his head, as if trying to scrape something horrible off of his skin. Bits of rock showered down on the chamber floor below, yet Frostwing lost no mass.

"And as for the fool who follows the fool," said the ancient power wielder, turning Frantisek's gaze on Grigori. "There is only one Mihas, my dear friend, and I am him."

A blast of withering heat threw Nicolau to the floor. The voices stopped filling his head. Either there were no more to come, or Mihas had found a way to close the path. Either way, Grigori wondered whether he had the power to withstand this new Mihas. Something was indeed different, something that had to do with the power wielder's hosts.

Then he realized why Mihas had taken the time to talk with Frostwing rather than simply punish the gargoyle immediately. There were no other hosts. There was only one. Mihas had drawn his collected fragments together into one body . . . but that was not supposed to be possible. None of his hosts had had the capability to contain so much power, so much of his life essence. Even Frantisek, as powerful as he had been, was not strong enough. Mihas had planned to use one of his own descendants, which had just happened to be Teresa, to achieve his ultimate goal, for one of his own had the best potential to contain his complete essence. The immutable law of like to like again. Grigori had prevented that, at least, but at the risk of himself being used instead.

He stared at the looming figure of Frantisek. The forces gathered should have burned him out, just as they had been doing to the other hosts of Mihas, only in this case it should have taken seconds instead of years. Frantisek should have been nothing but dust, yet here he stood.

"A power wielder must trust no one, Grigori Nicolau, not even his obedient servants. A little hidden knowledge is a wondrous weapon at the strangest of times."

Bone-shaking cold surrounded Grigori, driving him to his knees. Shivering, he drew upon his own power and created heat from the memory of his adversary's previous attack. The heat countered the cold.

"Yes, you are more me than we were both willing to

admit. It would be so much better if you would see your proper destiny and join me. Become a part of me, Grigori Nicolau. Accept that, and at least you will be a part of the glory that is Mihas! Decline and I will make certain that no trace of you remains. You will cease to exist.'' Mihas/Frantisek indicated himself. ''You see that nothing is impossible to me. Give in to the inevitable.'' Mihas extended a hand, as if offering aid, not death. ''I will make it swift, I promise you that.''

Grigori rose to his feet again, eyeing the sinister figure looming over him. He came to a decision, possibly the last of his long life. He reached out to take the other's hand.

A flutter of wings was all the warning that Grigori had before the massive form of Frostwing descended upon them. The gargoyle's flight was erratic, a sign that he still suffered from his master's punishment. Nonetheless he broke between the two power wielders before they could touch and, hovering, tried to strike Mihas.

The blows never landed. Each time Frostwing swung, his taloned hands stopped short. It looked at first to Grigori that some impenetrable wall blocked the way, but then he noticed that it was the winged golem himself who was responsible. Frostwing would pull his hand back just before it touched Mihas. The angry snarls of the gargoyle, snarls tinged with pain, indicated Frostwing's frustration with his own inability to strike his master. The compulsion laid on him by his creator still held. Betray him Frostwing might, but causing physical harm, even to a body that was not technically that of his master, was beyond his abilities.

Mihas had no such compulsions to confront. He whirled on his treacherous servant and glowed with the release of power, sending the gargoyle spinning away in a ball of blue flame. Yet, as Mihas struck, a change came over him. Gone was the perfection that he had radiated but moments before. He still held the form of Peter Frantisek, but the face was sunken in and blotches, like burns, covered his hands and head. He also seemed to be fading around the edges, as if he were partly a ghost or some such spirit.

The other image had been a lie. Mihas had been gambling. He could *not* long contain all his power within the shell of Frantisek.

The revelation strengthened Grigori Nicolau's resolve. As Mihas concentrated his anger on the gargoyle, Grigori stumbled forward and seized his adversary's hands.

"What are—?"

Those were the only words to escape the ancient power wielder's mouth. His eyes locked on Nicolau's, first in triumph, then, when he realized just what was happening, in shock and, perhaps, fear.

I am Mihas, Grigori thought over and over again. *I am the rightful one. Like to like. This is the body from which all were driven, and this is the body to which all must return if we ever hope to become complete again. Complete.*

The voices came again, but they were fewer than before. He had taken the fragments outside the confines of this sanctum without killing. Only the ones within remained, the ones whose lives this shadow of himself had carelessly usurped. Yet, they, too, deserved to join, to recreate the one who had been shattered for so long.

"Release . . . my . . . hand!" snarled Mihas, all trace of his condescending air a thing of the past. Peter Frantisek's face was little more than skin wrapped over bone now, and the blotches had spread to cover almost every inch of flesh. Only the eyes, which still burned with anger, remained constant.

"Your grand design is almost . . . fulfilled, my wondrous master!" roared Frostwing from afar. Grigori could not see him, yet somehow he sensed that the gargoyle was once more on his perch, one wing drooping, but otherwise intact. The gargoyle's smile was at its widest.

He saw through the eyes of Mihas. The link between the two of them was now as great in its own way as the one between Grigori and Teresa.

Teresa! Even as he thought of her, Grigori realized that somehow he had made a mistake. He should not have called her to mind; if he was so tied to Mihas that he could see through the other's eyes, then it might be possible for his foe to read his thoughts—

"To me, my daughter!" His free hand more like a blackened claw now, Mihas reached forth to empty air.

Grigori saw a shimmering. Teresa began to materialize. As she did, the link Grigori shared with her faltered.

"Come to me," Mihas commanded again. Teresa struggled to resist, but she was losing the battle.

"Teresa! No!" Grigori's shouts went unheeded. His companion could not resist the will of even a weakened Mihas. Yet if he released his hold on the other power wielder for even a moment, he might never regain it. Mihas was too clever to be allowed such a second chance.

Frostwing! It was time to see if what the gargoyle claimed was true. "Frostwing! Do something! I am your master! You must save her!"

"At last!" The winged golem let loose with a harsh laugh. "At last! As you command, so I very *willingly* obey, my lord!"

He had only been awaiting an order. That was all. Even in the midst of the struggle, Grigori Nicolau could not help but marvel at the gargoyle's perverse nature. There would be no understanding Frostwing, even if Grigori lived a thousand years.

Providing, of course, he survived the next few minutes.

A streak of gray and white landed before Teresa, cutting off her path to Mihas. Frostwing enveloped the blonde woman in his wings, completely obscuring her from the sight of both combatants.

By now the body of Peter Frantisek was a gaunt, horrific thing that might have risen from the grave, but the fiery will of Mihas somehow kept it moving. "Move away from her, foul gremlin! Move away, I command!"

Frostwing turned, grinned, and obeyed.

Teresa was no longer there.

The gargoyle laughed at the fury on the macabre figure's face. He stretched his wings wide and glared at his creator. "I feel no more compulsion to obey you, tattered and decaying Mihas! You are nothing more than shadow! He is truly my master now! This final command was the proof. I could obey without hesitation, truly a tasty moment for me!"

"Then you shall have that memory of your own to cherish . . . and that is *all*." Outrage overcoming reason, Mihas ignored Grigori and pointed a decaying finger in the direction of, but not *at*, Frostwing.

In his mind, Nicolau saw an image of the arch that stood over the great gate of the house. It was only a glimpse, but that glimpse was enough, for he saw the arch suddenly struck by *lightning*, lightning out of a clear sky.

The image faded even as the bits of stone scattered over the ground and the street.

Frostwing roared in pain and began to crumble. It was as if time had been sped up and the rock from which he had been hewed was eroding. Fragments dropped to the floor, an ever increasing pile of rubble consisting of gray rock and white bone.

To the surprise of both men, the roar once more became laughter. Familiar, mocking laughter. The gargoyle spread his wings—one snapped and crashed in pieces to the floor. He did not seem to care.

The toothy grin that had haunted Grigori for so long was there, but now it mocked the ancient power wielder and not the centuries-old wanderer named Grigori Nicolau. "And so it ends! But I will see you in *Hell*, Mihas . . . and quite *soon*, too!''

The rest of Frostwing shattered, pelting both Grigori and his other self.

At the same time, Mihas lurched forward, the shell that had been Peter Frantisek finally burning out. The vengeful destruction of his former slave had been too much for his host body.

The hand that Nicolau held tight slipped through his fingers, no more substantial than the wind. The empty shell collapsed to the floor, but it never touched the stone. It sank through. In less than a heartbeat it had vanished, fading away as the other hosts had done earlier. The suddenness of the collapse was so great that Grigori simply stared at the spot where the body of Frantisek had been.

The battle, however, had not quite ended.

Grigori was no longer alone in his own mind. Even as he recovered from what he had done, he felt the second presence within, a pitiful remnant that could not accept the inevitable despite once having expected others to do the same.

I am Mihas! it proclaimed in hollow protest. *I am the master! I am the god!*

It attacked Grigori through his thoughts, but the attacks were so weak, so pitiful, that he pushed them aside with ease.

No, thought Grigori in return. *I am Mihas. I am also Grigori Nicolau . . . and that is who I shall be from this point on. Mihas is dead.*

No, came the other voice, but it was already dwindling away, merging with the whole. This body possessed a controlling mind, one that had been made strong and determined through the efforts, however wrongly performed, of a bitter creature that had not asked to be brought into the world. It was the personality, the guiding force, with which the body was most familiar.

Mihas, on the other hand, was only an ancient, bad memory, one already well on its way to being forgotten.

A hand fell upon his shoulder even as he tried to orient himself. He stiffened, but then heard a female voice anxiously whisper, "Grigori?"

And he could answer with great satisfaction, *"Yes, I am."*

XXIII

WHEN EXACTLY THE HOUSE RETURNED TO NORMAL NEITHER of them could agree. Grigori knew that it had happened before Mihas vanished. Teresa was fairly certain that it had occurred only a breath or two after Frostwing had enveloped her. As far as she could tell, he had sent her to the living room. She had discovered Grigori there a moment later. Teresa could not, however, recall exactly when he had materialized. She had been too relieved to see him.

There was much she did not recall, most of which Grigori promised to tell her when they were finally able to relax. Both agreed their most pressing concern was to escape the house and never come back.

Grigori did not fear reprisal. There was no power, no magic left within. All of that he now contained within himself. He was a little in awe of his newfound abilities, but Nicolau had already sworn that he would not fall prey to ambition and vanity, as he had in his time as Mihas the Great.

It was night outside. Judging by the moon, Grigori estimated that it was only a couple of hours before daybreak.

Neither his watch nor Teresa's agreed with that, both indicating that the evening had barely begun.

"They may actually be able to sell this place now," his companion could not help remarking as they stepped through the front door. "That is, if anyone is still interested in it."

"You will probably find that someone is, but there may be trouble locating the most recent owners when it comes time to deal," he reminded her.

She paused, mulling that over. "That's right."

"Whatever happens, dear Teresa, it is not something with which we need be concerned—" The dark man froze and stared ahead of them.

"What is it? What do you . . . *oh!* What happened?"

The gate was a ruin. Rubble from the arch lay everywhere, but the majority of it had collapsed onto the gate itself. As with the house itself, Grigori could detect no trace of power left amidst the chaos. The destruction extended to the entire entranceway. One side of the metal gate had come completely off, leaving a gap large enough for both of them to step through.

"Lightning struck," was his only reply. Something in the midst of the rubble caught his attention even in the dim light of the moon. He hurried forward.

The high wall surrounding the house blocked enough moonlight that he chose to create a light of his own. In the glow of the blue sphere that formed in his palm, he was able to verify his suspicions.

It was a wing. A wing carved from stone. It was the same wing that had been damaged during the battle with Mihas, the one that had fallen off when Frostwing had crumbled.

He did not lie. He was here when I entered. He has always been here.

The Frostwing he was more familiar with, the one that had aided him in the end, had been something of a dream after all. Perhaps he had existed only in that magical realm within the house or in the nightmares of those linked to Mihas by birth or by curse. He had drawn others into that world or left signs of his passing in the waking world, but he had been unable to depart his arch. Grigori would never know the full story, for not all of the memories of Mihas were accessible. The merging had given him much power, but had eradicated all but a few traces of those lives from which the fragments had come.

Frostwing's hatred for his creator became even more understandable if the physical form of the gargoyle had been trapped upon the arch. Only when the arch had been moved from destination to destination by Mihas's unwitting offspring had the stone sentinel's view ever changed.

Only in dreams could Frostwing live and move at all. Small wonder that he stole memories from Grigori. Perhaps he had felt them his due for saving and nurturing the broken form of his master.

Perhaps. It was all idle speculation now.

Squatting, Grigori released the sphere to float a foot or two above his head. He began to dig through the rubble for pieces of the shattered gargoyle.

"What are you doing?" Teresa asked, kneeling beside him. "Shouldn't we leave? Someone must've heard the arch fall."

"No one heard anything. Frostwing assured that. When we leave, I will restore most of the arch. No one will be the wiser."

"*Most* of the arch?" She glanced down at the growing pile of pieces that he had so far gathered, shuddering when she realized what they would form when assembled. "What are you going to do with those?"

"There is a place, I believe it is in what is now Rumania—perhaps as part of the Carpathians—where I wish to bring these pieces and bury them."

"You're going to Rumania?" Her voice almost broke.

He looked up. Teresa had an unreadable look on her face. He reached out and took her hand. "Only for a few minutes. I would like to remain in Chicago for a time. It seems a most fascinating city."

Teresa smiled. "I'll be happy to show you around." The smile faltered. "Did you say 'a few minutes'?"

Grigori went back to gathering pieces. He had most of the body and now, at last, he succeeded in locating the head, which was virtually intact. The grin seemed hollow, and the eyes were once again simply dark pits. The horns had been snapped off; although he was able to find one, the other eluded him. "Yes, only a few minutes. I can go there after we return to your apartment. It will not take long."

"You—you can do that now? Just travel from one point to another in minutes?"

He placed the head on top of the other fragments, eyed it a moment longer, then looked up into eyes the same color as his, but so much more beautiful despite that. He hoped to see those eyes for the rest of his life, but that was a subject he would broach when both their lives had settled. "I can do that. I can do many, many things that I could not do before." Grigori gave her a smile. It was the first truly pleasureful smile of his life. That he knew as a certainty, regardless of his much battered memory. He had never had such a reason to smile before.

"And when I do them, it will be by *my* choice."

ABOUT THE AUTHOR

RICHARD A. KNAAK lives in Bartlett, Illinois. Besides the Dragonrealm novels, among which are the titles *Firedrake*, *Dragon Tome*, and *The Crystal Dragon*, he has also been a longtime contributor to the Dragonlance® series, having penned several short stories and two novels including the *New York Times* bestseller *The Legend of Huma* and its sequel *Kaz the Minotaur*. His other works include the Chicago-based fantasies *The King of the Grey* and *Frostwing* and the forthcoming *The Janus Mask*. In the future, he plans more fantasy, science fiction, and also mystery. Those interested in finding out more about future projects may write the author care of Warner Books.